ATWOOD MANOR
1860 – 1869

A Novel

By

Donna Benn Powers

CreateSpace Independent Publishing Platform
North Charleston, South Carolina

This book is dedicated to ~

Kay Summers   ~   My "Editor"
John & Patti Latson   ~   My Guardian Angels
My "family of friends" at Palmas Del Sol   ~   My Strength

Thank You

Atwood Manor
1860 – 1869

By
Donna Benn Powers

Chapter One
Liverpool, England
June 1860

Long days, low pay, and total exhaustion made James count the days until he could flee his gloomy existence. England was his homeland, but for as long as he could remember, dreams of America filled his nights, accompanied by visions of a big house surrounded by land, a lot of land. The dirty dock life he had lived for the past two years worked on his mind. He made it tolerable though, knowing he would eventually sadly leave his beloved family, friends, and England for a home with religious freedom and many more opportunities.

At the age of twenty, James finally had the nerve to share his dream with his father, Thomas Atwood. "Why James, you're a fool to think 'bout goin' to 'merica! You will just find more of the same there, ya will, lad!" James admired his father, loved him deeply, and patiently listened to his hasty words. Thomas had worked the Liverpool docks for thirty years, just as his father had done, as did his father's father. Thomas' body felt broken at times, but his English spirit carried him onward. Thomas and his ancestors had spent their entire lifetimes under the heavy royal thumb yet he did not share his son's American dream nor understand it.

Thomas Atwood married lovely Mary, who was always humming, and did so during good times and bad and he loved her for that. She not only kept and loved their small row house yet also enjoyed helping others and loved delivering babies. She saw hope in the new generation.

Looking back, James remembered when he came home from school to the smell of fresh bread and a song coming from his mother and would be overwhelmed with a sense of love and family. His younger sister Emily always trailed behind him, skipping home from school, and humming, like their mother. They both carried on the Atwood family traits, blonde hair, and brown eyes as big as dinner plates. James was a skinny child and caught hell from bullies at school, but his father had taught him enough to defend himself, much to his mother's chagrin. Therefore, he could never show his bumps and bruises to his mother with pride after winning schoolyard scraps.

He remembered how he watched his father come home from working the docks long after dark; he was dirty, hungry, and spent. James wondered how his father did it year after year. His mother Mary always tended to her husbands tired muscles and each night had a tub in the kitchen by the warm hearth for him. She boiled water to add to the tepid water she had retrieved from the public pump over a block away, bucket load by heavy bucket load. Each night Mary would rub and scrub his back and arms until they were blood red. His groans of relief filled their small home. James and Emily watched from the small table in the kitchen, mesmerized by the glow of the fireplace flames on the side of the cold steel tub.

Their father then sat hunched over the table and scooped up the night's hot stew, containing mostly vegetables and very little meat. Their mother emptied the tub only after she scrubbed Thomas' filthy clothes in the cooling, dirty bath water. James would often help his mother empty the tub, scraping the bottom with the bucket, which made a horrible noise that always made Emily draw her little legs to her chest with her hands over her ears. During winter, it was worse because the door was open so often from emptying buckets into the street; she would often slowly scoot closer and closer to the fire for warmth. Then in the morning, there would be thick ice covering the street after many emptied buckets from all the row houses, that froze into odd peeks and valleys as the water and other wastes followed the brick-shapes of the street.

At night, James shared his bed pallet with his younger sister, Emily. A piece of cloth acted as a door between them and their parent's thin mattress on a pallet near the fireplace. James, usually still awake, often heard his parents' whispers and sometimes giggles from his mother after she thought her children were asleep only eight feet away. Daily, Mary carried coal, when they could afford it, or broken wood pieces home with the day's bread and vegetables from the market. Sometimes Thomas brought home pieces of wooden crates from the dock hidden in his coat, so his family would have warmth. Their family time was usually short since Thomas worked long days, six days a week. Mary was forever helpful with the children's schoolwork as she awaited the arrival of her loving husband. The children's education was very important to her, and she would help as much as she could with her limited knowledge. She and Thomas both had to quit school at young ages to work for family income. "You can be whatever you want to be," she rhythmically sang to them over their shoulders as they studied. She then wiped their slates clean for the next day's lessons. However, Mary thought differently than her husband - his glass was always half empty.

Thomas' father had worked the docks up to his early death at age 50 from a heart attack. James witnessed many early deaths on the Liverpool docks in his young life, and he knew he wanted more out of life. Yet, he now worked on the same docks, next to his father, knowing in his heart, it would never be his life's work.

James often sat up-wind from the grimy dockworkers while eating his lunch as it was difficult to enjoy food while smelling the dirty, odorous men, especially in summer. Instead of listening to the men bolstering about the antics at the pub from the previous evening or gossip about the days absent worker, James gazed West over the ocean waves with dreams of life in America.

He was seldom able to buy the daily newspaper and often saw the headlines only in passing. He never knew nor asked how his mother gathered the aged papers, but she always managed to have plenty to wrap their daily bread and dollops of homemade jam for his and his father's lunches. Today it was peach jam. He could smell the sweet fruit as he removed the string binding on top of the burlap bag. Thomas always gave his son a larger bread portion first, yet Thomas took his portion of jam first, scraping the bread along the paper, while James waited so he could swipe the paper clean with his bread to be able to read the article his mother had carefully selected, knowing James was always hungry for knowledge.

James loved his younger sister Emily, now grown into a blonde beauty. She married the love of her life, John Bryce. Being very involved in city planning, John had dreams of climbing the political ladder to visions of being Liverpool mayor one day.

Now happily teaching grade three, John felt forming young mind's was essential and strongly believed war was a waste and meaningless. He thoroughly enjoyed engraving peace of heart and mind into his young students in hopes they would carry on his beliefs and be part of maintaining a peaceful country. However, the American Civil War had affected England when families that fled to America to find better lives, only days after they disembarked their ships and were soon entwined in Civil War battles. Many of England's young sons were cutdown, as they believed the $300 offered by army recruiters was the answer to their prayers. This hurt John Bryce to his core.

Chapter Two
April 1861

James ate his lunch with fellow dockworkers and did not listen to their conversations or gossip. He had an inner hunger to learn and grow; and their blather did not interest him. James' ambitions were much higher than these blokes ever dreamt of, which included his father. As he looked to the West and visualized his future, the sound of horse hooves on the wooden dock turned his head quickly in that direction. James saw a very fancy black carriage approach the office with a black suited driver sitting tall and proud in the front seat, as the wheels loudly pronounced each wooden plank of the dock. Behind him was a man in a dark suit and shiny top hat, looking very stern, who was paying no attention to the lovely female vision in pink sitting across from him. James looked at the woman more closely, chewing his lunch very slowly and he could not believe who it was - Jessica Strong. He recognized her from school and knew she was Emily's age, one year younger than he was. She had raven black curls then and was the prettiest girl in school and he had a mad crush on her back then, but he never let on to anyone. She and Emily were good friends then and Jessica would sometimes come home from school with Emily. He never got the nerve to say any more to her other than hello, and still regretted that he had never approached her.

As the carriage got closer to him, he now had a clearer view. His jaw dropped when he saw that she was now even more beautiful.

As the carriage driver assisted her down from her seat, James could not take his eyes from her. The curls had disappeared and her black hair, now twisted into a large bun under a tilted pink hat as wide as her shoulders. The hat matched her long, beautiful pink dress that flowed softly with every small step she took. As he watched the smoothness of the fabric covering her small hips, he suddenly forgot how to breathe. His trance was broken when he bit his own tongue while eating his lunch. Never before had a woman actually astounded him like this. She glides, he thought, actually glides. Her father's steady pace made it hard for her to keep up with him. She carried a small pink parasol and seemed to be struggling to open it. She was now lagging far behind her father, Edward Strong, who lived up to his name. He walked as a confident man who definitely knew where he was going, and had a powerful male presence. It looked as if he gave no concern to his daughter, until he reached the office door. He impatiently waited, glanced back to Jessica, lowered his gaze to the wooden planks, and began to tap his foot.

Edward Strong, President of Strong Lumber, the largest lumberyard in Liverpool, was a very prominent man. Since most of the lumber he sold was imported, he was a very familiar face on the docks. However, today his daughter was with him, much to Edward's discontent, or so it seemed. James watched in awe. He watched as Jessica finally gave up opening her parasol since her hat sufficed in blocking the sun. Now she seemed to be deciding which hand to hold it in, or was it caught on her glove? He could not tell due to the distance between them. It was Jessica, of that he was sure and she had grown to be a most beautiful nineteen-year old woman. As she finally reached the office door, her father held it open for her to enter before him.

James continued to eat his bread and jam, hoping he would still be sitting here when she and her father exited the office. He looked up to the sky, regarded the beauty of the day, the warmth of the sun, and noticed there was not a cloud in the sky, a rarity for England. Now, seeing her, the day was perfect. He ate slowly but soon noticed the dockworkers were starting to gather their lunch sacks and empty pints. They had stopped work for lunch only twenty minutes ago, but the boss was impatient and gave the men a whistle. James quickly folded the sticky newspaper article that he had not finished reading since sidetracked by the lovely Jessica, and shoved the paper in his pocket to read later. He looked toward the office one more time, but the door remained closed. He followed the men back to a huge stack of crates to put aboard the ship by day's end. He never got another glimpse of Jessica that day.

Now that he knew the possibility of seeing Jessica with her father again at the docks, he found himself often watching the office. Yet, day after day, he watched to no avail, but that hope made his days more pleasant and they passed faster than ever before.

He had to see her; had talk to her.

Emily, he thought, she might know a way he could get Jessica's attention, and decided he would talk to his sister about Jessica when he saw her at church. The week dragged slowly without seeing Jessica again. In addition, when he and his father got home from work, his father got first use of the tub, which left dirty water for James to bathe and he was tiring of that quickly. However, now that it was summer, he would take advantage of the shoreline to wash both himself and his clothes after the long workday. One thing he was glad to do was to combine his pay with his father's so they could buy more at the market. Now there was meat on each dinner plate for his family.

James was twenty-one now, and knew his life was going to have to change soon. Together, the Atwood family had saved money a long time for the wedding Emily deserved. She was a beautiful bride and John looked like a man who had just won the lottery. John and Emily met at school and both knew their love was forever. John wanted to be a teacher and worked his way through college doing bookkeeping. Emily, a seamstress for a dress shop that catered to the well-to-do. Together they saved money for their future. They also both wanted to start a family quickly as they adored children.

James had witnessed many of his school friends marry and start families, while he worked long weeks, and wondered when his time would come to "settle down". Therefore, he worked and saved what he could, month after month toward his dream. He loved his parents, but knew his leaving England was approaching quickly.

Sunday morning he arrived at church with his parents, searched for Emily and John to no avail, and anxiously squirmed in the pew. The sermon seemed longer than usual, but at last, they were outside with fellow parishioners. He finally noticed Emily alone when he approached her.

"Sis, how are you?" He leaned in to kiss her on the cheek. "Marriage agrees with you. You are glowing."

"Thank you James. You look good as well. I would prescribe marriage for everyone. I am very happy." Her smile gave away her heart.

"Do you remember Jessica Strong?" James looked at his feet and noticed how he had nervously kicked dust onto his church shoes.

"I do, yes, of course," she said and looked down where James was looking. "But I haven't seen her in some time. We used to be good friends in school but since then we've lost touch."

"Where is she employed, do you know?" James shyly questioned his sister.

"Strong Lumber - she works with her father."

"I should have assumed that I suppose. I saw her with her father at the docks and she was a vision in pink." James twisted his feet, stirring up even more dust.

"Oooh James - a vision?" Emily started giggling and was now searching the crowd for her husband John. She had seen him talking to a fellow bookkeeper a few moments ago.

"Do you know if she is unmarried?" He squirmed and hoped she said yes, as he felt his face warmly blush.

"I haven't heard that she has married. As far as I know, she is still living at home with her parents. Who would not want to live there? It's such a beautiful home." Emily again searched the crowd for John. She finally saw him under an oak tree with two young boys and appeared to be scratching in the dirt with a long stick.

"Please don't say anything to Jessica, if you happen to see her. I will approach her in my own time." He felt the warmth of his cheeks increase.

"That's fine, James. I will mind my own business." She started to walk away after she hugged her brother, who was smiling over his shoulder at his embarrassment, and then walked toward John and the two boys. When she arrived at John's side, she discovered he was scratching 2 + 2 in the dirt. The boys scratched their answer of four below the line as she approached. John smiled as Emily put her arm through his arm and squeezed tight.

James watched this and felt blessed to witness their love, and prayed silently that he too would have a love like theirs.

Many weeks passed before he finally saw Jessica with her father at the docks. It was his only chance to talk to her and he had to take it, yet he could not think straight. He found himself heading toward the office, without finding a reason to be there. When he opened the door, he took a deep breath, and saw her standing near the corner of the room with a look of boredom on her pretty face. Yet he could tell she was trying to pay attention to her father and the dock master, who continued to talk to Mr. Strong, totally ignoring Jessica. As the door opened, she turned to meet eyes with James who was now breathless. He ran his fingers through his blonde hair quickly and raised his head to meet her gaze.

"Hello!" His mouth dried instantly. He tried to smile, and his dry lip actually stuck to his teeth.

"Hello - James? Is that you?" Jessica did not break her stare.

"Yes hello - Jessica? It is so good to see you. How are you?"

The two men broke their conversation for a moment and then quickly returned their attention back to their topic.

"I'm fine. And you?" She nervously laced her fingers and then unlaced them, only to do it again.

"I'm well, thank you. Emily married John Bryce recently. You remember my sister Emily, don't you?"

"Yes, of course. I saw the announcement in the newspaper. She must have been a beautiful bride. She was always dear to me. Please give my congratulations to her and John." She briefly broke her gaze from James and looked toward her father who was still heavily engaged in his conversation.

"Yes, um...yes I will. She was a beautiful bride and has become a beautiful young woman. John's a good man, I think they'll do well together and make beautiful children." James started to giggle slightly at the end of his statement.

James shuffled his feet, looked at the floor, not knowing what to say next. He started to search his pockets as if looking for a reason to be in the office, only to find the sticky, daily newspaper article from today's lunch. He felt himself blush and his mouth went even drier. Just as he was about to speak Jessica spoke first.

"Are you employed here?"

"Um, yep." He mumbled his reply since he felt no pride in his answer.

"I see. My father has to come here now and again regarding his lumberyard. He has employed me...to assist with....paperwork." She scrunched her face, which said without words that she was unhappy. James smiled, for he understood how she felt.

"What is it you do here?"

"We load and unload crates on ships." He still looked at the floor. "My father is also employed here and has been for years." James put both hands in his pockets now to hide his nervousness.

"My, my. How hard you must work. Do you still live with your parents?"

"Yes. We needed to save for Emily's wedding and..." James started to mumble.

Jessica saw his hesitation and broke in quickly, "Oh, I understand. Times are hard. I too still live with my family. But someday I intend to ....well, you know."

James shook his head in agreement and finally raised his eyes to hers. "There's an ice cream social Sunday, ...this Sunday, at my church. I...I was wondering if you would like to attend it with me, Jessica. You can have all the ice cream you want. I am attending with my family, and Emily.....Emily will be there. You two can catch up?"

"I would love to, James. What time shall I be there?"

"One o'clock would be fine," he said through a blissful grin. He wanted to jump into the air, but kept his composure. "I will look for you there at one o'clock. It's at the corner of First and Hadley," he added too quickly, from nerves.

Jessica started to curtsy out of habit. Her father taught her to close professional meetings in that way, where men shake hands. She suddenly remembered this was not a business discussion and straightened herself promptly. She slightly twirled her blue parasol, and nervously pulled at her white gloves and began to finger the pleats in her dress for lack of knowing what to do.

James started to back out of the office when the dock master caught his attention, "What is it James? Do you need something?"

"Uh..... No sir, I am sorry. I will be off now," said James through his embarrassment.

"Off with you James," he barked, "Back to work!"

He turned and struggled with the door handle and pulled on the door only to meet resistance, then finally was able to push the door open. He turned slightly to face Jessica and nodded his head before he exited the office. "See you Sunday." His face was so hot with embarrassment from fiddling with the door, he wondered if and how he could face her on Sunday – but he knew he would. He then realized his feelings for her had never faded from school days, and he was so happy she accepted his invitation so quickly.

James waited until he was completely clear of the office window when he actually jumped and clicked his heals. As he neared the dockworkers, he realized they saw him jump for joy when they teased him relentlessly.

"Oh, James, seems you have a reason to be giddy as a little girl? You weren't terminated?" Frank O'Mally, the manager's assistant was an insecure man.

"No, I was not terminated. However, I will be seeing that young lady at the ice cream social on Sunday after church." James now had a wide grin.

"With Strong's young-un?" James' father feared for his son, as their class difference was obvious.

"As a matter of fact, it is Jessica Strong, thank you very much."

"Oooh, aren't you the lucky one!" teased another dockworker. "She's a beauty,"

James started to hum to block their tormenting and then remembered it was only Monday. He knew then it was going to be a long week with never ending ribbing from the men.

Saturday night, after his father bathed he emptied the tub and filled it again for himself with great effort, from the public pump. He wanted everything to be perfect for Sunday's meeting with Jessica. Sunday's sermon seemed to last forever, but when they finally dispersed, he quickly started his walk home for lunch and did not stay in the churchyard to mingle. Once home, he checked his clothes before he left the row house, then made the six-block walk back to church, and arrived thirty minutes early. Better early than late, he thought. Church members asked him to help set up tables and chairs on the lawn, which he did. He was so thankful it was a perfect day - it had to be. He looked to the heavens and thanked the Lord.

When putting chairs around the trees a lavender blur caught his eye. It was Jessica. He watched her scan the people looking for him and they finally met eyes. He smiled as he started the short walk to her as she too walked toward him.

"James, it's so good to see you again," Jessica stated, shyly looking at her gloved hands.

"And you also, Jessica!" He too looked at her dainty hands.

"Jess, please, my friends call me Jess." She said through a smile.

"Jess it is," he said, and added, "You look very pretty today."

"Thank you James. It's a beautiful day, don't you think?"

"Yes, 'tis beautiful." He held out his elbow to her and together they walked slowly toward the man who was repeatedly churning ice cream with his right arm. They both stood watching him for a short time, then scanned the yard for a place to sit and found two seats under a huge oak tree. He held the back of the chair for her to sit and sat next to her. His hands were shaking and he quickly checked them to make sure they were not wet with fear. He wanted to wipe them on his pants, but knew better. Jess sat with her hands in her lap after she placed her parasol on the ground between them. How he wanted to hold those small hands and yearned to feel the softness of each finger.

They continued to talk, all the time watching people at the social. Jess looked forward to seeing Emily again, yet she secretly envied her. She was already married and probably starting a family. Jess wanted what Emily already had, and so badly at times that it actually hurt her deep inside. Most of her friends were already married and some with babies.

Working at the lumberyard was not her cup of tea, yet she would continue to work hard, for her father's sake. She loved her father through his sternness, admired his strengths, and did appreciate how hard he worked for all they had. In her heart though, she knew money was not everything, though her father thought differently. He worked long days and weeks.

Finally, James noticed a line had started for ice cream, and he promptly excused himself from Jess and got into the waiting line. It was not long before he returned to her with two small bowls of ice cream. She thanked him and tasted the cold, creamy ice. She had not had ice

16

cream for some time and it felt so good and cool on her tongue. They ate the cold dessert quickly before it melted, when his mother shyly waved to him from the line. She and his father walked to the shade of a tree to enjoy their treat, as they did not want to intrude on their son and the girl he was with, and soon disappeared into the crowd.

There were games to play that day and James wondered if Jess would participate due to her lovely lavender dress. Yet, when the hoop rolling started, she was first in line. He watched as she led the pack to the finish line. When she won, the first face she searched for was his. He clapped his hands over his head and happily smiled and whistled for her win. He worked his way through the people to be near her while she accepted the blue ribbon the churchwomen made for the game winners. She was laughing so hard, she felt like a child again. She stood at James's side, out of breath, but glowing and proudly showed him her blue ribbon. He hugged her, as if they had done it a million times. She reciprocated with her arms around his neck. They both thought at the same time how natural their hug felt.

The day was passing too quickly. They watched the children's races and James could not refuse to participate in the tug of war. His team won and they each gladly accepted their blue ribbons and James proudly waved it at Jess, searching her face for her smile. He shyly wiped his hands on his pants and caught up with Jess, who was sitting with Emily and John. They had all watched James win the tug of war, whooping and hollering the entire time.

Jess and Emily were chatting about old times when John reached out his hand to shake James' hand in congratulations. Emily knew James waited for this day anxiously and was so glad to see they were together. The two couples walked and talked together for some time until they found the shade of a tree, where John put his arms around Emily's shoulders and said they had news. Emily beamed with delight and blushed as she looked to the ground and nodded her head in agreement.

"We're in the family way." John grinned from ear to ear with pride and excitement. He reached down with the palm of his hand and rested it on his wife's cotton gown and flat stomach. She put both her hands over John's and put forth a smile James had never seen on her face before.

"I am so happy for you both my dear sister. So happy for you both!" He stepped closer to his sister and hugged her tightly, kissing her cheek. He then shook John's hand a long time. "This is great news!" Jess stepped forward and hugged Emily and then John. She felt her envy inside again.

"Do Mother and Father know yet?" James was so excited and sounded like a young boy.

"No," giggled Emily, "We wanted to tell you first."

With a twinkle in his eye, James smiled wide. "Well let's find them and tell them the news," as he searched the crowd for their parents. He nodded briefly then cocked his head at John in the direction of the church. His parents stood near the church steps with a group of parishioners. They all walked quickly toward their parents. John shared the news with them after he got them away from the others. Thomas shouted out with glee, shook John's hand, hugged his daughter, and gently kissed her pink cheek.

"I am going to be a grandfather!" He shouted to the group of people, and they all came forward with congratulations and backslapping. Mary's smile and sudden tears showed her happiness. She hugged her daughter tenderly, as if she might break.

"When will I be able to hold my first grandchild?" Mary was beaming.

"In spring. The doctor told us early spring," she said as she blushed bright red.

"Spring is a wonderful time to have a baby, Darling Emily. How are you feeling?"

"Good, this afternoon. This morning was different, however."

"Well, we'll have to get you started on some herbs, and that will all be behind you." Mary then stepped to Jess and introduced herself and Thomas. James scuffed the dirt with his shoe in embarrassment. He forgot to introduce Jess to his parents.

"I'm Jessica Strong," she said to both of them. "It's so nice to meet you."

Thomas nodded his head to Jess and said nothing. Mary, however, took her hand and held it briefly, smiling. Mary stepped back to her husband's side, caught James' eye and smiled at him too.

As a group, they strolled around the church grounds until Thomas told Mary it was time they started their walk home; and with that, they said their goodbyes. Suddenly, James asked Jess, "May I walk you home?"

"Thank you, but I have a carriage waiting." Jess was so wishing she did not.

"Very well then, may I walk you to your carriage?" He would have walked her to the moon.

"Of course, James, I would like that."

"May I see you again in the near future?" James crossed his fingers. They slowly made their way to the rear of the churchyard. When they arrived where carriages and horses waited in the shade, James saw the same fancy carriage, with the same driver he saw on the docks, who waited in his seat. He sat stiffly with his back very straight and his clothes were dark and very neat. When they approached the carriage, he promptly jumped down to assist Jess into the velvet seat. He stood at attention as if she was an army general he was assisting.

James waited patiently for her answer and she finally turned to him with a smile. "I *would* like to see you again, James. My nanny, Lizzie, will be my chaperone. I hope you don't mind." She opened the carriage door, yet never removed her eyes from his.

"We can picnic at the beach, if you'd like. Maybe next Sunday?"

"I look forward to it, James. I will get permission and send you a message at the dock, which Lizzie will deliver to you. Would that be satisfactory?"

"Of course. How will she know who I am?" James was truly curious.

"She will find you," giggled Jess as she took the drivers hand as he assisted her up into the carriage. Jess giggled to herself as she climbed up adjusting her full skirt as she sat. It was then she remembered shopping with Lizzie in the past when they once saw James on the street and she pointed him out to her and they giggled like young schoolgirls. Jess had been sweet on James as long as she could remember. When she and Emily played together in the schoolyard, she would secretly watch him, never letting Emily know of her feelings. She often dreamt of what life could be with James. When she started to assist her father at the lumberyard, she told her father she wanted to learn more about the business, and why she *had* to go to the docks with him. He agreed that she needed to learn and took her with him on his business adventures. However, once they were in business meetings, he ignored her. He never asked her if she had questions, she was just a woman, after all.

Jess loved the days they went to the docks to get a glimpse of James, although some days she never saw him. Often, when she did see him, it was just a glimpse, but she saw him.

The days crawled slowly that week for James. He searched for her in each approaching carriage more often than he should have, often not paying attention to his work on the dock. Then on Thursday afternoon, a small black carriage approached the workers, coming much closer than any other carriage ever had before. A woman sat proudly in the driver's seat as she neared James. She smiled as she slowed the horse. When it stopped, the horse snorted and she delicately lowered herself to the dock from the carriage. James walked toward her and they met halfway. Lizzie smiled, and asked, "James?"

"Yes, ma'am," said James as they met eyes.

"I'm Lizzie, Miss Jessica's nanny. Are you a true gentleman, sir?"

"Yes ma'am." James swallowed hard.

"You must be, young man, Miss Jessica is a lady and deserves only the best. Always know I will be watching you." Lizzie smiled wickedly as she stared him in the eye. She did not blink as she studied his face for the truth. Lizzie decided he had kind eyes and handed him a folded paper.

"Yes ma'am, I'll remember that, and I agree, Miss Jessica does deserve a gentleman," said James as he took the paper and instantly noticed it smelled of flowers.

Lizzie murmured at him under her breath and began to climb up to the carriage seat. James jumped forward to assist her into the carriage seat. She turned her head and gave James a pleasing look. That he did that made her happy and thought he was a gentleman after all, despite his lower class. She let him help her and gave him one more look with a slight smile as she took the reins and slapped the horse's rump. "See you Sunday."

James stared after her. He watched the horse and carriage make the large turn and Lizzie only looked straight ahead, never looking back.

He opened the note after Lizzie was off the dock and out of view and took another whiff of the flower-scented paper. "James - I will meet you Sunday on North Beach at 1:00 p.m. I look forward to seeing you then. Respectfully, Jess"

James received relentless ribbings from the workers when he returned to the pile of crates they were to board on a freight ship that was leaving for America the next day. Thomas looked as his son in an understanding way and smiled.

Saturday night, after his bath, he asked his mother for his monthly hair trim. She gathered the small, cracked looking glass and scissors and smiled saying she would be glad to trim his hair. James then looked through the two "church" shirts he owned, trying to decide which one he would wear the following day. He decided on the gray shirt, asked his mother for her assistance again, and she pressed it for him with the hot iron from the cook stove surface. She was happy to do whatever she had to do to help him make his day perfect.

After church, he walked home and quickly gathered plates, glasses, silverware, water, and put it all in a wicker basket and headed for the market, where he selected fried chicken, a bread loaf, and two cheeses for their lunch. He then walked over a mile through the streets of Liverpool to North Beach.

James checked his timepiece and had plenty of time to find the perfect spot. He spread the blanket and arranged all the items from the basket. He wanted to present flowers to her when she arrived and quickly scanned the sandy mounds above the beach. He was gathering some beautiful white flowers growing in a bunch out of the sand a short distance away just as the small carriage appeared. Lizzie held the reins and Jess softly bounced on the velvet seat behind her, holding a white parasol over her head. He had never seen such beauty. Her black hair was cascading over her shoulders, shining in the sunlight and slightly curled. James noticed how it softly entwined in the lace that covered

21

the bodice of her white dress. They met each other's eyes and both smiled as James approached the carriage. He first assisted Jess down to the sandy surface, and then helped Lizzie from her stiff perch, when she asked him what his plans were. He knew when he was nervous he spoke too fast and tripped over his words, so he kept his explanation brief. Lizzie nodded her head in approval and announced she would now move the horse and carriage into shade some distance away but would be watching them. James told her he had enough food for all. Lizzie thanked him, nodded, then took a few small items on a plate and excused herself to the carriage.

James and Jess had a wonderful time as they shared their lunch on the blanket. She loved the flowers, thanked him shyly, and then assisted in cleaning dishes. He wanted their conversation to continue and hoped to hold her hand when he suggested they walk along the water. Her heels proved to be a problem in the sand, but with James' help, she insisted they continue. She politely refused to remove her shoes, for a "lady" should never show her ankles.

They talked as they walked as if they'd known each other forever. Laughter came easily and they were both very comfortable. When James took her hand in his for the first time, he looked over his shoulder toward Lizzie, where she sat very tall on the carriage seat, never taking her eyes off of them. Lizzie did not seem to disapprove, as far as he could tell, so he laced his fingers in hers. They fit together perfectly. Jess knew then his was the hand she wanted to hold the rest of her life. Her heart leaped, which actually astounded her for just a moment, as she sidestepped to be closer to James.

As the afternoon neared its end, they made plans for the next Sunday afternoon. James walked Jess to her waiting carriage where Lizzie still sat stiffly. He assisted Jess into her seat and kissed the back of her hand before she needed it to adjust her skirt folds. Jess blushed, said goodbye, looked into his eyes, and sweetly thanked him. Lizzie then offered James a ride home. He gladly accepted, went back to their picnic sight, quickly gathered everything into the blanket, and ran back to the carriage. He jumped up quickly, closed the small door, and turned to tell Lizzie where he lived. Lizzie's brow rose slightly when she heard his address, and then started the horse in that direction. James sat across from Jess, and as they bounced through the brick streets, had no conversation, yet shared loving looks. Both would blush at times and look away, but only for a moment. He knew then she was the one he wanted to share his life. He then silently prayed that her parents would accept him, being from a lower class.

They saw each other two additional Sunday afternoons, and it was then Jess told James that Lizzie had tattled to her parents of their meetings, and they were insistent on meeting him. James nervously said he would like to meet them, and then told his parents that he had been seeing Jessica Strong, and her parents have asked to meet him. They said they would like to get to know the young woman to which he was so attracted.

Edward Strong and his wife Victoria, both agreed with the philosophy of "the apple doesn't fall far from the tree", and asked to not only meet James but also his parents. They would all attend dinner at their home the following Sunday. They wanted to meet the young man their daughter fancied *and* his parents. Lizzie drove Jess to the docks on Tuesday to tell James of her parent's invitation and asked if they all would be available late Sunday afternoon. He started to laugh and told her his parents wanted to meet her also.

When James told his parents, they were nervous and concerned about their class difference, yet they finally agreed they would go to the Strong home for dinner with their son. Thomas shared his fear with James that the class differences might be what breaks-up this relationship in the making. James feared the same, but explained that he had total confidence in their love. He hoped and prayed their love would be evident to their parents and would overlook their class differences.

Saturday night arrived and the nervous atmosphere at the Atwood home was obvious. Sunday after church, the Atwood's ate a small, late lunch at the market then together they walked to the beach to admire the ocean for an hour before they walked two miles to the Strong's home.

When they arrived, Thomas, Mary, and James, were astonished at the size of their house. Someday, James thought, I will have a house like this, maybe bigger.

They followed a prune-faced servant to the library who told them to wait there for the Strong family. They had never seen so many books in one place except in Liverpool's library. The Atwood's were quiet while waiting and stood, nervously, afraid to sit on the beautiful furniture or scuff the waxed wood floors. None of the Atwood's had ever been in a home this fine. The more James looked around the room, the more nervous he became, yet thought of their love to get them through this day. He silently said a prayer that Jess would be his forever. It seemed they waited hours. Finally, Edward and Victoria Strong appeared in the doorway and Jess shyly followed them into the room. She looked as nervous as James felt.

After introductions, Edward went to a cabinet, retrieved a cut glass decanter, and poured six glasses of brandy. With Victoria's help, everyone held a glass. She asked everyone to sit as small talk began. Jess sat by her mother with her hands in her lap and could hardly look up she was so nervous. James tried to get her eyes to meet his to ease her nerves, but she never looked up. Thomas had never tasted such fine brandy and sipped it slowly. James wanted to drink his all at once for nerves, but watched his father and sipped slowly. The two mothers seemed to have a lot to talk about, where Edward sat sternly and observed. Thomas knew he had nothing in common with Edward Strong, and found him difficult to talk to unless it was about lumber. Soon a different servant arrived and whispered in Victoria's ear then quietly announced dinner was ready to serve.

She led the Atwood's into a grand dining room with James at the end of the line. Never before had they seen such a beautiful room. The dining table was almost as long as the room. It was exquisite. Three lit candelabras centered the table and there were place settings fit for Queen Victoria. The walls were covered in huge paintings and there were two closed doors that led to who knew where.

The dinner went more smoothly than they all expected. Thomas, Mary, and James watched the Strong's carefully to know which fork to use and the proper way to eat soup, and then they all quietly ate their lamb dinner, which was superb. Thomas thought there was enough lamb and potatoes for ten people. James was glad there were no servants watching them eat. At least they weren't that "high and mighty" he thought. Their conversations had few lulls and then it finally seemed comfortable for all. Then the question James had been dreading the most finally came from Edward Strong, "So what are your plans with my daughter, James Atwood?" Edward's forceful voice resonated in the room and sent a nervous chill through James.

James never thought the conversation would get to this level at their first meeting, but Mr. Strong was living up to his name, and the question dropped heavily into the room, and silenced all at the table. James took the opportunity and spoke his heart. "Well," James said, starting to stumble. All eyes turned toward him waiting for his answer, "I intend, sir, to make your daughter my wife. I am in love with your daughter, sir. I would like to spend the rest of my life with her. I also have a dream of a house like this one someday sir." As he squirmed in his chair during his answer, his napkin fell to the floor. He waited until he finished talking to swipe it up quickly and hoped no one noticed.

Edward coughed at his reply as Victoria cleared her throat and first looked to Edward then moved her wide-eyed stare to her daughter. Jess returned her mother's look with a nervous grin and acted as if it was something she had not heard before, which she hadn't. Jess turned to look at James, whom had not broken eye contact with Edward. She then saw James' strength and knew he meant what he said. It made her smile and she felt very excited. Knowing her father's sternness, she prayed then his heart would warm and recognize their love and not keep his hard outer exterior the entire afternoon, as she knew he would at times.

"How do you plan to support my daughter and build this house you speak of, young man?" asked Edward. Jess silently prayed again that her father would soften.

"Well, sir, I have been saving money a long time and I am hoping sir, to be a laborer for you at your lumberyard, as I have a great desire to learn the lumber business. Are you looking for any hands at this time, sir?" He cringed inside for calling him sir so many times.

"Let me think upon that, son. I like your ambition. You are a man with goals, and I like that also," said Edward, sounding softer and less harsh. Edward thought it might be enjoyable to teach a young man all he knew about the lumber business, since his son Grant took his career

25

in a different direction. Edward had always wanted his son to join him in the lumber business but respected his desire to be a doctor.

It did not take Edward long to think about it. The more he talked with James and his parents, the more he liked them. He especially admired James's tenacity and confidence.

After Victoria delivered bread pudding to everyone, Edward leaned back in his chair and told James that he would employ him at his lumberyard, and asked him if he wanted to start work the first of the following month. "If you want to marry my daughter, I'm going to have to make sure you can support her."

Jess wiggled in her chair across from James and stretched her arm across the table in an attempt to hold his hand. James did the same and they were barely able to meet in the middle to touch fingertips. This, James assumed, meant everything was fine; more than fine – it was wonderful.

"A fall wedding then?" Victoria jumped in quickly. She recognized their love and was more than happy for her daughter. Jess felt giddy inside. Victoria looked at her daughter, whose eyes were locked on James' eyes. She saw a joy on her daughter's face she had never seen before.

"Oh, yes mother, yes." Jess was very excited now and looked at her mother with a big smile. She then turned to James' mother, who was also smiling. Mary remembered her own wedding ceremony - at the Liverpool courthouse, then quickly recalled Emily's wedding, which was beautiful in every way. She was glad to see that James would probably have just as wonderful a day as Emily did.

"You should marry in our back yard. It's beautiful in fall, it will be lovely!" Victoria was smiling and imagining how stunning the wedding will be.

"My!" gasped Mary. "This is all moving so fast," she added, rubbing her forehead.

After more discussion over sherry, the wedding date was set for the first Sunday in October.

Chapter Three
Fall 1861

Jessica Strong woke Sunday, 6 October 1861, her wedding day, to a chilly English morning. She ran to the window to discover the sun shining brightly and prayed it would last throughout the day.

James had been working at the lumberyard a few months and had become Edward's right-hand man. James remained living with his parents until the week before the wedding, and then moved into what would be the newlyweds first home together, a flat not far from the lumberyard. He still did not own a horse or carriage, so being close to the yard would be advantageous, especially in the wee small hours of the cold winter mornings. James had partially furnished the flat and the Strong's gave an early wedding present of a fiber stuffed mattress. It was the first one James had ever slept on. It was heaven. He had only known straw filled lumpy, scratchy burlap mats on wooden pallets.

He was so in love with Jess and could not wait to make her his wife and start their life together. He hoped his new clothes would be sufficient for the wedding. He knew Jess would be a dream in white walking beside her father. A carriage was waiting for his parents at 2:00 p.m., and they felt like royalty when they rode through the streets of Liverpool. The row house neighbors gathered to watch them as they rode away. It had been a long time since this neighborhood had seen anything like it. They sat proudly all the way to their son's neighborhood, to his door. Mary was tickled to see her son looking so gallant. He was a prince in her eyes. He sat across from them in the carriage and held his head high. He was actually so nervous that later he would hardly remember the carriage ride to the Strong's home.

When they arrived, a man in a tailored suit helped the three of them down from the carriage and led them to the same memorable library. James looked around and thought to himself that he could get used to living like this and he wondered if they have actually read all these books? Suddenly the door opened, the same gentleman who led them there appeared and asked if they were ready to begin the wedding. When James and Thomas nodded their heads, he waved his hand to direct them out the door. They all exited into the foyer and were led down a long hallway toward the back door. James looked up the long staircase in hopes of a glimpse of his bride but he only saw a shiny table displaying a huge vase of flowers.

James saw the beauty of the back yard and all the people that filled the seats, who were mostly on the left side of the aisle, the bride's side. He saw men in suits, women's large hats, and children dressed like angelic dolls. On the groom's side were many fellow dockworkers and their wives. Then he spotted his Uncle Paul and Aunt Bess, his father's older brother and wife. Beside them were their sons John and Matthew and their wives Barbara and Heddy. He had not seen his cousins since Matt's wedding in York, Yorkshire County in the spring of '60. His Aunt Bess was smiling ear to ear. She loved Mary's children as her own. James' Aunt Sarina, Thomas's younger sister had been ill for some time, and James hoped she would be able to attend the wedding, but she was seen nowhere. That was not a good sign and made him feel sad. He knew if she were well, she and Uncle Richard would be at his wedding.

The crowd turned to watch as Thomas and Mary walked up the aisle with James behind them. James waited as his parents seated themselves next to Paul and Bess. He grinned, turned, and nodded to the pastor who would be performing the service, as he stepped to stand near him. James looked to his sister Emily, Jess's maid of honor, who looked lovely and glowing in her long pink gown. He sidestepped a bit to stand next to Grant, his best man, who shook his hand, and then turned to face the aisle, as he wanted a perfectly clear view of Jess as she came down the aisle to him.

Suddenly, there she was, with her father. Violins played as everyone stood to receive the bride. A vision, James thought, she's a beautiful vision in white. The dress covered her from chin to toe and the train went on forever behind her. Her veil was simple yet long and blended into the dress, to where one could hardly tell where it truly began down her back.

Edward walked very tall and proud next to his beautiful daughter. He led her hand to James' hand, kissed her on the cheek through her veil, and turned to sit next to his wife. The pastor then motioned for all to please sit. James and Jess said their vows and when the pastor said you may kiss the bride, it would be the first time their lips would meet. When they did, he thought they were as soft as a cloud, and as sweet as molasses. He felt then he was the luckiest man on earth.

"May I present to you, for the first time, Mr. and Mrs. James Atwood," said the pastor as he turned the bride and groom toward the seated crowd. James thought he was going to burst with pride and love for his new wife. As they walked down the aisle as husband and wife, Jess' arm tightly inside his elbow, she hung her hand just so, to show off her new golden wedding band. They then stopped at the end of the aisle to greet their guests.

The Strong's put on quite a feast for their daughter's wedding, serving roasted pig, and three kinds of fish. The violins played through dinner then suddenly changed their tempo so all could dance. The bride and groom were first to sway to the music, then the area filled with many dancers. John and Emily were among those on the dance floor and James noticed her stomach was starting to show small evidence of a baby. They danced through the evening with their well-wishers when suddenly James' cousin Matt, grabbed him by the arm, and started rushing him through the crowd to the top of the rear house steps. Jess saw what they were doing and worked her way through the crowd to join them. Grant did the same. Matt hugged Jess then announced to the crowd, "These newlyweds need to start their honeymoon." He yelled loud enough to where the violins stopped, and the wedding guests turned to look his way.

"Let's all wish James and Jessica good luck and let them get on their way!" By this time, Matt's brother, John had joined them, hugged his cousin James, then Jess, and wished them well. Grant held his sister for a long moment then released her after a long kiss on her cheek. She swore she saw tears in his eyes.

Victoria made her way through all those that gathered to see the bride and groom, got to the top of the stairs and joined her daughter and new son-in-law. She hugged her daughter with tears in her eyes. While still holding her, she searched the many faces in the crowd for her husband. Edward's feet were firmly planted, as he waved his glass of champagne in a toast to the bride and groom. The entire crowd joined him in the toast. She saw that he was not about to move, and hung her head for a moment with disappointment. She kissed her daughter's cheek, which was now wet with tears. Victoria then reached to hug James and found it hard to let him go. His caress back was heartfelt, and he then reached for his wife's hand as they stood together, waving to the crowd. Grant then led them through the house toward the front door and out, to a waiting carriage. The chill in the air was crisp, so James wrapped his wife in a blanket as the horses started their way around the circular drive. He held his wife as close as he could, while they rode silently through the streets of Liverpool until they arrived at their new home, their third floor flat.

James helped Jess down from the carriage and assisted with her dress, train, and veil as they climbed three stories of winding steps to their door. He then swept her up in his arms and struggled with the lock and door handle. Jess made a whooping sound when he scooped her off the floor. "Guess I should have opened the door first, My Love. Please bear with me," It finally opened and they practically fell into the small room. He twirled her in circles for a moment before putting her down. She had not yet seen the flat, so James quickly ran from oil lamp to oil lamp lighting them as he went, illuminating the room. She twirled as she viewed the room, picking up her dress as she spun. She laughed, threw her head back with joy, then ran to James, and wrapped her arms around his neck.

"I love it, James. I'm home," giggled Jess. He held her close then kissed her deeply. Her kiss in return was loving and sensual. Their tongues touched for the first time and his excitement drove him on, ravenously kissing his wife, and slowly moved his kisses gently around her face and down her neck. Jess melted in his arms. She softly moaned and let his kisses and hands go where he wanted on her body. His kisses traced the lace around her neck as he softly stepped around Jess and started kissing the back of her neck. He reached up to release her hair starting with the first hairpin he found, carefully removed many more and finally her beautiful black hair was loose and fell softly to her shoulders.

He started undoing the many wedding dress buttons down her back, as her head tilted forward and she helped by parting her hair so he could see each button as he undid them. James noticed her breathing was quickening with each undone button just as his excitement grew. James hardly knew anything about making love to a woman, as Jess was his first, but he moved with her reactions and sweet feminine sounds. He started lightly scratching her back as the dress opened to him. He saw her small back and with each soft stroke of his fingers, her back started to turn pink. She leaned into his motions with sweet moans that he had never heard from a woman before. He moved to her shoulders to lower her dress as she sucked in a breath, turned her head to James, and begged him not to stop. He continued running his hand up and down her back and slowly worked his right hand around to Jess' breast, inside the dress. She gasped so loudly, he thought he had done something wrong and started to pull his hand away. He stopped quickly as Jess shook her head no, grabbed his hand through the fabric, and led it back to her right breast. He felt the weight of her breast in his hand and while caressing it moved his fingers in search of the young, erect nipple. He discovered it to be hard like a small rosebud. He twirled the bud between his finger and thumb as she groaned and laid her head back on his chest. She turned to kiss his cheek, and then twisted her body around slowly, which worked his arm up, lifting the dress off her shoulders. When face-to-face he started lowering the dress, until it dropped to the floor. James took a step back to look at his wife, who was blushing, yet she did not attempt to cover herself.

"Oh James, I love you so," she whispered as she neared him and began taking his coat off and lay it on the chair nearest to her. James reached for her, but she moved his arms aside as she started undoing the buttons of his shirt. He assisted by pulling the tail of the shirt out of his pants as he let her finish undoing the buttons, removing his shirt, letting it drop to the floor. The oil lamps were throwing a soft yellow glow across his muscular chest and she could not stop herself from tenderly running her fingers across the tight skin of his chest. As she did this, his nipples became erect. She stopped at each with both hands and flicked them lightly with her thumbs. James' eyes closed at the wonderment of the feelings he was experiencing at her touch. He had never felt such heat and desire. His body ached for her.

He pulled her close to him and it was then she felt the full length and heat of his erection. She slowly lowered her hands, arriving at the waist of his pants. She found the top button and slowly undid each of them one by one. James wanted to take Jess to the floor right then, but looking into her eyes, he saw her desire and kissed her deeply. Their tongues entwined which made their hunger grow. Jess broke away from his kiss to catch her breath when their eyes met again. She lowered her look and said, "Shall we…" and before she could finish the question, James was pulling her by the hand toward the bedroom.

She stopped briefly when she entered the room to take in the view. It was too dark to see it all and she started for the oil lamp next to the bed, but he beat her to it, lit the lamp, and then turned quickly to his new wife. He again scooped her into his arms, only to kneel on the bed and lower her to the soft bedcover. She raised her arms to pull her hair out from under her and fanned it over the bedcover above her head. She looked like an angel.

Jess struggled beneath him trying to remove her pantaloons, when he raised himself slightly to give her room to move, he then took over the deed. He slowly peeled them from her long legs as he stood to eye her nakedness. While taking in the sight of his beautiful wife, he removed his shoes and pants and lay next to her. He began combing her long black hair with his fingers, then traced her face with one finger and then down her neck. She reached with one hand to caress his face and touch his fingers on her face with the other. James kissed her lightly before he kissed her chin and neck then found her erect nipple with his mouth. Jess' eyes closed tightly as she saw stars. Never before had she known such wonderful sensations. His tongue lightly teased her nipple before he began sucking and soon heard her groans of delight. His hand found her right breast when he then moved his mouth to suckle the waiting erect rosebud.

Jess was running her hands through his hair, when she found herself holding his head in the place where he was so involved. His left hand started down her taught stomach and traced her navel with his fingertip. She swallowed a groan as his hand searched further until he found her warm patch of hair. He moaned through his nose and turned his head to see what he found with his fingers. The lamp light was dim but he could still watch as his wife spread her legs slightly so he could investigate further. He reached lower, to find a warm wet opening where he inserted his middle finger. Jess nearly came off the bed to meet his hand in motion. James moved closer to his wife when his hot stiffness met the side of her leg. With that, he looked up to his wife's contorted face. He watched as her finger neared her own mouth when she gently bit down on her middle finger. James' finger traced her hand and replaced her finger with his. He ran his finger softly over her lips, then the edges of her open teeth. She then began to suck on his finger but released quickly to catch her breath. They met eyes and she grabbed his hand to lick slowly up and down each finger as his other hand explored her heated opening, which was now even slicker than before. He probed her until he found a spot deep inside that made her hips rise to his touch.

She dropped his hand when her head went back until the top of her head was on the bed, her neck straining. He saw that what he was doing was driving her to ecstasy. Jess held her breath briefly then exploded with wonder, muffling her own screams through closed lips. He continued his finger movement until her hand rushed to his, when she suddenly stopped his hand from moving. He watched her entire body stiffen then slowly lower to the bed. He listened to her contented sounds, which filled his erection to the point where he thought it would burst. As she slowly came back to earth and could breathe again, she turned to her husband, kissed him with fervor, and began exploring his body with her light touch. She stroked his hard muscular shoulders and arms, went across his chest and delighted him again by twirling his nipple between her fingers. She lowered her head to kiss the tip of each, then suckled one and gently squeezed the other between her thumb and finger. With her tongue on the raised bead on his hard chest, it was now her turn to listen to her husband's guttural tones.

She raised her head to watch her husband's face as she lowered her hand and traced the thin blonde hair trail down his stomach until she found his hard member, now throbbing in her hand. She held it tightly, not knowing what to do, when his hand lowered upon hers and directed her to do slow, gentle strokes. His head fell back onto the bed and his eyes clamped shut when loud moans escaped his lips. She tested different ways to slide up and down his manhood, squeezing tighter then softer, until he thought he would lose his mind. He had never felt anything more wonderful and could not imagine anything better. However, he was wrong.

He quickly raised himself off the bed, over his wife, where she gladly parted her legs to accept her husband for the first time. Neither one could wait for what was to come, yet they never wanted these feelings to stop. He reached down to direct his throbbing hardness into the sweet, warm, wet opening, and slowly began to glide it deeper into her, where he met resistance. He kissed his wife softly, then tenderly plunged harder and deeper and broke through her virginity. Her nails were digging into his back as she dealt with the pain, which to her surprise only lasted a moment. Then that wonderful feeling of him deep inside her retuned and overtook her entire being. He waited a moment, then saw the ecstasy return to her face and he started thrusting his hips, moving deeper, taking longer strides. She soon found his rhythm and met it. Soon their bodies were moving faster together, when he lowered his head to tickle her nipple again with his tongue. Their thrusts became more determined as he searched his wife's face. Her eyes were closed, blowing her breath through pursed lips, moving his blonde hair with each huff. It was getting difficult for James to hold back when her body rose off the bed and her groans intensified. The sounds started in her throat, then came through her nose until she finally opened her mouth and let the inner eruption out.

Her head had gone back and James watched as he drove her even farther, past heaven. With his sweat now dripping onto her heaving breasts, he took a deep breath and thrust even deeper and faster until he was close to exploding. He finally let go to an ecstasy he had never known before, spilling his seed deep inside of her. Jess heard her husband's guttural sounds, until he buried his face in her shoulder and cried out, trying to dampen his loud eruption. They had become one.

When he caught his breath, he opened his eyes, to see his wife reach for his face, smile, and turn her head to meet his. She kissed him with so much love. It was a long, loving kiss between husband and wife.

They pulled down the bedcover and quickly slipped between the sheets for warmth and slept the entire night wrapped in each other's arms. James woke a few hours later as the room had gotten cold from the autumn night air after the fire died. He slowly and quietly got out of bed, went to the fireplace, and added wood to the fire. Jess surprised him from behind with a hug and kissed the back of his neck. When he saw the fire roaring again, they once again found ecstasy and happiness in each other's arms.

Chapter Four
1861 - 1864

Edward Strong was kind enough to allow James off from work at the lumberyard Monday and Tuesday, those days were their honeymoon. For the next two days, James and Jess hardly got out of bed. They even opened their wedding gifts in bed. They cooked quickly together in the cool room, or had bread and cheese, only to return to their warm bed and enjoyed each other to exhaustion many times. They napped and read, totally entwined in each other, staying as close as they could to one another. They snacked and enjoyed the wine her parents gave them as part of their wedding gift. They also gave them, along with the mattress and wine, a monitory gift, which they desperately needed.

Wednesday morning arrived too quickly. James bathed in the warm tub they prepared together, and then he was off to work. Jess had prepared his lunch of bread, cheese, and sweet strawberry jam she had made herself in late summer. At lunch, he was excited to eat the first lunch she prepared for him for work when he found a note she slipped into the bread wrapped in newspaper saying "I love you!" The men at the lumberyard teased him, probably with envy. James just smiled, shrugged his shoulders, and ignored their remarks. "Eat your hearts out!"

Meanwhile, Jess tried desperately to remove the small bloodstain left on the bedcover during their first lovemaking. She could not remove the stain and reminded herself to ask Lizzie how to get it out. She then filled her day putting a feminine touch to their home. Lizzie brought over a wagon full of Jess' things and clothes from her old bedroom.

"There are a lot more clothes to come, wherever will you put them all?"

"I'm going to have to decide which clothes I truly want here for the winter season. I will ask James what to do when he returns home."

After Lizzie's visit, Jess looked around the flat and hoped James liked the changes she made, which were slight alterations, and she was very happy with the welcoming feeling the flat now had. She washed the sheets and even ironed them before she returned them to their bed. She knew James' favorite meal was roasted pig, which they shared on their wedding day. She bought pork at the market two blocks away along with fresh bread and green beans, for their first meal at the dining table in their home, as husband and wife.

When James arrived home, he smelled the pork roasting in the fireplace, yet, there was something else that made the flat feel warmer, what was it? After he kissed his wife hello, he removed his dirty clothes and hugged her at length. His bathtub waited for him near the hearth, just as it did in his childhood home. Jess poured the boiling water into the tepid tub and watched her husband lower himself into the welcoming tub. She started to wash his back when suddenly she stopped. James turned to watch Jess quickly remove her clothes. She stepped out of them and tiptoed over to the tub, rose one leg and waited for James to move his legs to make room for her. She dropped into the tub, almost on top of him, which aroused him instantly. She felt his erection, smiled and leaned forward to kiss the love of her life. She loved to look into his deep brown eyes. She adored his blonde hair and ran her wet fingers through it as they stared into each other's eyes. Jess thought he was the handsomest man she had ever seen, and was so proud of her man, and loved him more than he could ever know. She then reached down to stroke his throbbing manhood, and teased it only a short time before she raised herself high enough to then lower herself over his erection, much to his surprise. It stayed buried deep inside her while she positioned herself in the tub, putting her legs behind his muscled bottom. He caressed her small buttocks with both hands and felt her muscles work hard while she rode his hot, rock hard penis. Jess continued to ride his staff until they were both blind to the world and breathless.

"Where did you....learn to do that?" James was trying to catch his breath.

"I didn't learn it anywhere, my love, I just thought of it while I was washing your beautiful back. Guess I should get that clean now, and then the rest of you." She giggled through her red cheeks.

"Thank you, my beautiful wife." James chuckled. She smiled as she started to wash him all over. James happily returned the "favor".

37

After their "bath" and the delicious pork dinner, together they emptied the tub, sat in front of the fire, and discussed the changes she had made in their apartment. James told her how much he admired the changes, when her clothes came into their discussion. He said he would make her an armoire, and scolded himself silently for not thinking of it before. They both happily enjoyed each other's company in front of the fire when James said, "I have been waiting to talk to you about our future, Jess, until I knew exactly what it is I want to do....I mean, what I would like us to do."

"What of our future, my handsome husband?"

"Well, I have been dreaming of going to America most of my life."

"What do you......"

He held one finger to her lips and asked her to listen to his dream before she asked questions. He took a breath and continued as he looked into her eyes, "Since I was 16 or so, I have been dreaming of going to America, owning a big piece of land with a lot of trees for lumber and building a beautiful home there. I have done research at the library and I think northern New York in America would be the perfect place for us. Now that you are my wife, whom I love very much," he kissed his wife tenderly, "I would like us to go there together, find the right area and start building our home and our family. Although, I would wish to be employed by your father a few more years to learn all I can about the lumber business. Then I would like to start my own lumber business in America and the rest will be what it is to be."

"That all sounds wonderful, James, but how can we leave our families? I don't know if I could be that far away from my family."

"I have thought of that, Darling Jess, and I'm hoping they will all cross the sea with us." James started to sound unsure. "They may not leave immediately, but possibly, eventually..."

"I hardly believe Father would leave his business and Mother her home and her many friends, let alone England."

"Your father will hardly work all of his life, Honey. In addition, your mother, I think, would follow you anywhere. Moreover, this would only happen if you want it to. It won't come about for a few years to come. There's a lot of time for all to adjust to the idea."

"I see." Jess looked at the flames in the fireplace, "So this is just food for thought right now?"

"Yes, my dear, food for thought - of our future," he added and smiled at the latter.

She snuggled closer to him on the small, tattered settee and sunk her head into his strong shoulder. They did not light a lamp, but simply sat together in the glow of the fire and discussed America and his many dreams. He verbally shared the floor plan of the house he wanted to build with her and how they would fill it with children. Her smile met his.

Their fire was about to die and soon it was time to retire to bed when Jess went into the bedroom, lit a lamp and waited for James to follow her into the room. He soon entered the room to find two new shirts that waited for him on the chair by the fireplace.

"Are these for me?" James liked surprises.

"Yes, Sweetheart, I made them for you. I hope you like them and hope they keep you warm at the lumberyard."

"They seem to be too nice for work. But I will gladly wear each with pride."

"I pressed both shirts. Please take your choice on which to wear on the morrow." Jess felt excited inside and loved the sweet look on her husband's face.

"I see that. I will wear the plaid one. I have never owned a plaid shirt before. I thank you, my thoughtful woman. You are too kind."

Jess smiled and kissed her husband. She was glad he enjoyed her surprise and that he did not ask where she got the money. She had saved birthday and holiday gift money for some time, not knowing how she would spend it. This would be her secret.

They lived the next two years in the third story flat. James worked six days a week at the lumberyard, to which he was very accustomed.

In those two years, Emily, James' sister, had her first child and named her Sarah Elizabeth Bryce. Her middle name was to honor John's mother. Emily was quickly in the family way again and delivered another girl, named Marylee Jane Bryce, both names chosen to honor

Mary Jane Atwood, Emily and James' mother. They were both perfect images of their mother, with blonde hair and big brown eyes.

Jess filled her days going to the market and library with girlfriends and sometimes visited her mother or met her for lunch near the market. Victoria could see the happiness in Jess' eyes and heard it in her words of love for her husband. Then the subject suddenly changed which stunned Victoria when Jess said, "James has a dream, Mother. He really wants us to go to America in hopes that you and his parents will move there with us."

"Jessica, my word! How could you possibly move so far away from home? The American War Between the States is currently bubbling to a full boil. Why would you want to move into the middle of that?"

"My home is with James, wherever that may be. His desire is to go to northern New York where the war has barely touched. He gets information from the men that sail back and forth from here to New York. He says there is a lot of land to choose from there and like I said, is barely touched by the war."

"Barely touched? What does that mean, barely touched? My dear we would worry about you both so much. Can't this "dream" wait until the war is over?"

"Well, it's not going to happen soon, but he often brings it up in our conversations. He now knows the lumber business rather well, thanks to Father, and feels he can start his own lumber business over there and build the home he has always wanted." Jess surprised herself on how strongly she was defending her husband.

"Why can't he do that here? As you know, your father has done very well right here in Liverpool." Victoria's face was now red with concern.

"He feels very strongly that there are many opportunities there and his place is in America." Jess lowered her head and noted her fiddling fingers, and stopped her obvious nervousness. She had tried so many times to have this conversation with her mother to warn her. She then worried about how James would feel when she tells him that she shared their dream with her mother. She decided she would cross that bridge when she came to it. Jess knew her mother would rush home and tell her father of their conversation, and this way the family would have time to soften to the idea. Maybe they might start to think like James and would want to follow them to America. Jess started to think aloud to her mother, "Maybe Father could sell his business and help James start another one in America."

"That's so much to assume, Jessica. Your father loves this country and I doubt he will ever leave it. Is there any way you can convince James to build the house he wants so badly here in England? Why, you could build it close to us and we could employ Lizzie again to take care of your...children, someday. She loves and misses you so." Victoria was excited, yet tried to grin through her nervousness.

"Yes, she does, I know Mother, but James is my husband and I will talk to him, but in the end, I will follow him wherever he goes." Jess now twisted the wedding band on her finger she admired and respected so much.

The two women talked a while longer, finished their lunch, and then kissed good-bye in the carriage in front of Jess' building. As she made the three-story trek with her packages from the market, Jess again worried about how James will take the news that she had planted the seed in her mother's mind of America.

James arrived home to the usual good-natured Jess, to a warm bath that waited for him and the smell of beef in the stewpot that hung in the fireplace. He kissed his wife hello, yet waited to hug her because he felt his clothes were dirtier than usual from work. While he sunk into the warm tub water, he watched his wife move through the room, as she gathered his clothes, brought clean ones from the bedroom and arranged their dinner table, which included one fresh flower in a small vase. She looked at James and searched his face for his mood, just as he smiled and commented it was all beautiful and dinner smelled wonderful.

Sales had been very good at the lumberyard, and James usually assisted loading wagons with lumber, though he was now a supervisor, which Edward made him only a month ago. James had watched his previous gnarly dock manager often times and he swore he would never be that kind of man. His muscular body and sun soaked skin were proof of that.

Jess was washing his back when James tried to convince her to join him in the tub, which she often did, but not on this day; she was too nervous. She knew she would have to share her discussion she had with her mother with James, as he would have to face her father the next day. She helped him dry after his bath and while he dressed, she served dinner, scooping the beef stew into large bowls. They ate dinner by the glow of the fire in silence.

"You are very quiet tonight, my dear Jessica." James looked at her and felt worried.

"James, I had lunch with Mother today at the market and we had a long talk." Jess wiggled nervously in her chair. She could hardly make eye contact with her husband.

"Oh?" James wondered why she was so unsettled.

"Yes, we started talking of the future and I told her about your dream of America and building your own lumberyard there," she nervously sputtered.

"Well, I'm almost glad you did that. I was wondering how we were going to break the news to them." James smiled and felt relieved in a way.

"Oh, I'm so glad you feel that way, James. I am sorry I didn't wait for you to be in the conversation, it just slipped out. Mother expressed her worries, but I made it plain to her that you are my husband, and I will follow you wherever you go." Jess tried to smile and moved her eyes from his to the empty bowl in front of her.

"Well, I'm glad to hear that, because I feel the time to leave is nearing. I was thinking about the war going on there, and it may be a very good time to go since lumber will be in much demand to rebuild war battered towns. We might even have a hard time filling orders and keeping up with the demand. It could all work in our favor in fact, and be a great benefit to the poor people left with almost nothing."

"I never thought of it that way. You could be right." She was delighted.

"I could be *very* right and I need to make your father understand this, in hopes it will convince him they should follow us to America." With that, his arm crossed the table to hold Jess' hand, to comfort her worries. She looked at her husband with a smile, and squeezed his hand in return. He rose from the chair, approached his wife, and kissed the top of her head. She in turn, raised her arms to hug him around his middle. They held their embrace for a long time by the glow of the fire.

After dinner, they pulled their chairs closer to the fire, not only for warmth, but also for light to read the books Jess had borrowed from the library that day. She thought he would enjoy "Uncle Tom's Cabin" an American tale of slavery, and for herself, a love story. She adored books and would sometimes read them twice before returning them to the library.

The next day James worried that he might have the first heated conversation with his father-in-law, but their discussion found an even level when James explained how it might be the perfect time to own a lumber business in New York. He said if they go far enough North not near battle sights yet close enough to assist in the rebuilding of northeastern America, wood will probably be in high demand. In fact, the two men stopped their work during the day and returned to the America conversation several times. James could see that Edward was thinking seriously about America and its many prospects; yet also saw the pain of losing his daughter in his father-in-laws eyes.

James excitedly shared this news with his wife that evening over dinner. When she heard about her father's enthusiasm, she was almost giddy with excitement at the thought that her parents might make the decision to move to America with them.

Jess knew if they did this move with James and Jess, it would leave her younger brother Grant alone in England, only to have aunts, uncles, and cousins for his nearest family. She now wondered how he would take this news. Grant, a medical intern in London, usually visited Liverpool for Christmas, weddings, and once in summer. He was very dedicated yet still several years away from becoming the surgeon he wanted to be. She and Grant wrote letters to stay in touch, but it usually took him a long time to answer Jess' letters, however, she understood. He was a good student, yet she worried about her brother. Was he happy; did he have friends; was he in love? His letters usually contained information about school events, his grades, thoughts about instructors, and not much more. This however, she thought, is not something you would share in a letter. In person would be much better.

Jess decided to discuss traveling to London with James to visit Grant as the America dream grew closer to fruition.

Chapter Five
June 1864

James received American war information from his previous dockworkers and ship captains and was getting more anxious to start their lives there. He told Jess about his anxieties and they discussed the many things they would have to do to prepare for the move. Jess said she would do whatever was necessary. He explained that they would not have the best traveling conditions, since they would have to sail on a ship that imported American wood to England and exported teas and spices to America. The ship would arrive in New York City, which he explained, was much larger and busier than Liverpool, the only city Jess had ever known. She felt her stomach do a flip when she heard this, but as long as James was by her side, she knew in her heart, she would be fine.

"Maybe now would be a good time to travel to London to visit my brother and explain all of this to him and say our good-byes," Jess said almost in a whisper.

James pondered what she said, then looked at his wife. "You are right. Let me think about that."

They were sitting on the settee, facing each other, legs entwined in each other's, and reading by the light of the fireplace. James found himself scanning the words in his book and not retaining the words. His thoughts were on their future. His main concern was how to find the perfect town and wooded area for their home and lumberyard. He could handle the big city, he thought, but how would they travel north, how would they know which part of the state to settle? He only knew a few Americans from the docks, and they seemed honest, but were all Americans trustworthy? Well, the only way to find out is to deal with what happens, day to day. He knew he was a quick study of people and situations and prayed that all would go well.

Edward now knew his son-in-law rather well and recognized he was on edge and getting anxious to go to America. He discussed the situation with Victoria several times at length, and together, they decided they would start the sale of the lumberyard, and after they talked with Grant in London, if he did not object, they too would move to America. Edward had inklings about who might buy his lumberyard, but times were hard and he knew it could take time to sell. They shared their news that night with James and Jess at dinner at the Strong's home and they both could not have been happier. Jess loved the thought of her parents living near her in America where they could see their grandchildren often and watch them grow. Jess jumped up from the table to hug her parents separately, starting with her father then lingered by her mother. She looked across the table at James, smiled at him in delight and blew him a kiss. She felt giddy inside and wanted to jump up and down like a little girl, clapping her hands, yet she kept her composure.

"We need to tell Grant. I think all of us should be present when he learns the news." Edward was adamant.

"I agree," said James. "When should we do this?"

"The sooner, the better." Victoria looked around her daughter at Edward.

Their discussion continued and they decided to travel to London, which was 178 miles away, together on the next Tuesday. It would take almost three days by carriage. Edward sent a telegram to Grant to let him know of their forthcoming visit.

Tuesday arrived quickly for Jess, yet she was prepared. They were all thankful it was the start of spring, which would make travel comfortable. The carriage arrived that morning at dawn. Edward sent his driver up the three stories to assist James and Jess with their trunk and miscellaneous items, then jumped down to aid in loading them onto the rear of the carriage. Edward could not help but comment that his daughter never traveled lightly and punched his elbow into James' ribs. They both silently laughed. Then James, being the last to enter into the covered carriage, said good morning to Victoria and nestled next to his wife. Victoria had needlepoint in her lap to busy herself on the trip. Jess and James had books to read, and Edward had maps of New York City and state. He was also prepared to take notes on their discussions about necessities to complete their voyage.

Being mentally prepared for three days travel in their carriage, the first day was busy with a lot of talk of the future. Periodically the women added their thoughts with apprehension. The overall feeling was anxiousness yet happy. Victoria and Jess both prepared lunches, which they ate while on the move. Having traveled to London to accompany Grant to medical school, Edward remembered where the inns were he and Grant had stayed in and asked the family to trust him in selecting their stopping points.

The first inn's dining room was dark but cozy. Edward ordered their dinner for them and emphasized to the server that she continue to serve ale pints after dinner. Jess sipped at her first pint, as did Victoria, and then they requested water as a replacement. Dinner was plentiful, which they also shared with their driver. After clinking glasses, they agreed to retire to their rooms, rise at dawn, and continue their trek.

The second day seemed longer than the first to all of them. They were all very glad to arrive at the second inn for the night. There was a bounty of food and ale for all and again they retired early.

Jess thought the third day would never end. Finally, before dark, Edward announced London was on the horizon. They all stretched to see the view. The buildings were the tallest Jess had ever seen. Her mouth fell open as she stared in awe. James reached over with one finger and tenderly raised her jaw to close her mouth, with a wink. She looked over to meet his eyes and they giggled together.

Chapter Six
Spring 1864

The carriage arrived in front of the hotel where Edward asked the driver to assist the bellhops with their trunks. The driver then took the horse and carriage blocks away to the stable. Edward asked if all were up to a walk to meet Grant, and all said or nodded yes, not knowing what to expect. "It's only a few blocks to the medical school. The walk will do us all good after being in the carriage for days." Edward grinned then gladly led the way.

Jess had never seen so many people on a city street. While holding James' hand, it was still a struggle for them to keep up with her parents. James wondered where they were going. He could hardly look up while they walked, as he wanted to admire the architecture. Jess had to hold up her dress to not stumble and keep up her fathers pace.

They finally arrived at a building that looked older than the last one. The grounds were neat and groomed, yet it felt as if they had stepped out of the middle of London. They entered under a large archway, entered the building, and approached an oversized desk where a man sat busy with papers. Although it was warm, he was dressed in a very odd suit, one Jess had never seen the likes. The man looked up, smiled, and asked if he could be of assistance. Edward stepped forward and proclaimed they were here to see his son Grant Strong. The man behind the desk looked through a large ledger, nodded his head, and then explained that he was currently in a class. He added that within the hour, he would be able to receive visitors. He rose and asked them to follow him. He walked across the shiny marble floor as they followed and heard each click of his hard-soled shoes. They reached two doors that looked to be twenty feet tall. Jess' eyes opened wide as she still held James' hand, and then followed him and her parents into a large room filled with tables. There were two oil lamps and four chairs at each table. The room was warmer than the entry hall. They finally arrived at the far side of the room to two leather davenports.

"When Mr. Strong is out of class, I will instruct him to meet you here." The man did a half bow before he left the room.

They sat and quietly waited, admiring the hundreds of books and their aged surroundings. There were ladders that glided on wheels to reach the highest shelves, which amazed them all. Several students were at tables studying with the assistance of the sunlight that came from the very tall windows. Edward felt the need to whisper to his family that he hoped their wait would not be long. He checked his timepiece in his vest and told them it was approaching three o'clock. They all sat in silence, and most waited patiently.

"Half past three," announced Edward as he checked his timepiece again. They heard the door open and Grant appeared, with a big smile. He had grown a beard and mustache and Jess was amazed at how much older he looked since she had seen him Christmas last. Grant approached them, hugged his mother first, and kissed her cheek. He shook his father's hand then stepped to receive his sister. Jess hugged him closely and kissed his hairy cheek before she let him shake James' hand. James clapped Grant's shoulder with his left hand, glad to see his brother-in-law.

"It's so good to see you all. Just how do I deserve this wonderful surprise visit?"

"Did you not receive my wire?" Edward's brows rose in question.

"Yes I did, but this is still unexpected – and all of you!" Grant was happy but still wondered. "Jess, I would say marriage agrees with you."

Jess smiled at her brother with love and soon her father's voice filled the room.

"Son, we would like to discuss that over dinner. Might you suggest a restaurant and join us there?" Edward stepped closer to his son and put his hand lovingly on his shoulder.

"Yes sir, I can join you and I know the perfect place," Grant replied as they followed him out of the room. He stopped briefly to talk to the man at the desk then proceeded to lead them out of the building. They kept up with Grant, all trying to talk at the same time with questions and comments until they were again on the busy street. They walked one block and arrived at Grant's favorite restaurant. Once inside the huge dining room, they saw many diners scattered throughout the room. Grant led them to the back to the room finding a large table. A woman approached the table with a ewer of ale and tray of glasses.

"Grant, so good to see you again. Is this your family from Liverpool?" asked the server with a smile. "I assume you'll want your usual?"

With Grant's head nod, she put the tray and pitcher down before him. "Thank you. Yes, this is my family. Everyone, this is Lilly."

They all nodded and greeted her as she began to pour a glass of ale for each. When she finished she announced she would return to get their orders and handed each a parchment menu. She especially grinned at Jess then turned and left the area and disappeared behind a door.

"Is that woman your...." started Victoria.

Grant stopped her before she finished the question. He knew what she was about to ask. "No Mother, she's a friend who serves our table often when I and others come here after classes."

Victoria bowed her head in embarrassment when Grant asked again, why the visit. Edward took a long swig of his ale, looked at James, not knowing if he should start this conversation or let James do it.

James took the opportunity to start, "Grant, I've decided to take my bride to America to live and start a lumber business. Your parents...."

Edward interrupted James, "Your mother and I have decided to go with them, once the lumberyard and house in Liverpool are sold. We don't know how you're going to feel about this news, but we are all hoping you will embrace our common dream and say you will at least come to visit us there once you are out of school."

"Goodness, Father, I never expected to hear this kind of news. I knew it had to be big news for you all to come for a visit. Yet I have to say that I truly thought you were going to announce that a baby was on its way, but not America," supposed Grant.

Jessica blushed and looked to her lap. She took James' hand and said, "Sorry to disappoint, brother, but there are no children to announce."

Grant broke in quickly, "America, mm. I've had thoughts of that myself. With the war that's raging on year after year over there they are in desperate need of surgeons."

Victoria practically jumped off her chair, "Grant, you wouldn't!"

"But Mother, that's what I do, I help people," exclaimed Grant. "But I have to admit, I would be very close to the fighting, and that does not entice me. So when do you plan to make this move?"

"Well, we discussed it in the carriage, and James and Jessica want to leave for America soon. However, your mother and I are concerned about how you feel and we will stay in England if you ask us to. We love you son, but we are not getting any younger, and I am really looking forward to assisting James on the start-up of another lumber business. He has been working very hard at the yard, has gotten to know the business very well, and I am sure he will do well in America. As James mentioned in the past, lumber will be in much demand to rebuild war torn areas for many years to come. Therefore, northern New York State, where trees are plentiful and away from the battlefields makes sense."

Grant sat back in his chair, having drunk his ale, filled his glass again and finally said, "It sounds to me you have thought this through very well and it sounds like a strong, sane plan. May I say that it is enticing to me, but we have one small problem, or should I say I have a small reason that will keep me here? I have fallen in love with Miss Kathleen McCarthy."

"Kathleen?" Edward was the first to ask.

"I haven't told you about her, Father, but I am in love. Kathleen is my favorite professor's daughter. She is a flaming red head with wild green eyes and loves me as much as I love her. We've been courting for a year now and have decided to marry when I finish school." Grant displayed a huge smile.

"Grant! Why haven't you told us?" Victoria was amazed.

"I was going to surprise you this summer when she would have accompanied me to meet all of you. I know you will love her as I do. She's not only beautiful but smart, possibly smarter than me," Grant giggled as he added, "Her father came to England from Ireland to teach medicine. I do admire him greatly. Dr. McCarthy and his wife have been very kind to me with many dinners and summer picnics on the riverfront. She loves horses and assists in training them for the city of London. She is quite a girl!"

51

James rose and stepped toward Grant to shake his hand, "Congratulations! She sounds like quite a lady. Good luck to you both. We can't wait to meet her."

"Thank you, James! I'm a very lucky man. You will all be able to meet her tomorrow at dinner. She is very anxious to meet all of you, but I warn you, she lights up the room!"

The family sat for a long time and discussed America at length before they ordered their dinner. They were all glad to visit with Grant but were exhausted from their trip.

After dinner, they parted ways at the arch of the medical school where Grant was living in a dormitory. The crowd on the street was lighter than during their first London walk and James was able to enjoy some of the building faces now that they were ambling more slowly as they returned to the hotel. In the lobby, they said their good nights and each couple started up separate staircases that mirrored each other in the hotel lobby.

Chapter Seven

"My Dear Family, this is Kathleen." Grant was beaming as he took a half step away from her, and then bowed with a wave of his arm, as if presenting the queen.

Kathleen looked nervous but displayed a big smile. Everything about her was perfect, thought Jessica - Grant was right, she is a beauty, even her teeth are perfect.

"Nice to meet you all," said Kathleen in her Irish brogue, and slightly curtsied.

Victoria stepped forward to introduce herself first, then Edward. Jess followed with a hug for Kathleen then introduced James to her and put her arm through his and he patted Jess' hand on his arm.

They returned to the same restaurant, where Lilly served them again, whom, it seemed, knew Kathleen very well. They exchanged whispers and giggles before they ordered their meals. Two hours passed quickly while they all conversed, laughed, and got to know each other. Marriage came up briefly in conversation, but Kathleen acted uncomfortable and the subject was dropped quickly when Victoria tapped Edward's leg under the table. He smiled at Victoria and speedily changed the subject. Lilly surprised them with a cake and a small candle glowing on top to celebrate their family reunion. This made Edward look at his family with admiration and ordered a bottle of Champaign. They all clinked glasses and cheered so loudly that others in the room turned to see what the excitement was.

They each kissed Grant and Kathleen goodnight, then went their separate ways. All spoke highly of Kathleen during the walk back to the hotel. Jess was especially happy that her brother found true love just as she had. It almost made her giddy inside.

James and Jess made love that night, for the first time other than in their flat.

They met her parents for breakfast the next morning and talked about when James and Jess would leave England. The two couples rode through London sight seeing in their carriage before meeting Grant for lunch. The sight of Big Ben, and to hear it ring out every hour was delightful. Liverpool had nothing so grand. They all toured

Westminster Abbey and Kensington Hall, and saw where Anne Boleyn lost her head. They saw so many things they'd only heard about all of their lives. It was a wonderful trip for all of them.

Lunch was brief because Grant had to return to classes and sorrowful because they didn't know when they would see each other again. Kathleen was not able to get away from her training position to meet them, but sent them all her love.

The three-day trip back to Liverpool was uneventful. Jess and James shopped in Liverpool for steamer trunks upon their return and for the first time, regretted they lived on the third floor. It was then James realized it would be worse after the trunks were packed. They then took a short stroll to the market area enjoying the summer evening and each other's company.

They woke before dawn the next morning and worked together preparing the trunks, and discussed what to take with them and how to pack their items. They decided Jess' parents would bring the armoire James had built and their wedding bed to America, since James' ticket would be more costly with furniture. James went to the dock office to purchase their tickets before going to the lumberyard. The next ship would be arriving the following Monday and leave Liverpool for New York City early Thursday, March 4, 1864. Their sea journey would take two months.

Jess worked daily and carefully packed their trunks. Almost every evening they walked the streets of Liverpool and took in all the sights since they didn't know if they would ever return to see them again. On this night, they discussed how they hadn't made a baby yet. They both believed God was in full control and it would happen when He decided it would.

They had dinner with James' parents, Thomas and Mary, Tuesday evening. James again tried to convince them to join them in America, if not now, maybe after Thomas retired from the docks. Thomas nervously explained that England was their home and it was there they would stay. He also added that he might never be able to retire from the docks. Hearing that broke James' heart but he understood. It made him sad that his son would be leaving them behind, but he felt James had to follow his heart, and knew he was doing the right thing. Emily and John brought their two girls with them to the last "family dinner" and say good-bye to her brother and sister-in-law. There was barely room in Thomas' row house for them all, but they sufficed. While they talked, they brought up great memories and at times laughed until they cried. After dinner, Emily announced that she was expecting their third child by the end of the year. She found it hard to bring it up in front of Jess, but her brother needed to know. When Jess heard the news, she hung her head, but only for a moment. She simply reminded herself, as James squeezed her hand, that their time would come when it was meant to be. Then she and the others gathered around Emily and John and congratulated them. All through the evening, James had his nieces, Sarah and Marylee, on his knees. They often hugged his neck and many giggles filled the room. Jess watched this and her heart warmed to see how much James loved children. She prayed that God would bless them with a child soon.

The evening ended with many tears, especially Sarah and Marylee who loved their uncle very deeply. Being a beautiful spring's eve, Thomas and Mary went with James and Jess as they started their walk home. When they reached halfway, Thomas and Mary said their long good-byes before they returned home. James looked back briefly because he could hear his father trying to comfort his mother's tears. James whistled loudly and his parents stopped and turned around to wave one last time. James thought his heart would burst and asked himself repeatedly if he was doing the right thing. His dream kept him going forward.

James accompanied Edward home from the lumberyard to join his wife and Victoria for dinner the next evening. Lizzie met Jess at the market, and together they rode to the Strong's home. Jess was so glad Lizzie had attended the dinner. They had seen each other only a few brief times since she and James married. Jess loved Lizzie so and truly did miss her. There were many times in their first year of marriage, when Jess wished Lizzie were near for Lizzie would know how to do this or that. She often recalled the many lessons she learned from Lizzie and was very thankful she had been in her life. Lizzie was only fifteen years older than Jess, and in the last five years, they were more like sisters than her nanny. On this night, they reminisced and shared laughter and tears. Lizzie was now a nanny in another home for two small children and said she was very happy with her position. Yet both Jess and Victoria could see in her eyes and hear in her voice that was not entirely true. Jess' heart broke when Lizzie announced she needed to leave. Their good-bye was difficult. Jess stood and watched her carriage leave until she could see it no more. James came to her side, held her around her waist to comfort her when she turned to cry on his shoulder. They stayed in their embrace a short time before they returned to her parents. They all had brandy in the library before James and Jess said good-bye. Between the brandy and her emotions, Jess' heart split in half. However, she would follow James to the moon. That her heart knew.

Victoria arrived at Jess' flat early the next morning to assist her daughter for the final day of packing. They enjoyed a brief lunch in the market area, eating fresh vegetables and fruits then returned to their flat and continued to pack the last of their clothes and shoes. They left room for the final dishes to pack after tonight's dinner and their bedclothes. Victoria was there when James arrived home that evening to say good-bye to them both but they knew they would be together again in America someday...soon.

Jess quickly prepared a bath before dinner where they both enjoyed the warm water and relished in the feeling. They both knew it was time to end their loving tub when his stomach growled so loudly they both began to laugh.

That night they made love in their bed and knew it was the last time it would happen in what was their honeymoon room and home for their first married years in Liverpool.

They woke very early and finished last minute packing. Men arrived from Strong's lumberyard to assist in moving trunks from the third story flat. They went to the dock where James' father and ex-work mates loaded them onto the ship. Jess stood patiently, but nervously, while they worked. She had a tearful good-bye with Thomas and finally walked up the ramp to what was going to be their home for a long time to come. They were the only two people who boarded the ship who were not part of the crew. James joined her on ship after his long good-bye with his father. "Love ya, son." It was the first time James heard his father tell him he loved him, which made their parting even more difficult. James hugged his father for a long time, yet he knew he *had* to go up that ramp to his waiting wife and life-long dream. At the top of the ramp, they both turned to wave good-bye to Thomas and England. When the ship cleared the docks and started out to sea, they were asked to follow a uniformed man to their cabin. They went down one level to a long hallway of doors. They arrived in the middle of the hallway where the man opened a door, led them inside to a small, confining room. It had a small bed, one very undersized, round porthole, one chair and a tiny bedside table with the only oil lamp in the small room resting on it. The man set their traveling bag on the floor and stepped to the porthole to show them how it operated. He announced that dinner will be served on the main deck dining room promptly at six o'clock and that they would be dining with the captain, and to please not be late. After he handed James the room key and left them alone, the first thing James did was look through the porthole and saw that they were almost at water level. They could hear the water slap the ship's sides and he wondered how loud it would be while at sea. Jess busied herself with unpacking their traveling bag, retrieved both their books, and then sat on the bed. She folded her hands as if waiting to be told what to do next. James sat next to her, put his hands over hers, and tried to comfort her anxieties. He commented how the bed is much smaller than what they were used to, but they will be nothing but close. He giggled at how obvious that was. The small closet door would not close after Jess stuffed their clothes into it. She almost came to tears because she knew this voyage would be all but comfortable. There was nothing opulent on this ship. However, she smiled at James to confirm that she was fine and would remain fine.

Dinner with the captain was pleasant; however, he excused himself after an hour. James wished there was more to offer his wife like dancing, but this was a ship carrying exports to America, having unloaded lumber in England. This was not a cruise ship and James prayed she would accept this voyage for what it was – the most inexpensive way to get to America. Over the following weeks, he would remind her repeatedly to look to the future. They knew they would never forget the voyage, however, would be very glad when the voyage was over and they were back on land.

The first two weeks were absolute misery for Jess. She wondered how there could be anything left in her empty stomach which she lost so violently and so often. James recovered from seasickness only a few days after departure, but Jess' symptoms were never ending. She would force herself to eat, only to lose it minutes later. To hear the water slap the side of the ship and its constant rocking with each wave did not help. When she looked out the porthole, she would groan, hold her stomach, and lay back on the bed. She found no preferable position, sitting, laying, or standing. James always slept next to the wall in bed so Jess would have easy access to the thunder mug. He felt so bad for her, but knew there was not much he could do, other than wait it out with her and help when he could.

Finally, at the start of the third week, she was able to join James for dinner. She ate very little, noted by all, but was making progress. Together they would walk the main deck, stare at the moon light on the water and thank God, it had been fairly calm sailing so far. They sat on deck chairs for long evening talks about their future and enjoyed the spring sea air.

Jess read many books and asked a crewmember if she could retrieve books from their trunks. When they arrived below in the baggage area, she could not tell one of their trunks from the other, therefore had to open two before she found their books in the third trunk. Before closing it, she hung a ribbon bookmark near the latch. Therefore, next time she would know which trunk to search for more books, which were her saviors from daily boredom. She also found more paper for James, for he spent much of his time making figures and lists for his future lumberyard. There was hardly room to do these things in their cabin. Often he would spread it over the floor and work by the small porthole light. He did not want to leave Jess alone for hours at a time. She appreciated this and would often coax him to do his work in the dining room where he could spread out. James would insist that he was fine. His pencil was near being a stub and he hoped he would be able to find another. When he reentered the cabin, there was a stack of paper and a new pencil on top of his papers. He was thankful

Jess thought of everything, smiled, and hugged and thanked her. She kissed him and smiled. She was tiring of the cabin and the deck chairs, laughed to herself, and wondered if the phrase cabin fever began with sailors.

While they strolled the deck after dinner that evening, they met the captain. Small talk occurred for a moment and at the first lull in their conversation, Jess promptly asked if there was something she could do to help on the ship to rid her boredom. The captain grinned and asked if she could sew. When she nodded positively with a smile, he said he had repairs that were necessary on the pad of the captain's chair and a few others also. Jess said she would be glad to be of assistance and asked when she could start. He asked her to return to the dining room the next morning a short while after breakfast and she complied.

It took her most of the day to do the repairs for the captain. He thanked her profusely, smiled and said, "I have a few uniforms that need repair also, would that interest you?"

"I would love to do that for you. Does anyone else need sewing or darning?"

"I will search that and I will have the clothing ready for you after breakfast on the morrow."

"Thank you, I will be ready," giggled Jess in anticipation.

The next morning when she and James arrived in the dining room, a table held a mound of uniforms and clothing that waited for her attention. The cook brought them their breakfast and thanked her for what she was about to do.

"We 'een needin' 'is fer a long time. You a angel on 'rth," grinned the cook. As he did Jess saw he had no teeth. She smiled at him and said she was glad to help.

When James went to their cabin to retrieve his mound of paperwork, he brought back her sewing kit, put it in front of her, beside the heap of clothing.

"You are quite a woman, my Jess." He smiled and kissed her forehead.

She separated the clothing by color and started the repairs. James worked on their future at the next table and a few times that day he heard her cry out ouch or ooh more than once. He knew the needle had most likely pricked her finger. When he looked her way, she had a finger in her mouth so she would not get blood on the clothing. She grinned at him and continued sewing. Time flew by for both of them that day. When the cook brought out their lunch, they were both shocked that it was that time of day already. Jess was not finished with the mound of clothes, but knew there was really no hurry to finish, because no one was going anywhere.

After dinner that evening the crew and captain gave her a round of ovation in thanks for the work she had done. She curtsied in reply and sat next to James, blushing. He hugged her shoulders and lovingly kissed the side of her face.

Chapter Eight
1864 New York City

The last few weeks of their voyage seemed to be longer than all the previous weeks combined, to both James and Jess. They were very thankful they had sailed on calm seas the entire trip. The natural motion of the sea was hard enough to stomach. It was near the end of May and both were anxious to be back on land. A crewmember who had sailed for years, warned them how "sea legs" stay with them once they were back on land and Jess heeded his words. She didn't feel like she had sea legs, yet she knew she had gotten used to the sound of the water slapping against the ship and actually had come to like it, and especially liked to sleep to the reverberation.

Washing clothes onboard was tricky for Jess. She tried to keep the water inside the wooden bucket as it waved with the ocean. She discovered early in the voyage she needed to hang her pantaloons in their cabin to dry for obvious reasons - she was the only female on the ship.

They tired of the cabin at times and found that sleeping on deck chairs; letting the sea breezes sweep over them was heavenly. They found that making love while at sea added excitement to what was already wonderful. They enjoyed each other's bodies as often as circumstances allowed. Discretion was important in their cabin, as it seemed there was always someone in the hallway or in surrounding rooms.

Jess wanted a baby so badly, but never let James know how deeply it concerned her that it had not happened yet. She prayed to God that nothing was wrong, yet maintained her faith.

At dinner that night, the captain happily announced they would reach New York City the following day mid afternoon. James squeezed Jess' hand then leaned his head to hers until they touched. They both said silent prayers of thanks then looked at each other with loving eyes. Yet a small fear remained inside them both of the next leg of their journey ahead.

The next morning Jess busied herself with packing. James gathered his business plans and shuffled them to order before they all gathered for their last lunch at sea. It had been a long trip which they were both glad was at its end. Together they roamed the ship saying their good-byes and thanks to crewmembers, saving the captain for last. He told them they should be on the main deck when the city came into view, as they did not want to miss seeing the New York City skyline.

The ship finally slowed and there it was – New York City. Never had James or Jess observed such a beautiful sight. The city was bigger than they had ever seen and would soon find out for themselves how big it was when they walked the streets.

The captain had suggested two hotels to seek when they arrived. James knew it would be a few hours before their trunks were unloaded from the ship so they started toward the city. They naively thought London was crowded and were amazed how busy and loud the New York streets were. Their sea legs were obvious before they left the docks, and hoped this feeling would disappear soon. They followed the captain's directions and found the first suggested hotel. They were not impressed with the lobby, as it was hot, dark and cluttered. When they asked the desk clerk to see the room before they agreed on the weekly rates, he looked at them as if they were crazy. James did not have a good feeling and prompted Jess to follow him out the door.

"James, what are.......?" started Jess.

"I can *not* see us staying here, Jess. I don't have a good feeling," interrupted James. He took her hand and together started to weave through the people on the street. They walked another block until they found the second hotel on the list. When they walked in, they both instantly saw and felt the difference from the first lobby. The desk clerk quoted James the weekly rates, which were a bit higher than the first hotel, yet James felt it was worth it. The clerk gladly showed them the room before James paid the first week's fare. James asked the clerk where the market and horse stables were and discovered everything they needed was within three-square blocks. Their room was on the second floor and faced the street, but they were accustomed to city noise. Both the room and bed were bigger than the cabin they had just lived in for weeks on the ship. James sat on the bed, fell back, and stretched his arms over his head, which felt good. He patted the bed beside him, to ask Jess to join him. She lay next to him where they stayed for some time and talked about the approaching days. It felt so good to be back on land and they laughed about how the crewmember was correct about sea legs. She wondered how long it would last.

When their conversation lulled, they both nodded off and slept over an hour.

James woke with a start, which woke Jess. The light had changed in the room while they slept and they realized more time had passed than they wished. Leaving the hotel, they made their way through the bustling streets of New York in search of the market. They both commented on the fact that the war was not very obvious in the city. They would very seldom see a man in a soldier's uniform. Finally finding the market, they were amazed how it was far bigger than the market in Liverpool. They had never seen so much food offered in one place before. In fact, it was difficult for them to choose which type of breads and cheeses they liked, some they had never heard of before. After they made their choice, they found tables and chairs and enjoyed their dinner. They made their way back to the docks and arranged their trunks delivery. They also left a letter with the captain to deliver to Edward Strong upon his return to Liverpool. The note was brief and contained information about their voyage and the address of their hotel. They then meandered through the streets once more and took a different route back to the hotel to see more of the city that was now their home, to get to know their way around.

They were not back in their room very long when a knock on the door startled them. It was the desk clerk, who told them their trunks had arrived. James followed him downstairs while they discussed the additional cost to store them. James offered him a lower price and they haggled back and forth and finally agreed on a price. James proceeded to assist the dockworkers, and moved their trunks into a storage room. When he returned to their room, he found Jess trying to light the one oil lamp in the room and he quickly stepped beside her and lit it for her. He brought their travel bag into the room and Jess quickly unpacked it. The small chest in the room was hardly large enough to hold all of their belongings, therefore, she decided, they would have to live mostly out of their travel bag. She laid out the few pairs of shoes they owned, found her hairbrush, and thankfully brushed through her long black hair, which needed attention badly. She then started to brush James' blonde hair, which he welcomed by sitting still and enjoying the feeling of each stroke, with eyes closed. When she stopped, he put his hand on hers, took the brush, and returned the favor. He brushed until his arm ached and finally had to stop. She turned and kissed him, took the brush, placed it on the chest of drawers next to the silver backed looking glass she had owned since childhood. To look at them reminded her of her family and England, and that she missed them all terribly, yet she would never let on to James how she felt. She turned with a smile, and found James on the bed with his arms behind his head watching her. He imagined what she thought as she tenderly stroked the silver backed brush and then the looking glass and knew he wanted only the best for her, and that she probably missed her family desperately. He had always known he would do whatever it took to make sure they have a good life, with her by his side.

"God, you are beautiful." James felt blessed that she loved him.

She smiled and James watched her glide across the room to him. She neared the bed, put her left knee upon the bed, and bent to comb his blonde hair with her fingers.

"*You* are beautiful, my love," she whispered. She bent to kiss him lightly, yet his return kiss was with a hunger she had not felt in him since they left England. Their kiss continued, while James started to undo the many buttons down the front of her long dress. He reached inside the dress to find her warm skin, while he groaned through his nose and continued to kiss his wife. He broke his kiss and lowered her dress until she wore only pantaloons. He began to take those down from her waist as she reached for the buttons on his shirt, undid them slowly while she stared into his deep brown eyes. He could see the love she held for him in her eyes as a wave of more love for his wife struck his heart. He wondered how he could love her more than he already did, but it happened – every day. He sat up, took off his shirt, and bent forward to suckle the erect nipple that was now in front of his face. It was the color of a tender pink rose petal.

When his arms were free from his shirt, he caressed her breasts and moved his lips to the waiting, hard nipple of the neglected breast. Jess' head fell back in delight. How she loved the attention James gave her entire body. No other man, she thought, could be more loving and wondered if that were so with the many couples she had known in England. Her thought did not linger long as the excitement James aroused in her quickly erased everything from her mind except how he was making her feel.

Her arms wrapped around his head while he buried it in her breasts, kissed them all over, and held the weight of each breast in his hands. He started to kiss lower, leaned her back to kiss her stomach, which made her breathless. Her hands still held his head, entwined her fingers in his blonde hair, and soon forgot where she was. James quickly jumped off the bed, removed his pants, and took in the sight before him. Jess lay in wait, anxious for her husband's return to their bed. He started to trace the sunken track of her stomach with kisses until he reached her curly patch and felt her warmth on his face. When he reached lower, he gently spread her legs then parted the curls to find the tender, pink skin that now glistened with moisture.

He tenderly kissed the inside of each leg and teased her with each kiss, then slowly kissed his way to the middle. When he found the hard button hidden in the damp folds, he could hardly stay with her body as she rose off the bed. He started to suck on the hard bead while he inserted one finger into her hot wetness. He found that inner spot that drove her wild and rubbed it quickly with his fingertip until Jess started her release. While her body writhed in ecstasy, she realized her fingernails were dug into his shoulders. When she let go and gripped the bedcover she hoped she had not drawn blood. James enjoyed her body motions and spasms and watched Jess explode to heaven. He listened while her breathing, which had all but stopped, slowly back to normal. Jess rose onto her elbows and reached to brush James' hair out of his eyes.

They stared into each other's loving eyes, and slowly smiled. She leaned over to kiss him then slowly ran her fingers across his chest. She loved to softly caress the hard muscles and tease his erect nipples. He laid back and let her touch him tenderly as she gently glided her stomach over his hard erection. She then lay on her side and listened to his spastic breaths. Her hand slowly worked its way lower and lower, until she found his rock hard staff and gently stroked it, slowing at the tip and teased him to near madness. She started to kiss his chest, flicked each nipple with her tongue, and she heard his gasps, which excited her all over again. How she loved to listen to him, and to feel his muscles work to please her. She never heard him make sounds like this in life, except here, in bed, with her.

She traced his navel with her tongue and kissed lower than she had ever kissed before. He lifted his head to watch as her black hair slowly fell from one shoulder, which blocked his view of her face going lower and lower on his body. He pulled her jet-black hair back gently with one finger, traced her jaw line as her kisses led her to the hair track on his flat stomach to his thick, curly blonde patch. His hard member rose from the course hair, which got harder with each of her strokes. Just when he thought he would lose control, he felt her warm mouth embrace the tip of his penis and lick it with the warmth of her soft, hot tongue. She had no idea what to do since she had never done this before, yet she needed to make him feel as good as he did her. James thought he would lose his mind. It was very difficult for him not to release, and the vision before him was one he never dreamt he would see. He had heard the men on the dock talk of this act earlier in his life and wondered what it felt like and now he knew. She lowered her mouth down his length and when the tip of his hardness hit the back of her throat; he fought hard not to explode. He quickly, but gently grabbed her head, pulled her mouth away and speedily flipped his wife onto her back. He got on his knees and buried his erection deep inside his wife's hot, wet warmth. She gasped loudly from the suddenness of his motions, pulled him closer to her, and placed her hands on the muscles of his working buttocks. She wrapped her legs around his waist and locked her ankles on his back then lowered her hands to feel the muscles of his legs at work, pleasing them both.

He kissed her with passion then broke away to watch his wife as he buried himself deeper than ever before, making long strokes then deeper again. Jess could hardly breathe and her eyes were tightly clenched shut. Her ride to the stars began as she met each of his thrusts with her hips and guttural sounds came from deep inside both of them. One could neither hear nor see the other any more, yet took their ride to heaven together.

Jess was first to open her eyes and saw her husband's blonde head still buried in her shoulder. He slowly raised his head and kissed her tender lips, both still breathless. He gently removed himself from her, rolled onto his side, and held her close to him. They lay together as they caught their breaths. They had not noticed the oil lamp had gone out because neither of them took the time from lovemaking to raise the wick. They lay and watched the city lights that danced on the ceiling and listened to the sounds of the city before either one moved. Finally, James got off the bed, relit the oil lamp, turned, and took at her beautiful nakedness in the glow of the lamp.

"That was wonderful, Jess. You are beautiful. I have got to be the luckiest man on this earth." Jess did not know when it happened, but she swore he had become more handsome. The light from the lamp cast on his shining skin made it hard to look away and into his eyes.

Jess smiled and began to lightly scratch James' chest with her fingertips. His body responded with goose bumps, which made her giggle.

Chapter Nine
Summer 1864

They woke early the next morning. James explained to Jess that he didn't know the city and it would be best for her safety to stay in the room as he traveled through the city in search of men that are familiar with the northern part of the state. She agreed and said she would spend the day doing laundry and reading.

He wanted to begin his search at the market, hoping some of the beef or chicken brought into the city came from the north. He had done research before they left England, but he needed to know if a carriage would make it through the wooded areas of New York, and the travel time.

After he finally found and talked with several men from the north, many told him about available land and thousands of acres of wooded land. He decided to gather Jess, have their lunch at the market, and do more research at the New York Library. She said she would gladly help in any way she could.

"I have talked to many men, Jess and you won't believe this, but by what they are saying, the best area for us is the small town of Atwater in Atwater County," he finished with a smile.

"That sounds so close to Atwood. James, it's meant to be! What do we do next?" Jess now toyed with the edge of the library table nervously.

"This may be the most difficult part of the trip, Jess. According to the men I talked to, the war has barely touched the northern counties and the real fears would be the weather, and animals in the woods, of which I have no fear. It will take two to three days by carriage, Jess, and inns are scarce but I know we can make it. I know, in my heart, this is the right thing to do, and with you. Do you want to stay in the city while I go in search of these areas? You may be alone here for weeks."

"No! I want to be with you! You could be gone a long time. No, James, please don't leave me here," Jess fretted. She could not imagine being without him that long. This was the first time he thought how hard this would be if she was in the family way or tending a baby. Another reason why he thought everything happens for a reason.

He rounded the table to put his arm around her shoulder to comfort her and said, "I wouldn't leave you here if you really want to go. It will be rough in a carriage, as the weight of the trunks will make it a hard ride. But I met a man that brings salted meats from northern New York into the city and he said he would gladly let us follow him if we were ready to leave day after next." James was getting excited now. Jess saw it in his eyes. It made her excited too.

"Yes, James, I'm ready. We should follow this man. Does he seem trustworthy?"

"I talked to others about him after meeting him, and many spoke highly of him. He's a rugged man, Jess, but he's been bringing meats to the city for many years. They said he's a hard worker and honest as the day is long," he smiled. "His name is Theodore, "Teddy" Garnett." He searched his wife's eyes.

"May I meet.....Teddy?"

"Tomorrow at breakfast. We've already agreed to meet at the market. He also mentioned that he wanted us to try bacon he smokes himself."

The next morning they woke to a rainy day. The city had a different smell in the rain, Jess noticed, as she attempted to cover her head with her shawl, trying to stay dry on their walk to meet Teddy. They arrived at the spot they had agreed and waited for a long time before he finally approached them with a big, hairy smile. Jess had not seen a beard or mustache that long or scraggly before in her entire life. Yet his eyes were very kind. His arm stretched out to James long before he was actually within reach to shake his hand. After their hello, James introduced his wife to Teddy, who warmly greeted Jess. He took her hand and graciously kissed the back of it softly.

James was slightly taken aback with this action, and started to think twice about their decision to follow this man for three days.

Teddy saw that James wasn't happy with his actions then said, "I'm sorry, James. I dint mean nothin' other tha' t' greet a beautiful English lady. Please don' take 'ffense. Ya said she was pertty, but yer words do her no justice." He then turned to Jess and bowed silently, then stood erect and apologized to her also. Jess smiled, blushed, and reached for James' hand. She took one side step toward her husband and watched Teddy who also took a step back.

"Everything is fine, Teddy. We both accept your apology," said James through slightly closed lips. "Shall we sit?"

Jess followed James, who followed Teddy through the market maze, when they suddenly stopped in front of a butcher stand of which Teddy was familiar. He talked to the man in the apron for a moment, who soon brought out a slab of bacon wrapped in paper, handed it to Teddy, then pointed his arm as Teddy thanked him. Teddy motioned to James for them to follow, which they did, and passed many fruit and vegetable stands before Teddy abruptly turned into a restaurant. He told them he would return shortly and disappeared into the back room, behind a curtain. He returned with a beaming smile and told them their bacon would be ready soon.

Teddy explained that the cook said she would fry the bacon for them if she could have two pieces for herself. He said she was adding two eggs to each of their plates and then they would have the "perfect" breakfast. He smiled again and Jess noted that when he smiled, his eyes smiled too. She liked him. She hoped James would not hold an offense against Teddy for kissing her hand. She smiled, looked at her lap, twisted her wedding band and realized that no one other than James had ever commented on her looks. It made her feel wonderful.

She sat silently and listened to the men who conversed about the trip ahead, and she gathered James had made up his mind that Teddy could be trusted and they would make the trip together and leave early in the morning. Teddy advised James where to buy a horse and wagon and agreed to meet in front of their hotel so he could help load their trunks with James the following morning.

The bacon and eggs arrived at the table by an older woman with gray hair, who wore an oversized dirty apron. She placed the plates down hastily, starting with Jess. When she smiled at her Jess noticed that most of her teeth were missing, yet she proudly displayed her pink gums. The aroma of the bacon was wonderful. Jess took her first bite and noticed a hint of maple in the bacon flavor.

"I smoke it wit' sap o' maple trees," commented Teddy with another smile.

"It's heavenly, Teddy. We would like to place our first order now." Jess giggled while she looked toward James, who agreed with the nod of his head.

They finished their breakfast, yet stayed at the table for a long time after the older woman cleared the table and told them, through her toothless gums, "'at bacon 'as good, Ted. What is the udder taste in thar?"

Teddy grinned and explained to her how he used maple sap in the smokehouse, and thanked her for her compliment. Teddy turned back to James to continue their conversation, and glanced at Jess often to see if she was listening. He saw that she was and admired her devotion to her husband. They finally parted ways and the Atwood's returned to their room and started packing. This was getting old, thought Jess, yet she knew it would be a long time until she would be doing the final un-pack in their "home". James left for an hour to buy a horse and wagon and returned looking very confident. He bought a front covered wagon with plenty of room on the uncovered wooden bed for their trunks. He also bought a pitch-black horse to match Jess' beautiful black hair. His young hide shimmered in the sunlight and he had good muscle lines and teeth. He was perfect for their needs, and James was anxious for his wife's approval.

The knock on their door at 4 a.m. to wake them startled James and Jess awake but they did not get out of bed instantly. They held each other awhile, then stretched and readied for the day. When they went out the lobby door to the street, Teddy waited on horseback, holding the reins of a beautiful black horse. Jess had never seen such a gorgeous animal. She ran to his side and immediately began to stroke his neck. The horse patiently stood and allowed Jess to touch him. James saw that he had chosen the correct animal. He was docile as a lamb and she loved him.

"What shall we name him, Darling?" James saw in his wife's face he had made the right choice.

"Ooh, I will have to think about that. It has to be the perfect name. Maybe as I get to know him better... does he not have a name?"

"He does, but it doesn't fit him. The men at the stables called him Frankie."

"You're right, James, it does not fit him," giggled Jess as she shook her head in a negative motion.

She watched as James mounted their black beauty to ride to the stable to fetch their wagon. He returned quickly with horse and wagon and the men loaded the trunks quickly. James covered the trunks with a large blanket and tied it all down. He settled their bill with the desk clerk and soon they were riding through the New York streets following Teddy. They saw parts of the city they had not seen before and eventually the buildings got shorter and farther apart. When they were an hour out of the city, she looked back and it looked so far away. The wagon was nice, but she had a difficult time relaxing enough to sit back and read. As they rode through the day, she saw hills in the distance. If they looked big now, she thought, they must be very big when at their foot. She wondered how they would cross them, but had confidence in James and Teddy. Teddy told them they would enjoy the first stop they would make in Albany at the end of day.

They stopped briefly for a lunch of bread and cheese and watered the horses. Teddy shared some of his smoked, dried beef, which was delicious but they didn't dawdle. The sun was setting and Jess felt like her back was going to break yet they trudged on. Teddy was determined to make Albany before dark. Suddenly, after a bend in the road, Albany appeared on the horizon and she was so thankful.

Teddy led them directly to stables where they left the horses and wagons then promised them a short walk to the inn. James struggled to carry their travel bag and rested once, briefly while they walked through the streets of Albany. They came to a building where loud music erupted from its open doors where Teddy made a sharp turn inside. They wove between tables to find one in the back and were so glad to sit still and to not be bouncing anymore. Teddy was very familiar with the server, ordered for all three of them and ales came to the table quickly.

"Do you drink beer, Jessica?" Teddy didn't know if such a fine lady would put her lips to, what some called, the devils brew.

"Jess, please call me Jess," she said with a smile. He nodded his head and understood. "Not often, but tonight beer sounds very good."

"Gotta wash th' dirt down our gullets."

Jess looked to James and noticed he had drunk half his ale already. He put his glass down and she laughed as he smiled at her while wearing a white ale mustache on his upper lip. If they were not in public, she would have helped him remove it her way, but instead she bowed her head, smiled, and then took a tiny sip of her ale.

"Ya'll like yer supper, 'cuz it's some o' my pork. Dis place is one o' my bes' customers, besides th' big city."

Their pork dinner was the best Jess and James had ever had. Jess whispered to James that she needed a bath and he made arrangements for a room upstairs and a bath for his wife. When he saw her settled and her tub prepared, he returned to Teddy, and together they drank many more ales.

After her bath, Jess welcomed the soft bed, and stretched out under the sheet and aah'd for a long time. It felt like heaven and sleep came quickly. She barely stirred when James finally joined her a few hours later. He had a late bath, which sobered him somewhat before he retired for the night. He kissed his wife's forehead before he lay his head down.

The next day was much like the first, a lot of bouncing and dusty miles. She tried to read, but found it almost impossible to do while bouncing continuously. The only thing different on this day was Jess wore only one petticoat under her dress. The days were getting warmer and her second petticoat proved to be unnecessary. Lunch was brief again and they were on their way.

"Stormy," Jess suddenly shouted out to James. "Let's call the horse Stormy. He is as calm as a lamb, but his color is like the blackest of storm clouds."

"Stormy it is." He smiled.

Before dark, Teddy pulled his wagon onto a long drive, which lead to a large white house with tall columns that fronted the porch. Horses lazily munched green grass on both sides of the fenced drive. The front door opened as they neared the house. A tall, slender man appeared who smiled as he came down the steps and made his way to the wagons arriving. He was clean cut and dressed like a cowboy, as they had seen in books in England.

"I was expecting you yesterday, my boy," said the man as he neared Teddy, shook his hand and slapped him on his dusty back.

"Yeah, I know. Sorry 'bout dat. I brought some frien's wit' me, so we left a day late. I hope you don' min' havin' two more for dinner," said Teddy, as he shook the man's hand.

"No, don't mind at all." The man stepped toward James with his hand out. James hopped down from the wagon to greet the gentleman, and shook his hand.

"Glad to meet you, sir. My name is James Atwood," and then waved his arm toward Jess, "and this is my wife, Jess."

"Gerald Paxton here. Nice to meet you both." He tipped his hat to Jess, "Ma'am". Then he added "British, ey? Been a long time since I've heard that accent."

"Yes sir, Liverpool," said James

"Liverpool - mm, don't know that one." Gerald broke eye contact and looked toward the grasses where a bucking horse caught his attention.

"West, sir, coastal shipping port. We have sent a lot of tea and spices your way." James added a proud smile.

"Mm, I see. Well, I for one thank you for them both. What brings you to these fighting states, James?"

"We are here to start a new life, and a lumber business."

"You might make it doing that, young man. You just might make it. Well, I wish you luck. Let's go inside, shall we?"

James helped Jess down from the wagon and it was now she wished she had worn her second petticoat. She dusted her skirt and followed the men into the house. Gerald talked briefly with a young man who approached them as they entered the house. With very quick steps, the young man left the house through the front door. Soon they heard the horses and wagons being taken behind the house. James looked out the window to see another young man who opened the white crossed barn doors for horse and wagon entry and soon they all disappeared from view.

"My men will rub down the horses, water and feed them." Gerald noticed James' concerns. James relaxed now that he knew the horses were in good care.

James turned away from the window and watched Gerald cross the room to a cabinet where he retrieved a cut glass bottle and four short glasses. He started to pour one finger of whiskey in each glass, when he looked at Jess. "Will you join us, Misses Atwood?"

Jess shook her head no, "No thank you, sir," shied from his look, and then turned her head to look around the room. The men raised their glasses in a toast to a safe wagon trip for Teddy and company. Then Gerald raised the bottle, pointed it to each of the other men, asked each man without words, if they wanted another. They both motioned with nods and soon they all downed another shot of whiskey.

"Sorry, ma'am, would you like to sit down?" Gerald motioned Jess toward the settee.

"Thank you," said Jess almost in a whisper and then gathered her skirt to sit. The settee had beautiful tapestry on it and she looked around the room and noticed everything was beautiful. She wondered how this man could afford such a beautiful home and fine things. She sat silently as the men talked about their trip. She noticed the planed wood walls and wondered how he got the shine on the wood. Candled sconces were on each wall beside beautiful landscape paintings. The fireplace was bigger than she had ever seen, then the men finally started to sit around the room, and James joined Jess on the settee. He worried about being too dirty to sit on the softly padded cushion when Gerald motioned to him to sit and made a face of acceptance. James took his wife's hand and sat close to her, as he felt the warmth of the whiskey course through his body.

"How about some roasted pig for dinner?" asked Gerald as he scanned the room for approvals. Everyone nodded positively and the conversation continued. Gerald went to the back door, whistled through his fingers, and soon the first young man appeared. They talked briefly and Gerald patted the young man on his back. "Dinner will be ready in a few hours. Jess, your traveling bag will be here in a moment. May I show you to your room?"

"Thank you, Mr. Paxton," answered Jess as she rose to follow him across the room. They stopped at the foot of the tall, wide staircase that led upstairs where he told her to go to the second door on the right. She climbed the carpeted staircase, opened the second door to a beautiful light blue painted room filled with white wicker furniture. She loved it all and studied it closely, as she swore to herself that someday she would have a room like this. Before she made it across the room to the window, there was a knock on the door. She told whomever it was to enter. The door opened and the second young man who was at the barn door appeared with her travel bag. He walked to a short wooden table where he placed the bag then asked if she needed anything.

"No, thank you young man, I am fine." He bowed his head and started toward the door.

"I am sorry, ma'am, but I'm also to tell you your bath will be ready soon," he added as he turned and left the room.

Jess looked around the room and wondered where the tub could possibly be placed in this quaint bedroom. She opened her bag and removed what she needed for her bath. She heard many footsteps up and down the staircase, but dismissed them. Then there was another knock on her door, where a woman stood who wore a black dress, white apron and white gathered cap. She almost curtsied when Jess appeared in front of her and said, "Miss Jessica? My name is Elizabeth. Mister Gerald asked me to assist you in your bath. Would you please come this way?"

Jess promptly followed her down the hall to an open door, walked into a small room where there was a large tub, dressing table with a huge looking glass on the wall and a small curtained window. Elizabeth motioned to Jess to enter and started to help her disrobe. Elizabeth held up a large cloth to block her view of Jess' nakedness. Jess stepped into the warm water, which came up to her neck. Never before had she been submerged this deeply in the welcoming warmth. Elizabeth lowered the cloth, handed Jess a small cloth and bar of soap, and asked if she needed anything else.

"No, Elizabeth, I am fine, and this is heavenly." Jess smiled to the kind woman.

With that, Elizabeth bowed her head and actually backed out of the room and closed the door silently. Jess savored the feeling, let her eyes roam the room and then stopped at the window, and admired the golden, pink sunset for a long time. She felt that her eyes had only been closed for a moment when she was woken by a knock on the door. It was then she realized she must have slept longer than she thought. The water that surrounded her had become cool and she welcomed the large linen cloth Elizabeth held for her when she rose from the tub. She surrounded Jess with the warm cloth and helped dry her body. Elizabeth reminded her so much of Lizzie, her childhood nanny with the same name too, thought Jess as she smiled at her wonderful memories.

When she returned to the blue bedroom, the sunlight was gone, an oil lamp had been lit for her, and clean clothes had been laid on the bed. She quickly dressed, opened the door and listened to the house. The sound of male voices seemed to come from outside. She started toward the room containing the tub to thank Elizabeth, where she found her emptying the tub and pouring the used tub water out the window, which ran down a wooden trough to a large wooden barrel on the ground behind the house. How ingenious, thought Jess. I will have one of those one day, she thought as she smiled and thanked Elizabeth for her help. Elizabeth bowed her head and advised Jess that the men awaited her presence outside, at the back of the house. She went down the rambling staircase, made her way to the back door and found the men surrounding a large fire in a pit made of stone. Gerald stood, turning a large pork roast on a spit over the fire. He smiled when he saw Jess, nodded to James motioning him to look in the direction of his wife. James stood, held out his hand to his wife, and guided her to sit next to him. She walked across a stone veranda to join the men and admired the chairs as she passed, then sat. The roast smelled wonderful and she noticed the men's conversation had come to a halt.

"Thank you, Mr. Paxton, for the heavenly bath. Elizabeth is a dear woman, and very helpful."

"You are welcome, Jess. Please call me Gerald; and yes, Elizabeth is one in a million."

"Gerald it is." Jess shyly smiled, then added, "What are we discussing?"

"Your future, as a matter of fact." Gerald slightly smiled.

"I see. What about our future?" She smiled sweetly at her husband.

James told her, "Gerald thinks we have a good chance of our dream coming true and he knows Atwater County very well and thinks he knows the perfect piece of land that will work out very well for what we are looking for. The cabin on this land is rustic but livable."

Jess smiled, more for his excitement than what she heard about the cabin. As long as they were together, she could accept any challenge.

The conversation exchange continued another hour before Elizabeth appeared again with dishes, silverware and ewers of water. She disappeared into the house and reappeared with glasses and bottles of ale. She arranged all of it for their dinner on a handsome wrought iron table. The men pulled the chairs from around the fire, placed them at the table and soon they all enjoyed roasted potatoes and pork from Teddy's ranch. The men followed dinner with brandy and cigars. Jess listened to the men's conversation, thankful she was sitting on a chair that was not bouncing. Gerald offered to accompany them to the Atwater County seat the following day and asked James if he wanted to see the land before he put a claim to it. James chuckled, said yes, and they agreed to start out early the next morning.

James knew Jess was tired of traveling, but he also knew she would not want to miss seeing the land. They left very early the next morning and after a few hours of riding through heavily wooded hills and valleys, Gerald started Teddy's wagon up a steep trail. They arrived at a mesa in a clearing, and saw a run down cabin, which had obviously been ignored for some time. There was also a failing barn, which barely had any kind of roof, and a smaller building with no windows, behind the cabin. The area was luscious and green, with woods that totally surrounded them, and many songs from birds filled their ears, while their minds reeled.

James jumped down from the wagon in front of the cabin, helped his wife down, and started to walk the property. He noticed the plateau went on into the woods before dropping off suddenly. It would be perfect for their first clearing, and would supply them with an ample amount of wood for repairs on the cabin and barn. He saw there was plenty of wood here to cut and sell after it dried through the winter, and more than enough to cut for years.

"This is perfect!" James was so excited. The sun was bright and shone on his face and blonde hair and Jess saw his huge smile. "We could start the wood shelter in spring!" he added as he ran toward the cabin. The door stood open gaining easy entry, where Jess followed him and they both scanned the large main room and saw a small bedroom to the right. James held the tattered cloth divider and let his wife pass under it. The room had two small windows where most of the glass was broken or missing. James mentioned to Jess that they would be easy to repair. She grinned, for she knew James could handle these repairs easily. He knew the roof could be finished in two days, while she cleaned. It was summer, therefore, they did not have to worry about staying warm at night, only rain. He accessed the repairs on the fireplace, which, he said, could easily be completed before winter. They would have to cook outside for the time being though. Jess smiled.

The men walked the land for another hour, discussing the many assets of the land, and soon they all started toward the town of Atwater and the county seat, which was thirty minutes away. They entered the limestone building's archway and waited a short time before they met with the property handlers. James and Jess were given a drawn plot of the land they were claiming and signed the proper paperwork. When they returned to the wagons, James picked up his wife at her waist and twirled her around, shouting with glee. "Woo-hee! We did it!"

She kissed him when he faced her and he assisted her up to the wagon seat and then followed behind Teddy and Gerald. They returned to Gerald's estate where, over dinner, celebrated their findings. Teddy announced he would be leaving in the morning returning to his ranch in Malone, New York, and waiting wife, Amanda and family.

"Wait 'til ya meet my beauty! She's a wonnerful woman. I'm sure she's awonderin' where th' dickens I've gone to. We got two strong boys, Theodore Jr. we call him Junior, and Samuel, well Sam. They're nine 'nd ten 'nd help me on th' ranch a lot. Both are spittin' images o' their mother wit' big blue eyes 'nd blonde hair jus' like her. I thank God ever' day that they're too young t' think 'bout fightin' in the war for the Nort'."

"I cannot wait to meet them, Teddy." James could see so much pride in the man since he had literally puffed his chest with pride when talking about his family.

They all sat around the fire pit again that evening, enjoying fresh chicken on the spit, from Gerald's coop, clinked more glasses in celebration and enjoyed the light of the full moon.

Gerald offered his home to them for as long as they needed while making their new home repairs. James declined but thanked him more than once. Before Jess excused herself, she said her good-byes to Teddy with a hug, many thanks for all he did for them and a kiss on his scruffy cheek. She knew he would most likely be gone before she woke the next morning.

She climbed the stairs to find Elizabeth made a bath for her, where she aided Jess into the warm tub once again. When she entered the blue bedroom, Jess found the bed had been turned down, awaiting her clean body. James joined her in bed shortly after she retired and was still awake. They lay next to each other talking for what seemed hours of what was to come.

Chapter Ten
The Cabin 1864

They woke the next morning to a wonderful maple-bacon smell that filled the house. James and Jess dressed quickly and went downstairs to see a beautifully set table as Elizabeth was adding fresh cut flowers to the centerpiece. Gerald was at the table drinking coffee, reading this weeks news. Teddy had brought him newspapers from New York City, as well as jars of jam, fresh fruit and vegetables. Gerald seemed oblivious to the goings on in the room, and then suddenly looked up from the paper and welcomed James and Jess to breakfast.

After they ate fresh eggs, Teddy's famous bacon, and cornbread, they could not thank Gerald and Elizabeth enough for their hospitality before they left for their new home and land. While at the county seat they were told, they claimed over one thousand acres of woods, about to live among a lot of wildlife and a river that ran behind the cabin, down the hill. They were warned about wolves, bears, coyotes and beavers in the stream. James had never owned a gun, started to think twice about breaking his own rule of having one in his home, and decided to buy a rifle for hunting and possibly protection, since they would now be living in the "wild".

They stopped at the general store before they left Albany and bought a small supply of nails, a hammer, and a handsaw, and planks of wood. They also ordered food they needed from the clerk who wrapped their goods on the worn-smooth wooden counter. Their wagon was now completely loaded.

James easily remembered the trail they needed to take, which boggled Jess' mind, because they all looked alike to her. Yet he made it directly to the long drive, climbed the hill to the clearing where their run-down, new to them, cabin stood which waited to be occupied again. They did not know why the cabin had been abandoned, but were thankful for their good fortune, as it was perfect for them.

James immediately unloaded their supplies, and Jess started to clean the rooms with the broom she found in the corner of the main room. She pulled her hair back and tied it with the ribbon she usually used as a bookmark. She pulled it so suddenly from between the pages that she scolded herself for not marking the page she last read somehow. She soon heard the pounding of the hammer and smiled, for she knew how happy James was.

She started to pull the broken glass from the window frames, using a rag so she wouldn't cut her fingers. Jess collected the broken glass into a wicker basket she found near the fireplace and put it on the front porch, and then began to clean there. She placed two porch chairs aside for repair, and noticed the hammering sounds were different than before which made her search the noise. She walked to the side of the house, where she found James had made a ladder of fallen wood from the forest floor and was now on the roof over the bedroom doing repairs.

"This room has to be done first," he shouted as he grinned and continued to hammer nails into the new piece of wood onto the roof over the small bedroom. "A pretty lady like you needs a secure roof over her head."

Jess gave him a big smile while she wiped her hands on a rag. She stood and watched her husband for a while and noticed the sweat glistening on his face and darkening his shirt. She wondered how he would get clean before dinner then asked, "James, where is the river they spoke of?" He pointed with his hammer behind the cabin. Jess looked through the trees and saw nothing but green trees, large and small.

"It's down the hill, Jess, but wait for me to accompany you," shouted James from the roof. He continued to pound nails to complete his roof repair.

Jess returned to the inside of the cabin and saw there was nothing more she could do without soap and water. She went back outside and searched the front yard for the best spot to place a cooking fire pit. She went into the shaded forest to pick up dead wood, and when she came back to the front of the cabin, she dropped it in a pile and returned to the woods to gather more wood. After she did this three times, she noticed the hammering had stopped and she began to search for James. He came into view from the other side of the clearing where he had been tying the horse to a tree closer to the cabin. He caught sight of Jess, smiled and went to the wagon. He gathered their new pots and pans and motioned to join him. Together they walked down the hill through the woods until they came to a beautiful river. It was wide and ran strong and the sound of the fast moving water was wonderful. James immediately squatted down to splash his face and got his entire head wet with the cool water.

"Aaah, Jess, this is nice and cool. Take a drink." James couldn't stop dipping into the water.

Jess stooped next to him, scooped up water in her hands, took a long, soothing drink then did it again. The water was so clear they could see fish swim by, watched a frog jump from a log into the water across from them and could not help but notice the many lovely bird sounds. They both looked up and down the river that meandered as far as they could see as it wound through the trees. The loud call from an eagle made them look into the blue sky and watched it soar above the river as it followed its bends and turns until it flew out of sight. James had not done much fishing in his childhood, but he knew he would fish here. His mind reeled as he thought about all their needs for the cabin. This was going to be a life like neither of them had ever experienced before, and James hoped and prayed deep in his heart that Jess would accept this life and enjoy the journey as much as he. "This is going to be a real test for us, starting out, Jess. I hope you stay with me through this."

She stood after he rose from the stream and hugged him to assure him that as his wife, she looked as forward to their new start as he did. They stood in their embrace by the river for a long time and enjoyed the beautiful sights and sounds.

Jess got her rag wet, dunked it repeatedly in the river until she felt it was clean and usable again. Together they filled the pots with water and started the trek up the hill, and returned to the cabin.

Jess dunked the rag into one of the pots, soaped it heavily with a bar of soap and began to wash the chairs and tables. She wiped the mantel over the fireplace clean then moved to the bedroom fireplace to do the same. James took his pot of water to Stormy, watched him drink long swallows and made a mental note of the need of buckets for the horse and the cabin. He decided to start a written list of necessities for their trip into Atwater. Teddy had showed them the general store, bank, hardware store, a small library, church, city hall, while standing in front of the Atwater county seat. There was also a hotel with saloon. The Atwater population was close to two hundred people before the war, but Teddy could not guess how many of the men had gone off to war.

They started the fire in the spot Jess chose earlier for the fire pit, they ate and sat by the fire for some time before retiring to their new bedroom. Although rustic, they made love and slept on the mattress left in the cabin, and had only a scratchy wool blanket and no pillows. They swatted mosquitoes all night.

After James hooked Stormy to the wagon, they went into town, and realized they had not seen much of the town when originally there with Gerald and Teddy, and they realized the town was bigger than they originally thought it was. Their first stop was the general store, where James made three trips out to the wagon with new supplies. The daughter of the storeowner was minding the store and giggled at their accents. She said she had never heard any like it before. Next, they went to the bank. They introduced themselves to the President of the bank, Mr. Nichols. He was a pleasant, rotund man with long, fuzzy, white "lamb chops" on the side of his face. His white hair was wavy, which he tried to comb flat on his head to no avail. While he started an account for James and Jess, Mr. Nichols said in passing that he was glad to see the "Smith's Place" was occupied again.

"Can you tell us more about the Smith's, Mr. Nichols?" James was so curious.

"Well," he started as he layback in his chair, looked to the ceiling, "Jed Smith and his wife built that place back in '55. I never did know what they were gonna do with all that land, but he and his wife lived up there on that hill for a long time. Sadie, his wife, worked here in town at the library and he did odd jobs for people in town and at the church. They never had much and don't know how they managed. But den Sadie got sick and died real quick 'bout four years ago. He buried her up there somewhere behind the cabin. When the war started, he joined up. Last I heard, he was fighten' in Pennsylvania. He fought at the tail end of Gettysburg, lived through that and 's still around there somewhere. 've never heard anything 'bout him comin' home," finished Mr. Nichols.

"Goodness," Jess was flabbergasted.

"Well, thank you for that information, Mr. Nichols. Can he reclaim my land if or when he returns?"

"Nope, nope, he's been gone too long to call it his again. Don't need t' worry 'bout that."

They were both relieved to hear that. The men started to small talk and Jess found herself wondering if Misses Nichols was as big around as Mr. Nichols was. Did they have plump, round children also? She put her handkerchief to her nose to hide her grin, and then turned to listen to the men.

"I plan to have a lumber business very soon, and I'm not sure if I'm going to build it here in town or closer to my place, but I want you to know." James looked at his wife who caught her attention and she started to listen to them again.

"Lumber, eh? You should do well with that, up here, young man. Don't know how yur' gonna get the trees to the south o' here, but lumber's in *great* need. There are lots o' battle sights and where Sherman did his destruction for hundreds o' miles," said Mr. Nichols.

Jess was glad to hear James' assumption about a lumber business was correct. They looked at each other and smiled.

Jess had written four letters to their families, and needed to mail them to Liverpool. Mr. Nichols directed them to the post office and telegram station. When she walked into the post office, she kissed the back of each envelope before she handed them over the counter to the postmaster. He saw her do that and said, "Do not worry, Miss, they'll make it. In these modern times, they'll make it."

"How long will they take to arrive?"

He looked at the addresses down his long nose through tiny glasses, scratched his head, and looked to the ceiling as if the answer would suddenly appear there. "Three to four months is my best guess, Miss."

"My," Jess gasped and put her hand to her mouth. She then remembered the letters have to travel to New York City and then would be on a ship as long as they were, so now his answer made sense. "Thank you, sir." When she added up the length of time for the letters to arrive in Liverpool and time for them to answer in return, she knew she would not hear any news until Christmas or after.

They left town slowly and went down several side streets to get familiar with the town. They both felt pleased with the town of Atwater of which they were now citizens.

They searched for Sadie Smith's grave several times on their treks to the river, but never were able to find it. They assumed Jed Smith had never marked it.

They spent the summer fixing up their little cabin and barn and bought two goats to keep Stormy company and especially to eat the tall grasses surrounding the cabin.

Gerald Paxton arrived on a hot August day to see how they were getting along. He stayed for two weeks and helped James cut down trees. They made the clearing around the cabin and barn larger as they had cut down many large and small pines, leaving some to shade the cabin. James and Gerald's horses worked hard and were able to drag only the smaller trees during those two weeks. James decided he definitely needed at least one draft horse for that job. Gerald suggested a horse ranch near Albany where he would definitely find a good horse for the job.

Jess learned to love their cabin, but when Gerald arrived, she was almost ashamed of how small and rustic it was compared to his beautiful home. Yet, he seemed comfortable and was amazed at the many repairs James had completed so quickly and alone. She could not wait for the day when they would be able to live in their dream home James talked about daily.

One summer day Jess made curtains for their bedroom to surprise James. When he lit the oil lamp in the bedroom that night, he was shocked to see them.

"I don't remember you buying fabric on any trip to town." James smiled and looked at his wife in wonderment.

"They are made from my wedding veil." Jess smiled proudly.

"You are amazing, Jess. Why would you do that?"

"I won't be using it again. It was a great way to put it to good use." Jess giggled as she blushed.

James repaired the broken windowpanes that summer and made shutters for each window preparing for winter. James and Gerald also repaired the two chimneys during his visit. Before winter, James white washed the cabin and barn, and split plenty of cut, dried wood for winter and stacked it on their porch. Teddy brought them plenty of salted meat and now they were ready for winter.

James made notices to sell his lumber, posted them in town at the general store, library, and the bank.

They spent more money on hay and oats than they expected to during winter, which came out of their lumberyard money. This frustrated James, but he had to do it.

They started attending the small church in town every Sunday, where they made many new acquaintances and friends. Yet when winter came, they discovered it was more difficult to get into town as winter got colder and the snow deeper. They had never seen so much snow.

Gerald told James of an old trick to deal with deep snow, which was to tie one end of a rope to the barn and the other end to the front porch rail, to make it easier to get through deep or blowing snow. James couldn't imagine such a need, but soon found out Gerald was right.

Two months into winter, a blizzard kept them in their cabin for two days. In the middle of the second night of the blizzard, James heard the horse and goats making very loud, excited noises. He quickly got out of bed and dressed, then pushed as much snow as he could with the door as he squeezed through the opening. Jess stayed cozy in bed under four blankets, yet she was still cold. The fire had died in the fireplace and she hated the thought of getting out of bed to stoke the fire, but had to do it. She heard the animals get louder and worried about James struggling through the deep snow. She prayed the rope had not broken because of the blizzard. The window shutters prevented her from seeing outside and she heard Stormy kicking the barn walls and neighing very loudly. Jess was scared now and started to dress for the cold. She pushed through the doors small opening, guided by the rope, and stepped in the same steps in the snow James had made as she worked her way to the barn. The barn door was slightly ajar in a snowdrift as she approached the barn when she was suddenly rushed by a blur of gray fur and a growl she had never heard before. There was no room to step out of its way and fell back, bottom first, into the deep snow. Jess quickly got back on her feet and entered the totally dark barn. The horse neighed loudly and she heard shuffling in the hay toward the back of the barn. She made her way to Stormy, patted his neck to calm him and searched through the dark toward the sounds.

"James?" Jess felt so scared.

"Back here," he mumbled from the dark. She hurried the best she could through the straw, stumbling, and feeling her way through the dark barn along wooden rails until she finally found him on the barn floor. She tried to help him up and put his arm around her neck when he cried out in pain. Not able to see in the dark, she tried her best to get him to the open barn door. James could not walk alone and leaned heavily on Jess as they slowly made their way to the cabin through the deep snow, heavily relying on the frozen rope. She finally got him onto the bed, where by the light of the fire, she could see his bloody right arm and the dark red bloodstain that was growing quickly on his right pant leg below his knee. Jess raised the wick in the oil lamp to make a larger flame to study his wounds. She then ripped the stained hole in his pants larger where she saw blood still spewed from the large gash in his calf.

"Wolf," sputtered James. "It got one of the goats. Did it hurt Stormy?" he asked as he laid his head back, finding little relief. She shook her head no and wiped her hair from her face with the back of her hand.

Jess started to tear one of her petticoats to make long strips and started to tend to James' wounds. She quickly started a pot of water on the fire and rinsed the bloody cloths as the water warmed. She discovered the large gash in his leg was deep, but all of his leg was still there. She thanked God. His arm was also bitten, but not as bad as on his leg. Jess wrapped his arm successfully, but the bleeding from his leg would not stop. James reached for one of the cloth strips and tied it tightly below his knee to make a tourniquet. He laid back, put the crook of his arm over his eyes, as if to block out the pain. He then told Jess to get ice from their water bucket on the porch and apply it to his leg. He hoped that would stop the bleeding, and kill some of his pain. Jess quickly searched the water bucket they kept near the fireplace in the main room, which used to be ice but had melted. She checked the bucket on the porch, and it was frozen, but the ice was not too thick, and she was able to break it into the pieces she needed. She quickly wrapped a large chunk of ice and tied it to his leg. James howled at first, and then relaxed. The ice helped to stop the bleeding, and Jess took a sigh of relief. She sat on the edge of the bed and gently stroked James' face to give him comfort. She rested a moment, and then changed both bloody bandages and retrieved another piece of ice for his leg. Afterwards, she rinsed the strips and hung them near the hearth to dry. She then sat closely to James and searched his face.

"Darling, I don't know what to do for you. What can I do?" begged Jess. She searched his eyes for assurance in what she did to make him feel better.

"You're doing fine, Jess. I need to see the damage," spurted James as he struggled to sit up and reached for his leg with his left hand. He raised the bandage slightly and his face screwed up in pain as he took in a deep breath and looked at the bite on his leg.

"It's not as bad as it feels. The bleeding should stop soon, Jess. Thank you my love. You are a strong woman," said James as he lay back on the bed. Jess started to help him remove his heavy coat and boots. His right boot contained a lot of blood and she quickly started to clean it. His shirt, now wet with sweat, needed to come off also so he wouldn't get chilled. She thanked God he hadn't gone into shock. He started to remove it as Jess undid the buttons of his pants. She tended to his arm again and cleaned the wound the best she could. The fire was dying, Jess noticed, added wood then returned to James on the bed. He watched as she tended to his every need, then he giggled slightly. She looked at him with questioning eyes.

"You need to wash your face, my dear. You have blood all over it." James reached for her face, and then quickly pulled his injured arm back.

Jess prayed quickly for her husband and for the animals as she retrieved her looking glass and he was right - there was even blood in her hair. She quickly rinsed her face and rubbed the dried blood from her hair with a wet cloth. She needed fresh water and threw the bloody water from the porch into the snow. She filled her bucket with fresh snow, to let it melt near the fire. She was exhausted but knew she had to go on. She knew his pain was intense and searched the house for something to prop his leg higher than his heart. The only thing she could think of was books. They had stacks of them. She made two stacks, six books in each pile on the bed, and tied them together with her aprons, took the pad from the chair in the main room to put on top of the books for his comfort.

James situated himself to lay straight on the bed and raised his leg to rest it on the cushioned books. She covered him with their blankets, and then undressed to lie next to her wounded husband. James was in a lot of pain, but exhaustion quickly took him to slumber. Jess made a point to stay awake until she saw he was truly comfortable. When his eyes stayed closed and his breathing became deeper, she let herself relax and slept soundly next to him.

James woke first the next morning and didn't want to disturb Jess, who was still in deep sleep. He lifted his arm and searched his bandage for fresh blood. He saw none, raised his brows and it was then he realized the pain had actually lessened. He thanked God silently, then tried to move his right leg from the padded books. The pain from his action made him wince. Jess felt him stir, woke quickly, and rose to attend to her husband. She realized then that his wounds and blood were not a dream. She bent to kiss his cheek and pulled the blankets back that covered both of them to check his leg. She was thankful there was no new red blood on the bandage. She scanned his arm for the same and found all the bandages were dry.

"I need to clean your leg wound, James," she almost whispered and felt very afraid. His eyes closed and knew the pain would be unbearable, but it had to be done.

"I know, Jess. I'm not looking forward to it, but please do what you have to do," he said through tight grimaced lips.

She cleaned the wound with whiskey, which she had to do, knowing the pain would be unbearable for her husband. When she heard his groans of pain, she tried to finish as quickly as she could.

"We need to check the animals, Jess. I hate that I have to ask you to do this with me, but we need to tend to their wounds as well, if there are any. I couldn't tell which goat was dead, or if the other goat was wounded. I also passed Stormy and heard him neighing last night. He's got to be checked, Jess. Please help me to the barn. I...."

"You will be going nowhere. I will tend to them now before I make your breakfast," Jess interrupted him abruptly. She had never sounded so stern before, which James noticed immediately and grinned.

Jess dressed for the cold and snow and headed toward the barn. The barn door still stood open and she saw that snow had fallen inside the barn and prayed that she would be able to stand the sight she was about to confront. She saw bloody red snow immediately. She approached Stormy first, checked him all over and did not see any wounds. He was settled now. She silently said a prayer of thanks and fed him oats and hay. She checked his water bucket and found it frozen, and knew she would have to melt snow for him in a separate bucket. She walked to the back of the barn, saw the bloody drag marks in the straw, then she found Abe, the goat, who was fine but cried out loudly when he saw Jess. She comforted and fed him and then followed the bloody trail out the barn door and saw that it continued into the woods.

She returned to the house and told James what she found, and explained that the wolf must have returned and dragged the female goat he killed into the woods. James closed his eyes tightly and wished he were able to handle this task. Then Jess took the bucket from the hearth of melted snow to the barn and watered the horse and goat. Jess returned to the cabin and prepared breakfast of toasted bread and jam, cornbread and dried beef strips. When the coffee was ready, she served James in bed and soon joined him for breakfast. James told her he needed a crutch and an arm sling. Jess made the sling from a strip of her petticoat and searched their woodpile for a long piece of wood but didn't find any that would suffice. She told James she would search the barn, and drudged through the snow to the barn. Soon she returned with a piece she thought was long enough, but the crutch would need a crosspiece. She went to the porch in search again and returned with a small branch. James attached the wood with a piece of twine, he wound it around both pieces until he felt it would hold, and his crutch was made. He got out of bed to test it, and it worked, but the throbbing in his leg put him back into bed quickly. She hung the strip of cloth over his head to make a sling and then tied the knot at his nape. James was right handed and he knew everything was going to be difficult until he healed.

The next month was difficult for Jess since she tended to James' needs and the animals. She was becoming exhausted. The snow continued to fall several more times that winter which made her trips to the barn more challenging with each new snowfall. As he healed and going stir-crazy, he tried to help Jess as much as he could, yet she was insistent that he rest often.

James was finally able to get to the barn by using the rope to guide him to tend to the animals, and to bring wood into the cabin for fires, but healing very slowly. His arm had almost completely healed, but his leg would take all winter to heal completely. James was afraid he would limp for a long time. The wolf had almost ripped off his calf muscle, but it was in tact on top and bottom, which saved his leg. Jess kept his wounds clean with whiskey, which prevented infection. He still had a lot of pain, yet it lessened each day little by little.

Christmas was dreary, but they were glad to be together. It snowed all day, which was beautiful on the pine trees, but made it impossible for James and Jess to go to church.

Chapter Eleven
Spring 1865

Spring arrived slowly, but thankfully, the snow around the cabin had melted quickly, which made getting to the barn much easier. However, it was still deep in the shadiest spots of the woods and made Jess' trips to the river still very cold and slippery. She had to clean her shoes and dresses many times a day.

James was still limping in spring, yet they were able to return to church services where many expressed their concerns and offered help whenever he needed it.

James approached a few young men at church when he decided to take them up on their offers of assistance. He explained that he was not able to pay cash for their labor, but he would reimburse them with lumber. Two of the three young men who listened to him said they would like to do that. The third teenager backed away from the conversation and returned to his parents. The two boys were only thirteen years old and thankfully, their parents had stopped them from going off to war. They quickly agreed to James' offer. He told them Jess would prepare their lunches daily, and asked them to arrive at his barn the following morning. James felt good inside on the ride home from church and excitedly told Jess that Atwood Lumber officially begins tomorrow.

The boys arrived on time the next morning and found James waiting for them in the barn. He instructed them how to work the two-man saws and they cut the drying trees into eight-foot lengths. This went on for weeks as they piled the wood into huge heaps before he taught them how to strip the bark using smaller saws. They built wooden racks to hold the wood then cut more wood into stripped beams. Jess made their lunches daily and she often joined them. They sat on hay bales in the barn as they ate. The boys arrived on the fourth Monday in a wagon so they could return home with a load of lumber as their payments. Both boys explained to James and Jess that they were both adding a room to their parent's small homes using this lumber, so they could have their own bedrooms. James recalled his childhood where he shared just a corner of a room with Emily, and understood their desires.

They had not seen Teddy since autumn, yet continued to include him in their daily prayers. Finally, in mid March, they heard the sound of a large wagon coming up their long drive. When Teddy appeared at the top of the hill, with a broad smile, Jess wondered if she would ever be able to convince him to trim his shaggy hair and scraggly beard, and giggled to herself as she widely waved at him and started the walk across the yard to where he settled his horse and wagon. They hugged in greeting and Teddy asked where her no-good husband was, through his laughter. Jess pointed to the area behind the barn. There they found James, Bobby and Tim, the two teenagers, hard at work. Teddy and Jess got rather close before James realized they were there. He waved with a smile and started walking in their direction, "Hey, Teddy. It is so good to see you," said James, almost breathless from moving wood.

"Whoa, James, what's with th' limp?" Teddy looked at his leg with a questioning look. James told him about the wolf in the barn and Jess jumped in periodically to finish James' sentences.

Teddy hung his head, wishing so badly that he could have helped. He was gasping now and hung his head lower, "James - if I'd known, I..."

"It was in the dead of winter, Teddy. There was no way for us to reach the other, for even if you knew, you couldn't get here through all the snow we had. I thank you, Teddy. You're a good friend."

Jess patted Teddy on the back and thanked him for his thoughtfulness.

"I feel so bad fer both o' you. Is there anything I can do fer ya now?"

"No, my beautiful bride did it all. She was very strong," James said with a wide grin while Teddy still had his hand on James' back and gave him a supportive shoulder squeeze.

They talked a while longer then Teddy started the walk back to where James and the boys had been working. James introduced Teddy to the young men and proceeded to tell him all they had accomplished. He also told of his plans to build a shelter for the cut wood.

James and Teddy stood on the cabin porch and waved good-bye to the boys as they rode past on their horses. Their workday was done.

While Jess prepared dinner at the fireplace, the men entered the room and Teddy complimented her on how good dinner smelled. "Sure smells like venison cookin'. Am I right?"

"Yes sir, James shot and cleaned it yesterday. He worries me when he hunts with his leg still giving him pain, but he insists he is fine," said Jess through a worried look on her face.

Over dinner, Teddy told them he was on his way to New York City with a load of meat, and would return in a week, if they would have him. They both told him how glad they would be to see him again and he could stay as long as he pleased. Teddy told them he brought salted meats for them. James tried to pay Teddy for the meats and he waved his hand and dismissed the thought of it.

They shared their winter stories after dinner, then Teddy stood and said he had to make it to Gerald's place yet tonight and started for the door. James and Jess thanked him again for the meat and watched him disappear down the drive and out of sight. Teddy waved good-bye before he rounded the first bend at the bottom of the drive.

Before the next week ended, they heard Teddy's wagon climb the hill to their cabin. He jumped down quickly, unhooked his horse from the wagon and prompted him to graze on the grass. Jess took notice how he never tied his horse to anything, even in the city, and his horse always stayed close to him.

James came from behind the barn, Jess walked toward him from the cabin, and the three met near Teddy's horse. Teddy stood, petting the neck of his horse while greeting his friends.

"Sales were good in th' city. Th' trip was worth it. Gerald says 'ello and t' tell ya he'd see ya soon," said Teddy, still patting his horse's neck and combing through his mane. Stormy, tied to a tree at the edge of the woods neighed because he wanted to be near Teddy's horse. James untied Stormy and let him join his fellow horse as they freely grazed the tall grasses together.

"Friends t' the end," laughed Teddy.

"How is Gerald these days?" James had not seen him in so long.

"He's good an' doin' fine," replied Teddy. "So where is it yer wantin' to build this wood shelter you're talkin' 'bout, James?"

95

"Let me show you," said James as they headed to the proposed spot behind the barn.

Jess watched the two men walk together, grinned, and felt warmth in her heart. She knew they would always have a friend in Teddy. He was heaven sent, and she knew it.

The following days passed quickly as the men and two boys built the shelter over cut wood. James wanted to pay Teddy but he refused payment again. "Ya know what I could use though?"

"What's that?" James truly wanted to reimburse his friend.

"Repairs to my wagon. It's afallin' 'part! It's done a lo' o' miles."

"Let's get those repairs done then." James put his arm around his friend's shoulders as they walked.

That night after dinner, the men began to take the nearly empty wagon apart starting at the rear. They placed the old wood planks from the wagon onto the firewood pile then searched the newly cut wood for replacement pieces. Exhausted and hot, they decided they would finish the work after breakfast the next day. They rose early the next morning and finished the repairs to his wagon, which took most of the day.

Teddy left the next day midmorning and promised to return in a month.

When James went to town that day, the postmaster saw him enter the bank. The postmaster ran across the street and into the bank, and breathlessly told him he had a letter. He handed him an envelope from England. It was from Jess' parents:

"Dear James and Jessica ~ We are so proud to hear how well you have settled and that you are both doing well. The house and lumberyard have sold. We will be sailing by the middle of March. Will you be able meet us in New York City? We will look for you near the middle of May at the dock. Grant and Kathleen are well and send their love. We love you both, Mother and Father Strong."

Mr. Nichols saw postmaster Frank Jones hand the letter to James and waited to approach him until he saw him finish the letter. Only then, did he approach James and ask how he could help him. He finished his banking business and started toward his wagon when Mr. Jones ran into the street and screamed at the top of his lungs, "The war is over! The war is over!" He waved a telegram high in the air and repeated his words. A crowd started to gather around Mr. Jones, as he told everyone that Lee surrendered to Grant and the war was over. The crowd grew larger by the minute and the entire town celebrated. James felt a surge of relief that the war had not touched their lives, and that they had made this move to America to help the country rebuild.

James decided to ask Teddy on his next visit to get the ship line schedule when he next went into the city and they would go from there.

James and Jess celebrated the war's end in front of their fireplace, where the glow of a small fire was the only witness to their lovemaking.

Sales of lumber were seldom to citizens of Atwater, yet James stayed positive and kept track of each sale. Then he noticed sales were happening more often as spring worked its way into summer.

Three days later, James was surprised to see Gerald coming up their drive. His smile was broad as he neared their cabin with his arms waving excitedly. The clatter from his empty wagon as it bounced behind him was so loud it frightened Jess to where she had to see what all the noise was. She looked out the window and wiped her hands on her apron as she ran to greet their friend. By the time she arrived at Gerald's side, James was already shaking his hand. They all hugged and soon the end of the war came up in conversation. Gerald said, with a smile, he was here to place a lumber order. That put a big smile on James' face. Jess told them she had just made lunch and would deliver it to them soon. James and Gerald walked behind the barn, where Gerald inspected available dried lumber and the new wood shelter with James.

"Every time I come here, there are improvements. James, you are doing well, I see."

"It's going well, Gerald, very well. Now, what are you erecting and how much lumber do you need?"

Gerald told him he needed lumber to build a small house behind his home for his workers. He explained, "I lost one of my hired hands. His family left to go west to find gold, and he of course had to follow. Then the other young man almost left because his father was killed in Gettysburg and his mother had nowhere to go. Therefore, I took them both in and put her to work cleaning and gardening. I don't really want

97

them to live in my house, so I've decided to build a small house for my hired hands." Gerald expressed that he would like the new house finished by winter.

"You're a very nice man, Gerald. We've also been lucky. I have the finest young men working for me, and I would never want to lose them. I'm sure James feels the same way." Jess truly admired this man and thanked God Teddy brought him into their lives.

James nodded his head in agreement and then asked Gerald if he had the house plans with him. Gerald reached under the wagon seat, retrieved the plans, and laid them out on the wagon bed. They both bent over the plans to discuss Gerald's needs. James started a list, and Jess returned to the cabin to leave the men to their business.

They enjoyed their dinner while they sat around the fire pit. Afterwards, the men stretched their legs out in front of them, leaned back in their chairs, and enjoyed two of the biggest cigars Jess had ever seen. They celebrated Grant's and the North's success in the war and talked of the future, and both of their personal futures and the new United States.

"Do you know if there are any men in town looking for work?" Gerald asked.

"I believe you may be able to find one or two. We can go to town tomorrow and start the search for men that you need."

"Let's do that. Thank you, James." Gerald smiled as he leaned forward and flicked his long cigar ash into the fire.

"We have brandy, gentlemen. Would you like some?" Jess rose with a grin.

"Woman, why didn't you say so!" laughed Gerald. He rose and said he would get it from the cabin, "Do I need to get two or three glasses?" asked Gerald while he looked at Jess.

She held up two fingers and smiled. He quickly returned to the fire with clinking glasses and a glass decanter of brandy. He poured both glasses, handed one to James and they clinked their glasses together and downed the small shots of brandy. He refilled their glasses and then they sipped the brandy slowly as they sat by the fire and told stories, laughed and reminisced.

The moonlight appeared over the treetops and shone into the yard where they sat, which meant it was very late. Jess laid her head back and studied the twinkling stars. The heat from the fire sent strange waves up in the air, which made the stars look as if they were in liquid. She watched for a long time, listening to the men talk, when suddenly she felt nauseous. She wondered if it was from dinner or maybe the heat. She raised her head and hoped the feeling would pass, but it got worse. She excused herself and went into the house to lie down. The room began to spin and Jess didn't understand why. She quickly undressed and got under the cool sheets of the bed. When she didn't return, James came in to check on her.

"James, I feel ill. Can you please wet a cloth for my forehead?"

As he laid the cloth on her forehead, he said he would return soon. He went outside and explained to Gerald that he needed to tend to his ill wife. Gerald then stood and said, "I will sleep under the stars tonight. Thank you for your kindness, my friend. I hope Jess feels better soon. I will see you both in the morning." James watched as Gerald retrieved a blanket from his wagon, returned to the fire pit and laid the blanket on the ground before he lied down, folding his arms under his head to gaze at the sky.

James quickly returned to the bedroom, rewet the cloth for her head, undressed and quickly slid into bed beside his wife. He took her hand in his and was relieved that it did not feel too warm, so there was no fever. He said a silent prayer and asked God to look over his loving wife. He stayed awake and watched over her until he knew she was asleep.

James woke suddenly to the sounds of his wife vomiting into a bucket. He quickly went to her side and asked what he could do to help, as she was ill again. He ran to get another cloth and wet it in the water bucket in the main room, using it to wipe her face and mouth. He rinsed it again and placed it on her forehead after he helped her back to bed. He waited until she slept again before he went outside to Gerald. He had made bacon over the fire pit, which smelled wonderful. Gerald asked what he could do to help with Jess. James told his friend there was nothing either of them could do and how bad he felt for Jess. Gerald nodded his head and then told James he would have to leave soon. They ate their fill of bacon and chunks of bread and saved some for Jess. When James took the bacon into the bedroom and Jess smelled it, she ran to the bucket and lost her stomach again. James quickly removed the bacon from the room.

He ran outside and explained to Gerald what just happened. Gerald's head flew back in laughter.

James was stunned at his laughter, "Why do you think my wife's illness is so funny, sir?"

"She is with child, my friend. I will lay you odds, she is in the family way," finished Gerald through his laughter.

James' jaw dropped as he stared at his friend without blinking. The look on his face must have been a sight. When Gerald saw the look, he started to laugh louder. It was then he put his hand out to James to be the first to congratulate his dear friend. James, in shock, raised his arm slowly to shake his hand. When Gerald started to shake his hand, he laughed again at the looseness of his flopping arm, instead of his usual firm handshake. Gerald continued to laugh as he returned his blanket and frying pan to his wagon. He returned briefly to James, shook his hand again, and asked if he was okay. James shook his head yes, still looked shocked and when he finally came back to reality, gave a hearty thanks to Gerald for the lumber order.

"I can go to town with you now, if you wish, to look for the hands you intend to hire," said James to Gerald's grinning face.

"No sir! You stay here with your wife – and baby – and take care of them. I can find hired hands myself. What is the President of the Bank's name? I can start by talking with him."

"Nichols - Peter Nichols."

Gerald nodded his head. James started to walk beside Gerald toward his wagon, when Gerald took him by the shoulders, turned him around and said, "Go to your wife."

James started toward the house, turned to wave good-bye to Gerald, and jumped over the steps of the porch, landed in front of the door, opened it quickly and entered. Inside he found his wife still asleep. He then heard two horses approach the cabin, looked out, and saw Tim and Bobby coming up the drive who waved to Gerald as he went down the drive with his heavy load of lumber. James told the boys of Jess' "illness" and said he would work today, but would be checking on his wife often. James did just that, running back and forth between the house and wood shelter where the boys were removing bark from downed trees. Each time he entered the bedroom Jess was either sleeping or vomiting. It was hardly a good time to talk.

Finally, after the boys left for the day, James found Jess sitting up in bed, reading a book.

"How are you feeling, Jess?".

"I am much better, thank you, but very hungry. Has Gerald left?"

"Hours ago. You have been sleeping most of the day, my dear." James giggled.

Jess' brows rose slightly, changed her gaze to meet his eyes and saw the serious look on his face.

"What's wrong, James?"

"I don't know how to say or ask this, but, when was your last ladies time?" He almost whispered the last two words.

"Why are you...." she hesitated, counted in her head quickly then sputtered "James, do you know what this could mean?" she said as her voice raised an entire octave.

He ran to sit next to her on the bed, put his arms around her and hugged her tightly. Her arms rose slowly to return his hug. Now it was her turn to be in shock. Her arms finally hugged his neck, where they held their embrace a long time. When they parted, James saw tears in Jess' eyes. He tenderly wiped them away and kissed both tear trails down her cheeks. They looked into each other eyes with love and both tried to imagine what the future was bringing.

Sunday morning James and Jess started their way to church, but she got ill again, and they turned around and returned home. She apologized and James shushed her when he put his finger over her lips, then kissed her cheek sweetly.

Together, they sat with a calendar to figure the due date for the baby. They counted the months and realized the baby would most likely arrive in November. They were not sure which day it would be in November, but it would definitely be in November.

Jess' parents were due to arrive in a month and she prayed she would feel better by then. Only time would tell. She started out each day being ill, but found as the days progressed, she started feeling better each day. She readied the house for the upcoming visitors, her parents. Jess would make sure they would have a warm welcome to America and to their cabin and wondered how long they would be staying; especially since it was so different from the home they were accustomed.

During the next week, Teddy stopped at their cabin quickly on his way to New York City with more salted meats when they told him their news. He was elated.

"It's th' bes' thing that'll happen to ya in yer entire life, James. I'll never forget when my boys were born. Proudest days o' my life! When will yer happy even' be?"

"November, Teddy. For right now, though, I'm looking forward to the day when she is not ill every morning," said James as he put his hands in his pockets. He felt helpless.

"That'll las' 'bout three months, ma boy. Soon, by my calculations." Teddy started to count on his fingers.

"Thank God! I feel so bad for her and so helpless."

"I know, James. It's hard t' watch. But I guarantee th' end result is worth it!" Teddy smiled at James with a knowing look and patted him on the back. "Can I see her?"

"Yes, of course, she's in the house. Please come in." James pointed toward the cabin.

When they entered, Teddy noticed the improvements she had made in the cabin. He grinned at how hard Jess had worked to make their cabin a warm home. Jess came from the bedroom, met eyes with Teddy and smiled. She skipped over to him and hugged his neck. She could tell he had already heard the news.

He backed away a step and congratulated her with a kiss on her cheek. He stepped one more step back and released her arms and he smiled at her glow, noticing her rosy cheeks and her angelic appearance.

"Yer beamin', my dear. I'm so happy fer ya both. As I was just tellin' James outside, it's the best thing that'll happen in yer lives. Enjoy the peace and quiet now, Jess; it'll be a long time 'til ya have dat again," he said with a lilt to his voice. His happiness for them spewed from Teddy and they could both feel it.

"Teddy, there is something I have wanted to do since the day we met, and that is to trim your hair and beard. Please don't be insulted, my friend, but would you allow me to do that for you?" Jess looked at him sheepishly and searched his face for his reaction.

"No one woul' know me ifn I done dat." He smiled so big, yet she couldn't tell if he was joking or not. She still searched his face and eyes, and she could now tell he was thinking about it.

"I guess so. "'manda sometimes does dat for me, but not offen. Where you wantin' ta do dis?"

She pointed outside and reached for the scissors and a comb. She then followed him to the chairs that surrounded the fire pit. Teddy was laughing all the way out of the house, and shaking and scratching his head. Jess quickly turned his shirt collar under and started to snip the scraggly ends of his hair, not removing much hair. She combed it gently, and cut more off the back. She moved to face him, held his head up with one finger, smiled, and nodded her head. She thought he looked so much better. She then shaped his beard and when she stepped back and gazed at her friend, she was very pleased. "James can you please get my looking glass? He needs to see the new Teddy!"

James quickly returned from the cabin and handed his friend the mirror and Teddy's eyes got huge when he saw how nice she made him look in such a short time. "We'll have ta do dis again in a few mont's, Jess. My wife will think she's in bed wid a stranger." He poked James with his elbow and winked at Jess. "Thank ya, my fine lady!" Teddy stood and bowed at his waist and Jess returned the gesture with a full curtsy, as she pulled her skirt out as wide as it would go.

Teddy thanked her again and was off to Gerald's home, and said he would have the ship's schedule for them upon his return from New York City in six days. He waved as he was half way down the drive. He was planning to stay at Gerald's two days, assist with the building of his hired hands house as much as he could, then on to New York City with his delivery.

The wood shelter had filled quickly with cut wood and James was thankful Jess' parents would arrive soon. He knew Edward would know what to do next. James could not yet afford to build the proper office and supply building in town, and hoped Edward would help with that when he arrived. His lumber sales had increased by word of mouth throughout the county and he sold lumber to people from towns he never heard of. He kept a county map on the barn wall and marked each town that bought lumber and quantities along with customer's names. He made more posters and decided to take a day from work to travel to each of these towns to leave his posters in general stores, and bank windows.

Jess assured James she would be fine alone so he could go as planned. When the boys arrived for work, he asked them, for their safety, if they would only stack and move wood on this day, and were not to use saws while he was away. He told the boys Jess would bring them lunch and for the first time, he was able to pay them cash for their work. They both had big smiles when he handed them their wages. He counted the money to them before they quickly and happily stuffed it into their pockets, as they all exchanged smiles.

James saddled Stormy and left with his posters, water and lunch in a burlap bag. It took him much longer than he thought to ride to four towns to post his notices. While doing this he saw other posters with pictures of Lincoln, draped in black fabric, which he knew symbolized death. He went to the post office in the last town he was in and asked if something had happened to Mr. Lincoln. The postmaster explained that an actor named John Wilkes Booth had assassinated President Lincoln, and they were still looking for the scoundrel. He pointed to the tin type picture of Booth on his post office wall, and then added, "Be on the lookout, sir. One never knows how far he will get tryin' to 'scape!" James studied the picture closely, and then asked who the new President was. The man answered Andrew Johnson and screwed up his face with a look of disapproval as he spoke. James knew nothing of Johnson, but he clearly understood, by this man's body language, he was not happy with the new President.

He had a long ride home and knew it would be after dark when he arrived. He had eaten his lunch by the side of the road between towns and shared his water with Stormy as the horse munched grass nearby. He rode over an hour before he finally rode down the center of

Atwater. He noticed they too had black fabric draped over Lincoln posters throughout the town. He hated the thought of having to tell Jess the terrible news of Lincoln.

She cried, as he suspected she would, when he told her the news. "How terrible!" She buried her face into her husbands shoulder as she cried for the country's loss and thinking of their American born child. James held his mournful wife for a long time.

Teddy arrived with the shipyard schedule as promised, which said Jess' parents ship would arrive 23 May, give or take a day. James did not want Jess to ride in the bumpy wagon for two and a half days to New York City and back in her condition. Yet he didn't want to leave her alone that long either. Therefore, James asked Teddy if he would be in the city around their day of arrival and if he would bring the Strong's to Atwater.

"I've already thought 'bout this James, and I'll arrange t' be there two days bafor that fer my meat sales and I will gladly lead them t' yer door," said Teddy and assured James with a pat on his shoulder.

"Oh, thank you, Teddy. I just don't want Jess going on that bumpy ride."

"I know, my friend. I unterstant!"

At the fire pit that night, Teddy told them that Gerald's little house was half finished and that he had found two good men in Atwater who now lived on his ranch while they assisted in building the house, and they would return to Atwater when the house was completed.

"Teddy, I would like to ask another favor of you," inserted Jess.

"Yeah?" asked Teddy. He turned his head in her direction, looking away from the fire.

"When you guide my parents from the city, could you please not tell them our news? We want to surprise them," Jess said quietly.

"I figured ya'd want t' tell 'em, 'tho by then they be able t' tell as soon as they take one look at ya." Teddy smiled as he watched Jess blush.

She smiled and watched her feet shuffle and twist in the dirt.

The following morning, Teddy left after he told them he would return on May 19 on his way to New York City.

105

Chapter Twelve
May 1865

James was working hard at lumber sales and deliveries in Atwater County, and was using their personal wagon. He knew he needed a bigger wagon to deliver efficiently, yet he was trying to save money to buy the ban saw he needed to do proper cutting, and their wagon was starting to show its wear.

Jess continued to make her trips to the stream for water and was very thankful for the barrel James built for her, so she could wash clothes near the house. He also put a pulley system among the trees for them that brought buckets of water up to the house, as carrying the buckets of water up the hill was exhausting. She knew when the baby arrived, they would need even more water each day.

Teddy arrived on the 19th as he said he would. When she saw him, it made Jess anxious knowing her parents would be here soon. She did what she could do with limited money to prepare for their arrival, and found more to do all the time. She wanted their stay to be perfect.

Teddy spent the night, slept by the fire and left early the next morning without waking James or Jess. He left them some of his tasty bacon, which he knew they enjoyed, and Jess prepared one entire package of bacon at the fire pit. She knew the luscious smell would waft to the boys and James. She soon heard them behind her and giggled. She knew it would not take them long before they arrived by her side after smelling the luscious pork and the four of them ate until the food disappeared. The men talked between mouthfuls about the needs of another man and horses to make deliveries. It was the first time Jess heard about the business growth. Until then, James had never discussed it with her.

"James, this is wonderful news!" Jess said with delight. "I had no idea things were going so well!"

He stood, hugged his wife excitedly, saying nothing, and then returned to work with Tim and Bobby.

Jess nervously busied herself, and cleaned what was already clean. Her parents would arrive with the armoire James made for her in Liverpool and their wedding bed. She was tired of living out of their trunks and anxious to have drawers for clothes again. They decided they would move their stuffed, scratchy bed from the bedroom and into the main room for James and Jess to sleep on while her parents would use their bedroom and sleep on the better mattress.

The next days passed quickly, and soon she heard the clatter of wagons coming up their drive while Jess was gathering flowers in the woods. She ran to the front of the cabin and saw Teddy leading up the drive in his wagon, then saw a massive black half-covered wagon where her father sat proudly in the driver's seat. Edward slapped the horse with long reins all the way up the hill. Her tiny framed mother sat next to him with her hand over her mouth and nose to protect her face from the dust rustled up from Teddy's wagon. When they finally stopped, Jess ran to hug her father, who squeezed her tightly, kissed her cheek and squeezed her again. He then helped his wife Victoria down from the wagon, who was smiling ear to ear.

"My baby!" Victoria cried as Edward lowered her to the ground. She too hugged her daughter tightly and stepped back to view her daughter. "Jessica, are you with child?"

Jess blushed as she ran both hands over her skirt and wondered how she could tell. Victoria quickly wondered if Jess was trying to show them the tiny bulge of her stomach or hide it. Regardless, Victoria noticed, where Edward had not.

"My little girl is in the family way?" shouted Edward.

"Yes, Father, I am. The baby will arrive in November," exclaimed Jess with excitement when she smiled at him, then looked to her mother, as if she needed her approval.

"Jessica this is wonderful news! How do you feel?" squealed her mother. She hugged her daughter again and wondered where time had gone. It felt to her that it was just a short time ago when Jess was a little girl and played with dolls while sitting on her lap.

"I feel good, now, Mother." Jess then recalled the many ill mornings.

"I am going to be a Grandfather! This is wonderful news!" boasted Edward loudly.

James approached from behind the barn and ran to his family. He put his arm out to shake Edward's hand, but instead Edward grabbed his shoulders, looked him in the eye, then wrapped his arms around his son-in-law saying, "Congratulations, son. You're going to be a father!"

James' face turned bright red as he hugged his father-in-law in return. Victoria beamed as she put her arm around her daughters expanding waist. She let go to hug James, who thought she was going to squeeze the life out of him. Teddy stood back and watched the beautiful family reunion, smiling and then took his turn hugging Jess and shaking James' hand.

Edward walked to James and told him he had brought him a letter from his sister. He reached under the wagon seat and retrieved a large envelope from his travel bag. He handed it to him with a smile, "I have protected that envelope for almost three months, son; I hope its good news."

James separated himself from the gathering and carefully opened the envelope that had something very stiff in it. He opened the seal to find a tin type photograph of Emily and John, their girls Sarah and Marylee and a new baby on her lap. He couldn't tell if it was a boy or a girl because it was too young. He searched the envelope further and found a letter. His first impression was admiring Emily's beautiful penmanship. James and Jessica were written on the blank side of the folded letter. As he opened it, Jess stepped to his side with a quizzical look on her face. He held it so they could both read it at the same time. It said ~ "James and Jess ~ I hope this letter finds you both well and safe in America. As you will see in the photograph, we have welcomed Michael James Bryce into our family. He was born on 5 November, 1864. He's a lovely boy and we are so happy. Mother and Father are well and send you their love. We all miss you both so much. We realize you have a dream and are pursuing it and we hope you find happiness in America. John is now working at Liverpool city hall, misses teaching, but is very content in his new position. You know of his mayoral dreams, James. I love being a mother and who knows how many children God will grant us. Please write to us and let us know how you are and about your new homeland. With all of our love, Emily and family."

Jess looked at James and saw tears trail down his cheeks. She kissed him tenderly and put her arms around his neck.

"I must send a baby gift. The next time we go to town, I will send all three children a nice gift, James. Do you want me to send your parents something?" Jess was near tears.

"Maybe we should have our photograph taken, Jess. They would like that. They have one from our wedding, but maybe one in front of our cabin?" His tears were now gone and replaced by a slight smile.

"I will arrange that, James. I think that would be a nice gift for your parents and one for your sister and family also." Jess smiled now too.

They held their hug for some time and Victoria gave Jess a wondering look. Jess smiled to her mother over her husband's shoulder. "All is well with Emily and look at the beautiful tin type they sent of them and their children. I think it's time we had a tin type made and you should also, Mother, for Grant and us, of course." Victoria agreed with a smile.

The men immediately began unloading the big black wagon of the wedding bed and armoire. Jess and Victoria filled the drawers at once, so glad to see her furniture pieces. Her mother insisted on doing almost everything, babying her daughter in her "condition". The men started to exchange the beds from room to room until Victoria saw what they were doing. Jess explained her wishes on where they all slept, and Victoria said she and Edward would never take their bedroom. Edward agreed and they switched the beds back to their proper places. After Jess and her mother made both beds, Jess lie back on her bed and put her arms above her head and aaahed very calmly. Her mother stood and enjoyed watching her daughter's happiness finally lying on her wedding bed again. Then Jess jumped up and placed Emily's family portrait on their mantel.

James whistled to the boys in the back and asked them to assist in unloading the Strong's trunks. After only two of seven trunks were in the room, they noticed there would hardly be room for more. Victoria quickly went through the trunks in the room and wagon and decided which two trunks she needed while at the cabin. She spent the next hour opening and checking the other trunks in the wagon until she was satisfied. The remaining trunks were stored in the barn.

After the boys left for the day, they all sat around the fire pit and Edward told James and Jess how Teddy found them in New York City. He explained their ship arrived in New York a day earlier than expected and they stayed in the same hotel James and Jess had. The following day they searched the market for James or Jessica, never to find them. Edward continued to tell how he and his wife toured New York City from a small rented buggy. The day after that their furniture and trunks were at last off the ship and after seeing what they had to load for their trip to Atwater, it was then Edward bought the big black, half-covered wagon and a huge white horse. The horse had the biggest hooves Jess had ever seen on a horse. James talked to Edward about his horse, offered to buy him, as he was a draft horse, and could handle dragging the biggest trees they had already cut from their woods. Edward agreed to sell him the horse as soon as he found a smaller horse to pull their buggy, which he intended to buy anyway.

"We needed a large horse to handle the load on the buggy from New York City and the draft horse is all yours!"

"How did you and Teddy find each other?" Jess was curious.

"I saw these two fokes that looked prim and proper walkin' by my meat stand, knew they wasn't from New York by the way dare clothes were, so I stopped dem an' assed dem if day were Edward an' Victoria." Teddy then turned to Jess, "Jess, you shoulda seen da looks on dare faces." He laughed as he slapped his knee and continued, "I tole them who I was and dat day were comin' wit me to Atwater and your mother actually backed away from me. We got ta talkin' and den day knew I was for real and was gonna bring dem up here to yur cabin."

Edward nervously shifted his stance and finally sat next to his wife without saying a word. Jess could see his and Victoria's discomfort.

"How was the voyage?" Jess was curious.

Victoria did not look forward to this discussion, as she knew their trip to America was much more elegant and enjoyable than what James and Jess endured. Edward, not realizing how this affected Jess continued to tell all about the opulence of their ship, explaining how beautiful their cabin was and the dinners were each better than the last. He then added that the music bands played delightful dance tunes, and about the many nights when they danced for hours.

Jess hung her head in envy. James saw this and reached to squeeze her hand. They exchanged looks; Jess smiled, when he leaned toward his wife and kissed her lightly. Victoria cringed as Edward continued to tell them the details of their wonderful voyage. Edward finally changed the direction of his details and began to talk about the wagon loading at the dock and their first day of travel before they arrived at Gerald's home. Victoria raved about Gerald's beautiful home, which also embarrassed Jess, which she knew her mother was used to living the way Gerald lived. Yet Victoria never commented on the small cabin James and Jess now lived in. She knew they were doing their best. Edward spoke of how he admired Gerald and then described the stage of construction the little house was in and said it would most likely be finished by autumn. Victoria then talked briefly, about how dusty and bumpy the ride was from the city.

The next day the women were so happy to be together again, and did a lot of little things, then prepared lunch and dinner together. James tried to work normally with Bobby and Tim, which was hard to do with Edward by his side. Edward made a few suggestions and redirected the boys a few times, which James noted that he was correct and said nothing. They finally sat on the front porch, made lists, and discussed the next steps to develop their lumber business. Edward was anxious to see the town of Atwater and talked James and Teddy into taking him there after dinner. They took James' wagon and did not return until well after dark.

Edward was filled with excitement and said he thought he found the area in town to build the new lumberyard. He explained there was a house for sale with a lot of land he liked, and that they were all going to return the next day to see it.

Jess was glad for her father's excitement and that they had all returned safely. They seemed to be adjusting to America rather well and quickly. That made both she and James very happy. They agreed to go into town the following day in two carriages to see why Edward was so excited.

Teddy left the next morning for his ranch after breakfast, and the two wagons left for Atwater. James showed them around the town when they finally arrived at the house and large property for sale.

Victoria admired the house Edward had chosen, being a big house with a columned porch, which Jess adored and envied. They looked into the windows and saw massive rooms and a tall, winding staircase. They then went to the bank to discuss the homestead with Mr. Nichols. He then followed them to the house, where they were able to get inside and found four bedrooms upstairs and a massive main room and dining room with beautiful fireplaces. In addition, there was a huge summer kitchen erected on the back of the house. Jess was actually able to stand inside its fireplace and was amazed at its size. There were ten acres available with the house, which was at the far west front corner of the property. The men discussed the price with Mr. Nichols, then they all returned to the bank. Jess knew the men would be at the bank for some time and she asked her mother if she wanted to walk to the post office and library, and then to the church. Victoria agreed and followed Jess out to the street. Jess introduced her mother to Mr. Jones at the post office and Miss Spring at the library. Then the two women made the dusty walk to the church, stepped inside the small building, and saw Pastor Brown standing near the altar. He turned when he heard the door open and greeted the women with a broad smile. He walked to meet them mid-way down the aisle and shook Victoria's hand.

"I am Pastor Michael Brown. Welcome!"

"Nice to meet you. I am Jessica's mother, Victoria Strong. Her father is Edward."

Jess explained to the pastor why the men were at the bank and that her parents had just arrived from England and were buying property in Atwater. He grinned again, welcomed them to their wonderful town, and assured her they would love living in their nice little town.

"I look forward to seeing your faces in the congregation come Sunday. I am anxious to meet your husband, Edward was it?"

"Yes, Edward. I promise, Pastor Brown, you will see us on Sunday."

They left the church, walked two blocks back to the bank, where they found the men still bent over a desk studying papers. The women sat a short time when Edward asked Victoria to talk to her privately. Jess watched her parents and tried to read their faces. She saw her mother put her arms through her fathers arm, smile, and kiss her fathers cheek. Edward then joined the men and all shook hands before they started to walk in Victoria and Jess' direction.

"Mr. Nichols has heard our plan and has convinced me that we should call a town meeting, letting the town's citizens know of our plan before we buy the house and property. He will arrange for the meeting on Sunday, after church services," said Edward to the women. With that, they left the bank and Atwater and returned to the cabin.

Over dinner that night, the entire discussion was the house, the property, and plans for the lumberyard.

They attended church on Sunday as they promised Pastor Brown when he at last met Edward. Both Victoria and Edward enjoyed the sermon, and Jess was so relieved that everything had come together so well. They enjoyed lunch at the saloon in the hotel lobby then walked to the town hall to prepare for the town meeting.

Edward explained his plan to the town's people and asked for any questions or objections. Not one hand went up, and their vote was unanimous to bring the lumberyard into their town. Edward proudly stood at the back of the room, introducing himself and his wife to every person at the meeting. The town's people seemed to be happy with the pending addition to their town and actually welcomed the growth. Bobby and Tim's parents were at the meeting and met James for the first time. They thanked him profusely for employing their sons, and thanked Jess for the fine meals she makes for the boys. They were both so glad to meet them and have new friends.

Chapter Thirteen
Edward and Victoria

Edward and Victoria bought the house and land and moved into it quickly, with James, Bobby and Tim's assistance. Their wagon looked crowded with furniture, but when put into the big house, it looked lost in the spacious rooms.

Jess, in a way, hated to see her parents leave their tiny cabin; yet knowing they were close to her again gave her comfort. She had missed them so much during the past year. She also missed Grant, yet she knew he was happily in love with Kathleen McCarthy and was doing well in medical school. Victoria told her of Grant's future employment with London Hospital, where he had been an intern for over two years. How they all wished they could be at his wedding. It actually brought tears to Jess' eyes every time she thought about it. She then said a silent prayer that maybe, someday her brother would also come to America, so they could all be together again.

Her parents loved their new home and Jess often visited and assisted her mother with decorating, and together they made drapes and curtains for all the rooms. She loved to do these things with her mother and could not wait until she had a "home" to decorate. Teddy told them of the many items available in New York City and gladly delivered rugs that Victoria pointed out to him when they were in the city together. They also bought silver servers, dishware, and silver ware then, and the house was becoming a home quickly.

Meanwhile, Edward had a white picket fence built around their home and left enough land in front for flower gardens and beautiful walkways. He also made a large vegetable garden plot and built a small shed for yard tools. Victoria was delighted with the changes, and saw her daughter almost daily.

Jess woke on a July morning expecting it to be like others, but as she stretched in bed before she rose, she felt butterfly wings fluttering in her stomach. She waited a moment, put her hand on her belly, and hoped to feel it again. There it was again. She ran to the door and rang the large porch bell James hung there in case she needed to call him quickly. She waited only seconds before she rang the bell again, and soon James ran to the house as if it was on fire, and found his excited wife who stood with both hands on her stomach with the most anxious look on her face.

"James, Honey, it's the baby!"

"Are you in pain, Jess?"

"No Dear, please follow me." She smiled, led him to the bed, lied down, and invited him to sit next to her by patting the bed cover. He did so quickly. She grabbed his hand and placed it on the small bump. He left his hand there a short time and kept it exactly where she had placed it. "I think the baby moved, James!" He felt nothing. He looked into his wife's eyes and she saw his questioning look, yet insisted he wait to feel the tiny flutters. He waited a long time yet felt nothing and kissed his wife. "I am sorry I missed it, Jess. I must get back to work." He smiled as he rose from the bed, turned from the door to check his wife's face. She lay there still waiting with a look of wonderment on her face. James felt bad leaving her without feeling the baby move. Jess found it hard to get on with her day without feeling the butterfly flutters again.

When she arrived at her mothers that morning, she couldn't wait to tell her what she felt. They hugged and kissed and Victoria placed her hand on her daughter's tummy and waited to feel the movements and felt nothing.

Edward employed three men who started to erect the lumberyards main building and fenced the entire boundaries of their land. Edward agreed they should continue to call it Atwood Lumber, but James surprised him with a newly painted sign and hung it near the main gate – Atwood & Strong Lumber. James loved and admired Edward, and, after all, they were now business partners. James also laughed every time he thought about the play on words of strong and lumber. "Strong Lumber" - He believed that was probably part of the reason Edward was such a success in Liverpool. In July, Edward made an arrangement with Teddy to ride with him on his next venture into New York City where he would buy the huge saws the lumberyard needed to operate. He returned with a new, proper sized delivery wagon, and two huge saws and two more draft horses. It took six men to unload them into a not yet completed building, which they eventually finished around the saws. Edward also sold his covered wagon in New York City and bought a fancy buggy for personal use and a beautiful roan quarter horse, named Once More. His draft horses became property of the lumberyard where they built a stable and barn behind the lumberyard's main building large enough for all the family's horses.

James' head was spinning - things were moving so fast. Edward asked Bobby and Tim to bring most of the wood from under the shelter on James' property to the lumberyard and to leave James enough scrap, dried wood for their winter fires. The lumberyard employees built new shelves in the new building to dry wood and the remaining shelves would display lumber for sale. They made the sales counter from a huge oak tree, after sanding it smooth to show its beautiful grain. It was not long before customers began to come to the lumberyard daily. Jess often came into town with James in the morning to help her mother, where they did laundry and tended the garden through the day. James then picked her up at the end of his workday. He did not want her to be alone in the woods and a half hour from town in her condition.

James was working six-days a week again, which he hoped would have ended when he left England, but he was doing what he had to do. James planned to talk with Edward to change this when the baby came.

Jess discovered a fellow parishioner of their church was a photographer and quickly made an appointment to have family portraits taken. He came to their cabin and took a proud photograph of James and Jess, and one with her parents. The photographer said the tin types would be ready by the following Sunday. When she saw her own image, she was shocked to see how big her stomach appeared. Nevertheless, she paid the photographer for six photographs. She would mail two photographs to Emily and James' parents with a letter to both families. The other photographs were for their and her parent's mantels.

Weeks flew by as Jess' stomach grew larger daily. James held her at night with his hand on her stomach, finally able to feel the kicks of the baby. He wondered how she could stand it, and thought it had to be painful, yet, he happily listened to his wife's giggles of glee. The bigger her stomach got, the more she glowed. She bathed at her

116

parent's home every day in a tub near the huge fireplace in the kitchen with her mother's assistance.

James and Jess woke early one morning and lingered in bed as they discussed names for the baby that was now actively kicking its mother day and night. James wanted Thomas Edward, after both their fathers if it was a boy. Jess still liked James Jr., but James did not like juniors, and thought they caused confusion in families. If it was a girl, they both liked Rebecca. They giggled over many other names, but still could not agree on a boy's name.

James decided they needed a second horse and bought a gray mare, which Jess quickly named Misty. Stormy and Misty became best friends and would cry for each other and kick the stall walls when apart. When he came home with Misty, he also had a baby goat straddled across the horse's neck, which Jess quickly named Baby due to her cute baby face. Abe had been alone since the wolf attack and was very glad to have a new pal. The goats quickly became very close and you never saw one without the other.

Jess had seen Dr. Charles Harris in Atwater two times regarding the baby and James insisted she have another visit with him, since November was approaching quickly. Dr. Harris, also from England, London, in fact, came to America twenty years ago and was the only doctor in Atwater. He also assisted with animals when it was necessary. He had delivered almost all of Atwater's babies since his arrival and James had a lot of faith in him. Dr. Harris happily lived with his wife in a small house in town and his office and waiting room were two small rooms in the front of his house, next to the church.

The mornings had become chilly, so James wrapped his wife in a blanket before he took her to Dr. Harris' office. After the doctor examined Jess, he invited James into the small examination room where she waited anxiously.

"You're young wife is doing very well, James."

"That's good to know, Doctor Harris. Can you tell when the baby will arrive?"

"I would say in two to three weeks, James. Where will the baby be born, at your cabin?"

"We have not discussed that," James quickly answered then looked at his wife to search her face and without words, decided it made sense to have Victoria's help, and it would be warmer at the Strong's house. "She will have the baby at the Strong's home, Doctor," finished James. "How will I know when to take her there?"

"You'll know. Even though it is your first baby, you'll know." The doctor almost had a giggle in his voice. They left the doctor's office full of excitement.

When they arrived at her parent's home, James helped his wife up the stairs to the Strong's front door. Victoria greeted them there and asked what the doctor told them. James told her everything and she smiled wide as she guided Jess to the nearest chair.

"Maybe you should start staying here from now on, Jessica." Victoria sounded stern.

"Not quite yet, Mother, but soon." Jess slowly lowered herself into the soft, comfortable chair, of which there were plenty.

The next two weeks passed quickly and James noticed Jess was having a difficult time getting out of chairs and bed and did not feel comfortable her being at their cabin in the woods any longer; it was just too far from the doctor and her mother. Monday morning he helped her pack their traveling bag to stay with her mother until the baby was born, but not without him.

While at her parent's house, Victoria insisted Jess stay in bed, or seated with her feet up. Jess did not like being coddled, yet she did like doing nothing but read or converse with her mother since she was now so big and uncomfortable. Victoria turned their library into a bedroom so Jess would not have to use the stairs. When James and Edward arrived home from the lumberyard, Victoria asked James to retrieve a book for her from the library; she then winked at her daughter. He came out with a white wicker bassinette with a big bow on its handles. He carried it to the main room and placed it in front of Jess on the couch. Together they read the attached note, which said it was lovingly from her parents.

Jess was so surprised. She did not know how her mother had hidden the bassinette since she had been there all day. "Mother, Father, Thank you so much!" Jess struggled to get off the couch. Her father prompted her to stay seated and he went to her for his thank you hug. Victoria did the same. James also hugged them both in thanks. Jess had planned to use a trunk as a bassinette at their cabin, yet hadn't thought about what to do at her parent's home. Jess had loved white wicker ever since she stayed in Gerald's blue painted room filled with white wicker, but could not recall ever telling her mother that fact. She assumed either Gerald or his maid, Elizabeth had told her.

James was almost finished with the crib he was making as a surprise for Jess and bursting at the seams to tell her. He now decided to keep it a surprise for a later time, possibly Christmas.

On Monday, Jess was delighted yet surprised to see James arrive at noon, when they ate lunch together, which he did every day that week. Jess loved to see him in the middle of the day, which didn't happen often. Edward saw James' nervousness and sent him home early at the end of each day.

"I can cover things here, James. You go to where your mind and heart are."

Sunday, Victoria and Edward went to church and left James and Jess alone. They stayed in bed, talked and giggled, knowing they might not be able to do this again, probably for years.

Jess started to feel strange and did not tell James, until it showed on her face. He saw her wince in pain as she rubbed her stomach. James did not know what to do, but got her a cool wet cloth for her head and asked her what he should do next.

"James, don't worry. It has begun, but it will not happen just yet." Jess started taking deep breaths and James put his timepiece on the table next to the bed and noted the time. He sat next to her and held her hand while they chatted between pains. James tried to keep her mind off what was about to happen to her body and continued to talk. He was afraid, for he knew many women died in childbirth, and for a moment his thoughts were lost. He did not know what he would ever do without her. He loved her so much, yet knew she was very strong. James shook his head slightly, as if he was trying to erase those thoughts. He knew, in his heart, that she would be fine.

When he heard the back door open and Edward's mighty voice, he went to them quickly and told them it was time.

Victoria ran to her daughter's side, rewet the cloth on Jess' forehead, and started to ask questions to understand the stage of her labor. Being her first child, Victoria knew her daughter's labor could take all day. She quickly went upstairs, changed her clothes and asked Edward to alert the doctor.

The doctor came quickly, examined Jess, and announced to the family that it would be at least a few more hours before the baby arrived. He left after he assured James that his wife and baby were fine and said he would return after dinner. "If you need me before then, please come get me."

James watched his wife carefully and timed each labor pain. He wanted to run to the doctor after each one. Victoria tried to comfort him but he remained very nervous, and it was obvious. She brought James dinner in the library, which he thanked her for but said he could not eat. Jess tried to get him to eat, yet after trying, he could not eat.

The doctor returned after dinner, examined Jess again, and proclaimed that it would still be a few more hours before the birth. James heard this, fell into a chair, and put his head in his hands. He hated to watch Jess in so much pain. What could he do? He continued to tell himself it was all normal and natural.

Jess was near exhaustion and tried to sleep between labor pains, but that was nearly impossible. She sweated through the sheets and expressed concern to her mother about the mess she had made. Her mother told her not to worry about that and tried the best she could to comfort her daughter and changed the sheets. When Victoria left the room, she cried and worried about Jess, yet she was determined not to let her daughter or James see her fear.

James thought his hand would break every time Jess squeezed it during a labor pain, yet never pulled his hand away. Finally, she screamed so loudly during a pain, that James could not stand it any longer. He ran out of the house and did not take the time to close the door behind him. Edward went to close the door and watched James jump onto Stormy in one hop, then ride away toward the doctor's office. He and the doctor returned promptly. Dr. Harris took one look under the sheet at Jess and asked the men to leave the room. The last thing James saw before the door closed was the doctor rolling up his sleeves and wipe his forehead on his rolled-up sleeve. He also saw Victoria wipe her brow with the back of her hand while she was ripping sheets into rags.

"It is a girl!" Victoria erupted as she bolted through the library door.

"How is Jess? How is the baby?" James swiftly headed toward Victoria in the foyer.

"She and baby girl are just fine. Dr. Harris said you could see them both in a short time. We need to clean them both so you can see your girls." Victoria had a wide smile. She swiped her hair from her eyes, twirled quickly and returned to the library.

James turned back to Edward, who smiled at him and held out both of his arms to James. When the men reached each other, Edward hugged his son-in-law and slapped his back.

"Congratulations, son! You have a daughter! A girl, this is wonderful! I know she will be as beautiful as her mother!"

James thanked him, and shook Edward's hand vigorously, "Grandpa! I am so happy! I cannot wait to see them both! You know she will be just as beautiful as her mother."

Both men sat and waited anxiously until Victoria returned in just minutes, which felt like hours to James. He continued to shake his head in disbelief. He has a daughter! Victoria nodded and waved her arm toward the library door as if she was presenting a princess.

James started toward the library, slipped on the rug, righted himself quickly, and then entered into the room where his wife and daughter waited.

Jess lay in bed holding their daughter lovingly, staring at her in amazement. When she and James met eyes, their love exploded between them. He approached them slowly and gently bent over his wife and kissed the mother of their daughter lovingly. She had never looked so beautiful to him.

"My Darling James, meet Rebecca," Jess said softly. She was beaming.

He looked down and saw a small blonde head, a very red face and one tiny arm that was out of the blanket. He reached to touch the small hand and her little fingers wrapped around one of his fingers.

James leaned into her and lightly kissed her wee fingers, then kissed the red forehead and lingered there. He then smelled the wonderful scent of his newborn daughter. He had never experienced anything so wonderful before in his life.

"I love you, Jess," he said kissing his wife again. "Nice to meet you, Rebecca. I am your Daddy. And I love you, too – so much." He kissed his daughter's cheek, and then the other cheek. He was amazed at how small she was. "Welcome to the world," he whispered, "We've been waiting for you for a long time."

Jess smiled at his words and reached for his face. She stroked his cheek gently, feeling more love for him than ever before, which she didn't think was possible. "Isn't she beautiful, James? She looks just like you."

"She does have my blonde hair. What color are her eyes?" James was in awe.

"All babies have blue eyes," she said through a smile. "Yet in time they may change or sometimes not. Only time will tell. Shall we call her Becca?" James nodded and smiled in agreement while still staring at his daughter in astonishment.

Jess raised her elbow and offered Becca to James. He sat next to Jess, readied himself for this deed then smiled and nodded saying he was ready. Jess slowly and gently handed Becca to her father, where he nervously took her into the crook of his arm and Jess held her head until she safely lay in her fathers arm. James proudly held her and never took his eyes off her.

When he finally looked up, he saw Edward's arm around his wife who both stood in the doorway displaying so much pride. James motioned for them to come in and they neared the bed to get a closer look at their new granddaughter. Edward quickly went to the other side of the bed and kissed his daughter's forehead then returned to his wife's side. They both were anxious to hold Becca, yet did not want to interfere with James' moment.

They all stayed in their places for a long time and simply watched Becca in her father's arms. Finally, James was ready to hand Becca over to her grandmother. Victoria anxiously took Becca into her arms, kissed her little face and happy tears ran down her face. She watched her come into the world but had not touched her until now. Victoria proudly held her to Edward's face so he could kiss his new granddaughter too. He gently stroked her tiny cheek, bursting with pride and love. Victoria offered the baby for Edward to hold and he would not do it. "She is too tiny for me to hold. She might break," Edward giggled. Just to touch her chubby cheek and to kiss the new baby was enough for him right now.

"Her name is Rebecca Victoria Atwood," Jess proudly announced. "We'll lovingly call her Becca." Jess could not feel more love for her family.

"Jessica! James! Thank you so much!" Victoria whispered, yet wanted to shout her joy from the rooftop.

"I like her name, Jessica, and thank you for thinking of your mother." Edward's eyes filled with tears.

James stayed by his girls' side for the entire next week. Edward ran the lumberyard alone and proudly boasted about his new granddaughter to all who would listen. Church members came to Victoria's door with baby gifts and begged to see the newborn.

James knew he had to finish the crib soon, but it was in his barn at the cabin. He could not make himself leave his girls to go to the cabin. He talked to Edward about it and he said he would have Bobby and Tim bring it to him, which they did. He worked on the crib an hour each day in Edward's barn, using the lumberyard as an excuse to be away from Jess, but would quickly return to Jess and Becca. He did not want to miss a moment of Becca's new life. Jess felt better every day and nursing the baby was going well. She was very glad to get her figure back, almost. Victoria assured her that in time, her stomach would be flat again.

Becca was born Sunday, 19 November 1865, and now three weeks later, although she appreciated her mother's help, Jess wanted to go home. She expressed her wishes at dinner that night, and saw her parents disappointed faces. James understood how Jess felt yet on the other hand; if they were to stay, it was beneficial for all. Oh how he wished they had more than a cold, drafty cabin. Her parents convinced Jess to stay until after the New-Year, if for nothing else than it was warmer in their home. Jess agreed after looking into her husband's eyes.

Christmas morning was white and bright with a new blanket of snow. James woke early, and let his girls sleep, as he snuck to the barn and brought the new crib into the house and put it near the Christmas tree. He had not thought of a bow until now, yet he knew Jess would still be surprised and would love it. He then slipped quietly back into bed beside his wife after he peaked into the bassinette to see his beautiful sleeping baby girl.

An hour later, James and Jess, holding Becca, went into the main room and joined Edward and Victoria near the Christmas tree. Her mouth fell open when she saw the crib near the tree. She knew immediately James made it and ran to him and kissed him.

They spent the morning opening gifts and Becca received too many presents from her proud grandparents. Jess' parents gave them a buggy for Christmas, which embarrassed them, since James and Jess only gave them an imported vase from Italy. Victoria loved it, but loved Becca more – her favorite Christmas present.

Regardless, it was a grand Christmas for all.

Chapter Fifteen
1866

Jess could not stay awake until midnight to welcome 1866, and went to bed early, as did Victoria. James and Edward celebrated in the main room drinking brandy and smoking cigars, as men do. At the stroke of midnight from the huge, oak grandfather clock in the foyer, the men toasted in the New-Year, the new addition to their family and Atwood & Strong Lumber, and clinked their glasses three times. They talked most of the evening of plans for the future, their necessary changes, and discussed how many new employees they needed to hire, since the business was doing so well.

Although Edward had put a lot of money into their business, James had given sweat equity, and Edward considered himself and James as equal partners. He was very proud of his son-in-law and thanked God every day Jessica had selected the right man. It could have gone very differently. Edward was glad Grant had selected well also. He and Victoria liked Kathleen very much, even though they had only met her once, but they trusted their son and his decisions.

On 4 January, they took Becca home to the cabin. James wrapped his wife and baby for the cold trip home in two blankets. The baby gifts and clothes from church members and Christmas presents filled an entire trunk. James tied the goats to the top rail on the wagon, with the bassinette and crib, where they would ride on the wagon bed and tied Misty to the back of the wagon. They all made it through the snow by following tracks of other wagons through town, up their icy drive and home. James started a fire in each fireplace to warm the cold cabin immediately and placed the bassinette and new crib next to the bedroom fireplace where they stood for more than an hour before the bassinette and room were warm enough to place Becca down for a nap. Jess unpacked what there was room for in their tiny home while James tended to the animals. He was glad to be home, but already missed the comfort of the Strong's warm home. This prompted James to work further on their house plans and that night, in front of the fire, he laid out the plans he had worked so diligently on. After they lived almost two months at his in-laws, he added things to the plans that they

126

benefited from at his in-law's home that he had not thought of before. He took the plans with him the next day to the lumberyard to discuss the changes with Edward.

"Where are you going to build this house, James?"

"I plan to put it in front of the cabin, making the cabin an employee cabin, just as Gerald has done," explained James, while he searched his mind for a better place.

"That is so far away from town, the business and us. Don't you think living in town would be better for all concerned?" Edward was getting to something, James was sure of it.

"I have thought about that, and I know it would be better for Jess and Becca." James scratched his head. "Where, then?"

Edward gave James a look he had never seen on his face before. "How about building on the lumberyard property, my property?"

"I think that is far too close, Edward, but I will consider looking at possibilities here in town." James rolled up the house plans and bound them with a string.

Edward grinned and put his hands in his pockets. He assumed James would not build on his property, yet he thought he would make the suggestion anyway. Victoria would be disappointed to hear of James' refusal to live so close to them, yet they would still be in town and not a thirty-minute ride out of town.

James took his lunch with him, rode around town that day, and searched for available property. It had to be right. He knew when he saw the right spot, his heart would tell him. He's had the picture of his house and its surroundings in his head for years. It excited him now that it was finally coming to fruition. He rode Stormy through the streets of Atwater and saw existing houses for sale, but they were not what he wanted and he would not settle, although it would be much easier than building a house. He admired and trusted his wife's strengths, and knew she would work with him while the house was in construction. He prayed that he knew his wife as well as he thought he did.

He directed Stormy behind the lumberyard, where no streets existed, and a forest of pines stood. He went farther into the woods, found the river that meandered through the trees, which he followed

127

with his eyes. The river was very wide at some places and James thought it was beautiful. He dismounted his horse and he stood silently, listened to and studied the wooded area. It reminded him so much of their cabin's setting, and was just as lush and breath taking. He knew Jess would love it.

He returned to the lumberyard and asked Edward about the river that ran behind Atwater. Edward explained to James, as Mr. Nichols had explained to him, it is the same river that runs behind their cabin. The river ran south, and through mid-state New York and emptied into Hudson Bay in New York City. He admitted to James then he'd been studying the river and found its depths were good so they could use it in the near future to ship lumber to New York City and all points south of Atwater, before it empties into the bay. James' brow rose, and was amazed at the way Edward thought. No wonder he had been successful all of his life.

"I had no idea you were leading the business in that direction, but that is exactly how we can expand the business to do what I initially wanted to do – to help American's that lost so much during the war. Well, I'll tell you now that if we can cut a road to the east of the lumberyard, into the wooded area behind the city I am sure I can convince Jess to build there once she sees the woods and the river. The first thing I have to do is go to the town hall and talk to them about expanding the road and building our house back there."

"I agree." Edward nodded in agreement the entire time James talked. "You should do that now. I can handle things here - go!" He waved his arm as if dismissing him.

James rode Stormy to the town hall, and after he talked with Mayor John Goldman, he found the town already had plans to put a road there in years to come. James was very excited now. He relayed everything to Edward upon his return to the lumberyard and saw his excitement and Edward sent him home to talk to Jess.

"Jess, I found property today that I know you will like as much as I do where we can build our dream home."

"I thought we were going to build right here?" She had a questioning look on her face.

"I've thought about it and discussed it with your father at length and I don't want my girls to be alone half an hour from town while I am at work. In fact your father even offered for us to build our home on their property." James was talking fast and very excited.

Jess' nose crinkled when he said the latter. "So what are you thinking about, James?"

"I have found wooded land, even closer to the river than we are now and *no hills* to go down to get to the river. In addition, it is not a half mile behind your parent's home. I always knew the town was built along a line of the trees, but I never thought about looking back there until today. Would you like me to take you there Sunday after church?"

"Yes, James I would love to see it. What will we do with this land the cabin is on?"

"We will keep it for the trees and let hired hands live in the cabin. What do you think?" James met her eyes, looking there for her answer.

"That makes sense, James. Can we afford it?"

"We will borrow from the bank to build the house and use this land as collateral. I have thought this through before I brought it to you." He was proud of himself.

"I see that you *have* thought it all out. I am proud of you, husband. You are very smart." Jess hugged his neck.

"Your father is the smart one." James explained to Jess how he had planned to use the river to deliver lumber to everywhere south. "Your father has taken it a step farther than my original dream by the use of the river. Jess, I can say nothing but good of your father. We make a great team. In fact, I just had a thought of Atwood & Strong Lumber growing to where we could own lumberyards in other states, following rivers and buying more wooded land for lumber along the rivers." James quickly made notes on his last thought, to remind him to go to the library to do research before he talked to Edward.

Chapter Sixteen
Early 1867

Sunday was a cold January day, but the sun was strong and warmed them in their new buggy. Jess wrapped Becca in two blankets for their ride to church. After the service, James took his girls behind the town, through the woods and found the frozen river. Jess loved the area. James jumped down from the buggy, ran through the snow and showed her where he would like their property lines to be. He screamed from the invisible property lines so she could hear his dream of the house here and the barn over there. He added the descriptions of the vegetable garden and flowerbeds, for effect, but Jess loved it before they approached the river. She looked so forward to a warmer house, especially now that Becca had arrived.

James loved to lay in front of the fireplace with Becca, noticing her changes daily. Her eyes were still blue and had not changed color. Becca favored the Atwood family traits and her blue eyes must be from his mother Mary, he decided. Mary's cornflower blue eyes always glinted in the sun and people often complimented her on her beautiful eyes. She was a plain woman, but her blue eyes were memorable.

Since Becca was born, it was difficult for James to keep up with the water demand, but did what he had to do so Jess had plenty to wash nappies; called diapers in America they discovered, which was hard for Jess to remember. He broke up river ice and brought huge pieces into the house to melt by the fire to keep the wash bucket full.

The bank approved their home and land loan and planned to give them money in stages, as the building progressed. Edward convinced James to take the lumber he needed without paying the lumberyard. James tried to talk Edward into the yard taking *some* money for the lumber and Edward refused. The lumberyard would take the trees from his cabin property, and those cleared to build the new house as payment for lumber used. Again, Edward was a step ahead of James in his ideas.

Even though the snow was deep, James went to their five acres of land and marked trees to clear for the new house and barn. He also wanted a path cut through the trees to the river for Jess. He took Jess there the next Sunday after church for her approval. She asked only that the barn be closer to the tree line and not be even with the front of the house. James scolded himself for not thinking of that, ran through the snow and changed the tree markings. She also thought about trees that should not be cut down and would be beautiful in front of the house. James agreed and marked those trees to be saved. He would tell the men that do the clearing how to read his markings, and hoped they would abide by them.

A month later at the beginning of March, the clearing was done. James rode Stormy to the property thinking the men would be half-finished. When he arrived, he found they were finished clearing and they had saved the marked trees for the front yard. Now that he saw the actual size of the clearing, he requested it be bigger by taking more trees out, all the way around the clearing, two trees deep. It was done the next day. When James saw how many trees came into the lumberyard, he realized it was far more wood that came in than the lumber that went out to build his house. Edward was right and it was another thing he needed to remember and use in the future with lumber customers.

James took one of the yard's draft horses and delivery wagon to a quarry 75 miles away to buy stones for the base of the house and the trip took longer than he thought it would. It was long after dark when he arrived at the property, unhooked the draft horse from the wagon and left the wagon at their property. He then rode him to the lumberyard where he found Stormy anxious to leave Edward's barn and rode him home. Jess was actually pacing when he arrived. "I have been so worried, James. What took so long?"

"Oh, Honey, I am sorry. It took them much longer to load the stones than I thought it would. How's Becca?" James calmed his wife with a kiss and hug.

"She is wonderful. She was making new sounds today; I swear she is trying to talk!"

James looked at her through squinted eyes and wondered if she was serious. He knew Becca was far too young to make words. He could tell by his wife's smile that she was joking, in a way. She, like every mother in the world, thought her child was more special than any other child.

"Tomorrow, the men will start stumping our land the best they can in the cold, and hopefully, by weeks end the stones will be laid for the house base. Jess, we should be able to move in by late July, if not earlier."

"That is wonderful, Darling. How will we fill all of that space? We've been so used to this small cabin, it will feel....well....." She was changing Becca's diaper; she tickled her tummy and kissed the bottoms of her plump little feet, which made Becca laugh.

"I'm sure you'll have no problem filling the house, Jess. I thought we were going to fill it with children?"

Jess turned to him, smiled, kissed him then shrugged her shoulders. She handed Becca to her father who started to kiss her face all over, which made Becca smile. James commented over dinner that Becca was almost too big for the bassinette now and that Jess should think about putting her in the crib at night. Jess had kept Becca in the bassinette next to her side of the bed at night, always within reach. If she put her in the crib, she would be four feet away. Jess smiled at him, "Soon, James. I'm not ready yet to let her be that far away from me."

James gave her a grin and let it pass. He knew Jess would soon recognize Becca was getting too big and moving more now to be in the bassinette. He wagered to himself it would happen by week's end.

James inspected their property after work, before nightfall and found that most of the stumps were out and in a huge pile to dry and burn later. He was impressed with his employees on how efficient they were and decided to talk with Edward about pay raises for them. Business was good, and from what he saw in their profits, they could now afford to do this.

James remembered when six years ago, they fell in love, shared their dreams, and now had a daughter and their dream house was underway. He was amazed, shook his head, looked to the heavens, said a silent prayer of thanks and he then rode Stormy home in the early evening spring air.

Two weeks later, he was anxious for Jess to see the progress of their home. After church he drove there so fast, she wondered where the race was. She was shocked to see the first floor completed, and men ten feet in the air, starting the second floor. He helped Jess with Becca, down from the buggy and avoided the muddy areas. They had to use a stack of wood to gain entry onto the wood flooring of what will be their main room. Jess was in awe at how big the rooms were. This was the first time she realized their home was going to be enormous. Then she thought about cleaning it all and winced a bit.

"James, it is huge!" James roamed around the rooms with his arms straight out, twirling in the open spaces. She could see through the studs to the other end of the house, which looked to be a mile away. She knew once the walls were up, she would then see the rooms realistically. They walked from room to room and James explained where they were in each open space. Jess' head was spinning. "Can we afford this, Honey?"

"We can afford it, Jess. Business is going very well. In fact, we are giving the employees raises soon. Your father and I have been discussing erecting another drying building, which would make the existing building strictly for lumber sales. The lumber demand is growing weekly and we have not yet started using the river to ship south. The business is bigger than I ever dreamed it would be, and much sooner too. People are coming from two counties over to buy our lumber. Jess, our barn will be twice the size of the house, because I want to make a play area for the children for rainy days. My dream is coming true only far larger than I ever imagined."

"James, I had no idea. Are you saying we're rich?" Jess whispered, so the workers would not hear her.

"We are, Jess. And a year from now there will be even more money than you can imagine in the bank!" said James, a little too loudly. He doubted the men heard him through the hammer sounds. "You will have the finest buggy, imported rugs and all the paintings you want!"

Jess just stared at James. For the first time in her life, she was speechless. She hugged Becca and was so thankful she came along when she did. Her stomach leaped with excitement.

The next morning her stomach was doing more than leaping. When she started to vomit again, she knew this time exactly what it was.

It was difficult to make coffee without getting sick from the aroma, and changing Becca's diaper was worse. James had his suspicions from what he was seeing, yet he waited to say anything to his wife. Yet, when he saw her at the end of the day, he was certain.

"Jess, how are you feeling?" he shyly inquired.

"James, I think our dream of filling the house with children is coming true. I think I will see Doc Harris soon to confirm what I think is another baby." Jess quickly ran for a bucket.

James finished making dinner and smiled with so much happiness. Becca was perfect in his eyes and he loved her so much, but a second child? Where do you find love for another?

Jess could not eat dinner, so James insisted she go to bed and he would take care of Becca. She did that and was thankful her husband was such a loving, caring man. She slept the moment her head hit the pillow.

The next morning James insisted she go to her parent's home, and let Victoria help her tend to Becca. He had to stop the buggy twice before they arrived when Jess was ill. When Victoria answered the door and saw Jess, she knew. "Jessica, are you in the family way again?"

"Mother, I have the symptoms, but I would like to see Doc Harris before we come to any conclusions," said Jess as she searched for the nearest chair.

That afternoon Doc Harris made a house call and confirmed she was in the family way. He estimated her due date to be in early October. He congratulated her and gave her a sweet smelling syrup to sip for morning sickness. She took a sip before the doctor left and within an hour felt more like herself.

When James arrived home with Edward, Jess ran to her husband with a wide smile, hugged and kissed him and told him the news.

"Jessica! This is wonderful news!" James radiated in happiness.

"Doc Harris said early October. He gave me syrup to rid the sickness and it works. I feel so good, James. I am so happy!" Jess was filled with so much love for her family and her life.

Victoria insisted they stay for dinner, which they did, and Jess was now able to eat.

They rode home in delight, discussing names again. She still wanted James, Jr. if it was a boy and James just did not like that idea and stood his ground. They had months to decide on names.

"We will be in our new home when the baby arrives, Jess. This time will be a lot easier for everyone. I cannot wait!" James was almost shouting. When they arrived at the foot of their drive, before making the climb to the cabin, James whooped into the dark, hearing it echo through the woods. Jess took his hand, kissed the back of it as he returned to sit on the driver's seat.

The next morning, she felt ill as soon as her eyes opened. She made it to the bucket on time then ran for the miracle syrup. She could not wait until it started its magic.

Once a week, Jess and Becca spent the day with her mother in Atwater. It was then she inspected the progress of their house. In June, she saw the house had walls, a tiled roof and the siding was almost completed. She walked the floors and dreamt of how their life would be. Decorating this big house would be a challenge, yet she felt up to it. They were a month from moving in, and her belly grew larger daily. It was the most exciting time of her life. She twirled Becca around each room and described to her what her bedroom will look like. She then reminded herself to start the search for white wicker with Gerald and wrote him a letter that day.

Two weeks after Jess sent the letter, Gerald drove up their drive with a wagon full of white wicker furniture. He found no people at the cabin, just two goats, and a horse munching grass. They put their heads up briefly, from their grass chomping and looked at their visitor, only to go back to keeping the yard trimmed. Gerald didn't know where to look. He checked the wood shelter behind the barn and only saw cut, stacked wood, and drying wood on racks. He scratched his head, stood a moment and listened to the woods, and only heard the river running and the intermittent swishing of the horse's tail. He then turned his wagon around and headed for Atwater. He hoped to find James in town. He rode the half hour to town and the first thing he saw was a huge fenced area, and at the gate hung a large sign - Atwood & Strong Lumber. His heart did a leap with joy for James. He knew he had it in him. He went through the gate to the building that had another Atwood

& Strong Lumber sign high at its peak. He jumped down and dusted himself off. He easily took the three steps up to the door with "Office" painted on a glass pane. He walked in to see James bent over a table while he inspected a large print with a customer, his blonde hair falling around his face. James heard the door, turned, and a huge smile came over his face when he saw Gerald standing there. They both held out their arms, approached the other and met in a hug.

"Well, well, Mr. Atwood, it seems you have been working hard!" Gerald was elated.

"Yes sir, I have. Welcome to Atwood & Strong Lumber!" James said with pride. He waved his arm to guide Gerald's eyes to see racks and racks of lumber, customers that dwelled about and Edward assisting one. Gerald and Edward met eyes and Edward smiled at him, excused himself from the customer for the moment, and took long, heavy strides to arrive at Gerald's outstretched arm. As they shook hands, Edward slapped his back and said, "Gerald! It is so good to see you, Chap! Welcome to Atwood & Strong Lumber. What brings you to Atwater?"

"First let me say, Edward, congratulations on your business. It looks like you're doing well," said Gerald as they finished their handshake.

"Thank you Gerald, James has worked very hard." Edward smiled as he rested his hand on James' shoulder.

"Now Edward, you must agree it takes...."

Edward stopped him in mid sentence, "Gerald, good to see you."

"Well, I received a letter from your lovely wife, and I have made a special delivery."

"A delivery?" James was curious. Gerald gestured to the men to follow him out the door. It was then James saw the wagon full of white wicker furniture. He didn't know Jess had written to Gerald and could only imagine what the letter said.

"She asked me where I found the "lovely", her word, not mine, white wicker furniture. She told me in the letter that your home was near completion and wanted to fill Becca's bedroom with white wicker. Therefore, I thought I would bring some to her. This is my gift to you for Becca and your new home." Gerald put his hand on James' shoulder. He clapped it a few times, and then added, "Where is your lovely wife, anyway?"

"She is with her mother and Becca at the Strong's home." James pointed to the huge house at the corner of the lumberyard property, with a white picket fence that stretched around an entire acre.

"I would love to see her and Becca. Are they there now?"

"They are!" James started walking in that direction. Gerald asked him to hop into his wagon and drove to the house, while Edward went back inside to tend to customers. Gerald tied his horse to the picket fence and they went inside.

"Gerald!" Jess shouted when she saw the two men in the foyer. She ran to him with arms extended, kissed his cheek and asked, "To what do we owe this pleasure?"

"You wrote and asked about white wicker furniture and I thought I would assist in the matter."

"I wrote you asking where I can get white wicker. What have you...." Jess started to say.

"Come with me, young lady," finished Gerald with a glint in his eye and winked at James.

When she saw the wagon full of white wicker furniture Jess actually jumped up and down. She ran to the wagon and inspected the furniture from three sides of the wagon, and then ran to Gerald and gave him the biggest hug he probably ever received his entire life. When they broke from the hug, he saw she had tears in her eyes. "I love it!"

"I do not mean to make you cry, lovely Jessica." Gerald wiped one tear from her cheek.

"They are tears of joy, Gerald. You are the kindest friend! Please tell us how much we owe you for the beautiful furniture and we will gladly pay..."

"No, no! This is my gift to you all as a baby gift which I never sent when she was born, and a new house gift from me to you all," said Gerald with feeling. "Where is Becca?"

Jess informed him she was napping and he could see her when she woke.

She hugged his neck again, looked at James in wonderment, and then asked the men to join she and Victoria for lunch. Gerald and

Victoria reacquainted, and they ate lunch telling Gerald about the new house and all their plans. It was then they told him about the second child due in October. Gerald was embarrassed that he had not noticed, apologized and congratulated them both. They talked of the due date and Gerald asked if he could see their new house. James assured him he would not let him leave Atwater without seeing their dream home.

As James and Gerald rounded the lumberyard fence onto the new road, which cut through the woods, James told him how the town happily allowed the new road just for them. They rode through an arbor tunnel and arrived at the construction site. Gerald was amazed at the size of the house being built, which must have shown on his face.

"What is it, Gerald?" James saw his excitement.

"It is huge, James. How many children do you plan on having?" Gerald was in awe.

"As many as God gives us," James answered with pride and giggled.

Inside the house, they walked from room to room as James explained each one. Gerald saw the pride in his friends face and heard it in his voice. Gerald slapped James' shoulder and congratulated him on his success. "I saw you must be doing well when I saw the lumberyard, but this, James, this is amazing!"

The two men inspected the second story where they could, and then James said that he needed to get back to the lumberyard. Gerald felt guilty taking up his time and nodded his head in agreement. They left the house and returned to the lumberyard office. Gerald spent the remains of the day sitting back watching James in motion. He noted how good he was at sales, and that he was always willing to do what it took to complete a sale, including loading lumber.

Edward, James, and Gerald arrived at the Strong's home to the smells of a wonderful dinner. They first saw Jess as she approached them from the kitchen with Becca in her arms.

"I have never seen a more beautiful little girl!" Gerald took Becca in his arms. Becca went into his arms easily, and Jess watched as he cooed and tickled her daughter until she giggled aloud. He kissed her chubby cheek and Jess felt her heart melt. She knew Gerald did not have children and had always wondered why. At dinner, she heard the reason, as Gerald sat at the table and talked of his beautiful wife, Marie.

James and Jess looked at each other with questioning eyes. Gerald had never before talked of his life, yet tonight, it seemed, he wanted to tell all.

"If I am boring you with my life story....." said Gerald as he looked at each waiting face at the table.

"No, Gerald, it is not boring. If you want to tell us, we want to hear it," explained James.

Edward, Victoria, Jess and James sat quietly as Gerald continued, "Marie was a beautiful girl, whom I met at the state fair when we were teenagers. I tell you, it was love at first sight, well for me anyway. She was the prettiest girl I had ever seen. Her beautiful brown hair was wrapped into a bun on top of her head, which I imagined had to be very long by the size of the bun. I was right, it went to her waist, and she had the most beautiful blue eyes. They would send me to the moon when she looked at me her special way. Well, she was with girlfriends and I could not get her to step away from them. Yet I would not give up. I pestered her enough to where she finally stepped over to me, and that's when she asked me what it was I truly wanted. When I looked into those blue eyes, all my dry mouth would say is "You".

Becca began to cry from her crib in the library, and Jess rose to fetch her and knew she would miss what Gerald would say because she needed to nurse Becca. Gerald gave her a nod and said, "I will continue when you return, Jess. Don't worry." He gave her a kind smile.

Jess fed Becca, changed her diaper and they arrived back at the table in twenty minutes. Jess smiled at Gerald as he reached for Becca's tiny hand, which he admired intently. He then continued, "Well, where was I? Oh, yes, when Marie heard me say "you" she blushed the reddest cheeks I had ever seen. It was only four months later we were married. We lived in a little, tiny house not far from the fairgrounds where we met. She was a mid-wife delivering babies and assisted older folks in their homes. She loved helping others. I was a laborer for the county gravel pit, and I would come home so dirty and tired, yet she would never complain. I don't know who loved who more, but I'd venture to say it was me who loved her more," he said as he smiled, paused, and took a sip of his wine.

He continued, with all listening intently, "Well, we went like that for years, never having babies, not knowing why. We would try and try, believe me," he snickered, elbowed James, and winked.

"Eventually we built most of the house you have all been in. I added the upper floor after she died," said Gerald as he intently traced the design in the tablecloth with his fingertip.

"We had only lived in the smaller version of the existing house a short time when she started bleeding. The doctor saw her and told me she would not live out the week. Well, you can imagine how lost I was." Gerald had a very sad look on his face.

Jess took James' hand and thanked God silently that they still have each other. Jess looked at her mother, who had tears in her eyes. Victoria smiled at her daughter and wiped her tears away.

"The doctor was close on his diagnosis, she died that Saturday. He said she had a tumor the size of his fist that was making her bleed to death. Doc said there was nothing he could do to help her. Marie said she never felt the tumor and just thought she was gaining weight when her stomach started to distend a little. She died in my arms. I buried her way behind the house. None of you has been that far back behind the out buildings. I have a small fenced area back there where she is and I will be someday." Then he looked up and smiled, "Oh, and there are a few of my favorite dogs back there too."

No one moved. Riveted, they were all stunned. Jess was the first to stir. She rose from her chair, handed Becca to James, walked to Gerald, and put her arms around his neck from behind, her hands resting on his chest. She stayed that way a long time, her face next to his. Gerald put his hands on top of hers, clasped them and squeezed.

James cleared his throat, to swallow away the lump. "Gerald, I am so sorry for your loss. I cannot imagine losing the one you love, let alone watching her fade away in your arms." Tears welled in his eyes and he had to look away from Gerald and everyone.

"Anyway, I worked at the quarry a few years after she died and tired of that quickly. I had saved money in that time, and when I saw the stable for sale in town, I bought it and soon built the racetrack and people started attending the races, which made me enough money to slowly expand it all to what it is today." Gerald started to sit more proudly and looked at all the waiting faces at the table.

"Well, enough of that!" erupted Gerald. He gave Jess' hand another quick squeeze before he let go and attempted to rise. Jess went back to her chair, caressing her husband's back as she passed him.

Gerald rose from his chair, gently slapped the tabletop, and said loudly, "Let's all have a round of brandy, shall we? And change the subject, eh?"

Edward was first to jump up. He went to the liquor cabinet, retrieved the decanter of brandy and started to pour five glasses. Jess saw what he was doing and she politely and quietly added, "None for me Father." They all clinked glasses, Jess' was water. Victoria then announced, "A toast to the future!"

"Yes," shouted Gerald, "a toast to the future!"

The next day Gerald unloaded the wicker furniture into Edward's barn then offered to accompany James on a lumber delivery fifty miles away, almost to the next county. James was glad to have the company, and time passed much faster. The two men were good friends, and they both knew it would last their lifetimes. Their conversations never lulled and there was always laughter in most everything they discussed. They talked about Teddy that day, both said how much they admired him and when they pulled the wagon into the lumberyard gate, low and behold, there was Teddy's horse and wagon. Teddy saw them pull in and ran out to meet them with a big smile.

"Well, look a' what th' devil brough' in!" Teddy yelled, and shook both their hands.

"We didn't expect you until next month, Teddy. What brings you in this direction?" James still shook his hand.

"Well, things 're kind o' slow on the ranch and I thought I'd come t' see my friends and it's a miracle, yer both here, together." Teddy slapped both their backs with each of his hands.

"I hope you brought some good meat with you, my boy," started Gerald, "I'm in the mood for a good pork roast!"

"As a matter o' fact, I have a whole entire pig! Funny ya should mention pork! In fact I started it 'n the spit hours ago when I heard ya both would b' gone all day, bu' comin' back hungry!" Teddy laughed, as he pointed to the side of the lumberyard building, where a fire was going in the pit and a young man turning the spit. When they got closer, they realized it was Tim. Bobby was sitting nearby, drinking beer and rose when he saw the men approaching.

"You have any more of that?" Gerald was thirsty after their long wagon ride. Bobby nodded his head and reached into a bucket full of cool river water. He pulled out three bottles and handed them to the thirsty men and all was well with the world.

They stayed by the fire for hours and took turns rotating the roasting pig. They took pork into the women for their dinner when it was ready and declined their invitation to join the men at the fire, and encouraged the men to have a good time. The men would periodically cut a chunk of meat off the pig and eat it with their hands. They washed their hands when they reached into the bucket for another beer. Bobby and Tim were young, but knew how to drink, James discovered. He had no idea how much fun they were until now. The men cracked jokes, told tall tales about one another, then James asked, "Teddy, how is it you and Gerald became friends, anyway?"

"It's like this, ya ready fer a sad story?" asked Teddy as he scoped each face for answers. The men nodded yes because they thought he was joking, but he wasn't. Teddy walked next to his friend Gerald, swatted him on the back "'member, ol' pal?" Gerald nodded his head in agreement and took another swig of his beer. "Well," started Teddy, "I was on my way back home from th' city wit' a wagon full o' empty wood crates, when my 'orse just up and died. Right there in th' middle o' th' road, up and died! When he went down th' wagon tipped up in th' air, crates went flyin' an' threw me on top o' my dead horse!"

The rest of the men did not make a sound but were on the edge of laughter. Teddy looked at them all with an odd look on his face and that's when they all broke out in rowdy laughter.

"I know, boys, twasn't funny then, bu' it sure as hell's funny now!" said Teddy through his own laughter. "So there I was, tryin' t' get th' reins off my dead horse t' get the wagon up-right when along came Gerald on 'is beautiful chestnut mare." He looked at Gerald then, "Man that was a beautiful horse. You still got her?" Teddy asked. Gerald just nodded his head positively and Teddy continued. "The two o' us worked a long time t' get that wagon undone from my dead 'orse; then we had t' drag the poor thin' outta th' road. It was a hot Augus' day, sun beatin' down on us, an' we really worked up a sweat. Gerald hooked my wagon up to 'is 'orse and drove us t' 'is 'ouse. We been friends ever since," finished Teddy.

"So what happened then?" Bobby had to know.

"Well, we got drunk by a fire behin' his house, just like were gettin' drunk t'night, and th' next day he 'ooked up one o' his big ol' work 'orses to my wagon and I went home. Ya still got that 'orse too, Gerald?" Teddy asked as he snorted laughter and beer shot through his nose.

"Yep!" answered Gerald, who now slapped his knee with laughter.

"'bout two weeks lataa.... I brung 'is 'orse back tied t' th' back o' my wagon," said Teddy as he started to laugh again. "I had t' feed dat big ol' horse fer two weeks; man can dat boy eat!"

All the men were laughing so hard by now, none could speak for a long time. Finally, there was silence and Tim walked to the pig, cut away another chunk of pork, and asked if anyone wanted any. A few took more pork, but their drunkenness was starting to take over. They were stumbling and all they could do was laugh. James went into Edward's barn retrieving five blankets and threw one at each man's chest.

"We're sleeping under the stars tonight, Gentlemen," James slurred. They drunkenly fiddled with their blankets and put them around the fire and soon all were snoring at the stars.

Jess peaked out at dawn when she was up with Becca and saw five men sprawled over the ground around what used to be a fire in the pit and a half eaten pig. She giggled and returned to bed, and took Becca into her bed, where the two of them slept, with Jess' arms wrapped around her daughter.

The men didn't wake until the sound of a customer's wagon arriving at the lumberyard woke them. James was first to reach the building, unlocked the doors and followed the man into the building as he combed his blonde hair with his fingers. When Edward came into the

143

office, James excused himself, went back to Gerald and Teddy, Bobby and Tim, who were just now starting to wake. They all looked horrible.

"Come with me," he whispered, "we need to go to the river and sober up!" James soon brought his wagon to the men, picked them up and all the men went to the river. They all stripped their clothes and jumped into the cool water.

"I have never been so drunk in my whole life!" screamed James as they all dunked themselves under the cool water to not only get sober but also clean. Gerald said he swore he could smell beer coming from his pores.

"It's been a long time since I was that drunk myself," said Gerald. Teddy submersed himself repeatedly, making every effort to feel better.

"My head is split 'n two, I swear!" Teddy shouted as they all dressed and got back on the wagon. Gerald sat in the seat next to James, and Teddy eased himself onto the back of the wagon, along with the boys, legs dangling, until Teddy finally lay back to somehow relieve his pounding head. That did not help and he sat up holding his head in his hands, wishing the world would stop spinning.

That night at dinner, when Victoria offered the men beer with their dinner, their refusals were loud and adamant. She just giggled, her brows rose to Jess, who was also laughing.

Before both Teddy and Gerald left Atwater, James invited them for a new home celebration party in August and said he would send them letters with the party date. He assured them they would be moved in by then.

"Teddy, bring your wife!" added James as Teddy got into his wagon.

"I will - I will!" he shouted back as he left the yard through the gate.

Gerald said he wouldn't miss it and waved back at James as he exited the gate after Teddy. James watched as his friends followed the other up the road, out of town, until they were out of sight. When he heard the empty wooden crates bouncing in Teddy's wagon, it reminded him of his dead horse story and he started to laugh.

Chapter Seventeen
Summer 1867

James, Jess, and Becca celebrated the Fourth of July with the townspeople of Atwater for the first time, where before they felt uncomfortable being English. When they heard American's celebrated this day to mark their freedom from English rule, it made them squirm a bit, but their friends in Atwater did not think twice about it. They were all part of their community and completely accepted by all. James especially, was relieved.

At the Village Square, there was a pie competition, for which Missus Jones, the post master's wife, won a blue ribbon and pinned it proudly to her smock. There were games for children and tug-of-war for adults, which James could not resist. As he was rolling up his sleeves, he handed Jess the keys to the office from his pocket, kissed her and they both laughed, remembering the last time he did this. He ran to the rope as Jess, holding Becca, watched on, pointing to James; "That's your Daddy!" She did remember the last time he did this at the ice cream social and their first meeting of their short courtship in Liverpool. She surveyed her husband with pride. She loved that he was so muscular and full of vigor, as he spit into each of his hands, grabbed the rope, and when the whistle blew, pulled on the rope with all his might. Sadly, his team lost this time, when the ribbon tied around the middle of the rope crossed a line scratched in the dirt. He hung his head as he approached his wife when she raised it with one finger under his chin. They met eyes, both smiled and kissed. He kissed Becca, rolled his sleeves down to be proper, as they walked to the pie-eating contest.

Five young men were sitting at tables, with pies in front of them for the pie-eating contest with their arms behind their backs. It was then James noticed one of the young men was Bobby. James pointed him out to Jess and they both watched as his face dove into a blueberry pie as he munched at it wildly. He came up for air, then drove his face back into the blue gooey mess. He did not win, but had fun losing. A young lady ran up to Bobby and offered him a cloth for his face. It was in the way she did so, and lingered by his side, that James realized they were sweet on each other. He quickly reminded himself to josh Bobby about his girlfriend the next time he saw him at work.

James and his family went to the dining tent, where just outside the tent, there were many sausages roasting on a huge fire. When they finished eating, they both agreed that Teddy's sausages tasted much better and agreed to tell him that he must sell his sausages to the Atwater general store.

Jess told James she needed to rest and he gladly took his girls to her parent's home to nap. Edward and Victoria were uncomfortable, being English, and chose not to join the celebration and James could not convince them all the townspeople accepted them. Edward and Victoria spent a leisurely day at home, which was something that did not happen often. Victoria was often frustrated on Sundays or American holidays, because Edward would usually look over the accounting books or busy himself somehow at the lumberyard. On this day, they took a walk by the river, where Edward found a very small willow tree. He took it from the river's edge, brought it home and planted it in their back yard. He envisioned it growing to grandeur and providing a lot of well-needed shade behind the house. He visualized picnics and parties under that tree someday, but right now, it was just a thin green twig.

James and Edward enjoyed a beer and cigar in the back yard as Jess, Becca, and Victoria slept upstairs. Edward could never stop talking about business with James, which was fine with him. He learned something every time they had these talks. Then they decided to ride to the new house. Edward had not seen the house-building progress for a few weeks, and was anxious to inspect it. They rode through the woods in Edward's buggy and when they arrived, Edward was amazed at how it was coming together so quickly. It seemed fast to Edward, yet James, with his daily rides to the house, thought it would never be done. After they walked through each room, the men agreed the move-in day would be in two weeks. The house would not be totally completed by that time, but ready enough to live in. The stone base for the barn was done and awaiting walls. Edward inspected the workmanship of the house and barn and was very impressed. James explained the house will be white and the barn would be red. He added that he wanted bold white trim on the barn and its doors. Edward complimented James on his designs of the house and barn and told him how proud he was of him. James blushed and accepted his father-in-laws arm around his shoulders as they gazed at it all before they left.

When they returned to Edward's home, they found Victoria folding Becca's clothes and she said Jess was feeding the baby upstairs. It was getting dark and Victoria agreed to stay with Becca, when James and Jess walked to the Village Square for the Fourth of July dance. They heard the band playing when they turned the first corner, and sped up their steps so they would not miss any more of the fun. They danced nearly every dance, until Jess' feet hurt so badly, that James asked her to sit right there. He told her he would walk back to get the buggy, so she would not have to walk back to her parent's home. She bowed her head, almost in shame, but gladly agreed to his kind gesture and thanked him. While she waited, she talked with several ladies who were admiring the music. They all asked how she felt and asked when her baby was due. She told them October as Doc Harris had told her, they all raised their brows. Her stomach looked like she was due any day, and they all agreed with nodding heads. Jess saw their faces and felt herself blush. She and James had been wondering the same. This convinced her it was a boy this time, yet she never said so to James.

Every night James put his hand on Jess' stomach to feel the kicks and movements of the baby. James secretly hoped it was a boy yet clearly, as long as it was healthy he would be happy.

With moving day near, Jess packed as much as she could with her big tummy. Their new furniture would arrive soon, which she was anxious to see, along with a settee and two chairs for the main room, all from New York City. James started to make a dining room table in Edward's barn, and felt guilty that he had not had the time to finish it. Once they moved into their home and did not have to ride a half hour to the cabin, he would have more time to work on the table. He thanked God silently that Jess was a patient, understanding woman. He had seen couples argue at the lumberyard or the general store, and he was so thankful they did not have that kind of marriage.

Becca was starting to crawl everywhere and was more work for Jess now and she tired easily. James would often be the lone parent at night when Jess asked if she could sleep. He saw, on this night, that most everything had been packed and understood why she was so tired. In two days, they would be in their new home and he shook his head in disbelief. His dream was really coming true, after envisioning it, beginning as many as fifteen years ago. He sat with his daughter on his lap on the rocking chair and started to recall all he and Jess had gone through up to this point. Then his mind turned to the future where he imagined Becca older, at play with her brother or sister in their back yard riding ponies. Time was passing so fast, he thought, before he could blink, he would be dancing at her wedding. It sent his mind reeling. He kissed the top of Becca's sleeping head then tiptoed into the bedroom and put her in her crib. He stood there and watched her sleep for a long time by the dim light of the oil lamp. He then turned and did the same with Jess, who was sleeping deeply. Yet he could see the baby inside her moving briskly. James could not imagine how that felt and how she slept through it.

Saturday, the lumberyard closed for the first time since it opened. The notice on the gate said "Moving Day". James was up before dawn, gathered the goats, tied them onto the wagon bed, tied Misty to the back of the wagon, and loaded as much as he could from the barn. Stormy then pulled them to their new home. When they arrived, he tied Misty on a long lead to a tree at the edge of the yard, and then did the same with the goats. Enough of the barn was finished in time for James to unload the wagon. James picked up Bobby and Tim and when they arrived back at the cabin, Jess and Becca were both awake. Becca had been fed and now played in her crib. Jess was busy packing the last minute items. They all got to work loading the back of the wagon, and soon it was full. The three men left with their first load. Two hours later, they returned to the cabin for the final load. Jess had finished packing clothes, sheets and the last-used dishes, now clean, and was ready to say good-bye to the cabin. James was thankful for a fine sunny July day and Jess told him she wanted to take a final walk around the property before she left. With Becca in her arms, she slowly paced the yard, enjoyed the sun coming through the trees, casting odd shapes onto the grass. She walked to the barn door, recalled the wolf that knocked her into the snowdrift and hurt James so badly. She blinked hard and tried to remove that image from her mind. They then went down the hill to the river, where Jess looked in both directions and admired its beauty and sounds. She slowly made it back to the cabin and put Becca in the grass, not far from the wagon that was now loaded.

Jess took one last walk through the cabin and did as James had done last night – she briefly remembered all they had gone through together up to now. She stood in the bedroom silently; this was where James bled so badly after the wolf attack, and it was where the new baby was created. She touched the door jam as if caressing it, turned her head, and whispered "Thank you". Tears welled in her eyes, which she dismissed quickly as she turned her head to the future, picked up her daughter and with Tim's help, got up to the wagon seat. James then wanted a moment to inspect the house one final time. Jess noticed he paused at the door and put his hand on the same spot she had, and did as she had done and took one last look before he closed the door behind him. He jumped onto the seat in one leap, slapped the reins on Stormy's back, leaned to his wife, and kissed her and the top of his daughter's blonde head.

"Here we go! You ready?" He was excited and as the horse finished the arc in the yard to reach the drive, he looked back one more time. He remembered the wolf and then his mind did a flip and he recalled the night he thinks was the night they made the new baby.

"We are ready!" Jess smiled and hugged Becca and they were off.

The half-hour ride to their new home was uncomfortable for Jess and felt as if they would never get there, and the heavy load made the ride bumpier than usual. She held Becca on her knee the best she could in front of her ever-expanding stomach. Becca enjoyed riding in the wagon and Jess loved to watch her face as she took in all the sights and sounds. Becca often pointed her pudgy finger at things like birds and flowers. Jess found herself smiling when she watched her young daughter. Finally, they approached the road beside the lumberyard, made the turn, rode through the arbor tunnel, and turned onto the drive to their new home. She relished this moment and imbedded it in her mind. This would be their final move. She knew they would live in this house the rest of their lives. This was it – their dream had come true.

As they approached the front of the house, the tall white columns stood out in the sunlight with grandeur. It was the first time Jess saw just how many windows there actually were in the front of the house. It was all surreal to her. She wanted to pinch herself. Edward stood on the porch, smiled, then started down the front steps to aid his daughter and granddaughter to the ground from the wagon seat. She kissed his cheek, thanked him, and then as she held her hat in place, put her head back, and looked straight up at the tall, massive, white house front. As a surprise, James had a piece of granite stone engraved which read "Atwood Manor", arched over 1867. It was not hanging over the magnificent front door; it was actually part of the front of the house. James shook hands with Edward, Jess went back down the steps to James' side, waited for the men's greeting to finish, and put her arms around James and kissed him at length.

"You think of everything! The keystone is beautiful!"

He opened his eyes from their kiss, saw his wife's expression and said, "It was worth it just to see your face, Jess. I love you. Welcome to Atwood Manor!" James waved his arm in a big arc toward the house, presenting it to her.

"I love you too, James. Welcome home to Atwood Manor. You have waited a long time for this moment. I am so proud of you," she whispered into his shoulder.

They stayed in their embrace for a long moment, while Bobby, Tim, and Edward walked around them as they took items into the house, unloading the wagon. They brought with them their wedding mattress, bassinette, crib and armoire James made in England. The remaining things to come into the house were trunks, crates and traveling bags. It did not take them long to put the items to where Jess directed them. Edward announced to all that lunch would arrive soon, made by Victoria and beer was waiting in cool river water at the back of the house in a half-barrel. Bobby and Tim ran through the house, exiting quickly to find the cool beer and shade. Victoria soon arrived with fried chicken, corn bread, and apple pie. After lunch, Victoria helped Jess get many things in place downstairs, and then asked to see the bedroom furniture that arrived, which Jess herself had not yet seen. She chose it from drawings of furniture Teddy brought to her from the city. She prayed it was as nice as she imagined. Victoria followed her daughter up the staircase, with a smile on her face. When Jess opened the bedroom door, her jaw dropped. The furniture was not only beautiful, but the bed was made with plenty of pillows. All the wood had been polished to a high sheen. Victoria had fixed the room earlier in the day to surprise her daughter.

"Mother, did you do this?"

Victoria blushed, went to her daughter's side and hugged her. "Darling, you deserve the best and the prettiest. I hope you like the bed cover."

"Thank you, Mother. I love it! Everything is beautiful! Did you pick out the paintings also?" Jess stepped from painting to painting. She inspected the furniture and found it to be grander than she ever dreamt. The four-poster bed was the biggest, fluffiest bed she had ever seen. She caressed one of the bed's wooden posts lovingly then ran her fingers across the silk bed cover. Jess adored the lace edged pillows and went to the chair, which had a beautiful needle pointed cushion. She sat in the chair to catch her breath. She could not believe her eyes. Her mother held out her hand to help her up.

"Come, Jessica, I want to you to see Becca's room."

Jess took her hand and a deep breath, and said, "Mother, this is all too much."

They walked down the hall, and Victoria opened a white painted door and there was the powder blue painted room filled with white wicker furniture, Gerald's surprise gift. The crib had not made it upstairs yet, but the room was so big; there was plenty of room for it.

"Mother, I don't know what to say. Does James know?" Jess was breathless.

"No, James doesn't know. I wanted to surprise both of you."

"How did you get this paint color? I love it!" asked Jess as she looked at it closely.

"Gerald helped me find it. It was painted yesterday, so I was glad you didn't do daily inspections, like James. It was hard to keep him from seeing it, but I think I managed," giggled Victoria as she watched her daughters eyes widen as she took it all in.

Jess could not stop smiling. Everywhere she looked, she saw something she had not seen before. There was a polished wooden box in the corner on the floor with a bow on it. Jess walked to it, lifted the lid to find all the toys Becca received at Christmas and more. She walked to the white wicker chair next to the box, picked up Becca's favorite stuffed bear, sat down, hugged the bear, and took several deep breaths.

"Mother, I have no words. You and Father are far too good to my family and me. I must get James. He has to see this." She walked to the hall rail, peaked over to see her foyer, empty now, but knew it wouldn't be for long. "James," she yelled from the railing.

It took a minute until he appeared below and looked up to Jess, "Are you well, Jess?"

"I am well! James, you must see what Mother and Father have done. Please, James, come up here, please," begged Jess as she looked into her husband's big brown eyes.

He took two steps at a time, got up the stairs, and arrived at Jess' side quickly. She guided him into Becca's bedroom and his jaw dropped. He tried to take it all in, and like his wife, kept seeing something new. "Let me get the crib to complete the room," he said in amazement. He walked to his mother-in-law, kissed her cheek, hugged her, and thanked her repeatedly. He started to leave the room but Jess stopped him.

"You must see the other surprise, James. Our bedroom is beautiful! Wait until........" She was so excited she was breathless and at a loss for words.

They walked the hall together, entered their bedroom and James had tears in his eyes. He tried to see everything at once, walked to the four-poster bed, and said, "Jess, I have never seen a bigger bed in my life."

"Isn't it beautiful? When I ordered it from a drawing I wasn't sure how it would truly be, but it is exquisite." Jess had been smiling so long her face hurt.

James examined one of the bedposts, just as Jess had done, shook his head and tried to believe all of this was truly theirs. His memories filled his mind - he came from sharing a small space with his younger sister in the main room of the little row house in Liverpool, to a rustic, drafty cabin in America to this big, beautiful home. He wondered if he was dreaming. When he looked up, Edward stood in the door. James ran to the smiling man, hugged him and thanked him and Victoria repeatedly. He stepped to kiss and hug Victoria, who gladly reciprocated. Three family members stood and watched James as he went to the paintings, the silk bed cover, the new dresser and chest of drawers. He instantly thought the only thing missing from the top of the dresser was Jess' silver looking glass and brush. Then everything would be complete.

Jess led the way down the staircase to Becca in the crib, where she lay and had slept through it all. Her eyes teared as she witnessed her innocence, and was thankful that she would wake to all the newness, beauty and love around her. She walked to her husband, put her arms around his neck and laid her head on his shoulder. He held her that way a long time. Edward approached his wife and took her in his arms.

"We are all so lucky to have each other and such wonderful lives. James, I am so happy to say that I am thankful for your dream and that we came to America to witness all of this. We should all bow our heads in prayers of thanks." They all closed their eyes and Edward led them in prayer. When they opened their eyes, they saw Becca was standing in her crib for the first time.

"Everyone, look!" Jess said, with tears still in her eyes, so filled with love she thought she would burst. James kissed the top of his daughters blonde head, picked her up into his arms, kissed her cheeks, and then leaned Becca toward Jess so she could kiss her also.

"What a big girl!" said Jess and clapped her hands at Becca. She was so proud and wondered how time had passed so quickly that already, her daughter was standing. She sat on their new settee for the first time, rubbed her hands on the fabric, and her smile showed how delighted she was.

"I have another surprise for you, Jess." James invited her to follow him. She was still holding Becca. He led the others through the house and exited to the back yard. There they met up with Tim and

Bobby who sat in the shade from the house as they drank beer. Tim stepped forward to tickle Becca's stomach in James' arm and made her giggle. James walked farther until he came to a short white picket fence, which made a square under the shade of a tree. Inside the fencing were a ball and a doll. He bent over the fence and placed Becca on the grass inside the fenced area with her toys. She was not sure of the feeling of the grass on her chubby hands, but wanted her doll more than the grass bothered her and crawled over to it.

"Now you can have her outside with you while you hang laundry or read a book," said James with a smile. Jess walked over to the fencing, and watched Becca as she played with her toys. "James, this is ingenious! This way she will never wander to the river or get away from me. James, thank you so much. Becca thanks you too," she finished as she kissed him again.

"You're welcome. I had a lot of spare small pieces of wood from building the house and tried to think of a way to use them, and it just came to me."

Edward walked to the fencing, inspected its small gate, "James, you're amazing. The hinges and latch are on the outside so she can't get her little fingers squeezed. Good thinking, young man." Victoria stepped next to Edward to see what he spoke of and she too was amazed.

"I wish I had something like this when you and Grant were small," Victoria said as she looked at Jess. "And something so simple!"

They all stood around the fenced area and watched Becca play. Suddenly James spoke with an excited tone, "Edward, I just thought of it - we should sell these pickets for baby safety, and they can be used for animals also."

"James! You are so right! I will have one of our men begin making these small pickets Monday morning. We already sell pickets for fencing now and I am sure, when customers see the use for the shorter ones they will definitely buy them. Jessica was right – ingenious!"

That night James would put both goats inside the short fenced area. He knew they would munch the grass overnight, which kept them safe and the grass short. He giggled aloud, and amazed himself at how clever his fence was and when he put it together, he never thought of all possible uses. It was just another thing he wanted to finish before they moved in.

Edward and James joined Tim and Bobby and drank beer in the shade for an hour before the boys left. After James thanked them both, they asked him if he needed anything else and James shook his head no. He thanked them again and they rode away into town where they lived and had finished building their own bedrooms onto their parent's homes.

The remains of the day they arranged furniture, emptied trunks and hung curtains. James and Edward organized barn items while all the females took a nap. They finished the fried chicken for dinner and before dark, Edward and Victoria left them alone in their new home for the first time. The evening air was cool so James built a small fire for the first time in the main room fireplace. They sat on their new settee together and watched Becca play on the new rug. They talked about the day and the many wonderful surprises, and thanked God for everything.

Chapter Eighteen
Late Summer 1867

The first night in their new bed was as romantic as it could have been in Jess' condition, as it made James uncomfortable to make love to his wife while she was in the family way. She tried to assure him that Doc Harris said it was safe, but James didn't want to hurt her. They lit a small fire for ambiance and enjoyed the dancing orange glow on the ceiling of their new bedroom as they lay in each other's arms in their new bed. They prayed together and thanked God for their new home, their daughter, their families, for the baby they were patiently waiting for, and for having each other.

Becca was put into her crib in her own room, for the first time in her life. She had always been just feet away from Jess and was now down the hall. Jess slept lightly that night, and kept her motherly ear open. Becca only woke once that night and Jess was immediately by her side. She rocked her daughter in the white wicker rocker and sung her back to sleep. It was difficult for Jess to place her back into her crib, yet she knew it was the right time and place for her to get used to being in her own bedroom. It was a difficult process for both of them.

James woke early and at first, could not remember where he was, then quickly recalled the truth when he smelled the freshly cut wood aroma that filled his nostrils. He loved that smell, because not only was it his livelihood, but also it meant he was actually lying in his bed in his dream home. He watched the sun slowly move across Jess' long, black hair as she slept, which glistened all the colors of the rainbow, as her hair cascaded over her pillow and across her shoulder. He could tell his daughter was awake and heard her talking to her stuffed bear. There were no words, of course; only she knew what she was saying. As he listened, he noticed she was actually singing. Jess sang to her often, so music was part of Becca's being. He suddenly recalled how his mother and sister were always humming. He loved that he had such happy women in his life. He watched Jess' stomach for a short time when movement under her nightgown caught his eye. He again wondered how she slept through such stirrings inside of her, yet she slept deeply. James felt so content, so happy, and very thankful.

Jess stirred then and when he moved his eyes, he met her eyes, blinking and waking. He put his hand on her tummy, kissed her good morning and asked her how she felt on this fine Sunday morning.

"I am good, my love, and you?" said Jess as she stretched a bit then put her hands on his as they both felt the baby kicking.

He propped his head on his elbow to gaze at his beautiful wife. He admired her strength and her kindness so much. Everything he ever wanted was all within the walls of their home. It was then Jess heard Becca singing and put her finger to her lips so James would hear her too. They listened to the lilt in her song, which made them giggle quietly then James whispered, "She's been singing for thirty minutes."

Jess whispered back, "You've been awake that long?"

He answered yes quietly then asked Jess if she wanted him to go get her. She shook her head yes. He jumped up quickly and Jess stayed in bed and listened to how he greeted his daughter. As he changed her diaper, she could hear their kisses, and how sweetly he talked to Becca. Soon, the two loves of her life entered the room, where James placed Becca between them in bed, and pulled the sheet back up to their waists. The three of them stayed in bed like that for an hour. Jess fed her, which James loved to witness. Then he kissed Becca's sweet little toes and then her nose. She giggled most of the hour.

"This is heaven, Jess. I am in heaven. Look at us, our family. All four of us are here, all snuggled together. This is heaven!" exclaimed James as he softly patted her expanded stomach. He held his daughter over him and let her legs dangle over his stomach. She laughed loudly, but then started to drool and he quickly brought her down between them. It made Jess laugh too, but for a different reason than her daughter.

Soon they rose, and together made their first breakfast in their new home then dressed for church. Jess was so thankful they have such a good baby, and *very* thankful that she behaves at church. Yet, she wanted to be close to Mommy, and because Mommy's tummy grew larger every day, she sometimes fussed. When she had her favorite bear and doll, she usually stayed reasonably quiet during the sermon. They always sat near the door just in case.

When they arrived at church, they found Jess' parents had waited for them before they entered the church.

"How is my beautiful family this morning?" Edward happily took Becca in his arms and kissed her cheek. He leaned to kiss his daughter, shook hands with James, then patted Jess' growing stomach. "All of you...." he added with a big smile.

Jess smiled and said they were all just fine and patted her tummy. "Very active this morning,"

Victoria kissed Jess and James, and then blew bubble kisses into Becca's chubby hands. They both adored their granddaughter and could not wait until the next grandchild was born. Victoria did not normally knit in the summer, as the knitted blankets were too warm on her lap, but she did knit during the cooler summer evenings for the new baby.

They survived the church service where Becca only fussed once, when Edward took her quickly and busied her with twisting his wedding ring. She always tried to remove it but was never able to. The bad part was Edward found that he studied Becca so intently he did not listen to the sermon. Yet he had a good excuse in case the sermon topic came up in conversation later. He just smiled and looked into his granddaughters bright blue eyes. He loved her deeply and sometimes, when he looked at her it made him wonder where time had gone. He knew when he held Becca that he had missed many years of loving times with his children and knew and felt that his heart had changed. He now understood love and family were the reason to live, not lumberyards.

They enjoyed lunch together at the Strong's, since the Atwood cupboard was not yet filled. Becca took a nap and all took pleasure in the perfect summer day. Edward decided they needed short picket fencing in their back yard for Becca also. He and James walked the grass and discussed the best place for it. Edward assured James it would be in place by next Sunday.

Meanwhile, Victoria had a conversation with Jess, "You seem much larger than you were with Becca for as far along as you are. Do you think Doc Harris might have been wrong on the due date?"

"We agree with you. I'm afraid he might be off a month or possibly more." Jess patted her active large tummy.

"I think it's a boy, Darling. What do you think? You are carrying this baby lower," Victoria eyed her daughter's stomach from all angles.

"I think so too. I haven't told this to James, but I hope it is a boy, but time will tell," Jess then took her mother's hand and placed it where it felt as if the baby was stretching. They both giggled with delight, which made the men turn to look at them. They smiled when they saw what the women were doing.

Jess loved the fact that her husband and father got along so well. They saw each other almost every day, and still enjoyed their talks and working well together. What Jess worried about was that James had not talked of his parents often but she knew he had to miss them and his sister too. Like she missed Grant.

"I find it strange that James' parents do not write often. I know the letters take a long time to arrive, but since we arrived in America, we have only heard from them three times. Recently we sent them news of Becca's arrival and another letter telling them about their second grandchild coming soon and we have heard nothing. Don't you think that's odd?"

"Mmm," started Victoria through pursed lips, "that is strange. I couldn't even guess on why that is, can you?"

"I haven't a clue," Jess said quickly and quietly as the men returned to where they sat.

"I am going to check on Becca and shall return either with her or without her," joked James as he walked by his family with a smile.

Jess spent the rest of July and most of August filling their home with new rugs, drapes, and decorations, with Victoria's help. Jess enjoyed doing these things, but her stomach had grown so large that some things were nearly impossible. She was so thankful her mother was near to assist with Becca.

After he saw the tub-room at Gerald's home, James designed a similar room in the back corner of the second story of their home and Jess loved it. He built the trough to remove bath water, as Jess requested to copy Gerald's idea, and James designed a pulley system to get buckets of water up to the room without having to walk each bucket through the house and up the stairs.

Victoria had worked with Gerald to get the powder blue paint Jess liked so much, and decided to use other colors in her own home. Gerald ordered the tinted paints for her, had them delivered to Victoria and she anxiously painted their bedroom light yellow. It turned out well, therefore she ordered two other colors. Soon Jess had two of her rooms painted in colors also. It struck her then that James should sell tinted paints at the lumberyard. James got very excited about this prospect and wrote to Gerald about this opportunity. Gerald connected him to the company he had worked with by mail. Soon a huge delivery arrived at the lumberyard of many colors of paints and it was not long before they needed to place their second order. When James showed Jess the lumberyard's profits on the paints alone, she was shocked.

"We make quite a team, Jess!" James was very excited. He kissed her and placed his hand on her stomach. "How's the little one acting today?"

"Very active, the little devil. I wish you could feel what it's like to have life inside your body, James. I cannot explain how wonderful it is," said Jess as she smiled and rubbed her belly in a circular motion through teary eyes.

"I think I will pass, but I see how it makes you glow. How many children do you want to have, Jess?"

"Only God has control over that, James."

"Well Jess, we could abstain to manage how many children we have, but I don't know if I can keep my hands off of you." He started to laugh and blush as he raised his eyes to meet hers.

"James, you devil," she laughed, looked down to where she used to be able to see her toes while standing, which was impossible now. "To tell you the truth, I feel the same way," she finished and one finger traced his chin sensuously before she kissed the tip of his nose.

Jess wrote letters to both Gerald and Teddy earlier in the month, which invited them to the new home celebration on Saturday, 24 August. They also invited friends from church, storeowners, Mister and Missus Jones from the post office, Bobby and Tim's parents, and their favorite librarian, Miss Lois Appleton. Preparations began for this massive celebration early in the week. James had fallen in love with watermelon and put ten of them in the river to cool them. He used the small pickets again to fence them along the river shoreline and not float away. He patted himself on the back all the way back to the house from the river, snickering. Bobby suggested to James to put the beer in there too. James slapped his back and told him "good thinking". The beer went into the river.

Later in the week, Jess made pies and breads and Victoria made cakes and cookies. Gerald arrived Thursday evening and assisted James to bring wood to their back yard to make tables and benches. They also brought plenty of scrap wood and searched the woods for dead, fallen branches to have enough wood for fires. Teddy and Amanda arrived Friday with enough meat, James thought, to feed the entire town. They only planned on thirty guests.

Amanda was a plain but weathered woman with wide, bright, blue eyes. One could tell she had worked hard all of her life yet had a delightful personality. Her dishwater blonde hair was literally tied in a knot at the nape of her neck and hung past her waist. She was missing several teeth, but expressed a wide smile nonetheless. She made a pie and a cake for the party and handed them to Jess upon their meeting. Amanda hugged everyone at introductions, of which James and Jess were not accustomed. Their brows rose as they watched her hug the others who took steps back also. It was obvious Teddy and Amanda loved each other tremendously, and they were both very proud of their boys, Junior and Sam. They were tall and muscular like Teddy, with blonde hair and blues eyes like Amanda. James questioned in his mind, how much education the boys had and he estimated between them, it was probably only a few years. They had good manners though and were nice boys. They acted shy at first not knowing everyone, but soon Bobby and Tim brought them into their conversation, which made them feel more comfortable. Soon they laughed and joked together, which made James feel better also.

James assisted Teddy and all the boys in unloading the salted meats, which was a side of beef, an entire pig, and many pounds of bacon and sausage. They decided quickly the beef would be tonight's dinner and the pig would roast all day Saturday, for the main party.

James had Tim place many of the small picket fences near Becca's original pickets, so the small children at the party would be safe and could play together, and they started a huge fire in the pit to roast the beef. Tim and Bobby agreed to start the huge roasted pig after the beef had been served, and would spend the night at the fire pit and turn the spit every hour. Junior and Sam asked if they could sleep by the fire pit also. Teddy laughed as he slapped his sons on their shoulders. "We may all be ou' hera wit' you!"

The women gathered in the kitchen as they prepared dinner. Amanda was shocked at Jess' stomach size, after she heard her due date in early October.

"Ya sure 'bout dat doctor, Jess? I'd say he is 'ff on 'is dates."

"James and I agree, Amanda. I feel as big as a house." Jess grinned as her hand circled her stomach, as if to soothe the baby.

"I am watching her closely, Amanda. I believe the doctor has miscalculated also." Victoria walked to her daughter's side and put her arm around her shoulders.

Becca cried from the main room where she played with Ellie, a young girl they knew from church. Jess started to rise to go to her daughter and Victoria, whose arm was still around her daughter, kept her from leaving the room, and then turned to the main room. She soon returned with her granddaughter on her hip with tears on her cheeks; she saw her mother, and reached out her little arms to Jess. She took Becca into her arms. "She is hungry. That's where Ellie can't help." Jess smiled as she left the room to nurse her daughter. She patted Ellie's back to assure her she had done nothing wrong.

Ellie Madison was twelve years old and loved kids. When she saw Becca at church, she always made a point to say hello and tickle or kiss her. Often, when Becca acted up during the sermon, Jess would let Ellie take her outside. They would swing together on the long rope swing that hung from the huge oak tree in front of the church. She would hold her on her lap while seated on the wooden slat and turn Becca's tears into laughter.

All the men were sitting at tables around the fire pit and Jess did not want to disturb their jokes and conversations by bringing them into a formal dining room. She suggested the women eat inside, and men outside and the women agreed. They took plates and silverware to the men outside.

Soon James brought in a huge platter of beef, placed it in the middle of the new dining table he had just completed and brought into the house two days earlier. As he placed the platter, he admired his own workmanship and the shine on the wood. He grinned because he knew he would do anything for his loving wife and felt the warmth of love run through him. He walked into the kitchen and put his hand on Jess' shoulder. She looked up with love and smiled as he announced the beef was on the table. He leaned to kiss Becca, who giggled when she looked up to her father. She then scrunched her pudgy hand, "waving" at her dad.

The women stayed around the dining table for hours, taking turns telling birth stories. The laughter around the table was loud, but the laughter around the fire pit was even louder. It was evident the men had planned to stay outside all night, and they did.

Jess and Becca were first to rise the next morning and when she fried bacon, the wonderful aroma filled the house, and soon Amanda appeared in the kitchen. Victoria shortly came through the front door with a basket of fresh eggs from their neighbor's chicken coop. Jess brought out three loaves of bread she had made the day before and sliced it for toast. Soon, the men arrived one by one, as they followed the aroma of the bacon into the house. The kitchen and dining room was now overflowing with people as they ate fried eggs, maple-bacon and toast with fresh strawberry jam.

Saturday began busy and hectic and stayed that way. It was not long before guests arrived with food and new house celebration gifts. Jess expressed no gifts to those invited, but many ignored her request. Many ladies made things for their home, which were beautiful. Jess was in tears at times, while opening gifts when overcome by their friend's kindness.

The Madison's arrived with Ellie, who instantly picked up Becca, and did not want to put her down, until she cried from hunger. She brought Becca to Jess with a look of helplessness. Jess would giggle, feed Becca upstairs then deliver her back to Ellie's arms, who anxiously waited at the bottom of the stairs. Jess was finally able to convince Ellie to put Becca in the children's fenced area in the back yard so both she and Becca could play with other children. She did that and soon Jess noticed Ellie was playing with all the small children.

The wonderful aroma of roasted pig soon filled the air and many would approach the boys at the fire pit and ask when it would be ready. All the women worked for an hour lining up bowls of food and necessities on the tables outside. At four o'clock, James announced dinner was ready. The guests got in line for silverware, plates, and food first then stepped to the roasted pig, where Bobby or Tim sliced pork for each guest. The women brought the pies, cakes, and cookies outside and soon another line began for desserts.

When Jess came from the house and saw all their friends and family, she felt so happy and so thankful. She loved her life and was never happier. James saw her standing on the back step gazing over the crowd and joined her there. "It's wonderful, isn't it?"

Her eyes filled with tears when she looked at him. "It is, Honey. It is." They stood there a long time and watched their happy mingling guests enjoying themselves.

James squeezed her hand before he started down the stairs, and then turned to his wife. "We must to do this often." He giggled as he walked through the grass to his friends Gerald and Teddy, and the many others at the fire pit.

Jess checked on Becca and Ellie and they were well. She was about to join the women who sat at a table near the men and fire pit, when she felt water trickle down her leg. She didn't know what to do. She put her hand on her mother's shoulder and gave her a look of helplessness. Just as Victoria turned to her daughter, there was a sudden gush of fluid. Victoria heard and saw it and stood immediately. She screamed for James, which hushed the crowd, and all turned toward Victoria. James rushed to her side and he saw Jess' wet dress and shoes. Victoria helped Jess sit.

"What is it, Jess? Is it the baby?" James became frantic.

"Yes, it is. Can you help me get into the house, please?"

The guests had started to gather around, and then suddenly split to give James and Jess a passage to their home. Edward and Gerald took control then and thanked everyone for being there, and politely asked all to pray for the Atwood family and that it was time for all to leave.

Edward promised he would let everyone know how things were the following morning at church. They all expressed concern, but cleared the yard quickly.

Victoria and Amanda followed James and Jess to their bedroom upstairs, while Teddy went for the doctor. Jess was very concerned about the bed cover, which Victoria removed speedily before Jess lay on the bed. "It's too early! Something is wrong, James. Dear God, please help us!"

James said a silent prayer, searched the room, and saw Victoria and Amanda preparing Jess and the room for the delivery. James put a wet cloth across Jess' forehead, held her hand, and assured her everything would be fine. It felt like a long time to James, but finally the doctor arrived. By this time, the women had undressed Jess and put her under the bed sheet. The doctor checked Jess and said it would most likely happen soon. James felt like it was only a short time ago when Becca was born. Again, the door closed as the doctor rolled up his sleeves. James started to pace the hallway and soon Edward was at his side.

"Son, you need to come with me." He smiled as he put his hand on James' shoulder and started to guide him toward the stairs. They went outside to the fire pit, where Gerald and Teddy waited with all the boys. They all gathered around James, clapped his back one by one, and assured him Jess would be fine. Bobby had filled the beer barrel from the river when James was inside and he was glad to see those bottles floating in the cool water and opened one immediately.

"Yer gonna be a father again soon, my boy!" Teddy was at his side and then asked him if he wanted to sit. When James shook his head no, everyone saw he was nervous. It was going to be a long night.

Gerald and Edward opened beers for themselves. "A toast to Jessica, my beautiful daughter! May God bless her and the baby!" Edward raised his beer in the air and the others clanked their bottles to his. All the men said various toasts and blessings at the same time as their bottles met. The men stayed by the fire pit until the moon shone over the tops of the trees. James repeatedly turned to watch their bedroom window and one of the men would talk to him, trying to avert his attention.

Ellie brought Becca outside and tapped James on his shoulder. "Would you like to kiss Becca good-night, Mister Atwood?" He smiled widely and he took his daughter into his arms, then put an arm around Ellie and squeezed once. He let go of her, turned away from the fire pit, and began to walk around the yard with Becca in his arms. Ellie and the men could hear him talking, but could not understand his words.

"My darling little girl, you are about to have a brother or sister whom you will love very much, although you don't know that now." Becca put her fingers on her father's lips and made her own sounds, as if to mimic him. James giggled, hugged her, and then told her more. "You will love him or her, and you will play together, fight together, and grow together. My Becca, you don't know how lucky you are. I love you so much, little one, and soon it will be four of us in this family." He kissed her smiling face. She still played with her father's moving lips with her dainty fingers. "I will do whatever I have to do to make sure your lives are wonderful and not want for anything. My precious daughter," he kissed her again, "your mother loves you to the heavens and back. I hope you know that. I'm sure you do. How could you not? She constantly kisses you, sings to you, and adores everything you do. Your mother thinks you are the moon and the stars, as I do," James kissed both of her chubby cheeks, "and your new brother or sister is a miracle too. I know you don't understand what I am saying to you right now, but know this, my pretty girl, you are loved by many. You are even loved by many that live far, far away that have never even seen your beautiful little face or heard you sing in bed." He had tears running down his face now and Becca traced them with the tip of her tiny finger, then put her finger back on his lips and felt each word he said to her. "I pray that someday you will meet your other Grandmother and Grandfather and your Aunt Emily and Uncle John. You also have an Uncle Grant, who loves you too. And you have cousins who I pray you meet one day." He held a long kiss on her tiny blonde head. "Soon, we will have another to hug and kiss and love." He quietly held her a long time as he watched her expressive face and found it hard to let her go. He watched her eyes as they searched his and she giggled happily then pointed to the moon in wonder. "Moon. Can you say moon?" She would try by saying "oon" and point to it again and crinkle her little nose, lay her head back and laugh. James adored his time with his daughter and laughed too as he squeezed her tight.

He walked back to the fire pit, kissed Becca again, then handed her to Edward, who kissed her goodnight and hugged her a long time. James thanked Ellie for being so much help tonight. She smiled up to him and told him how much she loved Becca. Gerald and Teddy each walked to Becca and kissed her good night. Edward handed her to Ellie, who then turned to take Becca to bed. Bobby and Tim stopped Ellie and each tickled Becca's tummy and softly patted her head, slightly messing her blonde hair.

James looked up to the bedroom window again, but there was still no sign of any change.

The men stood around the fire pit for what seemed like hours, keeping James occupied. In reality, he laughed when they laughed, but never heard their words. He could not stop worrying about Jess. He sipped his beers, which hadn't affected him at all. He continuously prayed for Jess and the new baby as he watched the moon silently glide a path through the night sky. He hadn't checked his timepiece for a long time, but knew it was rather late. He thanked everyone for staying by his side and told them they could sleep and did not need to stay by his side. They all made excuses, slapped his back and stayed. He knew they would all wait as long as he did. He was very thankful for his many good friends.

Finally, Victoria came out the back door, but did not look as excited as she did when Becca was born. "It's a boy! Everyone, it's a boy!"

James was so relieved and all the men gathered around him as they shook his hand and slapped his back. He started toward Victoria through the dark. "How is Jess? How is the baby?"

"She's still in a lot of pain and the doctor is helping her with that. James, you have a son! He is very small but fine!"

"But how is *she*? Victoria, how is she? How is the baby?"

"This time was a little harder, James, but she will be fine."

"Can I see her...them?"

"Not right now, Dear. I must get back to Jess, but I will let you know as soon as I can. I must return." Victoria turned quickly and disappeared into the house.

Gerald approached James and congratulated him again. "James, how are they?"

"Victoria said this time was harder and Jess has a lot of pain but my son is doing fine."

"She is strong, James. She will be fine, I assure you!"

Just as Gerald comforted James, Victoria rushed through the back door again, with a look of shock on her face, which James could not read.

"James, you have two sons! Her pain was labor for a second baby. Two sons, James. You have two boys!"

James was in shock. He didn't know what to do. He actually had to remind himself to breathe. Gerald announced the news to the others and they all ran to James' side. Everyone whooped and hollered, jumped up and down and congratulated him repeatedly. Finally, there was silence when James put his hands in the air. "We have not decided on boys names! In fact, we had not decided on any names, because we thought we still had a few months. I have two boys!" The reality just hit him and soon he whooped and hollered and they all joined in. Their celebration sounds echoed through the pine trees.

Edward hugged Victoria as James approached them. "Can I see all of them?" His smile was so big he thought his mouth would crack.

"You can, James. I need to get back up there. Are you ready?"

He started up the stairs behind Victoria, but soon took the stairs two at a time, passed her quickly and went through their bedroom door in a rush. The lamp was dim, but he saw his wife lying in bed, her black hair was soaking wet with sweat as it rested on the pillow. She turned her head when she heard the door open. "James. Two boys, do you believe it?"

He flew to her side, knelt on the floor, and took her hand and kissed the back of it repeatedly.

"I am so proud of you Jess. Are you okay? Do you need anything?"

She closed her eyes to rid her tears to see him more clearly and shook her head no.

Soon he stood and kissed his wife at length, then heard two small cries start at the same time from across the room. He saw Amanda kneeling on the floor over a folded blanket where his twin sons lay together. When he looked at the tiny beings, all he saw were little arms and legs flaying in the air and two blonde heads. They were the smallest babies he had ever seen. Amanda tried to comfort them as she cleaned them, when suddenly one of them peed straight up in the air, into Amanda's hair, and she turned to James with the biggest smile, giggled while she dried her hair, and then shrugged her shoulders. "Do you want to hold them, James? Congratulations! Two boys! It's a miracle!" She hugged him quickly and returned to her task. She wanted them to be perfect when the boys met their parents the first time.

James didn't know what to do first. Amanda now washed the baby farthest away from her, and then he reached under her stretched arms and picked up one of his sons. Victoria quickly stepped over and held a small blanket under the baby in James' hands. He placed the baby in the blanket, wrapped it around him, and brought him up to his face. He kissed his tiny son, turned toward the bed and sat next to Jess. The doctor was finishing with Jess, which James chose not to watch, so he turned, putting his back to the doctor and faced his wife. He could see she was exhausted and soaked in sweat, but she still wanted to see her son. She pulled the blanket away from their son's face and tears instantly filled her eyes. "James, he's beautiful. Is he okay? He is so small." James shook his head yes and kissed his son again before he placed him in her arms. They laughed together when he told her how he had just peed on Amanda.

She was now eager to take him and propped herself up on one elbow. She looked down to the doctor, around James, and the doctor nodded approval for her to sit up. She winced in pain, but sat up with Victoria's help as she plumped a fat pillow behind her daughter. She took her son in her arms and kissed his tiny red face. "Mark" was all she said. James smiled through his tears as he watched his wife and son together for the first time. He could hardly see through his tears, but soon a thin, little red arm popped out of the blanket. James remembered when Becca was born, and her tiny little hand that wrapped around his finger. He held his finger up to his son's wee hand, and the smallest fingers he had ever seen wrapped half way around his little finger. Amazing, he thought. "Jess, look how tiny his fingers...." he started to say as he looked at his wife and saw how amazed she was too. She gently touched the top of her sons tiny fingers wrapped around her husband's finger and had to catch her breath through her tears. "Where's Luke?"

James looked at Jess, smiled until it hurt. "Luke?"

"Our sons, Mark and Luke. The names just came to me when I saw the doctor hold them up at birth. What do you think? Do you like the names? They are from the Bible."

"Perfect Jess. Mark and Luke. Which one was born first?"

Amanda spoke from across the room, "The firs' born is in your arms, so he is Mark. This one is Luke?" James shook his head yes. "This little man came 'bout two minute' after 'is brother. God bless their tiny little bodies." She had finished cleaning Luke and had him wrapped in a small blanket. She stood with him in her arms, kissed his cheek, and walked to James. James took him from Amanda, kissed his tiny face, which was identical to his brothers, then leaned him toward Jess so she could see him closely. She reached over and touched her son then raised her eyes to meet James' and he saw in her expression that she had to hold him. He placed him in her other arm, as he held his tiny head until it rested in the crook of her elbow. He could not believe his eyes - Jess sat in bed with a son in each arm. The sight put him to his knees. He stayed there a moment, put his elbows on the bed, and said a prayer out-loud. "Thank you God, thank you." Jess saw and heard her husband, and reached the best she could to put her fingertips on his praying hands. He looked up at her and they both had tears of total joy and thanks in their eyes.

He rose to sit next to his wife and two new sons when Victoria whispered in his ear asking where Becca was. "Ellie put her down hours ago." She nodded her head, and found peace in his answer and left the room. She met a grinning Edward in the hall as he walked toward her. When she asked him why he was grinning, he crooked his finger, which invited her to follow him. He arrived at Becca's door, opened it slowly, and stepped aside so Victoria could see into the room. Becca was sound asleep in her crib and Ellie was asleep on the floor with one of Becca's blankets under her and a cloth doll under her head for a pillow. Victoria put her hands to her mouth, but could not stop her tears. They both stood and stared a moment, turned down the wick on the oil lamp and gently closed the door behind them. They tiptoed down the hall back to the master bedroom. She stepped inside and waited to see Edward's face when he saw his daughter holding two of the tiniest babies he had ever seen. He had instant tears of joy. He walked to the bed, put his hand on James' shoulder, and looked up only a moment and smiled. James could not stop looking at all three of his miracles. Edward leaned to kiss his daughter's forehead and briefly touched the babies separately through their blankets. Jess looked to her father's eyes, smiled and held out her right arm the best she could without disturbing Luke to take her father's hand. "Beautiful, Jessica! My lovely girl, you have two miracles. They are so tiny." He was whispering, and raised his other hand to wipe his own tears away.

"Father, Mother, this is Mark Thomas," as she raised her left elbow a bit higher than it was at rest, "and this is Luke Edward," as she raised her right elbow. Edward looked at his glowing daughter and mouthed silently – Thank You – to her, and put his hand on his son-in-law's shoulder again. He then reached for his wife, put his arm around her shoulder and they stood in amazement as they gazed at their beautiful daughter, her new sons and her husband; a vision neither would ever forget. They both silently wished Grant were here to witness this.

Edward could not resist saying, "Our family is very blessed."

Suddenly James thought of Becca and started to rise and go to the door. Victoria saw the look on his face and could tell what his worry was and as she eased him, she asked him to follow her. She led him to Becca's door, opened it, where James was able to see the sweet sight they witnessed earlier of his daughter in her crib and Ellie sleeping near her on the floor. His eyes filled with tears as they backed out of the room. "Her parents must be so worried about her." Victoria told him that Ellie had asked permission of Edward to spend the night before her parents left and that they were aware of where she was. His face eased and he quickly returned to Jess, Mark, and Luke.

Chapter Nineteen
August 1867

Victoria woke early the next morning on the main room settee, where she had slept all night. The house was silent, but only for a moment. She heard a tiny cry from upstairs and bolted up the stairs to Jess' door, cracked it open very slowly, and peeked through the small slit and saw her daughter breast-feeding a tiny little boy. James slept on the floor after an exhausting night. He was lying beside his son who slept on the blanket next to him. He was on his side and faced his son's face, which were not six inches apart. She tiptoed into the room and to her daughter's bedside. Jess saw her and smiled, then quickly looked back to her feeding son. Victoria sat on the edge of the bed and put her hand over Jess' hand, which supported her son Mark.

"Jessica, how are you, my dear?"

Jess smiled and said she was fine. Victoria motioned for her to see her son and husband asleep on the floor. Jess smiled wide when saw them. Amanda rose from the chair in the corner and approached the bed.

"Good morning Victoria. How 're ya?" Amanda whispered quietly.

"Oh, Amanda! Have you been sleeping in here all night?"

"Took some cat naps 'ere 'nd thar. Would you mind if I got some sleep?"

"For heavens sake, Amanda, you should have wakened me. Yes, please do."

Amanda put her hand on Victoria's shoulder, smiled at Jess, and left the room. Victoria heard her walk the length of the hall and a door close in an unused bedroom.

"I feel so bad. I fell asleep on your settee downstairs after two this morning, and.... Well, you know" Victoria hung her head as her emotions took over.

"Mother, it was a long night for everyone and we are all exhausted. Don't feel bad. If she did not want to do all she did, I am sure she would have wakened you. She was amazing though, and so much help. You both were."

"When I saw the doctor out early this morning, I sat on the settee and I was only going to rest a moment and I must have fallen asleep. I don't remember anything else."

"I am sure she understands, Mother."

"Which one is this?"

Jess giggled quietly and delicately opened Mark's blanket, and showed her a blue ribbon tied loosely around his tiny ankle. "This is Mark Thomas Atwood. James thought of using ribbons because we cannot tell the boys apart. That is only because they are perfect," she giggled again, "and there is not a mark on either one of them."

Victoria whispered back, "What does Luke wear?"

Jess smiled wide. "He wears nothing. James thought we would put a ribbon on Mark for a day or two, give his skin some peace, and then Luke will wear a yellow ribbon for a day or two. Therefore, we need to write down these colors so we all can tell them apart. James found my hair ribbons and began using them because we were starting to mix them up. At first, we could tell them apart by where they lay on the blanket and knew that method would vanish as soon as others held them. Can you get the bassinette out of Becca's room today? I am sure they can both lie in there together since they are so small. What do you think?"

"Of course, Jess, whatever you need. How are you feeling?"

"I feel good Mother. I am very tired, but by the looks of things, I am going to be tired for a very long time. It is worth it. They are so perfect and beautiful. Is Becca awake?"

Victoria shook her head no, and then began to tell her about Ellie sleeping on Becca's floor. Jess smiled and asked her mother to bring Becca to her when she woke. "James must be awake, though, when Becca sees her brothers for the first time. I know he would not want to miss it."

Victoria agreed, checked James and Luke quickly, and saw they still slept soundly. Mark was done with his breakfast and Victoria offered to burp him on her shoulder. Jess gladly handed him to her then slid down in the bed and fell asleep very quickly. Victoria held the baby for a long time as he slept, for she couldn't make herself put him on the blanketed floor. The door cracked open quietly and Edward stuck his head in. He smiled at the view, stepped into the room, and went to Victoria's side at the chair by the fireplace. They didn't have to speak, and quietly watched most of their family sleep. Suddenly Luke started to cry and as Victoria attempted to rise from her chair, she saw James quickly wake and tend to his son. He looked around the room, nodded and smiled at his in-laws and picked up his hungry son. He quickly changed his tiny diaper then walked to the bed with the baby in his arms and looked down at his sleeping wife. He hated to wake her, but no one else could feed him. He giggled quietly, then bent and kissed his wife to wake her. She opened her eyes slowly at first, saw James, and came around swiftly. James helped her sit up with his free hand, then handed her their swaddled son, Luke. She spoke softly to him, kissed his tiny face, and proceeded to feed him modestly under the sheet, since her father was in the room. She looked at her father and smiled. He knew then he could approach his daughter and her son. He kissed her forehead after he pulled her hair back from her face, and then kept his hand on her shoulder for a long time. He could hear his grandson greedily suckle under the sheet.

He asked which one she was feeding and Victoria snickered from the corner and told him about the ribbons. Edward shook his head in amazement. "James your mind is constantly working, isn't it?"

James looked at him and just smiled. "The trouble is, when they get a little older, I don't know what we will do. So you, dear Edward, can help me come up with something."

Edward nodded his head at James with a smile.

"Do you want to hold your grandson?" Victoria looked at Edward, who gave her a doubting look, but then he agreed. She rose and he sat in her chair and put his arms out. Edward was a big man, and when she put the tiny wrapped soul into his arms, he was amazed at how light he felt. Soon he was mesmerized by his grandson's wee face, kissed his forehead, and introduced himself quietly. Mark hardly moved until the first kiss from his grandfather when his tiny arm flew out of his blanket. When Edward took his hand to ease him and saw how tiny it was against the palm of his hand, he found it hard to believe that this warm, little bundle in his arm was a complete human being. "God made you perfect, Mark, and I am so happy to welcome you into our family. You and your brother have a beautiful sister. Did you know that?" His voice was so soft and Victoria could not recall *ever* hearing it like that before, or such tender words.

Jess' eyes teared as she watched her father and son. James sat beside her on the bed and first looked at Mark in Edward's arm then at Luke at his wife's breast, then back to Mark, then back to Luke. He was still in shock and literally could not believe his eyes. It still felt like a dream. A quiet tap on the door broke his trance as he rose to open the door.

Gerald stood there sheepishly, as he had hoped he did not wake anyone. James motioned for him to enter the room. Jess quickly covered her feeding baby even more than she had before, then looked at Gerald, and smiled. "How are you, sweet Jessica?" He then asked through body language if he could come close to her. She nodded her head yes. He put one fist on the bed, leaned to kiss her forehead, then quickly stood erect.

"I am fine, Gerald. This is Luke," as she pointed to the bump under the sheet, "and that is Mark." She pointed to her father and son sitting in the corner. Gerald approached them quietly, shook Edward's free hand quickly, and then bent at the waist to see the tiny face inside the small blanket in Edward's arm. He touched Mark's tiny cheek tenderly, and simply stared.

Edward watched Gerald study the small bundle. "Amazing, isn't he?"

Gerald whispered, what Edward thought was "yes" but the lump in Gerald's throat made it come out choked. He cleared his throat and it came out clearer the second time. Victoria put her hand on Gerald's back to ease him. He turned and looked at her and she saw a tear run down one cheek. He stood and cleared his throat again, turned to James and told him Teddy was waiting on the stairs. James went to the door, looked out, and saw Teddy patiently waiting his turn. James went to him, their eyes met and Teddy smiled wide. He stood and shook James' hand and quietly asked how everyone was.

"We are all well, my friend. Please come in and meet my sons."

"Gladly." He softly followed James into the bedroom, where Jess had handed Luke to her mother, who was burping his wee body over her shoulder. Teddy didn't know where to look first. Yet the gentleman in him went to Jess first. He held out his hand to her, which she delicately grasped, he bent and tenderly kissed the back of her hand, then held it softly between both of his hands. "Th' last time I di' 'his in New York City at our first meeting, young lady, yer husband was up a' arms. Do ya think he wi' do dat again?" He started to laugh.

Jess got teary eyed. "I think you're safe, Teddy." She started to laugh also. She leaned forward as far as she could under the circumstances and met his kiss to her forehead.

Teddy walked to each tiny bundle with their grandparents, touched each of their small backs tenderly, and shook his head in amazement. They all stayed in silence a moment before he asked where his wife was. Victoria answered quietly that she was sleeping in the bedroom at the end of the hall. Teddy nodded his head and smiled. He shook James' hand again and silently backed out of the room.

Gerald shook James' hand also and patted his shoulder with his left hand. "Congratulations, James, Jess." He turned to her and bowed. "I will leave you to your family. I will tell the boys at the fire pit that all is well and I will wait for you there before I leave."

James told him he would be down soon, and stepped to the door and closed it behind Gerald.

He quickly went to his wife's side, sat next to her, leaned to kiss her and she quickly responded. They sat for some time and watched the boys asleep with their grandparents. Then there was another quiet tap on the door. James answered the door and there stood Ellie with Becca on her hip.

"Dada!" Becca said, as she stretched her arms out to him. He quickly took her into his arms and turned to the room. He wanted to shout, but needed to stay quiet. "Did you hear that?" His face lit up and his smile was huge. Jess was in shock. "Did she say Dada?"

"Yes! Dada, can you say it again?" His face was close to hers and kissed her so excitedly. As soon as their faces parted, "Dada." Everyone in the room got as excited as they could, yet stayed quiet for the boy's sake. Victoria swiftly stepped to Becca, kissed her, and then stepped back.

James took Becca to Jess, placed her on the bed, where she started to climb on Jess, when James quickly took her back into his arms.

"Becca – you have two baby brothers!" Jess was so excited and wanted to hold her so badly. James let Jess continue to talk to her daughter, as he took her to each baby.

"This is your brother Luke with your grandmother," as James let her look at him. Her eyes widened and she started to reach for her baby brother, but James held her back. "And that is your brother Mark with your grandfather!" James took her to him where she tried to touch him also. James realized then that Becca had dolls bigger than her brothers were, and she probably thought she had two new dolls.

"Can you give your brothers a kiss?" Jess' eyes teared, as she badly wanted to be the one that held her when she kissed them. James leaned Becca close to Mark as she puckered her lips and tenderly kissed her brother on his nose. Edward giggled then leaned close to his granddaughter.

"Give me a kiss too, precious girl." Becca quickly moved from Mark to her grandfather and kissed him, making a smacking sound. Everyone giggled. James took her quickly to Luke and Victoria, saw that Becca had kept her lips puckered for the next kiss, and then kissed her brother on his nose too. Victoria's smile was so big. "Grandmother needs a kiss too." Becca's lips remained puckered and she gladly kissed her grandmother and again made the smack sound.

"Mommy needs a kiss too, Becca." As James walked her to her mother, he took a kiss from his daughter, she again smacked, and then she kissed her mother, once, twice, then three times. Jess' eyes filled with tears and took her daughters face in her hands. "My beautiful girl, I love you!"

"'ov ooo!" Becca replied quickly. Jess was amazed, as she watched her husband kiss their daughter's chubby cheek repeatedly. "It's as if she just discovered, this morning, that she can talk!" Victoria shook her head in agreement with Jess, and could not believe her ears.

Edward sat with a slacked jaw. Victoria handed Luke to Jess and said she would return soon. It was not a minute later, when she returned with the bassinette. She quickly placed a blanket on the bottom of the bassinette and then a clean sheet. She took Luke from Jess and placed the baby in the small wicker bed. He quickly relaxed with his arms above his head and slept soundly. There was plenty of room for Mark so she took him from Edward and placed him next to his brother headed in the opposite direction in the wicker bed. She asked Edward to lift the bassinette and place it on the far side of the bed and close to Jess. The babies were like magnets, and immediately drawn to each other as they touched hips and legs. Mark then put his arms over his head and they both fell soundly asleep. Becca watched all of this from her father's hip, then suddenly blew them a kiss as they slept. They all watched in awe.

Edward announced that it was time to go to church, as everyone was probably anxious to hear the news. He and his wife kissed their daughter and shook James' hand, kissed Becca and left to dress for church. When they left the room, they found Ellie waiting quietly. Victoria told her she could go in and when James saw her, he felt terrible that he all but forgot her when he heard his daughter say Dada. He apologized to Ellie and asked her if she wanted to see the twins. She shook her head wildly as her eyes searched the room. She walked quickly to the wicker bassinette, put her hands on the edge, and stared at the babies. Her eyes widened and she quietly said "Aaaww. They are *so* tiny. When can I hold them?" Jess giggled and told her it would be some time, probably when they got a little bigger. Ellie smiled in anticipation and asked if she could touch them. James had worked his way to the bassinette and watched Ellie as she reached in when Jess said she could. She delicately touched each tummy, and smiled so happily.

"What are their names?" Her hands were back on the edge of the bassinette, which held a grip so tight, the ends of her fingers where white. Jess told her their names and watched her face, which froze in wonder. She studied them for ten minutes then suddenly turned and asked if she could feed Becca her breakfast. When Jess nodded yes, she quickly took her from her father's hip and left the room. It would be the first time that James and Jess were alone with their sons. He sat next to her on the bed, held her hand, kissed his wife and they quietly talked about the births and the future, and then sat silently, listening to their son's typical baby noises and their breathing as they slept.

James suddenly remembered that Gerald said he would wait by the fire pit before he left, and, he and Jess needed their breakfasts. He kissed his wife, told her to rest and that he would return in awhile with breakfast. He quickly went outside to the fire pit where Gerald stood with Bobby, Tim, Junior, and Sam. Gerald turned to greet James quickly and asked if he could start the bacon for breakfast. James was almost embarrassed that they had all waited to eat. James nodded his head yes, as Gerald began to unwrap the pork. James asked where Teddy was and Junior said he was upstairs sleeping with his mother, Amanda. They all talked about the twins and Jess and then James told them that Becca had said Dada. The way they all got excited, made James feel like they were all family.

Ellie brought Becca outside and put her in the fenced play area as the men ate bacon and eggs. James took Jess her breakfast and she was sleeping so deeply that he did not have the heart to wake her. He checked the twins and they too slept heavily. He returned to the fire pit where he and Gerald, somewhat separated from everyone, talked for over an hour about his beautiful family, and then Gerald said he must return home. James walked Gerald to his wagon when Edward and Victoria pulled their buggy into the drive.

"Gerald, are you leaving?" Edward was carrying a crate under his right arm, which he switched to his left to shake hands with Gerald.

Gerald nodded his head yes, as he looked into the crate. "Is that a scale?"

"Yes it is. The Johnson's at the general store gave us permission to use it." Edward put his hand on Gerald's shoulder and let out a short laugh. "I want to weigh the twins, because I don't think they weigh five pounds each. Do you mind, James?"

James clapped his hand on Edward's back and laughed. "I think it's a good idea, Edward. Let's go see if they are awake."

Gerald hesitated, but he had to know the weigh-in results, and followed everyone into the house. James looked back at Becca, who was happily playing with Ellie.

Everyone waited at the foot of the stairs while James went up and into their bedroom. He found Jess feeding one of the boys and told her what her father wanted to do and she smiled and thought it was a good idea also. James waved everyone up and Jess quickly covered her feeding son and greeted everyone with a smile.

"Mark is almost done here and Luke should wake up hungry soon." She giggled. "They do everything together, and I mean everything."

Victoria quickly went to the bassinette and saw Luke waking and stirring. She picked him up and lovingly snuggled him into her neck. He wiggled in her arms, and then started to fuss. She looked at Jess, who had taken Mark from her breast and was burping him over her shoulder.

"Do you want to trade?" Victoria knelt next to Jess and they easily swapped babies.

Edward set the scale on the floor and Victoria approached with a small blanket and Mark. Edward weighed the blanket and then knew what to subtract from the total weight when they weighed each baby. Victoria unwrapped her grandson, removed his clothes and diaper, and placed his tiny body on the scale. The needle on the scale barely jumped but finally settled on 4 pounds and 8 ounces. Edward picked up his grandson, and placed him back on the scale to confirm his weight and got the same results. When he subtracted 4 ounces for the blanket, he announced his weight to all in the room. James shook his head in amazement. They were not able to weigh Becca at her birth, but he knew she must have weighed almost twice as much as one of the twins.

Victoria quickly dressed Mark in clothes much too big for him, and continued to burp him over her shoulder and gently tapped on his tiny back. His small blonde head finally rested on her shoulder and slept. She did not immediately place him in the bassinette, as she wanted to hold him and study this wee being. She could not move her eyes from his sleeping face.

Luke was done nursing, and James burped him a short time before he placed him on the blanketed scale. Edward did the same as before, and weighed his grandson twice. Both times the needle rested on 4 pounds and 6 ounces.

"No wonder I was as big as a house!" Jess sat in bed, tried to see around everyone then assisted James in redressing Luke when he laid him next to her.

"That means Becca was probably around 7 pounds, maybe a little more when she was born." James coddled his son in his arm, and thought about how his son weighed less than a bucket of paint.

"Well, now we know." Edward returned the scale to its crate and scuffed his palms together, as one does when they've completed a job. "I figured they weighed around 4 pounds, but I had to be sure. Thank you Jess, and thank you James." He nodded his head to each of them.

"Father, I for one, am glad you did this. I was anxious to know also." Jess smiled at her father, put her hand out to him, which he took and held for a minute, as he sat next to her on the bed.

"How are you feeling, my beautiful daughter?"

Jess laid her head on her father's shoulder and smiled. "I am better every hour, Father. I will be out of this bed, hopefully by tomorrow. So who do you think they look like?"

Edward giggled and looked his daughter in the eye. "They are too small to look like either one of you, right now. Hopefully they will gain weight quickly and we shall know the answer to your question soon."

Victoria finally placed Mark in the bassinette and James put Luke there too and watched how they searched for the other. As soon as they were touching hips, they settled down and quickly fell asleep.

Gerald stepped around the bed to the bassinette, gently stroked each of the boy's stomachs, kissed his fingertips, and touched each of their cheeks with transferred kisses. He stared at them for a minute, and then walked around the bed to say good-bye to all. He leaned to kiss Jess' forehead, kissed and hugged Victoria, shook Edward's hand then approached James. As he shook his hand, James said he would walk him to his wagon. They left the room after Gerald waved to all in the room, and then turned to Jess. "You take care, Jess. Please let me know if you are in need of anything." He then turned to Victoria and nodded. She smiled and nodded her head to him in return.

One month later, Edward borrowed the general store's scale once again and discovered that the twins had gained over one pound each. Jess was so glad to hear that. She had been so afraid she would lose one or both of the boys since they were so small. Doc Harris checked on them every four days, and always gave a good report.

Becca wanted to be around her brothers as much as was allowed. Jess would let her hold them, one at a time, on her lap, next to her while they all sat on the bed. However, Jess watched her closely, as she tried to hold them as she did her dolls. Becca's kisses were never ending.

The twins were getting used to all the attention, especially from their grandparents. James had built one crib and was making a second when he brought the first completed crib to their bedroom. Jess loved it, yet found it difficult to put the boys into it from the bassinette. She did admit she could see them better in the crib from the bed and then relaxed.

"James, I wish I could know what you looked like as a baby. I bet if your mother were here, she would say they look just like you as a child." Jess smiled as she placed Luke in the crib after she had fed both of her sons. "I am concerned, Honey, and wondering if they are getting enough milk. They both eat more often than they should and I don't know if my body is making enough milk for both of them."

James had a concerned look on his face and scratched his chin. "We need to talk to Doc Harris about this, Jess, yet they are gaining weight. We never used a bottle for Becca, but do you think I should get bottles for the boys?"

The next day, James ate his lunch quickly at the lumberyard, and went to Doc Harris' office and told him of their concerns. He shook his head and said he had never dealt with twins before, but it all made sense. The doctor joked that James might need his own dairy cow, but James knew then he had to buy a cow. He talked to Edward about the predicament and Edward agreed and said he should keep the cow in the lumberyard stable with the horses until he made the proper space in his own barn.

The next day, while Victoria worked in her garden, she laughed at the sight of James as he came into the lumberyard with a cow tied to the back of his buggy. She watched as he put the cow into the grazing area with the horses and giggled as the horses, one by one, came to the cow, sniffed her, and then went back to grazing. She noticed the cows engorged teats and wondered who would be the one to milk her every day. She dusted off her hands and prepared to walk to the lumberyard to talk with him.

"James, I was wondering who is going to milk the cow daily." She didn't want to admit that she knew nothing of milking a cow, nor did Edward.

"I will." He looked at her with pride, although, truth known, he knew nothing of milking a cow. It was then he looked at his hands and saw how callused they were from handling lumber for years. He wondered if they would be too rough for the cow, and then giggled quickly, thinking about when he touches Jess, and recalled that he never had any complaints from her. He then turned his attention back to his mother-in-law.

Victoria looked at his hands, as her eyes followed his. "Do you know how to milk a cow, my dear?"

"No, but I can learn. At least I hope I can learn." He giggled again, yet felt positive.

"Well, my dear boy, I hope all goes well." She giggled all the way back to her house.

James cleaned a bucket and took the metal cup from the water barrel along with the four glass bottles he bought at the general store, and walked to the stable behind the lumberyard. He took a deep breath, got a short rope, and approached the cow, which was happily grazing in the green grass. He led her to the stable, tied her head close to the rail, set the bucket under her, and took another deep breath. He brought a crate near to sit on and rubbed his hands together as he prepared to milk her. He squeezed, pulled, and squeezed again with no results. He looked at the cow's face, which was turned and straining to look at him. He chuckled aloud, rubbed his hands together again, and prepared for another attempt. As he laughed, he wondered how hard could this be. He heard stirring at the stable door, looked up, and saw Bobby, who stood there giggling, with his hand over his mouth. "You need some help there, James?"

"It seems I don't know how to do this, Bobby. Do you know how to milk a cow?"

"I do. I have done it so many times, I could prol'ly do it in my sleep!" Bobby walked toward James as he stood to let Bobby sit on the crate. Bobby reached under the cow and James saw his arms move swiftly, and soon the bucket was half-full of milk. James shook his head repeatedly.

"You have to show me how you do that!" Bobby let James sit on the crate next to him and bent to watch his hands squeeze and pull, with results. Bobby showed him in slow motion how to handle the teat. James tried, and at last, got milk to squirt into the bucket. The cow still strained to watch the men, but when she was relieved, she turned her head back to the stable wall and again chewed her cud.

"She got a name?" Bobby now stood next to James and let him milk the cow without supervision, as he patted the back end of the cow.

"They told me her name is Bess, but I have an Aunt Bess and just cannot bring myself to call her that. I'm sure Jess will come up with a name for her. Or do you have a suggestion?"

"Betsy! If she knows her name, it's close enough to the sound of Bess. How are the twins?"

"They are growing like weeds and they are well. You should visit them, Bobby. Jess is doing well, and she would love to show them off to you. You should bring Tim too."

"I will do that Sunday, after church. Or are you taking them to church now?"

"Not yet, Bobby. When we do, that will be a hectic day. Victoria continues to ask us when we will return to church, so I suppose we will soon."

"Well, Tim and I will visit after church. I can't wait to see them."

"You won't believe how they have changed in one month. We were scared for awhile there because they were so small, but I think we should have no worries now."

"That's great! Does Becca love them?"

"She kisses them to pieces. She can't understand why we won't let her drag them into her room, like she does her dolls."

The bucket was almost full and James stopped milking the cow. He removed the bucket and untied the cow. As he walked her out of the stable, Bobby followed.

"Sounds like you have fun with your kids. You are a lucky man, James."

James untied the rope from the cow, and slapped Bobby on his back and agreed.

"Bobby, I am one of the luckiest men on earth!"

The two men stood in the stable door and watched the cow and horses glisten in the sunshine for a long time.

"Hey, are you still seeing that young lady I saw you with at the pie eating contest a long time ago?" James didn't look at Bobby, in case he would be embarrassed.

Bobby hung his head shyly, kicked the dirt, and there was a long pause before he answered.

"I am, James. However, I may lose her, 'cuz she wants to go to New York City to learn about fashions when she finishes school here." Bobby bent to pull a long blade of grass from the ground and put it in his mouth, where it hung loosely from his closed teeth.

"Who is she?"

"Samantha Madison. She's Ellie's older sister."

"Oh! Well, she sure is a pretty girl."

"I know! I'm afraid some New Yorker will steal her heart and I'll never see her again."

"All I can say to that is if it is meant to be, she will be yours. I had a crush on Jess a long time before we finally got together. You just have to have faith, Bobby. If she truly loves you, she will be back. If she doesn't come back, although I know it's hard to take, then she just wasn't meant to be yours. Faith, boy, Faith." James put his hand on his shoulder and squeezed it for assurance.

Bobby continued to chew on the blade of grass, in deep thought. "Well..."

Soon, Bobby went back to work and James quickly took the bucket of milk and the new bottles to Jess. He told her quickly how he learned to milk the cow from Bobby and they laughed together, while she washed the bottles.

"The boys are going to be hungry soon, and I will try the bottles then. I hope they accept them." Jess smiled and kissed her husband before he left to return to the lumberyard.

186

It was a difficult day for Jess, as the boys refused the bottles, strongly at first, yet gradually got used to them. It took a week to feed them with the bottles without fussing. She also had to express her own milk, which she mixed with the cow's milk, until her body finally stopped making milk.

James was concerned about the cabin and asked Bobby to check their now empty cabin and barn before the snow started. Bobby returned with the news of two squatters who were living there. James decided to take Bobby, Tim, and two other young men from the lumberyard with him to see for himself. When they rode up the drive on horseback, they saw two men run out the door and head for the river. All the men dismounted swiftly and Tim stayed to tie the horses as the rest ran after the men running through the woods. The squatters were now running in opposite directions through the trees, close to the river. James and his men tried their best to catch the fleeing men, but they disappeared into the woods and were out of sight quickly. James hushed his men, as they all stood quietly catching their breaths, listening to the forest sounds, and heard nothing but birds and the running river. The men slowly climbed the hill back to the cabin where James entered and inspected each room. They gathered the squatter's blankets and their few personal items, put them into three saddlebags, and then walked to the barn for its inspection. They found nothing disturbed there and returned to the back of the cabin and toward the river to see if their culprits had returned. They stood and listened again for possible sounds of rustling leaves or broken branches, and heard nothing.

"I guess we scared them away, boys. I thank you all, but it looks as if there is nothing else we can do." James had a look of disgust on his face and brushed his hair out of his eyes with the back of his hand. "I will lock the door and we will come back in a few days to check it all again."

In an attempt to lock the door, James found the squatters had broken the lock, and realized there was nothing he could do to repair it. They all mounted their horses and rode back to Atwater.

Two days later James took the same men back to the cabin where they found the invaders, who must have been angry for them taking their blankets and belongings, had tried to burn down the cabin. They were not successful, and James thanked God for that. Flames that for some reason did not burn long had extinguished yet blackened the outside of the bedroom wall. James realized they must not have had enough of whatever they used to light the fire, to relight it once it went out. On the inside, they had pulled Jess' wedding veil curtains off the walls and ripped them to pieces. They also cut the old mattress left there into shreds. James thanked God that was all they did as they all helped clean up the mess. He inspected the burnt wood on the cabin and saw it would be an easy repair.

It was then he asked his men if any of them wanted to live in the cabin to prevent this from happening again. James knew it was a half hour ride to town from here and offered to whoever lived here would start work at the lumberyard a half hour later than usual each day. All the young men stood silently, looking at each other for their replies, and heard nothing.

"Well, it was food for thought. Let's get back to town, men, and pray these culprits don't return." James truly thought one or two of the men would jump at the chance to live in the cabin.

They rode back to town in silence and James could tell they were all thinking about his offer. His real concern now was how to tell Jess about her wedding veil curtains.

After dinner and the children were in bed, James sat next to his wife in front of the fireplace, where they enjoyed the dancing flames.

"I have not told you everything about the cabin, Jess. I waited until the children were asleep, because it's not good news."

"You are safe and sitting next to me, Love, so all is well." Jess smiled at her husband, put her hand on his knee, and patted it several times.

"There was destruction inside the cabin and I am sorry to say, they destroyed your wedding veil curtains. I'm sorry, Jess."

"Really? Why would they do that, I wonder?"

"They were angry that we took their blankets and things. I'm sorry."

"Ooh, don't be, James, you didn't do it." She actually smiled. James was shocked.

"Well, the veil served more than one purpose and like I said before, I had no plans to use it again. I just pray they don't go back to the cabin and destroy more. What are we going to do?"

James told her about the offer he made his men and that he truly thought one or two of them might still decide to live there.

They sat by the fire discussing the cabin and their children and soon retired, to make love by the flames in their bedroom fireplace.

The next day, James rode Stormy to their cabin to fix the broken lock. The invaders had never returned.

It was Sunday, and a beautiful Indian summer day when James and Jess had all three children in their back yard. They watched Becca play in the fallen leaves, while each of them held their sons. Ellie had come home with them after church when she begged to play with Becca.

The twins were two months old and now weighed seven pounds each. They were finally the size Becca was as a newborn. Doc Harris had done research on twins since their birth, and told Jess that it would take them a year or more to catch up in size to other children their age, yet they should treat them as they would any other baby. Sometimes that was difficult for Jess because of their size and often prayed for strength and courage not to coddle them, which would make them dependent on her forever. She knew, as they got older and started to bump things or fall, it would be *very* difficult for her.

James told Jess the mayor has called for a town meeting on Monday night and that he would be attending. "I will go there directly from the lumberyard and have my dinner after the meeting. Is that fine with you?"

"Of course, James. What is the meeting about?" Jess, who held Mark, started to bounce him on her lap as he began to fuss.

"I'm not sure; Hon. John Goldman came into the yard office yesterday and asked that both your father and I attend. I will always attend those meetings, anyway. But this is a special meeting, according to your father."

Jess grinned and told him she would keep his dinner warm and that she would ask her mother to stay longer than normal to assist her

Monday. James nodded his head, lifted Luke to his face, and kissed his son, who crinkled his face as if he tried to smile. James could not read his tiny face.

They sat in the yard as they enjoyed what was normally the last warm day before the cold and snow arrived. Jess told her husband how much she had been enjoying the friendship of Addie Higgins, Bobby's mother, since the twins were born.

"She came with gifts for the boys when they were born and we got along right away. She comes to help me three, sometimes four times a week, as you know, and we have become good friends. I am so glad to have such a good friend, as I miss my friends in England so much. I have written to Ashley twice and she has not written in return. I do miss her so and wonder why she has forgotten me."

"I am sure Ashley has not forgotten you, but some people were actually angry that we left England. Maybe she is one of them."

"She did act strange when we said good-bye, but I never thought about her being angry."

"People are odd, Jess, and you should write again. Maybe she has lost our address or the mail was lost for some reason. Give her the benefit of the doubt, my love, and I would bet you hear from her soon." James smiled and hugged her shoulder with his free hand, then quickly took hold of his son, who was beginning to fuss.

"I guess I will, Hon. I don't want to lose her friendship even though we are so far from each other. I would love to hear what's happening in her life. I haven't written to her about the twins yet, so I will write to her soon." She wrote her friend again, but never got a reply.

The boys were not happy and obviously getting hungry. She rose to heat some milk when Becca walked to her. "I hungy, Mama." Jess smiled, patted her daughter's head lightly, and asked her to follow her into the house and she would take care of that.

"Ellie, would you like something to eat?" Ellie shook her head yes and followed Jess into the house.

James sat a short time trying to appease Mark while the milk warmed before he went into the house, as he sat and admired their property. It was so peaceful, with the songs of birds and sounds of the river in the distance. He loved that they lived among the tall pines and the river and suddenly thought of his family in England. He knew if they were here, they would not only love his children and be proud of his success, but they too would love the woody area and the massive house. He looked to the azure blue cloudless sky and prayed for them and asked God to bring them all together again someday. He raised his son with outstretched arms and talked to him lovingly, as he walked to the house. Jess prepared the girls lunches while the milk warmed on the wood stove, which was still warm from breakfast. Jess had finally told Ellie she could hold the boys, separately, and she was so happy. They talked about her school lessons while they ate and each baby got a warm bottle. It wasn't long until everyone returned to the back yard to enjoy the beautiful weather.

Their peace and quiet was suddenly broken with the sound of a wagon that pulled up between the house and barn. It was Edward and Victoria, but another person was with them, but neither James nor Jess could tell who it was. Edward helped his wife to the ground then assisted another woman who stayed hidden behind Edward's large stature. Victoria laughed aloud at something the other woman said. As her parents and the hidden guest approached the Atwood's, the woman continued to walk behind Edward. When they were close to where Jess and James sat with the boys in their arms, suddenly, Lizzie stepped out from behind Edward. Jess screamed and rose so fast that Mark began to cry. She swiftly handed him to James as she ran to Lizzie and hugged her a long time. Both women hopped up and down during their long hug, laughing loudly the entire time.

"Lizzie! What a wonderful surprise!" Jess was in shock and overcome by tears. She could no longer speak.

Lizzie held her precious Jessica for a long time, before they finally parted and she asked to see her children. Jess proudly pointed to James, who held both crying boys. Lizzie took Mark into her arms and soothed the sobbing baby instantly. "His name is...?"

"Mark Thomas. Oh Lizzie, it is so wonderful to see you. It has been so long! I have missed you so!" Jess' tears continued. She almost tripped on James' feet and then introduced Mark's twin. "This is Luke Edward." James stood and put the baby closer to Lizzie so she could see

192

him and easily place her free hand on his stomach while in his father's arms. She held her hand there a moment, then raised it to James' face and stroked his chin lightly. "James, you look well. I hear you have worked hard and I see you have," as she swept her hand toward the house, "and that you have become very successful." Her smile had never stopped and soon tears ran down her face. She bent to kiss the baby in her arms, and then leaned to kiss Luke. She then kissed James hello. She turned to look down at Jess' feet at the little girl clutching her legs. "This is Becca?"

Jess had her hand on the back of Becca's head and proudly looked down at her daughter.

"Yes, this is our Becca! Becca, this is Lizzie. She is someone whom Mommy loves very much. Can you say hello to my friend?"

"'ello, 'issie." Becca still clung to her mother.

"Hello, my name is Ellie." She proudly came forward, put her arms out, and hugged Lizzie the best she could, which included Mark in her hug.

"Hello Ellie. I am Lizzie. I used to be Jessica's nanny!"

"Nanny?"

Jess laughed through her tears, smiled, and put her arm around Ellie's shoulders. "She took care of me like you take care of Becca."

"Oh. Nice to meet you. I love Becca...... and the boys too."

"That's wonderful, Ellie. I love them too."

Ellie's face looked questioned, since to her it was too soon, as she had just met Becca and the twins. She shrugged her shoulders then asked Becca if she wanted to play with the ball. When Becca shook her head yes, they both ran off to play in the grass. Then they all heard a bark from the idle wagon.

Edward and Victoria had stood by quietly, and watched the wonderful reunion with tears in both of their eyes. They had forgotten about the dog tied in the back of their wagon and hidden by Lizzie's trunks. Edward turned and quickly went to the back of his wagon, untied the dog and suddenly the cutest dog Jess had ever seen ran to Lizzie, where it stood on it's back legs with it's front paws on Lizzie's knees.

"Oh dear! Everyone, this is Truffy. He is a Cavalier King Charles Spaniel and wouldn't hurt a flea."

Jess immediately bent to pet the anxious dog, which had changed legs, and now begged at Jess' knees. "Can I pick him up?"

"He would love it if you did!" Lizzie was amazed at the sight. When she bought Truffy, she never dreamt that he would someday be in Jess' arms. Jess picked him up and he swiftly started to lick her face, which Jess turned and twisted to get away from his lapping tongue. She withstood this for a minute, and then placed him back on the ground. Victoria bent to pet him when the dog saw the girls that played in the grass. Truffy ran to them and Becca gave out a squeal. Ellie gladly pet the dog. James ran to his daughter, comforted her, and assured her that he would not hurt her and that he was just happy to meet her. Truffy had started to settle and James took Becca's hand and showed her how to pet him. She liked his soft fur and continued to pet him without her father's assistance. Soon she ran from him as he followed and she pet him again with laughter.

James joined the adults and found Jess and Victoria in a long hug.

"Mother, how could you keep this from me? It's Lizzie!"

"Darling, it was so difficult. When you were in the family way the second time, and the business was such a success, I had to send for her. She would have been here sooner, but she had to give a long notice to her employer's because they had a hard time replacing Lizzie."

Jess turned to Lizzie. "How long is your visit?"

Lizzie chuckled and kissed Jess' cheek. "I am here to stay, my sweet Jessica. Forever!"

"Eeeeeeeeee! That's wonderful. James, she is here to stay!"

"That is wonderful! We have plenty of room for you, Lizzie, and you are more than welcome to live right here."

"I was hoping you would say that. Well, I guess it's settled then, because nothing would make me happier than taking care of you again *and* your children, Jessica."

Edward scratched his chin in question. "I thought......"

194

Victoria put her hand on his arm, with a strange look in her eyes. "We can settle all of that later. Let's all enjoy this wonderful moment and the beautiful day!" Edward smiled and sat back.

They decided to have roasted beef for dinner so James and Edward started a fire in the pit. They all spent the afternoon together, talking about old times and the future. James mentioned that Lizzie's trunks should come into the house before dark and Edward held his hand up for all to see.

"We need to discuss where Lizzie will live." Victoria hung her head and waited.

"What do you mean, Father?" Jess thought that had been settled.

"We brought her here to assist you and your children and also to cook and clean for us. Granted, she would be closer to the children if she lives here, and you do have room for her now, but I will bet in two years those rooms will be needed for children." He winked at Jess.

"Father..........."

Lizzie put her hand up to stop Jess. "I think if I live here and work at your home also would work well and probably would for a long time. Does it bother anyone that I have a dog?"

They all said no and she went on. "James, do you work on Saturday's?"

"Used to be every Saturday, but since the twins were born, I have only worked a few."

"Well, if I live here Monday through Friday, can I cook for all of you here on Friday's? Since James is most often here on Saturday's, I will clean your house then and have Sunday's off. Then I will return here on Monday mornings." She looked away from Edward, to check everyone's faces. "The only thing we have to figure out is how to get your meals to you Monday through Friday. I assume you are here often, if I know you Victoria." Victoria blushed and nodded her head yes. "So problem is solved. I love to cook and would love to do that for all of you. Therefore, we will enjoy some dinners together and some dinners we will be apart. Does anyone have a problem with any of it?"

They were silent, and each waited for objections. It seemed Lizzie had solved the dilemma. "Now all I have to do is figure out which clothes go to which home." She laughed and felt total happiness to be among her "family" again.

They learned Lizzie's sea voyage was wonderful and was ten weeks long.

"Traveling with a dog must have been difficult at times. On a ship, where do they..... well, you know." Jess blushed yet knew everyone was wondering the same.

"Isn't that why they call it the poop deck?" Lizzie laughed and they all joined in the laughter. The laughter was so loud that both Becca and Ellie nearly came off the floor, where they played in front of the fireplace.

"Lizzie, you will never change! That's an order!" Jess smiled and blew her a kiss.

"Ellie, it is time for me to take you home, young lady, you have school tomorrow." James sounded like a real parent. He actually scared himself.

Ellie went around the room and kissed everyone good-bye and saved Becca for last. Soon they heard the horse and buggy leave the barn. The women took the children upstairs and prepared all three for bed. Edward watched the flames in the fireplace while he sipped brandy and was not alone long before the women returned.

James returned shortly and Lizzie said she was very tired from her travels and needed to rest. She told Jess she would return in the morning after she made her parents breakfast. Jess did not want the evening to end and found it difficult to say goodnight, but finally let her go. She ran into her husband's arms when he asked if she was happy. She sunk her head into his shoulder and shook her head yes and he smiled as he kissed the top of her head.

After breakfast, as James headed for the lumberyard, he passed and waved at Edward and Lizzie on their way to Atwood Manor.

Lizzie washed their breakfast dishes as Jess bathed Becca in a small tub near the hearth. Jess was so at ease and elated when the twins cried from upstairs and she did not have to split herself into three people when she saw Lizzie dart past her toward the staircase to tend to the boys. Her mother and Addie had helped in the past, but never this early in the morning. Often she felt spent by noon. As she finished

Becca's bath, Jess, as she did every morning, said the alphabet three letters at a time, while Becca worked hard to repeat each letter. She warmed milk for the boys, and before it was ready, two babies came into the room, one in each of Lizzie's arms, and started to cry as soon as they saw their mother. They quickly prepared their bottles and each woman satisfied the hungry boys. Jess told her how she would normally attempt to feed them at the same time, which was difficult when they fussed at the same time. Lizzie grinned. "I am glad to be home!" Jess almost came to tears when she heard her words.

Their daily rhythm fell into place easily and quickly, as if they had never spent a day apart. Victoria and Addie arrived after lunch and they too were amazed at their ease in getting things done without telling each other. "Watching you two is like watching a fine tuned clock's works." Victoria was amazed but not surprised at how well they worked together.

Truffy, the dog, fit into both households comfortably, and Lizzie was very relieved.

James and Edward both built a small picket fenced area for the dog, and Lizzie was astounded at James' idea and thankful.

"I am preparing chicken for all tonight. Victoria, would you like to dine here or at home?"

"I would like to dine here. When I take Addie home, I will stop to tell Edward."

Victoria took Addie home at four o'clock and returned to Atwood Manor by 4:30. The four women enjoyed their first day as they jumped into their routine, without knowing they had done that. They had prepared Lizzie's bedroom at the end of the hall, which was easily accomplished by four women.

The men arrived home later than usual after they attended the special town hall meeting. When they entered the back door of Atwood Manor, the men sounded very happy. As they approached the women in the main room, Edward had his arm around James' shoulders and looked at the women with a wide smile.

"Ladies, you are looking at a young and very modest man." Edward patted James' back as James looked at the floor and shuffled his feet. "The town took a vote tonight and it was unanimously voted to name the road that starts at the corner of the lumberyard and winds through the woods to this beautiful home "Atwood Lane". The Johnson's, as you know own the general store, want to build a home at the bend in the road and it made the mayor more aware that the road needed a name, now that two homes will exist on the road. This, ladies, is another reason to be proud of our James here for his hard work and success." Edward was so proud of his son-in-law because he had come so far from his dock days in Liverpool.

"I suggested that it should be named Atwood Strong Lane, but your father shot that down before they all heard it. I feel honored that the town's people think that much of us to do this." James looked at his wife with wide eyes.

"Mayor Goldman told us all that the lumber business has brought so many people into the town, and they have spent money at the general store and other businesses, that the least they could do in thanks was to name a road after James Atwood." Edward stood proudly next to his son-in-law where his arm remained around James' shoulders.

Jess ran to her husband, hugged his neck, and told him how proud she was of him and that she always had been. His face remained red as everyone gathered around him with pride. Lizzie was especially thankful that she made it to America and Atwater in time to witness this event. She took special notice, on this night; how Edward had truly changed from his very stern presence, she had known in England. She realized a change in the man when she first arrived in New York City and on their trip to Atwater. She now saw a man who truly loved and cared for his family. She never thought she would see the day, but it was here.

As a family, they continued to converse about the meeting and events of the day which regarded Lizzie being settled and of course, the children. Lizzie jerked her head toward Edward when she heard he was the first to ask about the children. She looked around the room and saw all were relaxed and obviously used to this new man's ways.

Jess was astounded, since Lizzie arrived, at the end of the day when she was no longer exhausted and anxious for sleep. Now, she and her husband could lie in bed at night and talk in the dark in the summer, which they both loved to do. In the winter, they had the glow of the fire and golden flames dancing around the room to talk by or make love. Their days were so hectic and at night in bed was the only time they were alone and could enjoy each other.

The soft glow of the fire on this night made Jess embarrassed to have her husband see her naked body. Her shape had returned quickly after she delivered Becca, but it had not since she had the twins. James tried to convince her that it did not matter to him and that she was the mother of his children, and appreciated and loved her just the way she was. She heard his words, but still found it difficult to strut and move sensually in front of him as she had in the past.

Their routine established quickly where Victoria picked up Addie three days in the middle of each week, and she and Edward would eat at their own home. The other days the entire family dined together. The Atwood's and Strong's were content to divide costs for food and Lizzie's pay.

James announced at dinner one night in late October he planned to build an icehouse. He asked Edward if he could borrow Bobby and Tim from the lumberyard for three days for its construction, and he agreed, since they all would benefit from the icehouse.

The men spent three days as they dug a huge hole four feet deep and twelve feet long. They then lined it with river rocks and built roofed walls over the rock-lined hole. It had front and rear doors, where they would bring ice from the river into the back door in winter and take the ice to the house through the front door. James hoped they would also be able to preserve food through July with the previous winter's river ice. The first summer would tell him if he was correct.

Lizzie asked Edward to help her buy a horse and buggy, as she did not want to rely on anyone. Edward said he would gladly help her, which took them to Gerald's stables.

Lizzie came to work for the Strong's when her parents died when she was 15. She had no siblings, had always been independent, and would remain that way.

Edward knew it was rude to appear at Gerald's door without notice, but there was not enough time to send a letter. He hoped he was not away and that he would assist Lizzie to select the proper horse.

When they pulled up his drive, they saw smoke rising from the chimney and Edward made a big sigh of relief. Gerald warmly welcomed them and said he would be glad to assist Lizzie in selecting the proper horse for her. When Elizabeth appeared and took their bags upstairs, Lizzie was speechless. No one had served her before; she had always been the one to serve. After a wonderful lamb dinner, Gerald offered them brandy and Lizzie drank with them. She thought, I could get used to this, and giggled to herself. Both men heard her giggles, looked at her, stopped their discussion, and gazed at her in wonder. She waved her hand, and coaxed them to disregard her. Soon Elizabeth touched her shoulder and told her a warm bath had been prepared for her. Lizzie's brows rose far into her forehead. She excused herself from the men and followed Elizabeth to her waiting tub. After she disrobed with Elizabeth's assistance, she sunk into the hot water up to her chin. Never before in her life had she been this submerged in a tub. "This is heavenly." Little did she know that she and Jess had said the same exact words when they first lowered themselves into the bath tub. It made Elizabeth giggle.

Lizzie remained in the warm water and thought about how much she loved Jess, and was so thankful for the Strong's, whom she thought of as family. She let out a large sigh and pinched herself. She was back with the Strong's *and* in America. Life was grand.

The following morning, they rose early and rode into the outskirts of Albany to a huge horse ranch. Gerald thought Lizzie would like Morgan horses and when she saw them, she was in love. They held their heads like royalty and pranced, not plainly trotted. Everything about them was proud. When she saw a black female Morgan, she knew she was the one. Gerald pulled her away from the other horses and looked to Lizzie for her final approval. She nodded her head so strongly up and down, she thought she hurt her own neck and grasped her nape. Gerald brought her over to Lizzie and the horse let her pet her face, her neck and nearly everywhere else. So far, she was perfect. "I am going to ride her first and if I can handle her easily, would you like to ride her?" Gerald waited for Lizzie's nod before he walked the horse to the stable and saddled her. Ten minutes later, he returned to Lizzie, who felt like a child on Christmas morning. Gerald pointed to another training ring that was empty and Lizzie and Edward walked there quickly. Soon she watched the most beautiful horse she had ever seen prance around the ring as if she was performing in front of the Queen. After he rode the Morgan around the ring several times, he rode past Lizzie and Edward with his thumb up. He rode her to the gate and motioned Lizzie to enter. He dismounted and assisted Lizzie onto the horse, which stood patiently, and Lizzie walked her at first then kicked her ribs slightly with her boot heel into a trot. Everything felt right about this horse. She could not stop her smile and the men saw that it was a good match. "What is her name?" asked Lizzie as she passed the men on the fence with pride. Gerald shrugged his shoulders. When she dismounted and handed the reins to the groom, she asked him the same question. "Lady" was his reply. Lizzie shook her head agreeing that she was a true lady, and the name fit her very well.

Lizzie selected a fancy buggy and asked the groom to have the horse and buggy ready in an hour. From a small restaurant beside the racetrack, the three of them had lunch as they watched many horses and riders prepare for the races. When they finished and went to the stable, the groom stood waiting for them, very much like a statue. Lizzie could not believe this horse was hers. Edward brought his horse, Once More, to meet Lady. They smelled each other briefly, had no problems and were at instant ease with each other. Lizzie was so relieved, as the two horses would share Edward's barn two nights per week. Edward happily paid Gerald.

They said their good-byes and Lizzie could not thank Gerald enough for his help. She offered to make payments to Edward, to pay him back, and Edward sternly denied her money, and said he was glad to help. Soon they were off. Lizzie felt like the most important person in world when she rode in her buggy behind Lady. She gallantly followed Edward in his buggy for the three-hour ride home. She could not wait until everyone saw her beautiful horse.

When they arrived home, Edward rang the bell on his buggy to alert all of their arrival. Jess, Victoria with Becca, and Addie ran out swiftly and could not believe their eyes. The black gleaming horse and black buggy were beautiful. Lizzie sat proud and tall in her new buggy. Jess smiled wide and felt Lizzie's pride. When she told everyone the horses name was Lady, they too all nodded in agreement with her name. Edward put Lady into James' barn with hay and water. He would let James introduce Stormy and Misty to Lady, which were at the lumberyard. Some days Misty would stay at the lumberyard as she was used to make small, local deliveries. On weekends, she would be stabled with Stormy, who now would have the company of Lady through the week.

Becca's first birthday was a wonderful day for the entire family and many friends, including Bobby and Tim. James and Jess had waited a long time for her, and they were stunned that she was a year old already. She could not blow out the candle on her cake, yet she had no problem opening her many presents.

Lizzie Younger's birthday was 24 November, and Jess would not let it pass as a normal day, even though it was her day off. When the Atwood's returned home from church, which included Ellie and Addie, Jess put the twins down for a nap and Ellie played with Becca in the back yard. The women quickly prepared many dishes for Lizzie's surprise birthday party. James started a fire in the pit and placed a small pig on the spit. Soon Edward, Victoria and Lizzie arrived in their buggy. As they entered through the back door, everyone jumped out and shouted "Surprise!" which scared Lizzie as she grasped her throat. Everyone took their turn hugging her, and wished her a happy day. They all gathered in the main room, where a table full of presents waited for Lizzie. Still in shock, she opened her gifts one by one and came to tears once as she looked around the love-filled room. Lizzie briefly remembered her previous ten birthdays, which had gone unnoticed. Now, life was very, very good.

The boys woke and cried from upstairs, when Lizzie quickly jumped up to gather the hungry babies. Jess insisted she stay put because it was her special day. They spent the afternoon together and soon the pork was roasted and they all gathered around the huge dining table, which James was glad he made longer and wider than he had first planned.

Christmas Day and New Year's Eve were just as pleasant. Jess tried to stay awake until midnight to welcome 1868, but again could not do it. Victoria and Lizzie were the same. As the tradition that started when the Strong's first came to America, Edward and James continued it as they sat in front of the fireplace, drank brandy, and smoked fat cigars. As the grandfather clock chimed midnight, they clinked their glasses and shook hands.

Chapter Twenty-One
January 1868

The snows were deep that winter, which made the lumber business slow. James and Edward used that time to plan for their future and put their heads together on ideas of what to sell in addition to lumber and paint. The small pickets had sold well, yet James wanted to do more and strained his mind for more ideas. They lived in the Adirondack Mountains and he had seen "Adirondack chairs" in his travels around the county and decided the lumberyard would create a similar chair to sell. He knew Jess had loved and appreciated the many types of furniture he made for her and their home and knew similar items would sell. He designed a chair and built one for Edward's approval. Edward sat in it and thought it was very comfortable, and suggested they make tables also. They kept their employees busy that winter and had them build both chairs and tables. Soon, there were chairs and tables everywhere.

In early March, they thought they had a customer when a wagon pulled into the lumberyard. James went to the door to greet them and saw it was Teddy, with Amanda and their son, Sam. James was amazed that they had traveled in their open wagon in the winter cold and deep snow for more than three hours from Malone, New York to Atwater. He quickly escorted Amanda through the door to the fireplace for warmth. Teddy and Sam were not far behind them. James and Edward heartily greeted their friends, but their returned greetings were very subdued.

"Is something wrong, Teddy? What is it Amanda?" James was anxious to hear their explanation for such long faces.

"Junior is gone, James. He ran 'way 'nd we got no ide' where 'e went to!" Teddy did all he could to not sob. "We were wonderin' if 'e came don 'ere, or if ya seen 'im?" Teddy questioned James in hope of a positive answer.

James shook his head in a negative direction, with sad eyes at Teddy, as Amanda looked at James with hopeful eyes. Sam stood close to his mother and helped to warm her hands and feet by the fire. James quickly got three chairs and added them to the two that were permanent fixtures in winter in front of the warm flames. They all sat after Edward hugged Amanda to comfort her. She was in tears now and looked as if she had been crying for days.

"Teddy, I am so sorry to hear this. When did he leave your ranch?" James patted his friends back to console him.

"'bout three week' ago. We 'ad a nice Christmas then in da beginnin' of Febary, we had a fight and we ain' seen 'im since." He put his face in his hands and stared at the orange flames.

Amanda burst into tears and James quickly stood behind her and comforted her by putting his hands on her heaving shoulders. Teddy held her hand and Sam held the other.

Teddy and Sam were speechless, as Amanda attempted to talk. Through her breathless gasps, she was finally able to talk. "'e left on are stallion in dis col' and snow. I am so worried 'bout him, James, dat he might be frozen somewhere or starvin' ta death." Her sobs started again

James and Edward were beyond words and had no idea what to do or say next.

"You all must be hungry. Let us all go to my home where Lizzie can prepare some hot food for you and we can decide there what to do next." James was anxious and felt lost. Soon they all rose as James went to Bobby and explained the situation to him and asked him to tend the fire after they left.

Jess heard the wagon's crunch through the snow and ice in their drive and quickly looked outside. When she opened the back door, Amanda practically fell into her arms sobbing. Jess held her tightly as she searched all their faces for an answer for her tears. James worked his way to Jess, and led them all closer to the fireplace in the main room as they shed their winter coats. James explained everything to Jess, Lizzie, and Victoria, as the women gathered around Teddy and his family and comforted them. Teddy told them he brought frozen meat from his ranch and he would help bring some in when James then told him about the icehouse.

Soon the aroma of beef filled the house. Amanda found comfort as she watched Mark and Luke, who were identical and she could not tell them apart. She could not remember which color ribbon went to which baby boy. Jess smiled and told her Luke wore the yellow ribbon on this day. Amanda enjoyed watching Becca play so calmly with her twin brothers in front of the fire. She talked to them constantly and instructed them like a teacher would. Everyone giggled when she was the instructor. Amanda was amazed to hear letters of the alphabet come from Becca. They were not in the proper order, but she knew many. The boys listened to her steadfastly, without blinking. Yet this reminded her of her sons and she began to cry again. Becca used Amanda's knee to raise herself off the floor and with wide, bright eyes, looked Amanda in the eye. "Sad?" Becca patted her knee and Amanda chuckled. Becca walked well now and side stepped to Teddy with outstretched arms. He gladly picked her up and kissed her rosy cheek. He hugged her closely as he closed his eyes and held their embrace for a moment. Becca loved her Uncle Teddy and giggled when his hairy kisses tickled her cheek or neck.

After they ate stew stocked with beef, they sat again in front of the fire and discussed what to do next. James had thought Junior had possibly gone to Gerald's, but they had not seen Gerald since the first snowfall. Teddy was at a loss, and so was James. Teddy explained that they had checked with all of Junior's friends and in all towns between Malone, where they lived, and Atwater with no results.

James and Edward felt terrible for their friend, but James had family and business responsibilities and he couldn't leave. Edward could not travel in the cold, as his nearly 50-year-old bones were afflicted with arthritis, which got worse every year. Teddy asked if Amanda and Sam could stay with the Atwood's while he went south in search of his son. James and Jess quickly nodded their heads and assured Teddy verbally that they could stay as long as necessary. Amanda fought this when she admitted she wanted to go with him, but Teddy speedily told her he would tackle the cold and snow alone. Lizzie and Victoria prepared food for Teddy's journey as Jess tended to her children's needs.

Soon Bobby and Tim arrived on horseback and wanted to know about their friend, Junior. After Teddy questioned them and they admitted they had not seen Junior, they offered to help any way they could. James asked if one of them would take Sam home with him to get his mind off of his missing brother, even if it's just for one night. Tim said he would gladly do that and they left together atop his horse.

The Atwood home was astir long before sunrise when they all ate breakfast together then helped Teddy load for his cold trip. Spring was around the corner, but had not arrived yet. Teddy hugged and kissed his sobbing wife and after his many thanks and goodbye's and was off into the still, white landscape. His plan was to check at Gerald's then go into New York City and search there for his son. He was only familiar with parts of the city, and Junior could be anywhere.

James felt terrible as he watched his friend disappear into the snow scape, yet he knew Teddy would make better ground alone. He and Jess discussed where Junior could possibly have gone, but they hardly knew him and could only guess. Sam came to the lumberyard with Tim and worked beside him all day. James insisted they all follow him home for supper. After they ate, James and the boys started a fire in the pit, cleared snow from the area the best they could and the adults drank beer.

"Sam, do you have any idea where Junior might have gone?" James was very concerned.

"Naw, but I know he sure was mad. Pa won't tell me what the fight was about, and I don' know if he tol' Ma or not, but Junior was really mad. He only took enough clothes to fit in two saddlebags and was gone. He dint take no food, nor nothin'."

James scratched his head and took a long drink of his beer. As he gazed into the fire, he thought about the future and his two sons and prayed to God this would never happen with them. He didn't know what he would do. He prayed for Teddy and Junior, and their safety and prayed that he found his son quickly. The night had gotten colder and they did not stay by the fire pit long.

After one week, Teddy still had not returned and James was scared for his friend. The weather had gradually warmed and the streets were nothing but mud. James asked Bobby, Tim, and Sam to break up the river ice and began to fill the icehouse to its roof with ice. They did this daily until spring was in full bloom.

To stay busy Amanda baked daily, made all the meals, and knitted half a blanket in one week. Whenever Jess found her staring out the window, she would get her involved with the twins or Becca. Then she decided it would be a good time to make summer clothes for the children. Lizzie and Victoria stayed with the children while Jess and Amanda went to the general store in search of fabrics. Jess found six flowered fabrics for the many summer dresses she wanted for Becca and the usual plain grays and browns for the twins. Amanda and Jess both prayed Teddy's wagon would be there when they got home, but there was no sign of him.

They all gathered for dinner at the dining table that evening. They replaced the usual grace they said, joined hands, and said a lengthy family prayer for Teddy and Junior. Amanda broke down quickly and Lizzie held her while she cried. She apologized then insisted everyone eat. They enjoyed leg of lamb, small potatoes, Victoria's jarred carrots, and winter lettuce. Edward said business was improving since the days had started to get warmer, and said they had sold six chairs and two tables already. He patted James' shoulder and winked at Jess. It warmed her heart.

They remained around the table and talked for hours. Lizzie attempted to clear the table, but James would not let her, as she was part of the family and dishes could come later. The grandfather clock chimed eight times and Jess picked up Becca to prepare her for bed. Suddenly they heard a wagon come up the drive and Amanda ran for the door. Everyone knew it had to be Teddy because she ran outside without a coat. James ran to the door while he put on his coat and carried Amanda's coat, lit a lantern and started outside. Everyone gathered at the windows, in hope to see Junior next to his father in the wagon. It was so dark they could not see a thing. Soon James' lantern lit up the front of the wagon and they saw that Teddy sat alone. They watched Amanda as she ran next to the wagon before it came to a halt. Teddy jumped down swiftly to embrace his wife and still in that hug, Teddy shook James' hand. Together they pulled the horse and wagon into the barn and disappeared into the darkness.

At this time, Jess took Becca to each of her family as they each kissed her good night.

It took time for the horse to be unhitched from the wagon, fed and watered, yet the family waited patiently by the windows in silence. Finally, they saw the light of James' lantern and saw that Teddy kept his arm around his wife as the three of them made their way to the back door. Edward saw that Teddy was exhausted and Lizzie asked if he was hungry. Teddy nodded his head as he greeted everyone with separate head nods and fell into a chair at the table. "Junior is alive!"

Lizzie quickly jumped up and prepared a plate for him. He hunched over the plate, devoured the lamb, carrots, and potatoes, and then asked for more. Lizzie gladly obliged, and they all silently watched him eat. Jess soon appeared in the room, ran to Teddy, and hugged him very tightly. She asked her father if he could prepare a whiskey or brandy for Teddy and Edward stood quickly and poured the tired man three fingers of whiskey. Teddy thanked him and drank half of the whiskey in one gulp. He rested the glass on the table without removing his hand. Teddy took two deep breaths, then downed the remainder of the whiskey, looked at Edward, and without words, Edward filled his glass again. Teddy nodded his head to the elder, and finished his dinner. Amanda sat next to her husband and fidgeted the entire time he ate, yet never said a word. Finally, Teddy sat back in his chair and patted his full stomach. He reached for his wife's hand, squeezed it, and said to the room of patient people, "Junior is 'live an' is at Geral's." Amanda sobbed into his shoulder and they all cheered and were instantly relieved. Teddy looked like he had been to hell and back. Jess and Lizzie went to the kitchen and pulled the tub to the hearth, and then filled buckets from the pump in the back yard. Jess filled the boiling pot with water and knew Teddy would want a very hot bath and started a second boiling pot.

"Ya see, Junior got mad a' me when h' wanted,...... well, he's bee' askin' fer me ta pay 'im fer 'is work fer 'bout a year now, I guess, an'....wel' I don' make 'nough money t' pay my boys an' eat too, so I kep' tellin' 'im I couldn do dat....an' he got mad. So he rode t' Geral's and got him a payin' job dere workin' wit' 'orses. I been dere tryin' t' tal' 'im into comin' 'ome an' he won' do it." Teddy looked into his wife's red and swollen eyes then. "I am sorra Manda bu' h' wants t' have money in 'is pocket an' ya know we can' pay 'im." Amanda bowed her head because she knew her son and just then realized he was gone for good. "Geral' tried t' make 'im unnerstand 'bout family an' all, bu' Junior ha' made up 'is mind. Geral' said he woul' take goo' care a 'im and said we coul' visit anytime. Geral' sai' he sen' a litter, but we aint neve' got it"

With that, he smiled and tried to get Amanda to smile, but she was not able to yet.

The discussion continued for another hour when Teddy explained that he stayed there for the week to try to convince his son to come home, that his mother's heart was broken, but Junior had made up his mind and decided to stay at Gerald's stables.

"I am just glad that he is safe and I am sure everyone here feels the same way, Teddy. Thank the Lord his is okay and is well, and is becoming a man. And you know Gerald will pay him well and work him hard." James laughed when he said the latter. "Junior loves horses and he will learn a lot working with Gerald. Again, we are all glad he is safe."

Everyone had listened intently and expressed their concerns to Teddy, Amanda, and Sam. Soon Edward announced it was time for him and Victoria to leave. Lizzie heard one of the boys starting to cry and ran up the stairs after she said good night to the Strong's. Jess kissed her parents and followed Lizzie up the stairs.

Teddy, Amanda, and Sam left the next morning for their ranch and life went back to normal.

Becca walked everywhere now and the twins had started to crawl. The staircase concerned Jess and asked James for a solution. He instantly made a picket fence gate at the top of the stairs. Jess kissed her husband. "I knew you would do something that made perfect sense." She was relieved, as Becca was getting out of her crib on her own and for her safety, James made her a "big girl bed" and they put her crib into the empty fourth upstairs bedroom.

They were still using ribbons to differentiate the twins but it was time to change their method. Mark, the patient, loving boy, never removed his blue ribbon. Luke, however, had a mind of his own and yanked his ribbon off his ankle the first chance he got. Jess decided the only way to "mark" them was that they have different haircuts. She hated the idea of cutting their beautiful blonde hair, but it was necessary. She knew Luke would never sit still long enough for a haircut and decided Mark probably would sit quietly. She sat him in the kitchen with Truffy in his lap and carefully trimmed his straight blonde hair around his ears. Luke's hair would remain longer. When she was finished, she told Mark he looked like a prince and asked him for a kiss. He swiftly puckered his lips to kiss his mother.

James was shocked that evening when he arrived home and saw Mark's haircut. He gave Jess a questioning look because he knew Jess adored their beautiful, almost white, blonde hair.

"Daddy, do you like Mark's prince haircut?" She winked at her husband and he then realized what she had done and why.

"My, young man, aren't you handsome! Let me hold my prince and get a kiss." Mark raised his arms to his father and they kissed hello. Luke was at his feet with his arms out too. James picked him up, a son in each arm, and kissed him too. "My other prince!" Soon Becca was pulling on James pants and wanted a kiss too. He squatted down, kissed his daughter, and put his arms around all three of his children in a loving, hug. Jess loved these moments and was very thankful to witness them.

After the children were in bed that evening, being winter, James and Jess took their usual posture in front of the fire, and in summer, they were outside next to the fire pit, letting the children romp in the grass until bedtime.

He added wood to the fire and said he had news tonight. He told her that two men from the lumberyard had taken his offer to live in their cabin.

"Do you remember Charlie Stone and Dave McHenry that work at the yard?"

"I do, dear. They are nice young men, if I remember correctly." Jess smiled and watched the reflection of the flames in her husband's wide brown eyes.

"They are going to live in the cabin for two reasons. It will prevent invaders and this summer they are going to thin trees west of the cabin and east of the barn."

"Thinning, what is that?"

"Thinning is not clearing; they take out bigger trees in an area and leave the smaller trees to grow. That way, there's now room for new growth and then someday, when the now smaller trees are big trees and we cut those, the new growth starts and on goes the rotation. That way, the land is never clear of trees and they keep growing as the lumberyard grows too. Do you understand?"

"Yes I do. That will take years, but it is far better than farming, since you don't have to mind the crops and such, it's just nature taking its course. How clever you are, my handsome man." Jess leaned her head into his chest and they both stared into the flames.

James tilted her head to kiss her tenderly, but their love took over, their kisses became heated and soon their passion overpowered them and James wanted to make love to his wife in front of the fire. Jess was not comfortable with that, yet did not like refusing her husband. He giggled, snatched her hand from his chest, and together ran up the stairs as if they were teenagers.

From bed, as they lay there talking, they heard the horses whinnying and two or three kicks to their stall walls, which was not normal. James said he would return soon, after he checked on the animals. In the barn, he checked each horse and the cow and found nothing, not understanding why they were acting up.

However, he did not know he was not alone in the barn.

That summer Lizzie spent her days-off working with Lady in the training ring James constructed for her in a new clearing behind the barn. She thought of entering contests, but had no way of knowing how to do that except through Gerald. When he arrived in June for a visit, Lizzie cornered him and asked him how she could go about doing this.

Gerald wanted to take Lizzie to his ranch and the racetrack for one week where she would gain the knowledge she needed. He knew after one week that she would know if she wanted to pursue training and showing horses. The Atwood's and Strong's were in agreement for her to take a week off.

The men stood near the fire pit while turning a beef roast on the spit.

"How is Junior doing on your ranch?" James prayed the answer was a positive one.

"He's doing a great job. He knows animals well and he gets along well with the other hands, which was a big part of whether I kept him or not. I am very happy with his work. I feel bad about the family separation and I pray Teddy and Amanda visit him soon. I think they would be surprised and be very content knowing he is a fine young man that works hard. Teddy taught him very well. He just needs to be appreciated and he's getting to that age where he wants his own things. It's a shame that Teddy couldn't provide that for him, but they should rest knowing I look after him like I would my own son." Gerald had looked away from the flames and kept constant eye contact with James.

James saw how serious he was and recognized his pride. Gerald and Teddy had been friends for years, and he had watched Teddy's son grow up. "How is Sam taking all of this?"

"I don't know if he understands it all, but what I saw when they were here, he spent most of his time comforting his mother. Amanda was very upset and probably still is. I just hope she doesn't blame Teddy. I know they all work very hard and things are what they are with his ranch. What's his ranch like, Gerald?"

"Well, I don't know quite how to explain it. It's big, but very rustic. He doesn't use the modern methods in hardly anything he does there. They get by. His meats are very good and he definitely knows how to make the right cuts. Their days are long and since it's just them, they are all very busy, so you have to hand it to the guy. I think he told me once, that he's the fourth generation on that ranch, and he probably runs it like his father, and his father's father did, so there won't be any changes made soon, if at all." Gerald then added a piece of wood to the fire, and both men watched as the flames grew around the new wood and soon it was enveloped.

"Teddy's one hell of a guy, Gerald. He would give you the shirt off of his back and I think a lot of him and know we will stay friends until death." James took a half step back from the heat of the fire.

"He *is* one hell of a guy. The day I met him and his dead horse," Gerald chuckled, "I knew he was a good man. Amanda, too, is a wonderful woman. I have never asked how they met, but it's obvious they were made for each other."

"She is a great girl. She was so wonderful the night the twins were born. I will always love her for that. Jess raves about her. I just wish they lived closer to us and you."

"Yes, I have often thought that myself. There's no way they would leave Malone. I would like to go there for a visit, but I think they need to see Junior at work first so they can see him in action with their own eyes and not just hear my enthusiastic words. Therefore, I will wait. He should need to go to Albany and New York City soon with meat and I hope he brings Amanda with him. Sam is old enough to stay alone now, so that shouldn't be a problem, if they don't bring him with them."

James nodded his head in agreement, as he stared, mesmerized by the flames.

The beef roast was ready and they took it into the house.

Gerald truly enjoyed the children and played with them every chance he had. He loved to spoil them with gifts and Becca was fully aware of that fact and now asked what he brought her when he arrived at each visit. She was upset when she saw Lizzie pack a travel bag and it took her a long time to convince Becca she would only be gone one week. Becca still cried when Jess put her to bed. She had to read two books until Becca finally slept.

Mark and Luke heard Becca's sobs and they cried too. Lizzie tried to settle them down but it took James and Jess to calm them both. They rocked them in front of the fireplace as Gerald read aloud. James heard his friend's voice lilt in the bedtime story and his heart ached for him, knowing he never had children, but loved them. When the boys couldn't fight sleep any longer, he offered to take Luke from Jess and put him to bed. Jess stayed in the rocker and watched the two men slowly climb the stairs with her sleeping boys held lovingly in the men's arms. It brought tears to her eyes.

Gerald laid Luke in his crib and stroked his back gently as he settled into slumber. He motioned to James that he wanted to peak into Becca's room to observe her asleep. James nodded his head and Gerald gently opened her door to see his "little princess", he called her, asleep on her back, with arms outstretched and gone to the world. He thought his heart would melt. He had never told anything but the truth and the truth was Becca was the cutest little girl he had ever seen. He loved when she talked to him and looked him in the eye with her big blue eyes. He wanted to squeeze her with love. When she attempted to say "Unal Gerral", he almost went to his knees. He also admired the way Jess combed her beautiful, long, blonde hair, which always had a bow or ribbon in it. Becca was petite, like her mother, and he thought at times, she looked like a china doll, and the spitting image of her father.

However, her personality and femininity were all Jess. Gerald often thought of Becca as an angel on earth.

He returned to the boy's room, where James stood and stared in amazement at his twin boys. Gerald took in the view, sucked in a breath and swallowed the lump in his throat, then gazed at Mark. He too, like Becca, slept on his back with arms outstretched. He and Luke too, were exact images of James. Their big brown eyes were even bigger than James' eyes. That, he thought, was what James must have looked like when he was a young boy. They crawled everywhere now and Jess or Lizzie, never got any rest when they were awake. Their personalities showed more every day and Mark was definitely going to be just like his father. Luke, however, was a different story. He had a mind of his own, fought for what was his, and let everyone know about it. Gerald envied James in so many ways, yet these two boys were going to give James a "run for his money" as they grew up. That he did not envy.

Gerald knew they wanted more children and wondered where they got their strength. Their home had six bedrooms and if he knew James, they would fill them with children.

Gerald had arrived on "Beginner", his black stallion. He was a beautiful horse that loved to show himself off and refused to pull a buggy or wagon. When Gerald and Lizzie left in the morning, it was difficult for James to decide which black horse was the best-looking animal. They both shimmered in the early morning sun, and both pranced down the drive to Atwood Lane. Gerald trotted Beginner next to Lizzie in her buggy as they made their way to his stables and racetrack.

The groom took Beginner and Lady to the stable for the afternoon as Lizzie learned her way around the horse ranch and racetrack. She stood next to one trainer in the ring as she watched him work with his horse on a long lead, giving verbal commands as he cracked his whip in the air. The second trainer that Gerald introduced her to, asked her to watch and learn from the fence, doing the same as the first trainer, with different verbal commands.

Lizzie felt as if she had found her calling. It was wonderful for her and she could not wait to work with Lady.

The next day two "Dressage" trainers taught and assisted her and Lady to learn the many "dance" steps with whip commands. Lizzie wished she could see from afar what they looked like because it felt grand and Lady's posture was perfect.

"Lady must rest, Liz. I will give you another horse to ride to my home for the next few nights. He's a gentle soul. I hope you trust my opinion." Gerald rubbed Lady's neck and noticed she was very wet with sweat. He handed her rein to the groom and asked him to rub her down and feed her oats. The boy nodded to Gerald and took the reins. Lizzie watched as Lady strutted away and never looked back. She realized Gerald was correct and that he knew horses very well. The horse she rode home on was a gentle soul, and she was glad to rest.

Elizabeth had dinner waiting on the wood stove and the aroma of chicken and rosemary filled the air. Lizzie had not realized how hungry she was until the plate was in front of her. She and Gerald spent a pleasant evening in the back yard, enjoyed the summer breeze, and talked about nothing but horses. Elizabeth asked her when she would like her bath and Lizzie, still not used to a servant, told her nine o'clock would be fine. The hours flew by and Lizzie was shocked when Elizabeth soon tapped her shoulder and told her the warm tub awaited her. With that, she let Elizabeth assist her bath and found the sheets turned down when she entered the blue bedroom with white wicker furniture.

Lizzie spent the next two days with Lady, and together they learned the steps and moves used in competition. She had sore feet and arms the second day, and was glad she was able to ride the buggy to Gerald's home.

"I am very proud of Lady, Gerald. She did great today. I can't tell you how much I appreciate all that you are doing for me and for Lady. This has been a dream of mine for a long time. In England, I never owned a horse and always fancied them from afar. Since I was a small child, I have always wanted to do this. I thank you from the bottom of my heart."

"You are welcome, Liz. I watched you today and I could tell you were in your glory. It warms my heart to see you so happy and it looks like we picked the right horse for you. Lady is beautiful in the ring and I would be willing to bet you will be winning blue ribbons in no time. When will you be able to do this, since you work six days a week?"

"I am not sure, but if there's a will there's a way." Lizzie smiled as she raised her glass to Gerald and he raised his glass to her.

Friday night, Gerald and Lizzie were stunned when Elizabeth came to the back to announce visitors. Behind her stood James, Jess, Edward, Victoria, and 3 children.

"Oh my goodness!" Lizzie had her hand at her throat as she approached Jess. She kissed her and James, took Becca in her arms, then kissed Victoria and Edward. Becca strongly wrapped her arms around Lizzie's neck, and they stayed there a long time. Their faces were stuck together, literally. She had missed Lizzie during the week and she told her so.

"We came to see what you are up to, Lizzie. How's it been going?" James put his arm around her shoulders and squeezed.

She looked at all of them, and tears came to her eyes. Gerald greeted everyone and gathered chairs enough for all to sit. Lizzie explained to all what she and Lady had learned, and although she was very sore, she said she would gladly show them tomorrow at the racetrack.

The twins quickly found themselves in trouble after they crawled off the stones, into the grass and tipped a potted plant over on their way to the next pot. Jess swiftly snatched up Mark and Victoria took Luke in her arms as James reset the pot, scooped up the lost dirt, all the while apologizing to Gerald. Gerald told him not to worry about it and asked James to sit and relax.

"I like the haircut on Mark. Now I can tell them apart!" Gerald smiled as he watched James finally settle after he had insisted to clean the mess the twins made.

"I think it was such a good idea too, Gerald. Aren't they the most darling boys?" Lizzie then turned to her family.

"I am shocked and very glad to see you all. This is wonderful!" Lizzie had tears in her eyes. "Wait until you see how beautiful and graceful Lady is. This week has been wonderful. Gerald has been the most gracious host and Elizabeth is so kind to me. You all must come and watch tomorrow."

"We plan to - all of us!" Jess smiled and was so glad to see her best friend so happy.

They all took turns minding the twins, while Becca remained hung on Lizzie's neck.

The next morning everyone arrived at Gerald's horse ranch and Lizzie quickly readied Lady. Gerald guided the group to the training ring where Lizzie would soon appear. Jess watched her lifelong friend swollen with pride enter the ring with her pure black Morgan. They all watched as Lizzie directed her horse in Dressage, doing tricky and amazing steps, and backward at times. They all clapped loudly when they finished. Lizzie's smile was broad and bright as she rode over to her family.

"We have worked hard, and there's more." Lizzie took Lady through the gate where the groom helped her remove her saddle. They re-entered the ring where Lizzie had Lady on a long lead and she led the horse to the middle of the ring. She had a long whip, stood in place and while she gave one-word signals and cracked the whip in the air, Lady did more complicated steps and beautiful prances. When done, Lizzie turned to her family and bowed, as Lady knelt down on one front knee and bowed her beautiful head. Everyone was amazed and applauded wildly.

Suddenly, behind them, came a shrilling whistle. All turned to see Junior, with his fingers in his mouth, who continued to whistle at Lizzie and her amazing black horse.

James ran to him, they hugged and walked back to the family. He was so glad to see everyone and was shocked at the children's growth.

"Junior, you look well!" Jess was thrilled to see their friend's son doing so well.

He joined them for lunch where he explained that he was a horse groomer and trainer. He told them he lives in the cabins behind the horse ranch, has many friends, and is paid well. He asked about his family and James told him all he knew, which wasn't much since they had not seen Teddy for months. Gerald invited him to dinner at his home with everyone. He gladly accepted then had to return to work.

"Lizzie, what are your plans with all that you've learned?" James had seen her happiness and feared they would lose her.

"Well, I would like to start a horse club for Atwater County, where others can train and learn in the ring you made for me and we can represent the County in competitions here, in Albany. Is that something that you would allow in your ring?"

"Of course! I think you may have more interested in what you are doing than you think. We can place posters at the lumberyard and general store and word of mouth will travel through the county. Lizzie, follow your dream. I will help you whenever you need it!"

"Thank you James. I will begin as soon as we return home. Thank you."

"Lizzie, you both were beautiful in that ring. I am amazed at what you learned in less than a week." Jess hugged her shoulders. Becca reached for Lizzie, who gladly took her in her arms. "'orsy!" said Becca, as she pointed to Lady.

"Yes, my love, horsy." Lizzie kissed her cheek and reached for each of the twins in their grandparent's arms, and gently stroked each of their chins, whose wide eyes searched everywhere as they tried to understand their new surroundings.

Junior arrived for dinner, where Gerald's hired hands had prepared seven chickens on the spit over the fire pit. They enjoyed dinner, served by Elizabeth, and learned from Junior that he had no plans of returning to his father's ranch and was very happy working for Gerald. James wished Teddy and Amanda were there to see their beaming son.

"Do you have a message for your family if we see them soon?"

"Jus' tell 'em dat I love 'em and miss 'em and day can visit me anytime." Junior bowed his head, yet felt he had found his new home, with no regrets.

"I will do that, Junior. I hope to see them soon. He should be heading for New York City soon, if I know your father." James prayed that his statement was correct.

The Atwood's and Strong's left Gerald's ranch early the next morning, and Lizzie followed in her buggy, with Jess and Becca by her side.

That evening, the photographer arrived at Atwood Manor after dinner and took many family photographs. He told them he would bring the tin types to church on Sunday. Jess wrote two long letters to Emily and James' parents, which she would mail Monday morning with the photographs.

When she arrived at the post office Monday morning to send her mail, Mr. Jones had a letter waiting for her from Emily. She did not open it after she decided she and James would read it together after dinner. James anxiously opened the letter from his sister, while his children happily played in their fenced area in the back yard. Jess stood closely to her husband as he ripped the envelope open.

"Dear James and Jess ~ I am sorry to tell you this news, but father died on 4 March. He had a heart attack while at work and passed quickly. Mother has moved in with us, where she deeply grieves. We all do. We buried Father next to his parents and it was a nice service. John and the children are doing well. I hope you are all well. Your children must be getting big.

I feel you should know the last time I saw Father he talked about how proud he was of you and how much he missed you. Mother agreed with him and she has asked me to send you her love. We all love you and miss you very much. I look forward to the next photograph of your growing family. I am sure they are lovely, James. It's not the same here without you, so please stay in touch. May God Bless you all and keep you safe. All my love, Emily"

James and Jess threw their arms around each other and both sobbed. Lizzie witnessed their tears and quickly ran to them when Jess handed her the letter. She read it and put her arms around both of them. "I am so sorry for your loss, James. Jess, my dear, is there anything I can do for either of you?"

"Can you please take this letter to my parents? I think they should know." Jess immediately went to her children and, after kissing each child, she watched them play. James joined her, placed his arm around her waist as they stood together, and watched their young children. It made them both sad that their children would never know their father's father, a kind, and loving man.

James deeply felt the loss of his father and had never felt farther away from England and his family than he did right now. He recalled how hard his father had worked and how his grandfather had died at the same age as his father, doing the same thing. He never wished so badly that his parents had followed him to America as he did now. He knew he would feel the loss of his father for a long time. Jess did not know what to do for James. Her grandparents both died when she was very young of consumption, and hardly remembered them, and had never had a family loss since.

Soon Lizzie returned and it wasn't long until Edward and Victoria came into their drive. Victoria ran to James and held him without words. Edward placed his hand on James' shoulder and then Victoria stepped to Jess as Edward hugged James. Jess cried into her mother's neck, and quickly stopped because she didn't want the children to see her cry. The five adults walked to the chairs near the rear of the house and talked about Thomas and Mary Atwood. James shared many good memories of his youth and his father with everyone, as they all listened intently.

Chapter Twenty-Two
August 1868

The 25th of August began with a deafening thunderstorm. Jess was so disappointed in the weather and had to change the twin's first birthday party plans from outside to inside. She and Lizzie quickly made the necessary changes after breakfast. They expected ten children for the party and Jess thought about canceling the party because the rain was coming down hard with no signs of stopping.

Mark and Luke both started walking in July and Jess felt they ran ten miles by the end of each day, and today was no exception. James installed pickets at the base of the stairs for safety, of which Jess was very thankful. Jess asked the party guests to arrive by ten o'clock and by eleven o'clock, only three children had arrived with their mothers for the party. The weather had definitely kept people home. They played pin the tail on the donkey and hide and seek before lunch. Lizzie had made separate birthday cakes for Mark and Luke, and after they tried to blow out their candles, which Becca had to complete, they both dove into their cakes. There was cake everywhere, including their hair. Jess could not remember laughing so much as she had when she watched her boys and their cakes. The third and bigger cake was for guests, and there was plenty left for family, after dinner.

James loved when he came home at night when his three children and beautiful wife ran to the door all wanting his kisses and hugs. He never felt more loved and alive as he did in those moments. Soon grandmother and grandfather arrived and the kisses and hugs were shared by all, and then the boys saw more presents in their grandparent's arms. Jess had a difficult time with Becca, when she did not understand why the presents were only for her brothers. She cried for a moment, and then saw that Luke needed help to open his birthday present, crawled down from her mother's lap, and helped him undo the big yellow bow. He had no trouble removing the paper.

James and Edward were planning an end-of-summer party for the employees of the lumberyard and their families. Bobby rode to the cabin to let Charlie and Dave know about the party and returned with a good report to James.

"They have almost completed the thinning you wanted beside the barn and are a week away from thinning the other side of the cabin. They told me they would come into town for the party, and then they would return with our draft horses to move the cut trees. They have cut down some mighty big trees, James. I don't know how you're going to get them to the yard's saws, but they have many trees cut and waiting."

"Well, we will have to figure that out. We need to get the trees here and cut so they can dry over winter. I will discuss this with Edward, as it might be time to start using the river."

"Using the river?" Bobby's face looked questioned as he waited for James to explain.

"Someone will float them down the river to behind my home, so we will have to erect a stop in the river."

Bobby scratched his head, and couldn't imagine what James was talking about, but he was willing to learn. He and James had worked together a long time and Bobby admired him greatly. He now knew the lumber business well, yet still learned something new often. He also appreciated the way Edward thought and had seen many times why he and James had become such successes.

"James, you know that I will do for you and Edward whatever it takes to get the job done and I am anxious to see what the heck you are talking about."

James chuckled at his latter statement, but then approached Bobby, shook his hand, and thanked him for being such a good friend and hard worker.

"You know the business well, Bobby, and you are about to learn more. But we have to move swiftly to create the stop in the river, because the weather will be changing soon."

James asked Jess to write letters to Gerald and Teddy, inviting them to the party, which she did. Gerald replied quickly saying he would definitely be there. They heard no response from Teddy, but assumed he and his family would attend.

Addie, Bobby's mother, came to Atwood Manor every day before the party to help the women prepare food for the party.

Gerald arrived Friday afternoon and after dinner, as usual, the men gathered around the fire pit and women at the dining table. James did not want the separation on this night and after he kissed his children good night, he insisted the women join them around the fire pit. Addie had to return home, and after their goodbyes to her, the women joined the men. Tables had been set up for the party, and when the women came outside, Bobby and Tim moved the tables to surround the fire pit. They shared stories and laughs for hours, when Lizzie heard one of the boys crying through their open window. Jess said she would go to him. When she returned she told everyone it was after midnight and she needed to say good night, for tomorrow was going to come quickly and be a very busy day. Victoria and Lizzie agreed, said their good nights, as Victoria looked at Edward with begging eyes. He took his last drink of beer and walked her to their buggy.

"You have quite a family, my friend. I am glad to know you all!" Gerald raised his beer to James, Bobby, and Tim, who returned his bottle salute.

James discussed the stop they needed to build in the river and Gerald remained quiet as he listened to the three men as they put their ideas together, and arrive at a final plan.

"I think it's going to take all the men you have to do this, James. Can I help in any way?" Gerald did not know much about working in a river, but would help his friend whenever he could.

"I appreciate your offer, Gerald, but I think I am going to have all the muscle I will need." James clapped his shoulder and squeezed it. "You are a good friend."

It was a nice evening, and the men decided to stoke the fire and sleep around the pit.

Suddenly, the men were awakened by a screaming horse and cracking wood from it kicking the stall walls. Everyone scrambled and quickly entered the barn, but it was so dark they could hardly see anything. James quickly went to Misty to calm her down and found blood gushing from her neck. He removed his shirt and wrapped it around her wound with Gerald's help. They thought they were alone with the horse, and just as they wondered where Bobby and Tim had gone, they saw their silhouettes through the door with the fire pit embers behind them. When James could focus through the dark, he saw four men standing at the fire pit. Bobby and Tim had each overpowered a man running from the back of the barn and had them secured in their angry grips.

Misty was still neighing loudly and kicking, which greatly worried James. He felt along the door and found the lantern, took it to the fire pit and lit it there. The two men Bobby and Tim were holding stood silently with hanging heads.

James quickly went to Misty and saw that his shirt around her neck was completely saturated with blood. He asked Gerald to take the lantern and look for rags in the far corner of the barn. Gerald did that and returned quickly with the few that he found. James asked him to hold the lantern to Misty's neck and saw a deep wound, still gushing blood. The horse was skittish, which made her heart pump faster, and James needed her to settle down, to help stop the bleeding. He asked Gerald to help him get her on the ground, which he did, while Gerald held the horses head in his lap. James had never stitched an animal before and was not sure where to start. The bell that had hung on the cabin porch, now hung on the inside of the big barn door and James quickly ran to it, and pulled the leather strap on the clangor and rang the bell for half a minute. He hated the thought of waking his children, but he needed Doc Harris' help. It wasn't long when Lizzie ran to the barn, after passing the men at the fire pit with a wide stance.

"James, what's wrong?"

"Lizzie, Misty has been stabbed, and I need you to hold pressure on her wound while I ride into town for Doc Harris." She nodded her head, acknowledged Gerald, and immediately went to Misty's neck. James saddled Stormy quickly and rode her out the door to Bobby, Tim and the two villains.

"Will you two be alright?"

"We have them, James. Go do what you have to do."

The fire wasn't big enough to throw light onto the four men, and James couldn't make out any faces. He pulled Stormy's rein to the left to start her down the drive when he saw Jess standing on the back porch.

"Get back inside and lock the door, Jess! I will return soon!" He waved his arms violently at her when he kicked Stormy's ribs and flew past the side of the house and onto Atwood Lane.

"What happened?" Lizzie had no idea why Misty was bleeding. "Who are those men?" She looked into Gerald's eyes, only seeing fear.

"Liz, we were awakened by Misty's screams and Bobby and Tim caught the two culprits running out the back of the barn. They must have stabbed her or tried to cut her throat. I just hope Doc Harris can get here quick, because she is losing a lot of blood." Gerald searched Misty's wide, fearful eye and pet her head to comfort her. "How's the bleeding?"

"It's not good, Gerald. I don't know how bad the bleeding was five minutes ago, but it is still coming out strongly with every heartbeat." Lizzie applied more pressure than she had before. They could hear the men talking but could not make out the words and Gerald leaned closer to try to understand them, but he could not.

Bobby and Tim still held the two men by the fire pit, when Bobby screamed toward the barn that they needed rope. Gerald gently laid Misty's head down and searched many places in the barn, and finally found rope, but it was one long piece. Bobby now stood in the barn door, still holding his captive.

"That's fine. We'll tie them together. Thanks." Bobby took the rope and his man back to the fire pit where he and Tim went to work tying their hands behind their backs, then walked around them several times, winding the rope around them as he went. They had to remain standing and couldn't sit, which Bobby did on purpose. Tim added wood to the fire, which made the flames jump around the new wood, yet he still could not see the men well enough and added more wood. When the flames were almost as tall as he was, Bobby pushed the tied men to the flames, so fast, in fact, that they screamed thinking they were going into the flames. They were able to stop short of the pit as Bobby and Tim stood next to them and stared at their faces.

"You know these men?" Bobby studied each face carefully.

"Nope." Tim studied them, trying to make eye contact, which the men would not do.

"What the hell are you two doing?" Bobby shoved one of the men's shoulders.

"You took our stuff!"

"So in trade you try to kill a horse? Are you stupid?" Bobby was getting very angry. He kicked the dirt around the fire pit and walked quickly around the pit and the men several times to tame his anger.

Tim reached into the bucket for two beers, opened them, and handed one to Bobby. He took a long drink, and sat next to Tim at a table and stared at the men. They still hung their heads in shame and fear. The men looked to be in their late twenties.

"You guys deserters or fugitives?" Bobby spit beer in his words he was still so angry.

"Naw! We fought for the North and we got lost sever'l times comin' home. We tryin' to make it to Malone."

"Well, you're about three, maybe four hours south of there, by horse. It looks like you won't be getting to Malone too soon. You are fools. Tell me, how did you connect the cabin with this house?" Bobby felt like he was defending his own home. James was family.

"Ya jus' gotta ax around." The man still would not look Bobby in the eye as he answered his questions. The second man stayed silent.

Soon they heard two horses approaching and saw James and Doc Harris running their horses straight out to get to the barn. James hopped down like a trick rider and took Doc's horse reins, as he dismounted and ran to Misty. Lizzie got out of his way and Doc quickly went to work inspecting the wound.

"It's deep, Gerald. What did this?"

"We are not sure. The men who did this are out by the fire. I don't know what they used."

James ran into the barn as soon as he tied up the horses. "How is she Doc?"

"She's lost a lot of blood, James. It's a deep wound. I'm going to have to stuff it and stitch it. Can you hand me my bag, please?" James did that, took the lantern off the barn floor, and held it higher, next to Doc's shoulder. He watched as Doc worked and then stepped to the other side of the horse and sat near her prone shoulder. He knew as soon as Doc started the stitches Misty would try to rise up. Lizzie had to look away when she saw the needle and thread start their deed. Gerald had trouble holding Misty's head, but soon Doc finished the stitching and said the horse needed to get on her feet.

"They can't lay down long or they'll suffocate." Gerald told this to Lizzie, knowing the men already knew. Lizzie shook her head to let Gerald know she understood.

They all had to help Misty up to her feet, but she finally stood with very shaky legs.

"Blood loss," was all Doc said as he watched her carefully. Doc checked the wound and it was barely seeping blood. They all stayed around her for quite a while before they felt confident enough to leave her.

"Thank you so much Doc. I didn't know what to do because I knew it was deep. Thank you. If you hadn't come we probably would have lost her."

"James, it was bad. You still have to watch the wound closely. If it comes open and she starts to bleed again, come get me! You have to keep her in here and calm!" James nodded his head as he shook Doc's bloody hand.

"Would you like a beer?" Doc said he would and they swished their bloody hands in the beer bucket, each found a bottle, opened them quickly, and took long swigs. Doc finished his beer and left a lot slower than he arrived.

It was an entire minute after he took another long swig of beer before James could talk. "We need to change that water, men," as he pointed to the beer barrel.

Tim acknowledged his suggestion with a head nod as he approached the bucket. He poured the water out carefully to not break the glass bottles. "They should be rinsed in the river, Tim. And thank you! So, who are these two men?"

"Well, they are still trying to make it home to Malone, where they were born and raised, from the war that's been over for over three years now. But that's what they tell me. They took it out on your horse because we took their blankets and things from the cabin." Bobby looked disgusted.

"I see. Well, it's three in the morning and I am exhausted and you all probably are too, so what we are going to do is this; we are going to tie them separately to the pump over there and we are going back to sleep around the fire. Can anyone think of something better?"

James was rubbing his face now due to exhaustion. Gerald walked to James from the barn, wiping his hands on a wet cloth.

"The stitches are holding James and she has settled down pretty nicely. What are we going to do with these two?"

James told him his plan; Gerald nodded and approached the men as Bobby and Tim were untying them. Gerald held the one now without rope, while the other two tied the first man, and then tied the second man to the pump, which was twenty feet from the fire. Gerald knew they would get cold, but he didn't feel sorry for them. As he walked away from the tied men, Gerald asked if there were any beers left. James explained about the bloody water and apologized, saying that he should have had Tim take the beers out first, but he wasn't thinking straight. Gerald nodded his head, took one of the beers out of the grass, and after he opened it, wiped the bottle lip with his wet cloth. "Lizzie said she was going to sleep in Misty's stall tonight. She is really worried about her."

"No she isn't." James went into the barn and after five minutes came out with Lizzie's arm in his as he walked her to the house. He asked her to explain everything to Jess, as he saw the lamp was still burning in their bedroom window. He opened the door with his key and kissed her cheek before she went inside.

James returned to the fire pit and had another beer with Gerald in silence. Gerald could tell James' mind was at work and he was exhausted, so he stayed quiet next to his friend. When James was done with his beer, he checked Misty with the lantern. The wound had stopped bleeding, and she was staying calm and he was satisfied. He then walked to the two men who were already sleeping and placed the lantern between them, so he could watch them from the fire pit. Soon all four men were asleep by the warm fire.

James thought he was the first to wake the next morning, but when he looked around the yard, Bobby and Tim were sitting by the tied strangers, acting as guards. James grinned, rose, and went to the barn to check on Misty. The stitches had held in her neck, and the wound looked good. She was lethargic but very aware. The rest of the animals were fine as he checked each one while feeding them. When James walked out to the fire pit, he saw a jackknife lying in the dirt, and realized it must have been their intended deadly weapon. Bobby or Tim must have confiscated it.

With the help of his men, James put a pig on the spit over the fire pit and stacked wood that should be efficient to keep the fire going under the roasting pork all day.

Gerald still lay sleeping and James left him quietly as he headed to the house. He pointed his thumb up to his men and asked if they were hungry. They said yes as if they were dying from starvation. When he entered the house, Jess had already made biscuits, the gravy was keeping warm on the wood stove, and she was frying bacon. She ran to her husband, wrapped her arms around his neck, and held him for a long time. She had heard everything that happened from Lizzie and knew her husband would give her the details later.

"Mommy!" Becca was hollering from the top of the stairs after she saw her parents were not in bed, through their open door. James held up his hand to Jess, who started to walk toward their daughter and he opened both stair gates to retrieve his little girl. She was so happy to see her Daddy and clung to his neck very tightly. When they entered the kitchen, she saw her mother and wanted down to go to her. Jess picked her up, kissed her, and held her on her hip for a moment before she had to flip the bacon.

"Let's change your diaper, little one." James smiled as he picked her up and took her back upstairs. When they returned, Jess had set the table for everyone and was placing the platters of biscuits and bacon there and going back to the kitchen. James went to the door and called everyone in for breakfast. Gerald was awake, heard the invitation, and was first through the door. He had passed the two men still tied to the pump and saw they were awake with scared eyes, but he was at ease to see them still tied securely.

The men gathered around the table as Jess brought in a huge bowl of sausage gravy and they dove into their breakfast. It warmed her heart to see the men's camaraderie.

Soon they heard one of her crying sons coming down the stairs as they saw Lizzie, looking very tired, carrying Mark, a hungry boy.

"Lizzie, I would have brought him downstairs. You should try to get some sleep." Jess looked very concerned. She took Mark from her arms, and went into the kitchen to prepare two bottles. Lizzie sat at the table and had biscuits and gravy with the men. Soon Luke was crying from upstairs and Jess put her hand on Lizzie's shoulder as she passed behind her on her way to the stairs.

Between bites, James began to think aloud. "Here's what I think we should do."

All eyes turned to him, as they continued to eat. James asked if someone would pass the coffee pot, and as he poured his second cup, he voiced his thoughts.

"We need to build a stop in the river, right?" All the men nodded in agreement.

"Today's party will go on as scheduled, and I am not sure what we will do with our angry men, except feed them well to build their strength; but if we put our heads together, we can come up with something. Anyway, I truly believe that all men have good hearts and these men are two lost souls just trying to make their way home from a horrible war. God knows what they witnessed in battle and what they have been through while walking through, most likely, many states with no money, no food, tired and hungry. I have decided they will help us construct the stop in the river as payback for what they have done. After that, I have not decided what to do with them. We all have to tie off to trees for safety while we are building in the river anyway, so we will just tie them to where they cannot escape their ropes. I cannot tell if they feel bad about what they have done, but they feel worse captured. I would like to put them to work and trust working beside them. I think deep inside they are good men. Is everyone in agreement?" James searched each man's face and saw some doubt in each face, but they agreed with him nonetheless.

"I am going to stay, James. I deeply feel that I need to be here and help, my friend." Gerald kept eye contact with James and he saw that his friend meant what he said.

"You don't need to stay, but I truly appreciate you and your friendship! Are you a good shot?"

Gerald shook his head no while he explained that he had only handled a gun in his youth while hunting with his father.

"I can shoot a tic off a deer's ass, James." Bobby spoke up quickly. The room busted up in laughter.

"I have seen him do that – almost – the tic was on the deer's neck and well..... you can imagine what happened to that tic." Tim laughed while he tried to explain how good a shot Bobby was.

"Well, I now appoint you as shore supervisor, Bobby, with a rifle. If one or both of our men try to escape, you will fire a warning shot first and if they keep running, shoot for the leg only. Got it?" James looked seriously into Bobby's eyes. Bobby nodded in acceptance.

Jess was coming down the stairs with both boys when there was a knock at their front door. James went to the door quickly, as Jess paused when she saw the County Sheriff as James opened the door. The boys were crying and wiggling so she swiftly went to the kitchen to feed them.

"Come in, Sheriff Graff. What can I do for you?"

"Well, I heard you had some troubles last night."

"We did, but I think I have everything under control."

"Now James, how can that be? Doc Harris told me everything that went on here last night and it sounds like we got two scoundrels that need to be taken in." The Sheriff sounded stern and adamant.

"Well Sheriff, let me tell what I am going to do." James told him his plan, including Bobby with a rifle.

"Where are these men?"

"They are tied to my pump right now, but we have a party planned for today and maybe you could take them in just for today. Tomorrow morning I will take them from you myself and put them to work."

"We could do that. Are you sure you don't want them arrested and put away for what they done?"

"I am sure. Sheriff, would you like some breakfast?"

"I smell something cookin'. Sure smells good!" The Sheriff raised his nose, taking in the wonderful aromas.

"Have a seat here where I was and I will get you a plate." James tapped the back of his empty chair as the Sheriff plopped himself onto the soft cushioned seat. He nodded to all the men and Lizzie at the table, as all eyes were turned to him. Lizzie passed James coming out of the kitchen with a plate and fork for the sheriff. She quickly took Luke into her arms, took a bottle Jess had prepared and both women took the twins into the main room with bottles in their now quiet mouths. As Jess passed James, she expressed her concern of feeding the two men outside. He smiled and told them he would feed them when the Sheriff was finished eating. She smiled at him, knowing he had complete control of the situation.

Becca wanted down from her chair at the table, which James helped her with and watched his tiny daughter run to her mother.

James first took cups of coffee to the two men outside and quickly returned to them with two heaping plates of biscuits and gravy. He watched as they ate like starving animals. As they ate, he explained what was going to happen to them. They looked up to him with wide eyes, not moving. Soon, the Sheriff joined James by the men as he was finishing his explanation. They did not speak or nod their heads, as they knew they were lucky to be treated so kindly by an understanding man, after they tried to kill his horse. They knew horse thieves were hung.

"I know you both have good hearts and have had a very hard time while returning home from the war and have made some bad decisions. After the river stop is completed, I will decide what to do with you then." The men nodded and hung their heads in shame.

The Sheriff saw the men had finished their breakfast, and told James he would now take them to jail in Atwater and would see him in the morning. James agreed as he watched the Sheriff tie the men with two ropes. He tied their hands with one end of the rope and other end tied to the horn of his saddle. By now, all the men were outside and watching the Sheriff. Jess and Lizzie watched from the kitchen window.

The Sheriff started his horse at a slow pace, with the tied men on foot, and they had no choice but to follow.

James shook his head in disbelief and knew the following days would be trying but productive.

Soon Edward and Victoria came up the drive with questioning looks on their faces. Edward assisted his wife from their buggy and they both took pies and covered plates from the floor of the buggy, and started toward the back door.

233

"What is going on here? We just passed the Sheriff with two men following him, tied to his saddle horn. Did they come from here?" Gerald took the items Victoria had in her hands and walked with them as they entered the house, explaining the events of last evening and how James was going to use them for labor.

James asked Bobby and Tim to help him move the tables, benches, and chairs in the yard, and prepare for the party. While doing this, they discussed how they were going to create the river stop and who, from the lumberyard, would be the best choices to assist. Soon Edward joined them in their conversation, and he was in complete agreement that Charlie and Dave, from the cabin, would be the best choices. Edward said he would keep the lumberyard open with three remaining employees. The project would begin Monday morning. James now had to decide what to do with the jailed men on Sunday. He told the Sheriff he would obtain the men Sunday morning, and would decide what to do with them sometime today, during the party. He was sure the men would be the topic of the day and if they put their heads together, he was sure they would come up with something. He didn't want to go back on his word to the Sheriff.

Teddy, Amanda, and Sam arrived at the same time as Bobby's parents and sister, Addie, Frank, and Sadie Higgins for the party. The events from the previous evening and nasty rumors were passing through Atwater swiftly and Frank had heard that James had to shoot the evil men. James cringed when he heard this and told the truth to all the new arrivals. Addie ran to her son Bobby and hung on his neck, crying. She feared for her son's well being and he assured her he was fine.

"Frank, I hear Bobby is a good shot!" James clasped Frank's shoulder as they walked to the closest table.

"Why he can shoot a tic off a....." James laughed and finished his sentence for him. Frank then laughed, realizing he had obviously heard this before.

Tim asked Bobby for his help in getting beer from the river in cool water filled buckets.

"That water is awfully cold. Being in it is going to be somethin'" Tim got goose bumps when he thought about the cold, running river.

"Yeah, I think you and I should take turns in the river and on the shore. You're as good a shot as I am, why didn't you tell James?"

" I dunno. He favors you, Bobby, and I dint want to step in front o' that."

"You're crazy, Tim. That's just in your mind. I don't see where he favors anyone!" Bobby slapped Tim's back, reassuring him and hopefully building his confidence.

Soon Tim's parents and two brothers arrived, whom James hadn't seen in some time. Mick quickly approached his son, and asked him if he was okay. Tim shook his head yes, as James approached his new guests.

"Do you remember my parents, James? This is my father Mick Albright, and my mother Hanna. These are my younger brothers Tom and Jake. My younger sister Betty couldn't make it today."

James stepped forward to shake Mick's hand, and went around the circle of Tim's family with greetings. Mick and Hanna had heard the rumors and asked James if he was okay and he comforted them with a positive reply and asked them to select a table and to hear the truth from his friend, Gerald. They sat near Gerald, who then repeated what he had just told the Higgins'. James placed his hand on Gerald's shoulder when he started his speech again, and then walked to the beer bucket and greedily took one, opened it and almost finished it in one tip of the bottle.

Eventually, the yard filled with a crowd of lumberyard employees and their families. Edward happily greeted each one with James, as they arrived. They all came with dishes, which Addie gladly took from each guest and placed on the food table. Jess and Lizzie were inside icing two cakes and soon went outside carrying the twins and Becca followed behind them. They put the twins in the fenced play area and Becca began to mingle with the many guests and soon found Ellie, who had arrived with her parents George and Francis Madison and her older sister Samantha, Bobby's love. Ellie swiftly picked her up and Becca happily was on her hip for the next few hours.

Bobby and Samantha remained a "couple" the rest of the day; where he went, she followed. Their parents sat together discussing their children, and all agreed they would wait and see what happened with their relationship. Francis knew her daughter's dream of going to New York City, yet she also knew she loved Bobby, and had no idea where their love would take their relationship.

Jess noticed that many people were drawn to the twins and gathered to watch the identical boys, who played happily with each other. They curiously listened to them talk to each other in what seemed to be their own language, which the boys easily understood.

James stood on a table and attempted to get everyone's attention. Eventually, the crowd silenced and turned in his direction.

"Edward and I would like to welcome everyone and thank you for coming to the Atwood & Strong Lumber picnic," he paused, scratched his head, "Um, heck, it's a party!" The entire crowed applauded loudly. "We have great employees, and we wanted to show our appreciation for their hard work and devotion to the lumberyard. The ultimate sacrifice was made by our guest of honor," as he pointed to the pig on the spit. Everyone laughed as they all gazed at the roasting pork. "and, we thank him, or her, I never asked." James giggled as the crowd laughed too. "I hope everyone has a good time today and if any of you haven't spoken to Edward or me by the end of the day please make a point of coming to each of us. Thank you, employees. We couldn't do what we do without each one of you!" He raised his beer as praise and everyone's arms raised in the air all through the mass of people lauding the employees. Edward shouted out "Here, Here!" as another wave of arms and cheers rose in praise.

The party went on without a hitch and the last guest left at nine o'clock, well after dark, except Ellie, who asked her parents and Jess at the same time if she could spend the night with Becca and Jess agreed, and made a bed of blankets on Becca's bedroom floor. Ellie happily read Becca to sleep.

Teddy, Amanda and Sam planned to spend the night at Atwood Manor, then leave early the next morning for Gerald's horse ranch to finally visit their son, Junior.

James was finally able to lay his weary head in bed with his wife. "What will tomorrow bring, darling?" Jess was snuggled under his arm, with her head on his chest.

"Ahhh, well, I have decided to have the two men clean and organize the lumberyard. So my dear, after church I will gather the men, and Gerald and I will supervise them until three o'clock and Bobby and Tim will relieve us then. The men will go back to jail for the night, then the hard part begins Monday morning." He kissed the top of his wife's head as he felt his body relaxing.

"Goodness. Is Misty going to be okay? I mean, will she go back to her wonderful self or..."

"She will need time to heal, but in a month or so, she will be her beautiful self." Doc had changed her bandages two times since the horrible night she was stabbed.

Jess smiled and thanked God, and she soon heard her husband sleeping deeply.

The next day went as planned and the two "convicts" fully cooperated. They moved dried wood from drying racks and into sale racks, and completed the rotation of lumber. They also swept piles and piles of sawdust into burlap bags, which the yard sold as fire starter.

James and Gerald were home in time to enjoy the remainder of the day with the children who had their naps and were full of energy. Gerald treasured these moments.

James rose early the next morning, kissed his wife, peeked into each of his children's rooms then rode Stormy to the jail. He had to wake the Sheriff to get the convicts from behind their bars. He tied them, as the Sheriff had done, to his saddle horn and walked them through town to the lumberyard. Lizzie had made a huge breakfast for eight men, but Victoria did not want them in her house. James understood and asked Lizzie to help him and Edward transport the hot food to the lumberyard. Bobby and Tim guarded the convicts and soon Charlie and Dave arrived shortly before the food.

While they ate, James thanked Charlie and Dave for successfully sending three huge trees down the river from behind the cabin, that would create the river stop, which were started afloat an hour apart. Then he thanked Bobby and Tim for stopping each floating tree that came down the river with horses and ropes. The stop, he told them, would be behind Atwood Manor at the narrowest part of the river.

After they ate breakfast, James instructed each man of their job and asked them all to join hands as he led them in prayer for safety and strength for all.

It took over an hour to measure ropes and tie themselves to trees. They put extra ropes around the convicts and James told them should they try to escape, that Bobby had been instructed to shoot as a warning, and then was to shoot to stop, not to kill. The two convicts, Jimmy and Henry, mumbled that they would cooperate and work hard. James would not trust them until he saw that he could. Jimmy was tall and thin, which worried James, but Henry was stout and looked strong. When James asked who could swim, all the men said they could. He was glad to hear that.

Bobby and Tim had agreed earlier in the day they would trade positions every hour with the rifle. At the river, they shook hands before Bobby found the right position with his rifle and Tim got into the cold water.

Jimmy, Henry, Charlie, and Dave knew it was their job to tie the massive, thick rope around the base of a huge, very old pine tree on the Atwood Manor side of the river then swim the other end of the rope across the river and tie it to another massive pine tree. With this done, the other men brought the first tree down that had jammed into the shore at the river's bend. While most of the men held the floating tree by rope, against the river flow, Gerald and James tied the floating tree to the cross rope. They did the same with the second tree, and the third tree went in front of where the first two trees were already tied together. Tying all the trees together, making sure the first rope would hold, had proved the most difficult part of the task. They then wound tie another thick rope around all the trees and to the original trees on land. The trees in the river did not cross the entire span of the river, so the water could flow normally on the far side of the tied trees.

It was then they all heard Jimmy splashing and struggling in the water, when he lost his hold of the floating trees. Knowing he was tied to a tree on shore, James did not hurry to save him, but then saw his thin body go under the river flow and somehow slipped out of his security rope. James quickly made it to shore, with Gerald right behind him, and speedily got farther down the shoreline while looking for a large fallen branch to assist Jimmy out of the water. It was then they saw Jimmy hit a large rock and go under the water. As James ran down shore, watching Jimmy closely, he saw him come back up, gulping for air, and doing his best to hold onto the rock while the water slammed against him. Just then, James felt his own rope tighten – he was at its full length, and there would be no way for him to reach Jimmy in the water. Gerald suddenly came up behind James without his safety rope, took a step into the water, and dove in toward Jimmy, leaving James on the shore.

"Bobby, get me a rope – fast!!" James was yelling as loud as he could as he saw all the men trying to undo their safety ropes and make their way toward James. Dave undid his rope first from the tree he was tied to, ran to James, handing him his wet rope. "Quick, let's make a loop of rope to toss into the water; they will need to be dragged back in!" James, still dripping wet, sputtered his order while he watched all the men doing what they could with all their ropes; and when satisfied, they threw the huge looped end of the rope into the river, and watched as it quickly followed the river flow and eventually ended up almost back at their feet.

"I am going to get into the loop and swim it out to them. You men tie the rope off to a tree!" James stepped into the loop of the rope and began swimming toward Gerald and Jimmy, who were now holding onto the huge rock as best they could. James reached them as they all struggled against the rushing river to hold onto the rock while putting the rope loop around all three of them. James pushed off the rock with all three in the rope and shouted as loud as he could to the men on the shore to pull. They all swiftly did their tasks and slowly the three near drowned men made it to shore, coughing, and stumbling. At that point, all the men fell to the earth in exhaustion.

Bobby made an effort to help James to his feet and James pointed to Jimmy, "Help him first, he needs your help." With that, Bobby sidestepped, reaching to Jimmy, whom he grabbed by the arm and out of the water. Jimmy, still struggling and spitting out water, made his way to the nearest tree and slumped against it. Henry approached him quickly and attempted to pat him on his back, then slowly sat beside his friend.

Everyone was finally out of the water, and checking each other for their well-being. They all sat in silence, gaining back their breaths and strength. Finally, James stood and started to gather the ropes and all the other men started doing the same. Together they made it to the clearing and started their trek toward Atwood Manor.

James had seen that Jimmy and Henry worked as hard as the others did, and he was encouraged by their behavior, before and after the scare. Now he had the difficult task of deciding their fate. The first thing they all had to do was eat. When they arrived near the house, James was very happy to see two tables set for them around a large fir log in the fire pit burning warmly. The men changed into dry clothes, except Jimmy and Henry, who owned only what they were wearing. James got some of his clothes for them, which fit Jimmy but not Henry. There was nothing to offer Henry except a linen sheet, which he wore like a toga. Henry and the men all laughed at the sight of him, but he was miserable in his wet clothes. Jess and Lizzie brought them dinner and they happily ate around the warm fire. Both women saw how Henry was dressed, raised their eyebrows, but decided not to ask. They had no idea what the men had just gone through while they patiently waited with food for them.

Soon, all the men were conversing as if they had been friends for years. Gerald and James seemed to notice it at the same time and gave each other questioning looks. Together, they decided to begin to send trees down the river to the stop two days from now. James asked that they again space them by an hour, and discussed what to do if a tree got caught-up coming down the river. James also decided trees would come down the river Monday, Wednesday, and Friday, so they and the horses could rest a day between these exhausting days. Dave and Charlie gathered their dry clothes, and rode back to the cabin on the draft horse and a chestnut mare.

James motioned Gerald away from the men at the fire pit, and asked him if he thought the two convicts could be trusted. Gerald admitted he was not sure, yet admired the way they had worked as part of the team in the river. James decided to follow his gut instinct and still believed every man had a good heart. They walked back to the pit and listened to the men, who again, were talking like old friends.

240

"I have decided that you four should sleep by the fire tonight and tomorrow we will check on the stop and see if the ropes have held, then all of us should go to the cabin. We need to count the cut trees there are and tally how many days its going to take to get them all to the yard. What do you think?" James looked at Jimmy and Henry first and they said yes, nodding their heads as if they were part of the group, which in a sense, they were.

James and Gerald left the four men at the pit and went inside to bed.

Early the next morning, James looked out his bedroom window and saw Henry stoking the fire and Jimmy gathering wood from the woodpile. Bobby and Tim were awake, talking near the fire. He took a big sigh of relief, quickly dressed and went outside, passing Lizzie in the kitchen making breakfast for all.

After they ate, James put Stormy in front of the smaller yard wagon, and tied Jimmy and Henry to the wooden bed. He and Gerald were in the front seat, and Bobby and Tim followed on their horses. James tried to talk to the men tied behind him on their way to the cabin, but they remained shy. When they arrived at the cabin, he untied the men and asked them to go to the cut trees near the river and begin to count the stumps. As they started toward the river, James realized he had started to trust them and hoped they didn't run away. He unhooked Stormy, while Gerald went to the back corner of the cabin to inspect the burnt wall and silently agreed with James that it would be easy to repair.

Together they headed toward the river and joined the six men counting cut trees. After the count, they deducted that seven trees would go down the river per designated day and it would take nine days to send all the cut trees to the stop. The trees Charlie and Dave downed while thinning on the far side of the cabin hadn't been moved from where they dropped.

James and Gerald went back the Atwood Manor with Jimmy and Henry, untied this time. There they found Teddy, who sat alone at the fire pit with a small fire burning.

241

"Teddy! It is so good to see you!" James jumped from the wagon swiftly to shake his friend's hand. Gerald was right behind him. "How is Junior?"

"Great! 'e's very 'appy and showed me 'lot of what 'e does and 'e is very good at what 'e does wid horses. Did I teach th' boy right?" Teddy looked at Gerald with wide eyes.

"You did, my man. He is very good at his job and gets along well with everyone. Yes, Teddy, you raised a good man." Gerald patted Teddy's shoulder assuring him of being a good father.

"Are Amanda and Sam in the house?" James walked to the fire pit, added more wood, and watched as the flames grew higher.

"Yep." Teddy was curious who the two strangers were, and James saw his questioning look.

"Teddy, this is Jimmy and Henry, who have been helping us out a few days."

"Jimmy? Is dat you? Jimmy Hart?" Teddy looked closer at his face, as he stepped closer.

"Yeah, Jimmy Hart. How do you know me?"

"You used to come to my ranch to buy meat with your father. You don't remember me?"

Jimmy scratched his head and looked at the ground as he searched his memory. "Oh yeah! Mr. Garnett, now I 'member. What are ya doing here?"

"James and Gerald, 'ere, are my best frien's. What are *you* doin' here?"

"Well, Henry here, and I are makin' our way home from Gettysburg, Pennsylvania. We been waylaid here an' dare for da las three yars and met up wid Mr. Atwood.......he needed some 'elp and we 'elped him." Jimmy hung his head during his lie. Henry stood silent, looking at his shoes.

"What a small world! Seems we have a lot to talk about." James put his hand on Jimmy's shoulder, who jumped and stiffened.

The men gathered around the fire pit where Teddy heard the entire story of how Jimmy and Henry came to know James and Gerald. Teddy shook his head as he listened while he stared at the golden flames.

"I have decided that both of you have worked off your debt to me and society and I am asking you now, Teddy, if you could take these two young men home to Malone, so they can end their long journey."

"James,...ah, Mr. Atwood, I want t' say how sorry I am for what I done t' yer cabin and yer 'orse. I don't usually do dat kinda stuff and done know what came ova me. I am sorry, and I want t' thank ya for all ya done fer me th's week. Henry?"

"Yep, I want to say that I am sorry, Mr. Atwood, for the pain I brought you and your family. I am not normally like that either. However, since the war, I have done many stupid things and I am angry about my brother dying. He was standing right next to me when he got blown away. One minute he was there and the next, not much was left of him. I guess I gotta learn how to get that outta my mind. I am a good man, went to school and dream of livin' like you do, someday, I do. I got no family in Malone no more and got no reason to go back dare. You need any more help 'round here?"

"I accept both of your apologies, men, and have seen that I was right, and you do have good hearts. I am sorry, Henry, but I don't need anyone at this time."

"My ranch is always looking for good men. Henry, I have watched you work the last few days and I see you do not fear hard work. Do you know horses well?" Gerald sounded anxious.

"I been 'round horses all my life, Gerald. I am sorry, I donno your last name." Henry looked to the ground.

"It's Paxton, Gerald Paxton. My ranch is affiliated with a race track, does that suit your fancy?"

"Yes sir, Mr. Paxton, I think I woul' like dat a lot! Where is your place?" Henry sounded excited and clutched his suspenders, then brought them together in the middle of his chest.

"It's in rural Albany, back south, I'm afraid. Are you familiar with that area?"

"We came through dare, I think. Did we, Jimmy?"

"Yeah, but I don 'member any race track."

"Well, I will tell you, Henry, that I will be leaving tomorrow and you are welcome to come with me then, and we can get you started at the race track. I think you will not only fit in well but you will enjoy it. I saw your eyes light up when I said racetrack, so maybe you have found a real home. What were you going to do when you got back to Malone?"

"I dunno, dint have anything planned. My folks are dead and ain't got no family dare no more..." Henry's thoughts trailed off and he thought of his dead brother once again.

"Henry, I am sorry for the loss of your brother, and maybe if we keep you busy and you're doing something you really like, you may find happiness and we'll work on that anger." Gerald suddenly felt fatherly to this young man and had a good feeling about him. "What's your last name, Henry?"

"Stewart, sir. Henry Stewart. Born in '46 and raised in Malone." His confidence was improving; that was obvious.

"Well Henry Stewart, I think we can do business together. You have to swear to me now, in front of God and these witnesses, that you will never harm another animal." Gerald tried to get Henry to look him in the eye, but he hung his head when Gerald said the word harm.

Henry kicked the dirt and then finally looked at Gerald. "I swear I will never do anyding like dat again, sir. I promise."

"Well, looks like both of you will be onto better paths. God works in mysterious ways, men, and obviously you were both brought here for a reason. I am hungry, are any of you?" James patted his stomach then stood and started toward the house.

Chapter Twenty-Three
Fall 1868

The next morning Teddy and his family took Jimmy back to Malone and Gerald and Henry left for the racetrack. Jimmy and Henry thanked James and Jess profusely for all they did for them and promised to let them know how they were in the future.

The first four days went well when they sent trees down the river, but on the fifth day, a tree coming down got caught-up in a river bend and it took five hours to find it and send it on its way. The tree stop continued to do its job and Bobby promised to check the ropes early each shipping day. So far, the ropes were still strong and holding well.

In early November, Jess was feeling run down and had no energy, and decided to see Doc Harris, hoping he would tell her it was from chasing three youngsters every day. He examined her, wrote in her record, and turned to her with a smile.

"Why are you smiling?" She started to giggle at the funny look on his face.

"You are in the family way, my dear! You couldn't tell?"

"My.....no I couldn't tell. I was so violently ill the last two times, I just assumed I was lacking something or just plain tired. A baby? Are you sure, Doc?" She was grinning from ear to ear.

"I am sure. I would say you will deliver in mid June. Congratulations!"

"June, I am going to have another baby in June." She was shocked yet very excited.

"Want twins again?" His smile was wide.

"Oh my, I guess I will take what God gives me. But I am not sick, Doc Harris."

"Sometimes that happens. Just be thankful, Jess."

"I am thankful, very thankful. May I go now, I need to tell my husband."

"Yes you may go. I want to see you back here before Christmas, young lady."

"I will, Doc. Thank you for everything." She finished dressing and flew out of his office to her buggy, turned Misty toward the lumberyard and prayed that James would be as excited as she was.

Victoria saw her come through the gate, not turning her horse to the house, but to the office. She and Lizzie were preparing lunch for the children, which they then delayed now to wait for Jess.

Jess ran into the office, to find her father behind the sales counter waiting on a customer. He winked at her and pointed his finger to the back of the building, knowing she was looking for James. She found him moving dried lumber from the drying racks with Bobby, Tim and two other young employees. James saw her pink dress first and looked to see his ecstatic wife as she was almost running to him. He knew she went to see Doc Harris today and was glad she had stopped to tell him what the doctor said.

"James, Honey, we are going to have another baby! Isn't that wonderful?" She ran to him, put her arms around his neck as he heard the news. He wrapped his arms around her waist, lifted her up, and swung her in a circle.

"A baby? Jess, that's great news!" He put her down but left his arms around her. "Hey, men, we are in the family way! Another baby, do you believe it?" He felt as if his face was going to crack, his smile was so wide.

All the men gathered around them congratulating them. James and Jess headed toward the front of the office where her father was shaking hands with his customer as he walked him to the door and thanking him for his business. "What's all the hollering about?"

"Father, we are in the family way. You are going to be a grandfather again!"

Edward hugged his daughter and then shook James' hand, which turned into a hug.

"We have to tell your mother. She will be so excited to hear this news."

James lifted his wife into the buggy, as Jess giggled like a little girl. Edward squeezed into the seat next to his daughter as they crossed the vast yard between them and the house. Lizzie was hanging clothes on the line and heard them coming, turned and stared at the sight of

246

the three of them tightly wedged in the buggy seat. Their faces were gleeful and she ran to meet them as James tied Misty to the granite hitching post.

"Lizzie, I am going to.....we are in the family way! Isn't it wonderful?" Jess hugged her lifelong friend and the two of them danced and giggled.

"What is going on out here?" Victoria heard the commotion and came out her back door.

"Mother....."

"Victoria, we are in the family way! We had to tell you immediately." James hugged her and then Lizzie too.

"My, my, that's wonderful, Jess. When will this one come into the world?"

"Doc Harris said mid June. I am so happy."

They all went into the house where Jess told each of her children about the new baby, and Becca repeated her words, but Jess doubted any of them understood. They knew everyone was happy and the boys started to dance and jump, and soon Becca joined them.

~

Before the first snow, Gerald visited the Atwood's and had good news about Henry. He obviously liked his new position at the racetrack, was well liked by others and all was going well.

"Shall we make a big fire to keep us warm, James? We should have one more fire before winter." Gerald clapped his back as they both walked toward the woodpile. James picked out kindling and together they started a huge fire. The chill in the air was getting colder as the day got longer, but soon they were warm.

"Another baby. That is wonderful. Jess is certainly excited. I am so happy for you both, for you all, really. When is it due?"

"Mid June and we can't agree on names again. It's funny, because we agree on most everything, but when it comes to names, we have a hard time." James giggled as he played with a twig before he threw it into the fire.

"You are a lucky man, James. Yet, you see, I am the one that has it made."

"Really - do tell me more."

247

"Because I can love your children and spoil them and when they act up I can hand them to you." Gerald laughed and grabbed James' shoulder as they met eyes and watched each other laugh.

"If you say so, but I think I am the one who has it made. The boys are growing fast, aren't they? I see changes in all my children almost daily. It is amazing. How I love to watch my beautiful wife interact with them. She loves them so and I am afraid at how many children she wants." Gerald had never seen such a look on his friends face as he spoke. He actually got a lump in his throat listening to him and watching his face.

"I thought I would visit before the snow but I have something to tell you." Gerald suddenly felt nervous and didn't know why.

"What is it Gerald? Are you okay?"

"I am better than okay, James, I am in love." Gerald's face lit brighter than the fire.

"Gerald, that's wonderful! When did this happen? Who is she? When can we meet her?"

"Slow down there, one question at a time. Yes, it is wonderful and it happened about three months ago. I met her before we put in the river stop, but when I fell in love with her, I am not sure. I think it happened rather quickly, for me anyway, but I was not sure how she felt then, but I know now. She loves me, James, me. I am a lucky man. Who is she? Her name is Rachael Longwood. She is your age, which makes her two years younger than I. You can meet her at our wedding."

"Your wedding! Gerald, I am so happy for you! When are you getting married?"

"We are talking about a spring wedding and it will probably be at the house or at the ranch. She's a lovely girl, James, and a lot of fun. We laugh a lot and get on well. She is a strawberry blonde and it is almost as long as Jess' hair. She is a horse trainer that started to work for me last summer. The first time I saw her I couldn't take my eyes off her. You know how your mouth goes dry and you forget your own name? Well, that happened. She is an excellent trainer. Her husband was killed in the war and her folks are dead, and she wanted to get out of New York City and somehow heard about my ranch and came there looking for work. She has always been fascinated by horses and has been around them all her life." Gerald paused as they heard the back door open. Jess came out wrapped in a wool shawl, pulling the shawl closer around her neck as she neared them at the fire.

"Darling, wait until you hear the news!"

"What is it? Ooh, it's rather cold tonight."

"You tell her, Gerald, it's your wonderful news."

"I am in love, Jess and we are getting married in spring!"

She ran to him, hugged him a long time, kissed his cheek, and then stepped back with delight in her eyes. "Gerald, I am so happy for you! This is wonderful news!"

"I was just telling your husband about her. Her name is Rachael and she is a horse trainer at my ranch." He told her what he had told James and then continued. "She rode and trained horses in her younger years and then her folks moved to New York City when she was a teenager. They both died after she married, but he was killed in the war. Anyway, it was love at first sight and I can't stop thinking about her. I know snow will fly soon, but I would like you all to be at our wedding in spring. I know you are due in mid June and I hope you will be able to make the ride in April. I will let you know by letter of the wedding date, but I want all of my friends there. James I want to ask you if you will be my Best Man. I am also going to ask Teddy to stand and witness with us." He looked away from the fire and turned to Jess. "When I leave here I am going to Malone to tell Teddy that she has agreed to marry me."

"Of course I will be your best man, Gerald. I have a black suit, will that be alright?"

Gerald stepped to James, shook his hand, and told him a black suit would be fine.

"Gerald, I am so happy for you! This is so exciting! We will be there!" Jess' smile never went away. She looked at James, who was still smiling too.

Gerald left the next morning for Teddy's ranch to tell him the news.

~

The lumber business was booming and James wished now that he had kept Henry in Atwater, as they should hire another employee to handle the work. Their records showed that one third of their business was coming from south of Atwater. That was when James and Edward had their first realistic conversation of building a second lumberyard. Their question was "How far south should they build?" James admitted to his father-in-law that if the second yard were to start in spring, he needed to stay in Atwater, since their fourth child was due in mid June. James would easily assist wherever he needed to afterward. Edward agreed. They also agreed that Bobby and Tim were the obvious next men in line to operate the second lumberyard.

One day in early November, they asked Bobby and Tim to stay after work for a meeting.

"Thank you both for staying for this meeting. It has become evident to Edward and I that a second lumberyard is necessary. One third of our business comes from south of Atwater and we would like to follow the river and possibly build just north of Gerald's ranch, in Lincoln, New York. It is not a large town, much like our fine town, yet near Albany and closer still to New York City, where the river flows to its bay. You have both proven yourselves to us as worthy of operating the new yard over the past four years repeatedly. We are offering this opportunity to you now and are asking that both of you think about it for the next month or two. Construction would begin in very early spring, although you would not be involved in the construction but would run and operate the second Atwood & Strong Lumber.

"You both would receive substantial raises and be given titles and would have to move to Lincoln, of course, so there is a lot to consider. Edward and I are planting this seed now for you to ponder. Do either of you have any questions?"

Tim stood to address his bosses. "I would like to thank you James and you Edward for this opportunity and I will tell you now that I am available for whatever you need. Will the new yard be the same as this one or will there be changes?"

"To be honest, Tim, Edward, and I have talked about that and we have our ideas, but are always open for suggestions." James was more than delighted at Tim's response.

"I too would like to take you up on this opportunity and look forward to the challenge." Bobby stood and shook James' hand then walked to Edward to do the same.

Edward stood and looked at each man in the room. "I must say, I am not surprised by your replies, yet I never thought you both would respond so quickly. I admire your devotion and at such a young age. How old are you two, anyway?" They both responded spontaneously with "18". Edward shook his head in disbelief, yet recalled he was only one year older when he started Strong Lumber in Liverpool. "Well, I think we have a good team here and I truly think this will work out very well for all of us. This all started in a cabin and a barn, and look where we are now."

The four men discussed the new yard for another hour then said good night.

~

Christmas was always wonderful at Atwood Manor. James had help from lumberyard employees making three wooden rocking horses for the children, and they were overly excited to see them near their huge Christmas tree. Becca rode hers immediately and enjoyed her 'orsy. The boys could climb into the seat on their horses but would instantly slide off. Once they had help from Lizzie and their mother staying on their horse, they did not want to get down. James gave Jess a blue sapphire ring, where diamonds surrounded the deep blue stone. She was so surprised and shocked, she sobbed into her husbands embrace. She had never owned anything so fine in her life. She gave James a full length, leather, riding coat. She knew he would look so handsome in it, and when he tried it on that morning, surrounded by her parents and their children, she got rather excited and wished they were alone. It made him look even taller than his height of 6′ 2″ and she was so glad he was *her* husband.

Her parents gave them a beautiful silk bed cover, to replace the one they surprised them with in their new home. They also had Edward's brother, Paul, send an English pram via ship, which arrived at the Strong's only two days before Christmas. Jess loved it.

They gave her parents carved wooden lions, for both sides of their front gate. They thought the lions were wonderful and Victoria asked four times that day how they thought of such a beautiful, creative gift. She hoped they would be mounted at their gate as quickly as possible.

New Years Eve went as many had in the past where Edward and James sat in front of the fireplace drinking brandy, smoking fat cigars and talking about business.

After the holidays, they received Gerald's wedding invitation for Saturday, 18 April at his ranch. The invitation was for five Atwood's, which Jess frowned at, thinking of Lizzie. Later she would find that Lizzie was included on Edward and Victoria's invitation. James was not surprised to hear that he had also invited Bobby, Tim, and their lady-friends.

Jess felt wonderful, which was so different than the first two times she was in the family way. She was so thankful. She depended on Lizzie for many things, especially with the children, and she couldn't bear the thought of Lizzie waiting on her too. Her stomach was growing already at five months and could not begin to guess the sex of the baby. Most women in her condition tried to hide away, but Jess was elated and proud. She loved children and wanted to fill the house with them, as James suspected.

Jess wanted a new dress for Gerald's wedding and wanted Becca's dress to match hers. Victoria picked up Ellie and delivered her to Atwood Manor, so the three women could shop for fabric. The general store had many fabric choices, and could order fabric from New York City if necessary. They were excited to see more fabrics to choose from in the store than they thought would be available. Jess found a beautiful and tasteful floral fabric for her and Becca's dresses. Victoria had two fabrics she really liked and could not decide which she preferred for her dress therefore, she bought both and would decide which she favored after the dresses were finished. Lizzie also had a difficult time making her selection, and finally chose a dark blue fabric. She owned many white tatted collars to choose from to wear on the dress, which she knew would be beautiful. They swiftly returned to the children and Ellie, and they found she had handled the children alone very well.

Jess and Lizzie put the children down for naps and Jess asked Ellie if she could stay for the afternoon and play with the children after they woke, which she gladly agreed to. The women immediately laid their fabrics on the dining table and began cutting their patterns.

Jess was holding the skirt of her dress up for the others opinions, when Mark saw his mother as he peeked through his grandmother and Auntie Lizzie and said, in a tiny voice, "Mama beautymus". Jess draped the new skirt of her dress over the back of a dining chair and ran to her son, picked him up and thanked him, kissed him and squeezed him tight. "Mama hug Mok", as he wrapped his little arms around her neck and pressed his cheek into hers, facing the same direction. Victoria and Lizzie watched this loving moment as they paused their sewing.

~

Horatio Seymour, the previous governor of New York, came into Atwood & Strong Lumber in early February asking who the proprietor was.

"I am sir. I am James Atwood and my business partner is Edward Strong. How may I help you?" James looked the man up and down, not knowing who he was.

"I am Horatio Seymour. I am running for President of these United States and you have the perfect place here where many people can gather to hear me speak."

Edward saw the well-dressed man talking to James and approached the two men, as he stretched out his hand welcoming the stranger. "Edward Strong."

"Horatio Seymour, sir. I am running for President of these United States and I was just telling your business partner here...I am sorry..."

"James Atwood." James was excited to have such a prominent man in their establishment and sternly shook his hand.

"Mr. Atwood, nice to meet you. Anyway, I would like to speak from your porch to the people of Atwater as part of my campaign and about the Democratic party. Do I have your permission to do that? I will post notices around town myself, and two days from now speak to all from here, which could possibly bring you customers as well. You have the space here for many to gather and the porch is high enough for me to be above everyone that gathers. What do you think?"

James and Edward looked at each other and asked Mr. Seymour to talk privately for a moment. He gladly agreed as he took several steps back as James and Edward did the same. They both agreed it would be a good business move, although neither man knew what his platform was, but they too wanted to hear what the Democratic nominee had to say.

"We have agreed, Mr. Seymour, Saturday, two days from now would work well for all of us. What time would you like to do this?" James was impressed that their English accents did not discourage the man from his desire.

"Well, thank you Mr. Atwood, Mr. Strong." Mr. Seymour shook both of their hands, with a wide smile. "I will start placing the posters in town and I will see you Saturday at one o'clock. I thank you both again." He turned to leave, and then turned to talk to James and Edward asking them about their business. They informed him about the lumberyard, also that a second yard was being built beginning in spring in Lincoln, New York, outside Albany. Mr. Seymour was impressed with the information of their beginning and use of the river and wished them luck on their second yard. He had grown up in the area and told them he thought they had made an excellent choice of placement for the second Atwood & Strong Lumber.

By noon on Saturday, there were almost one hundred people filling the property in front of the lumberyard, even though it was a cold but clear day, which proved they were anxious to listen to the Presidential candidate. Jess, Victoria and Lizzie were part of the crowd, after Jess promised Ellie and the children they would return within two hours.

Mr. Seymour talked over an hour, promising a peaceful country and stating his experience as Governor made him a better candidate than a Civil War General, Ulysses S. Grant. The crowd applauded and cheered for Mr. Seymour several times during his speech.

Democracy was very different to the English Atwood's, Strong's, and Lizzie, as royalty ran their homeland, generation after generation. There were no elections. They all knew they wanted to be part of this election and agreed to register to vote at the town hall.

Mr. Seymour lost the election to Ulysses S. Grant that year. Grant won 53% of the votes, and was inaugurated as President of the

United States on 4 March. All of Jess' family enjoyed being part of American democracy and found an inner pride; especially for Becca, Mark, and Luke, born as American citizens.

Chapter Twenty-Four
Spring 1869

Spring arrived early and the snow melted quickly. James and Edward created and delivered quotes to build wooden walkways in front of the general store, post office, bank, and hotel. James knew once these walkways were completed, it would not be long before other businesses would want the same, creating long walkways on each side of town. All the businesses accepted their quotes and the walkways were soon completed. Now one could walk the length of the town without walking through mud. Most all of the townspeople, especially the women, thanked and lauded James and Edward when they saw them at the yard or in town for their ideas and efforts. Pastor Brown praised their *donation* of the walkway in front of the church after his sermon and joked about the back door needing a walkway, while winking at James. After church that day, many men of Atwater gathered, including James and Edward, and volunteered their time to build the back door walkway if the lumberyard would again donate the lumber. By the following Sunday, James walked to the back of the church to check their progress, and was delighted to see it was completed, *and* with handrails. His heart warmed.

This made James now think ahead of doing all the streets of Atwater with wood. He scratched his head, knowing it would take more dried lumber than they had or would ever have to do the job, shrugged his shoulders, and thought "someday".

James and Edward had been to Lincoln, New York once since February, in search of property for their second lumberyard and came home disappointed. There were no properties large enough for a lumberyard, and none by the river. On their second trip, they stayed with Gerald. After dinner of roasted chicken, which they ate hungrily with Gerald, James was eager to hear about Rachael.

"When can we meet Rachael? Will she be here tonight?" James asked his friend in a teasing manner.

Gerald laughed, studied the grain in the oak table, and traced the edge of his glass with his index finger. "She is training tonight and was sorry to hear she would miss meeting you both. You will all be here for the wedding, correct?"

"Yes, we will all be here, Gerald. We would not miss it for anything. Jess' stomach grows daily, I swear," James laughed as he studied Gerald's face seeing his nervousness for the first time, "yet, she says she will make the trip, even if she has to walk."

Gerald's brows rose as he looked at James and smiled. James returned the smile.

"You all mean the world to me and I wouldn't want any of you to miss it. She is planning a very big event with a musical quartet. It's going to cost me a mint." Gerald laughed and rose to retrieve the brandy bottle from his liquor cabinet. He offered a drink to both men and they gladly accepted.

"We can't find the proper land for our lumberyard, Gerald, even though we have searched the properties you suggested and more. Do you have any other thoughts on this?"

"Well, I have been thinking about this, Gentlemen, and I have a lot of excess land next to my horse ranch where I seldom let horses graze because there is no fence that far east of the existing grazing area. I haven't talked about it before because only a very small portion of that land unites with the street and I didn't think you would want to see it for that reason. You are welcome to look at it though."

James looked at Edward, who shrugged his shoulders. "Gerald, I think we should take a look at your land and decide then. We also need to talk price." Edward took the initiative to begin this conversation. Gerald told them the land was a half mile from the river and asked how they would get trees to and from the river. Edward told him, "We will have to construct long wagons to handle two to three logs. The three draft horses we bought from you last year, along with the draft horses we already have, could easily pull two trees at a time." Gerald's eyes widened as he nodded his head, understanding.

"I wondered what you were doing with all those horses."

"We are going to need four more horses when this yard is completed. Bobby and Tim will be operating the new yard, so if we buy your land, you will be seeing a lot of them." James grinned and squeezed Gerald's forearm as they met eyes.

"They are good men; young, but good men." Gerald smiled at James and looked toward Edward, who was finishing his brandy with three small sips. Gerald placed the brandy bottle in front of Edward, who then replenished his glass.

"First thing in the morning we will go to the land and see what you think." Gerald then poured himself another brandy. He then rose and added wood to the fireplace. They all watched the flames grow around the new log, lost in their thoughts.

The next morning they rode to Gerald's horse ranch and inspected the property he proposed to sell to them. James and Edward walked the entire circumference of the ten acres and then returned to Gerald.

"If we fence the back eight acres for horses, would you want to combine the grazing areas or fence them off?" James waved his arm in the direction of the existing fence.

"I have paying customer's horses that would need to be kept separate. Therefore, I would leave the fence where it is and you would only need a back and side fence. Does that sound good to you?"

"I like it. You are right about the shape where not much meets the street, but we only need an entrance with a gate and I think it widens just about at the right place to build the office and sales building. What do you think, Edward?"

"I agree with James. I am concerned about your growth, Gerald. If you want to expand your ranch someday..."

Gerald put his hand in the air, "Edward, I own another fifty acres behind the fence east of the existing grazing area. I have enough land back there to expand in that direction if I need to."

"I would say we have a deal, my friend." James slapped his friend on his shoulder with his left hand and shook hands with Gerald, who obliged his friend with his hand shake.

"We have drawn the building plans, Gerald, and we will be sending men down this way to erect the new fence first for the new draft horses we need from you and then a few more men to start erecting the drying shed and sales office."

"Sounds like we need to look at some horses." Gerald motioned his friends to follow him to the stables.

Bobby and Tim left Atwater Monday morning with a wagon full of fencing. They bunked with Junior at the ranch, who helped them put up the fence, which was done in one week. Soon four draft horses pulling a large wagon full of lumber arrived from Atwood & Strong Lumber along with two additional men. When the lumber was unloaded, the two men drove the horses and wagon back to Atwater for a second load of lumber and returned with two builders who started building the drying shed and sales office. Two weeks later James rode Stormy to Lincoln to inspect the new fence and buildings and drove the draft horses and wagon back with Stormy tied to the back of the wagon.

~

The Atwood home was hectic the morning of 17 April, as Lizzie helped them pack for Gerald's wedding. She left Atwood Manor to assist Edward and Victoria pack and then packed herself. Three buggies left at noon toward Lincoln, with Lizzie and Lady in the rear. They arrived almost four hours later, as Jess asked James to stop twice to rest her aching back and change diapers.

Elizabeth had the dinner table set for all of them, and then directed them to the back patio where Gerald and Rachael waited for them.

James was first through the door to greet Gerald and finally meet Rachael.

"Everyone, this is Rachael Longwood, my bride-to-be." Gerald beamed as he introduced her to each guest separately, ending with the twins, Mark and Luke; who were wiggling, wanting down from Lizzie's arms. She placed them on the patio, and when Gerald saw them both walk with ease to Victoria and Jess, who both promptly picked up the boys, he was amazed at how they had grown.

"Uncle Geral'!" Becca ran to him with raised arms, he picked her up, kissed her rosy cheek, then kissed every female cheek on the patio, not neglecting the twins.

"Rachael, it is so nice to finally meet you! We have heard so much about you and I have waited for this moment. In addition, I love seeing Gerald so happy. Please, let's sit and get to know each other." Jess held Rachael's hand with her other hand, put Luke onto his feet, and then placed her hand on her expanding stomach, and then around to her aching back.

"I would love to, Jess. I too, have heard a lot about you all. Gerald loves you all so much and speaks so highly of you. When is your baby due?"

Jess now patted her stomach and looked down at the dainty flowered fabric covering it. "Doc Harris says mid June, but the baby will come when it's ready. They always do." She giggled slightly.

"Your children are beautiful, Jess. You must be so proud." Rachael glanced at the children and back to Jess.

"Thank you. But I can't take all the credit." Jess smiled as she looked at her handsome husband, who was laughing with Gerald and Edward.

"They all certainly take after him. Maybe this one will look like you." Rachael giggled, hoping Jess did not take offense.

"That's up to God, but it would be nice to have one that takes after me." Jess smiled as she watched her blonde children play on the stone patio.

Victoria and Lizzie joined Jess and Rachael while they talked together for some time.

Elizabeth then appeared from the back door with a huge platter of steaks, placed them on the table next to the fire pit for Gerald to put onto the fire, and then went from person to person asking if they wanted something to drink. Jess hugged Elizabeth, who stiffly hugged her in return then disappeared into the house. She soon returned with a tray of drinks and the special order for Jess of lemonade. Jess snickered as she took her glass from the tray and thanked Elizabeth. "How do you make your lemonade? Yours is so much better than mine, please tell me your secret." Elizabeth simply smiled with no reply.

They enjoyed dinner at the dining table getting to know Rachael. She talked of how much she loved Gerald and the many wedding plans she made. Her love for him was obvious. Everyone adored her and her beautiful strawberry blonde hair. It was going to be easy to bring her into their circle of friends. Rachael was petite like Jess, and Jess wondered how she controlled and trained large horses being so small.

They lingered around the dining table an hour after dinner and chocolate cake, and then Rachael announced she had to leave to prepare for her wedding the next day. They all rose, gathered around her with hugs and kisses good-bye and she gladly returned the love. Gerald excused himself, and walked her to their horses and they rode off together. Everyone praised Rachael, and soon Lizzie and Jess put the children to bed. Gerald returned from chaperoning Rachael home, and although he was all smiles, James could see his friend's nervousness.

"So, what do you think?" Gerald's smile made his entire face light up. Everyone spoke at once, telling him how wonderful she was and how happy they all were for him.

James woke very early the next morning and found Jess still asleep. He watched her sleep for a moment and then softly placed his hand on her active stomach, feeling the new life they created. He rose and pulled the drape back, seeing that the sun had not risen over the horizon yet, and noticed men walking to and from the big red barn. He quickly dressed, padded quietly down the stairs, and walked through a barely lit, silent house to the back door. He made his way to the barn, thinking Gerald was there with his hired hands. Not seeing Gerald, he asked if they knew where he was and they all pointed to the rear of his property.

"Where is he exactly?" James didn't know what their pointing meant.

"Walk past the fenced grazing area and you'll find him back there." James thanked them, left the barn, and walked the length of the fence past ten grazing horses. When he reached the corner fence post, he saw Gerald's silhouette in the distance against the morning sky with his back to James. He had no idea what Gerald was doing this far back on his property until he got closer and realized he was standing inside the wrought iron fenced area, standing at Marie's grave. When he saw his friend with his head down, James turned to return to the house quietly. Gerald heard his footsteps and called to him. James shyly waved and motioned with his hands that he would leave him in peace.

"James, come back here please." Gerald waved his hand, inviting him to come into the fenced area.

"Gerald, I didn't mean to bother you. I am sorry. I will..."

"Please James, come in."

James walked through the gate, closed it behind him, and then stood by Gerald's side, as he looked down to Marie's headstone. He saw three crosses behind the headstone with names roughly painted on the cross bars.

"This is my small family plot I told you about." Gerald spoke without taking his eyes from the headstone.

"Gerald, I feel I am intruding."

"Not at all. I was just telling Marie, that although I now love another, she will always have a piece of my heart. I wish you could have known her, James. She was a wonderful woman." Gerald was still eyeing the headstone, and then pointed to the crosses. "They were great dogs. When I buried the second dog, there was barely shade back here and now look how they are all in the shade; even Marie."

James put his hand on Gerald's shoulder and left it there to show support for his friend. Finally, Gerald broke his trance and put his hand on James' shoulder, where they stood for a minute. Eventually, Gerald broke away and kissed his fingertips, bent to the headstone and placed his fingers on the stone. He turned to leave and James followed, closing the gate behind him.

"I just wanted to tell her that I am getting married today. You may think that's strange, but I have found comfort in talking to Marie many times in my life."

"I don't think it's strange at all. You miss your wife and best friend. It's understandable."

Together, they walked back to the house where Elizabeth was frying bacon, Teddy's maple bacon, and removing corn bread from the wood stove. James went upstairs to gather his family and soon all were around the dining table again.

The wedding was to be at the horse stables at noon. After breakfast, everyone scrambled to various rooms to bathe and dress for the wedding. Of the women, Lizzie was ready first and brought the twins down dressed like princes. James asked if Jess needed help and Lizzie shook her head no and waved her hand to the top of the stairs where Jess appeared in a beautiful floral dress, holding Becca's hand, donned in her matching dress. Jess had curled her and Becca's hair, which had many ribbons throughout her beautiful blonde curls. James met them on their way down the stairs, kissed them both. "My two favorite ladies! You are both breathtaking. The bride will have a lot of competition today." He lifted his daughter into his arms, and took Jess' hand inside his elbow and aided them down the remaining stairs. Lizzie waited at the landing with the twins in light blue shirts, dark blue shorts, and white knee socks. James was bursting with pride. Gerald was watching from the end of the hall. "You have one beautiful family, my friend." He leaned to kiss Jess' cheek, kissed Becca, who eagerly puckered her lips to kiss her loving "uncle". He patted the twin's blonde heads and kissed Lizzie's cheek. "I must dress for my bride." He turned toward his bedroom at the end of the hall and disappeared.

Edward and Victoria soon came down the stairs, looking like English royalty, including his black, gold-tipped cane.

Jess prayed their children would behave at the wedding, and her prayer was heard. The children were mesmerized by the horses with flower braided manes and the rose blankets that draped their backs as they walked past the stables, into the green grazing grass. The fences were covered with flowered garlands. A long white fabric aisle ran between two areas of rowed chairs for guests. At the end of the fabric aisle, stood a tall wooden arch covered in red and white roses. All of the ranch and racetrack employees were well dressed - the women had white rose corsages and the men had red rose buds in their lapels. They were each directing and guiding guests to their seats. James kissed Jess as Junior led her and the entire family up the aisle to their seats.

While standing in the back James got a tap on his shoulder. He turned to see Henry with a hair cut, shaved and in a suit. They shook hands, exchanged happy greetings, and then talked about how beautiful everything was. Henry thanked him again for giving him a second chance and soon two guests needed assistance up the aisle as Henry grinned at the guests and offered his arm to the woman. Then James gladly walked two of the bride's friends to their seats. His heart swelled while watching Henry, who had obviously come a long way from the horrendous night he and Jimmy stabbed Misty. He was so glad that he had correctly speculated the good hearts of the two men.

Soon most of the chairs were filled with wedding guests when James felt another tap on his shoulder. Gerald stood next to him, looking happy yet nervous. He handed James a red rose bud for his lapel as he put his own rose into the lapel hole of his black suit. They turned to each other for inspection and waited for their cue from the pastor conducting the service, who stood under the flowered arch.

"Have you seen Teddy?" Gerald scanned the people behind them toward the stable, and saw no sign of him.

"No I haven't, Gerald. Junior hasn't said a word either. Have you heard from him before today?"

"Yes, he agreed to stand up with me when I asked him in the fall and I last saw him six weeks ago when he was coming back from New York City." Gerald continued to scan the people but did not see Teddy, Amanda, or Sam. They stood together until the pastor finally invited them up the aisle with the nod of his head.

Gerald and James walked side by side up the aisle, smiling at guests as they went, and soon arrived at the flowered arch and stood to the pastor's side. They then waited for the harpist and pianist to change their music to the song Rachael selected to walk up the aisle with her best friend's husband, Roger. Soon the selected song started and Gerald stared down the aisle toward his beautiful bride. Who was that by her side? He elbowed James and gave him a quizzical look and he too shrugged his shoulders, for he had only met Roger once, yet this man did not look like the man he met. Suddenly, Gerald knew it wasn't Roger. The bride and her escort slowly walked up the aisle and as they got closer, both Gerald and James realized at the same moment, it was Teddy. His beard was gone and his hair cut, parted, and slicked back. Most of the guests could be heard whispering, as it seemed no one knew who this man was. James looked at Jess just as she too recognized Teddy, and saw her put her hands in front of her gasping lips. It was then Amanda and Sam made their way to the back row of chairs to their seat.

Gerald was flabbergasted and his mind went blank. However, he quickly turned his attention to his beautiful bride in her glorious ivory colored wedding dress. Her headpiece was tiny white rose buds holding a long veil that ran down her back. She was holding a long draping bouquet of white roses. Her train went on behind her for five feet. Gerald almost wanted to pinch himself. She was absolutely stunning and smiling from ear to ear. When they reached Gerald, he stepped forward, shook Teddy's hand firmly with a wide grin, and then took Rachael's hand and guided her to stand with him in front of the pastor under the adorned arch. Teddy waited a moment, and then turned to stand next to James. They shook hands and James could not help putting his left hand on Teddy's shoulder and squeezed hard. The whispering among the guests that knew Teddy continued until the pastor spoke his first words.

After the ceremony, Gerald and Rachael walked down the aisle all smiles, followed by James and the maid-of-honor, then Teddy and Rachel's bridesmaid. They walked to a tent and lined quickly to greet their guests, but Gerald and James could not wait to talk to Teddy.

"I did not know who you were! I kept wondering who the stranger was walking my bride up the aisle. You look so different! What possessed you.....?" Gerald was floored.

"Teddy, what a shocking surprise! You look great!" James hugged him before the guests started to arrive at their line.

"I wante' ta suprize ya! Do ya like da new me?" Teddy bowed when he finished his words.

"Teddy! I did not know who you were. It is amazing how different you look, not that you looked bad before, it's just so different than how we have known you for years!" Jess hugged their friend and stood back to look him over with her hands still on his arms.

The wedding celebration went on all afternoon and into the night while the quartet played and many danced. Jess sat with Amanda, who wore her nicest dress. Amanda was so happy to once again be in the presence of both of her sons and watched every move they both made. She laughed and clapped her hands as she watched Junior dance with a female ranch employee. She and Jess teased each other about a possible wedding in the future while watching them dance.

Jess saw Elizabeth sitting alone and invited her to sit with her and Amanda. "You look so pretty today, Elizabeth. It was a beautiful wedding, don't you think?"

"Yes ma'am, it was very beautiful. She is a stunning bride." Elizabeth sat with her hands folded properly in her lap and watched the dancers.

Bobby and Tim came to the wedding together. Samantha was not allowed to go that far with a young man without a chaperone, and Tim was alone. Before dark, they said goodbye to James and family and rode back to Atwater.

The photographer took photos of the wedding party and then two of Rachael on her flower adorned horse. Her dress train draped over her horses rump with Gerald on the ground at the horses neck, holding the reins in one hand and his brides hand in the other. The second photo was the same pose, but looking at each other lovingly.

Jess and Lizzie hated to leave the fun, but needed to get the dancing children to bed. Becca had to kiss her "Uncle Geral'" good night and happily kissed her new "Aunt Rachul" too. Edward and Victoria were tired and returned to Gerald's home with Jess and the children. James could not stay without his family, so he went to Gerald and Rachael, and apologized. They both understood.

James never asked where the bride and groom were spending their wedding night, but he knew they were leaving early the next morning for Niagara Falls, New York for their honeymoon.

Early Sunday morning, James' family thanked Elizabeth for her assistance, loaded the buggies, and headed back to Atwater.

Monday morning Lizzie arrived early as she always did on Mondays and started frying bacon and eggs, and making cornbread for the Atwood family.

"Your mother said she would be along shortly, as she has errands to run in town." She smiled to Jess as she poured a cup of coffee for her husband while humming a tune. Soon the children woke in time to kiss their father good- bye before he went to the yard.

After their breakfast and baths, they heard Victoria from outside, coming up the drive in her buggy, screaming "Jessica! Jessica!"

Jess ran out to meet her mother, who jumped from her buggy, which startled the horse. Jess quickly grabbed the reins to settle the horse. "Mother! What is wrong?"

Victoria wrapped her arms around Jess and started jumping up and down. Jess' stomach kept her from jumping with her, but felt her mother's excitement.

"Jessica! Your brother is coming to America! I stopped at the post office this morning and his letter was waiting. He and Kathleen will be here the middle of June. Can you believe it?"

"That is wonderful! My handsome brother! I cannot wait to see them both. Mother, the baby is due then. May I see the letter?" Jess took the envelope from her mother and read the letter carefully. "They will be coming into New York City by June 10th and it will take two days or more to get here, so we should see them by the afternoon of the 13th, if the ship arrives on time. He sounds as anxious to see all of us, as we are to see him. I wonder how he talked Kathleen into leaving England."

"My boy is coming!" Victoria was still excitedly skipping as they went in the back door. Lizzie jumped up and down in Victoria's hug when she heard the news, and soon the three children were surrounding their legs and joining in the excitement.

Victoria had to share the news with her husband, whom she knew would be happy beyond the stars. She knew he missed his son terribly, as he talked of Grant often. Jess rode with her mother to the lumberyard to tell their men the wonderful news.

When Edward heard his son was on his way to America, his eyes teared and had to sit down. When James heard their date of arrival, he was very concerned for his wife and new baby and hoped the excitement did not harm either one of them, perhaps making the baby arrive early.

"We should start looking at houses for sale in the area immediately – for Grant and Kathleen. They can stay with us as long as they want to, but if I know my son..." Edward had put his arm around his wife's shoulders after he rose from the chair he had practically fallen into when he heard the news.

"Edward, you don't know yet if Grant and Kathleen are coming to stay; and if they are it may not be in Atwater." James, thinking logically, patted his father-in-laws shoulder.

"Why wouldn't they want to live here?" Edward looked at each of his family's faces.

"He's right, Father. His letter says nothing of their plans other than they are coming to America." Jess shyly responded to her father, and then looked to James for reassurance.

"I think we can look, Edward, for now, but Jess is right. Although Doc Harris could use help and *is* getting older, but only Grant knows what he wants to do. If Grant has other plans, we may be able to convince him to stay in America and in Atwater when he sees the situation." James stepped next to Jess and held her hand. He then laid his hand on her stomach and looked at Jess with raised brows.

"We are all doing well, Honey." She smiled as she placed her hand over his. He kissed his wife tenderly. They started toward the door and Edward and Victoria followed.

On the ride back to the manor, Victoria was dancing in the buggy seat with excitement.

Chapter Twenty-Five
Summer 1869

Spring gave way to summer early in '69, which Jess dreaded. As her pregnant stomach grew, she became more uncomfortable with each hot summer day. Victoria and Lizzie spent three weekends preparing a spare bedroom at the Strong's home for Grant and Kathleen's arrival. Wallpaper went up quickly, and a new satin bed cover and drapes arrived soon after Victoria ordered them through the general store from New York City. Every morning Victoria inspected the room, hoping she had thought of everything they would need. Grant said nothing in his letter of meeting them at the boat in the city and all assumed they would find their way to Atwater on their own, since they would need a horse and buggy nevertheless.

Jess loved watching her children play outside on summer days, and was so thankful Lizzie was not only there to help, but was so much help with everything to do with the family. She expressed her thanks very often, yet at the same time felt guilty that Lizzie's entire life was to help others. Lizzie had Sunday's off and feverishly worked with Lady's Dressage training, and had made many new friends that also trained their horses in the corral behind the barn. Lizzie always seemed happy, yet it bothered Jess that Lizzie had no love in her life other than loving all of them.

Early in June, James, Jess, and Lizzie were sitting by the fire pit after the children were in bed and Jess could not help but mention to Lizzie what was on her mind.

"Lizzie, you know how I love you, but I have concerns about your life. It totally consists of our family and Lady. Don't you miss having someone special in your life?" Jess reached over to Lizzie's lap and placed her hand on top of Lizzie's resting hands.

"Well, I appreciate your concerns, but you all are my loves." She twisted her feet in the grass, clasped Jess' hand, and squeezed it.

James looked at Jess and gave her a questioning look, having never heard her concerns before. Jess smiled at him with confidence.

"But Lizzie, we all can't be the only people in your life. I feel as if I am holding you back from what you really want."

"Not at all, Jessica. I have worked for your family since I was 15 years old and I consider you my family and I am very satisfied." She smiled as she patted Jess' hand reassuring her.

"We all feel the same way, Lizzie, yet still, you are such a nice person and deserve to have a good, full life."

"I do have a good, full life, Jessica. I love your children as if they were my own..." Lizzie reached over to pat Jess' large stomach, then added, "and this little one too. Lady is the horse I have always wanted and she is doing well with her training and all is well."

Jess reached around Lizzie's shoulders with her right arm and hugged her close. She thought of Lizzie as a sister and could hardly remember what life was like without her in it.

"Well, Lizzie, we love you very much; all of us do. Anytime you want time off to do something with Lady or perhaps you do meet someone, and, well....you know." James now stood and added wood to the fire to cover his nervousness.

"I love all of you too, James, and thank you. If that situation should arise, I will let you know." Lizzie smiled, and felt the warmth of love rush through her and felt very happy.

On Friday, 4 June, Gerald and his bride Rachael arrived just as the summer sun set in the west, casting an orange-pink glow around the setting sun. Jess noticed how happy they looked and how they not only stayed by each other's sides at all times, yet held hands constantly. James hugged Gerald as he would a brother when they greeted each other and shook hands a long time.

"We have news." Gerald was beaming and smiling ear to ear. "If you can't tell by my happiness, my family, we are in the family way!" His voice raised an octave and got louder, his arms raised to the heavens, as if he wanted to tell the world.

Everyone gathered around them in congratulations, clapping his back, hugs were everywhere and the cheers were boisterous.

"It is the best thing that will ever happen to you, besides loving Rachael!" James was so excited for his friend. He knew Gerald would be a great father and the only thing that made him happier than he ever thought he could be was when his wife told him they were about to have a baby. He hugged Gerald and then Rachael and then hugged them both at once.

"When is your little bundle due?" Jess asked Rachael as she motioned her to a chair near the fire pit.

Rachael sat quickly and watched to see that Gerald would sit next to her before she answered. "Thanksgiving. The baby is due in late November. I am so thankful that I have hardly been sick, as I have heard so many women are."

"That's wonderful, Rachael. That was my next question; how you felt." Jess sat next to Rachael, while watching James and Gerald place more logs atop the existing fire in the pit. The logs caught quickly and the men stepped backwards to sit next to their wives. Lizzie soon came out the back door and asked what the celebration was all about. When she heard the news, she hugged Gerald and Rachael with many congratulations, and then sat next to Gerald. They all sat and conversed around the fire for hours. Babies were the main topic until Gerald heard Grant and Kathleen were due to arrive in a week or so and he was elated.

"If he is as nice as you, Jess, it will be a pleasure to meet him. Does he plan to open a practice here in Atwater?"

"Thank you. We are not sure of his plans, Gerald, but we are all hoping they will stay in America and here in Atwater. We have not seen him in over five years. I cannot wait until they get here. I just pray that the baby comes at the right time." Jess patted her active stomach.

"Have you chosen names yet?" Rachael asked anxiously, hoping they had not chosen her favorite names for her baby.

"We are prepared, this time. Matthew if it's a boy and Abigail if it's a girl."

"Those are nice names. We are still discussing names and having a difficult time agreeing. We have six more months to decide, so...." Rachel gazed down at her still flat stomach wishing time would fly to six months from now, but she knew that was wishing life away.

"Rachael wants Ulysses if it's a boy in honor of Ulysses Grant, but I am not too happy with that name, but I'm sure we will find a name we both like." Gerald leaned toward his wife and kissed her cheek. It warmed James' heart to see his friend so happy. He looked to the heavenly sky filled with stars and a full sliver moon and thanked God for his life and all of those in it.

Gerald and Rachael left the next day after lunch, yet not before Gerald could play with the children in the green grass, playing tag, kick the can and hide-and-go-seek. Truffy, Lizzie's dog ran beside Mark or Luke at all times. The children loved the dog so much, Jess asked Lizzie if she could leave Truffy with them over the weekends while Lizzie worked at Edward and Victoria's, and trained Lady on Sundays for the boy's sake. She quickly said of course, knowing it helped her also. After watching Becca and the boys run and play so happily with Truffy, Gerald decided it was time for them to get a dog, a big dog.

~

Teddy pulled into the Atwood Manor drive early in the morning while James was eating breakfast before going to the yard, which made him wonder why he was out-and-about so early in the day. He ran out to greet his friend, seeing a huge smile. Jess pulled back the kitchen curtain to watch her husband and his good friend greet and talk like brothers. The men talked for a while before they came in the back door. "Somethin' smells awful goooood," said Teddy as he smiled at Jess with his nose in the air, then kissed her cheek.

"You hungry, Teddy?" Jess began to set another place at the table.

"Always!" Teddy plunked heavily into the chair next to James, holding his silverware in his fists, waiting patiently for breakfast. His eggs were finally ready to be served with his biscuits and gravy and he dug in as if he was famished.

"What brings you out so early, Teddy?" Jess sat at the table with her breakfast and looked at Teddy, getting no reply as he ate then gave James a questioning look. James simply smiled.

"Oh, was in th' city yesterdee, at Gerald and Rachel's las' night an' felt antsy ta git home, so I started out early th's morn, is all." Teddy first looked at Jess, and then turned to smile oddly at James. Jess noticed this, thought something was peculiar, but said nothing.

When Teddy was done eating, he pushed his plate away from him, leaned back in the chair and aahed for a long time, put one hand on this stomach before it joined his other hand behind his head. He gave James a wink, which Jess noticed and started to hum briefly.

"Something is going on here. Do you have a secret, Teddy?" Jess was suspicious of something between the men that were acting strangely.

"Nah, no secrits here, Jess." He winked at James again. "Beefer I head back t' Malone, I sure would like t' see the chil'ren, will they be risin' soon?"

"Oh, it will not be long before they wake." James quickly answered. "I think today we should all picnic at the village green in town. What do you think, Jess?"

"That sounds nice. Will you be staying for that, Teddy?" Jess finished her breakfast and waited for his reply, as she checked both men's faces.

"Twould be nice; think I will." Teddy smiled oddly again.

Soon the entire household was up and the usual bustle began. James left for the lumberyard and told Jess he would join them all at the village green at the noon hour for the picnic. Lizzie quickly bathed the children and helped Jess make their picnic lunch and pack their basket. Teddy unhitched his horse from his meat wagon and led the way to downtown Atwater as Lizzie and the Atwood family followed.

The children quickly started playing in the green grass at the village green and Luke actually was trying to climb a huge oak tree in the middle of the green in front of the courthouse. Lizzie laid a blanket in the grass, placing the basket at one corner and sat, and then assisted Jess to sit on the blanket, where they both kept an eye on Truffy and the children as they happily ran and romped. Teddy walked the grounds and Jess noticed he was often checking the sky, which was pure blue and cloudless. He finally joined the ladies on the blanket, stretching out his long legs, and added to the girl's laughter as they all watched the children. It was not long before James walked through the grass and joined their picnic. Lizzie started to unload the food basket when James put his hand on hers. "Let's wait a while, Lizzie. Edward and Victoria are going to join us for lunch."

"What is the occasion, James, to do all of this in the middle of the week?" Jess studied her husbands face yet saw no hint of what he was up to.

"Oh, you will see soon." He smiled at her, turning to smile at Teddy and Lizzie. Edward had left the yard earlier to pick up his wife, soon to unite with their family, carrying a blanket and a picnic basket of their own. Victoria was very curious of the mid-week picnic, asking the same questions Jess had, to get no real answers from anyone. Jess looked at her mother and shrugged her shoulder then assisted Lizzie in preparing food for all.

After lunch, Teddy started to walk the grounds again, searching the sky and finally seemed fixated on something above them all. He motioned to everyone to come to where he stood, and everyone quickly ran to him and looked up. Teddy pointed excitedly, "Thar it is!"

Everyone looked up to the sky, first to see something they had never seen before – a huge balloon with a wicker basket hanging under it. Then the noise it made alarmed everyone, as flames suddenly shot up from the basket into the hole at the base of the balloon. The children were mesmerized.

"James, what is that?" Jess held Mark close to her as she gazed at the strange contraption, which seemed to be lowering from its height in the sky, almost like it was going to land where they stood.

"It's a hot air balloon, Jess. They used them in the war to silently spy on their enemies. Jess, you need to keep your eye on the basket."

Victoria and Edward stood near Jess in wonder, yet could not keep their eyes from the odd machine now coming toward them. As the balloon started to lower, the three people in the basket began to wave and the man was screaming something to them all.

Victoria was the first to recognize the familiar shape of the man, his hair color, and then finally his face. "Grant!! That is Grant in that basket," she screamed, putting her hands to her mouth.

James and Jess could not make out the peoples features, and the man in the basket had a dark beard; but finally Jess saw it was her brother, and then noticed Kathleen's bright red hair glistening in the sunshine. Grant and Kathleen were waving feverishly, and Grant was whooping and hollering as the basket finally landed in the grass of the village green. Many people of Atwater started gathering around the strange attraction and all waited to approach it as the huge balloon began collapsing as it lost its hot air. When it was finally grounded, Grant hopped out of the basket, and then eagerly helped Kathleen out safely. The balloon pilot busied himself with gages and ropes, then soon jumped out also and began tying the basket to stakes he hammered into the ground. Everyone was gathered around the basket by now and Grant and Kathleen did not know who to hug and kiss first. Victoria worked her way through the people with Edward right behind her when they both took their son into their arms and hugged him for a long time. Edward stepped back, breaking their embrace and began rubbing his sons chin, jesting with him about his beard. It was then he saw Kathleen was free from Jess' arms and took his turn to greet her. Jess sidestepped, to at last, be in front of her brother where he took a long look at her from her head to her toes, stopping to stare at her huge belly. He held her as close as he could, kissed her cheek for a long moment. "You look great, Sis. It is so good to finally see you again. Are these your children?"

"Yes; these are my beautiful babies. Haven't they grown since you've seen the tin types?" As she introduced each child by name, she was beaming with pride and could not stop smiling. Her large tummy was obvious as she was due at any time. Grant placed his hand on her stomach for just a moment, looked at his happy sister and smiled.

"When are you due, Jess?"

"Any time now, Grant. I hope the baby comes soon." Jess put her hand on her aching back as they walked; eventually their arms were around each other.

"I would say it's going to happen soon, Sis, very soon." Grant smiled and wished he could help his sister with her pain. Jess looked up to her brother, smiled, and then squeezed his waist with her hand. She was so glad he was here. She had truly missed him.

"Mother and Father must be so happy you both are here. I know I am. Kathleen looks great. Marriage agrees with both of you."

"I am a lucky man, Jess, very lucky." This time he squeezed where Jess' waist once was as they caught each other's eyes and smiles.

Eventually everyone was able to greet one another, saying their hellos. The village green crowd stayed around the huge balloon and basket in awe, as Edward's entire family worked their way to the picnic blankets.

Everyone had the same question for Grant and Kathleen; "Are you staying in America?"

Coming Soon .... *The Atwood saga continues in ~*
Atwood Manor The Second Generation

About the Author

Donna Benn Powers is originally from Plainfield, IL. Various careers through the years have allowed her to travel throughout the entire United States, where she studied people and places, and used these experiences to create the story and characters of her sagas. She has lived in Illinois, Oklahoma, New Hampshire, and now resides in Arizona. She has two children, is a breast cancer survivor, and now follows her passion ~ writing.